MIKE MAIHACK

CLEOPATRA
IN SPACE

BOOK FIVE
FALLEN EMPIRES

graphix
AN IMPRINT OF
■SCHOLASTIC

Library of Congress Control Number: 2017962946

ISBN 978-1-338-20413-1 (hardcover)
ISBN 978-1-338-20412-4 (paperback)

10 9 8 7 6 5 4 3 2 1   19 20 21 22 23

Printed in China   38
First edition, April 2019
Edited by Cassandra Pelham Fulton
Book design by Phil Falco
Creative Director: David Saylor

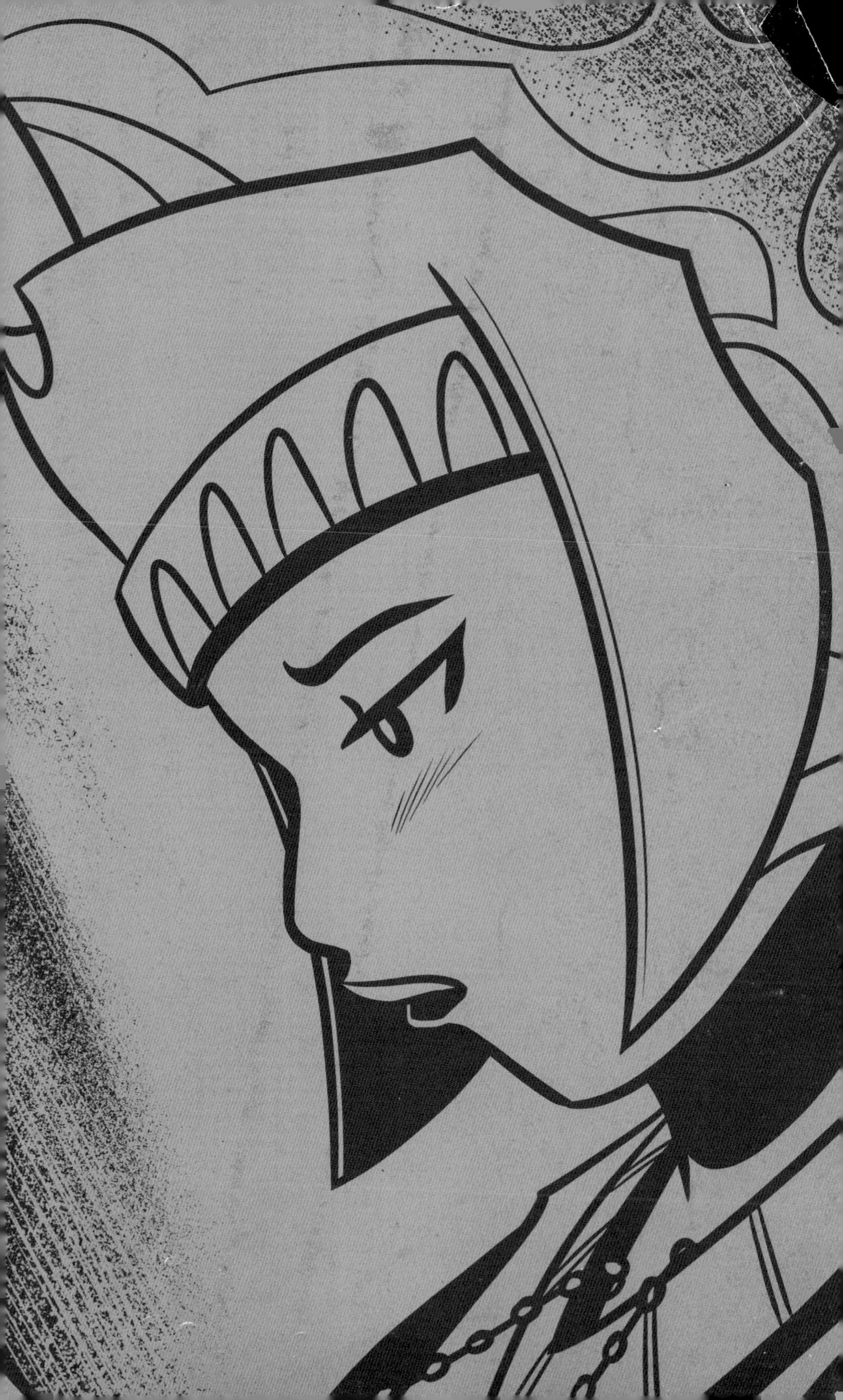

CHAPTER ONE

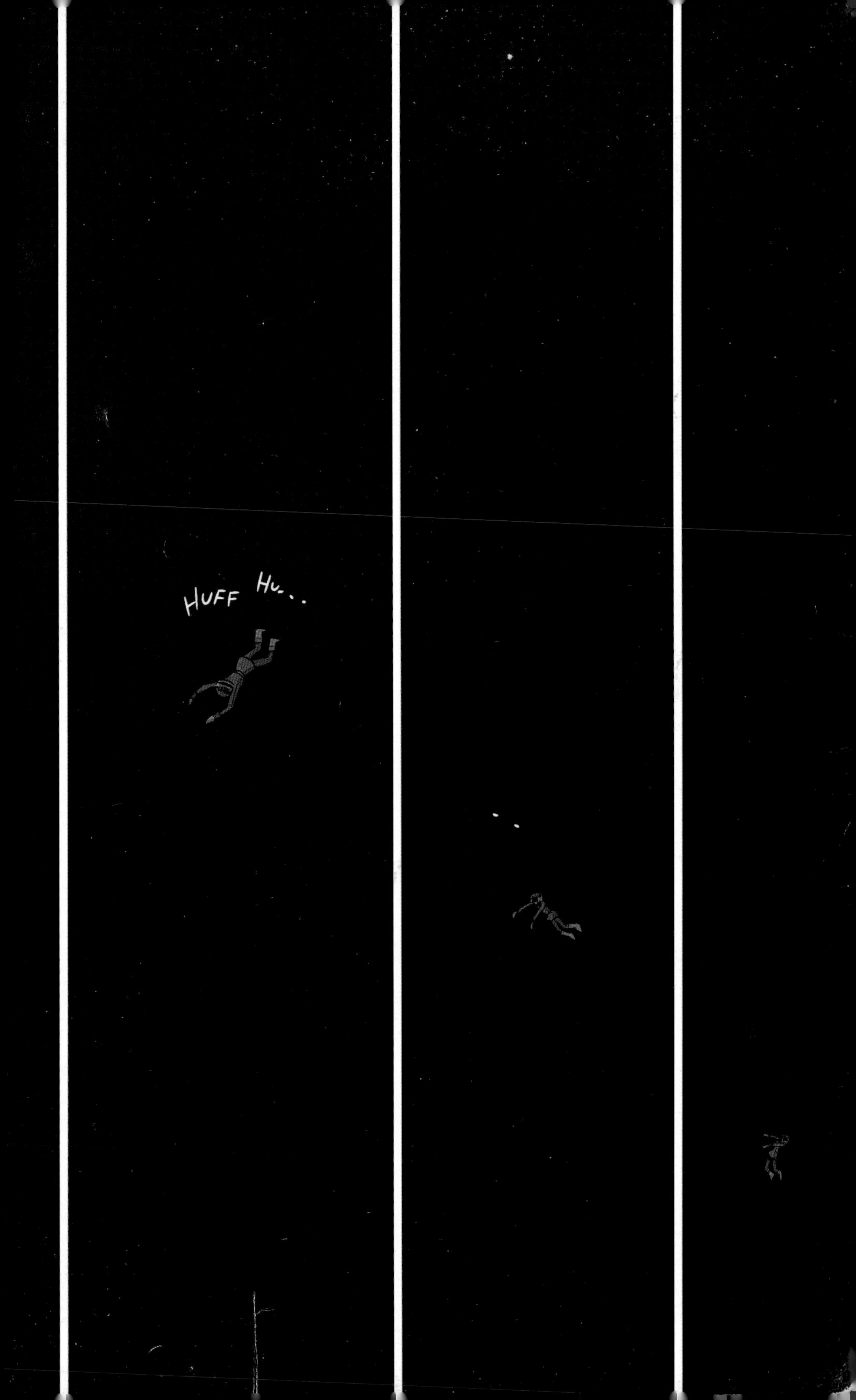
HUFF Hu...

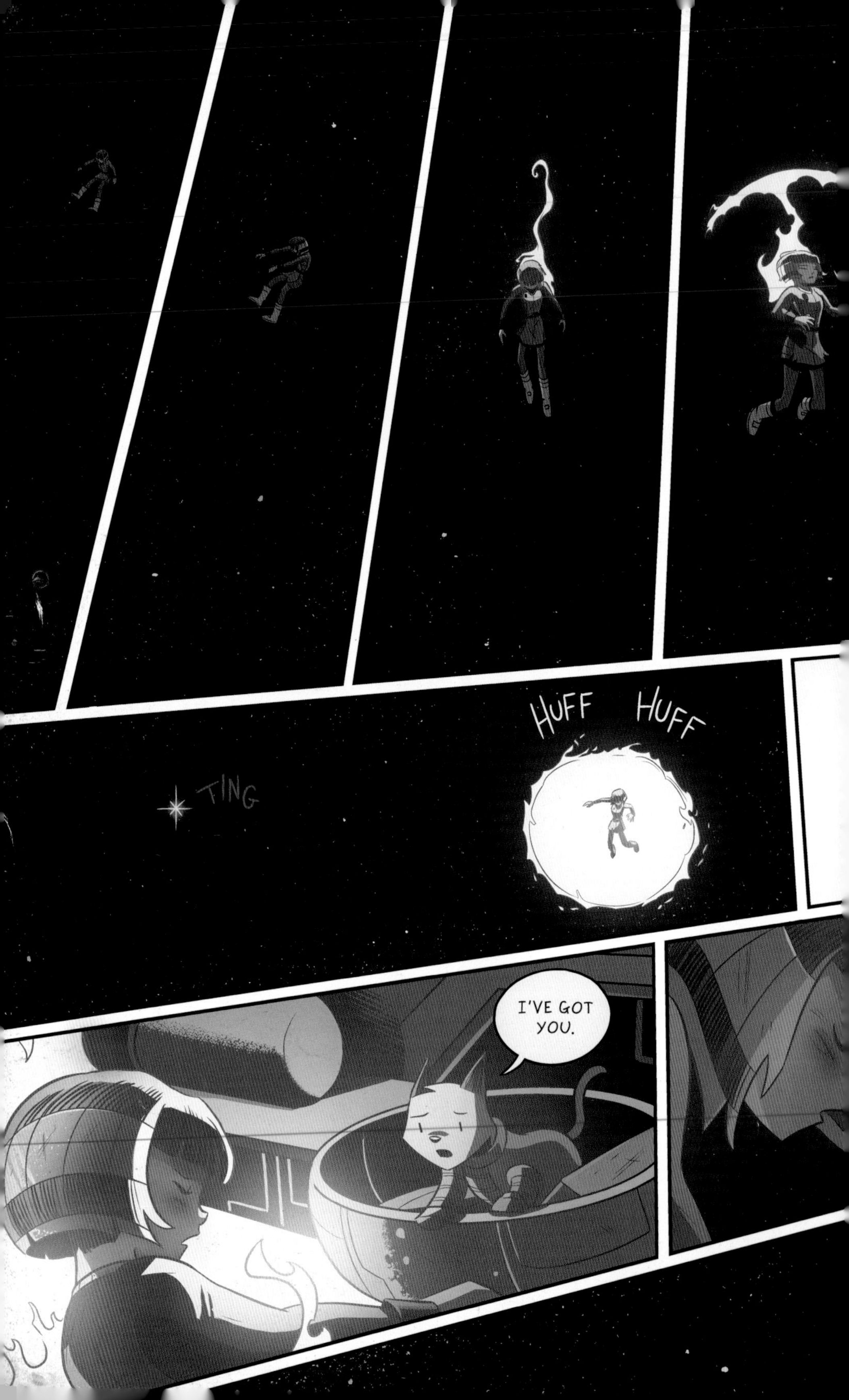
TING
HUFF HUFF
I'VE GOT YOU.

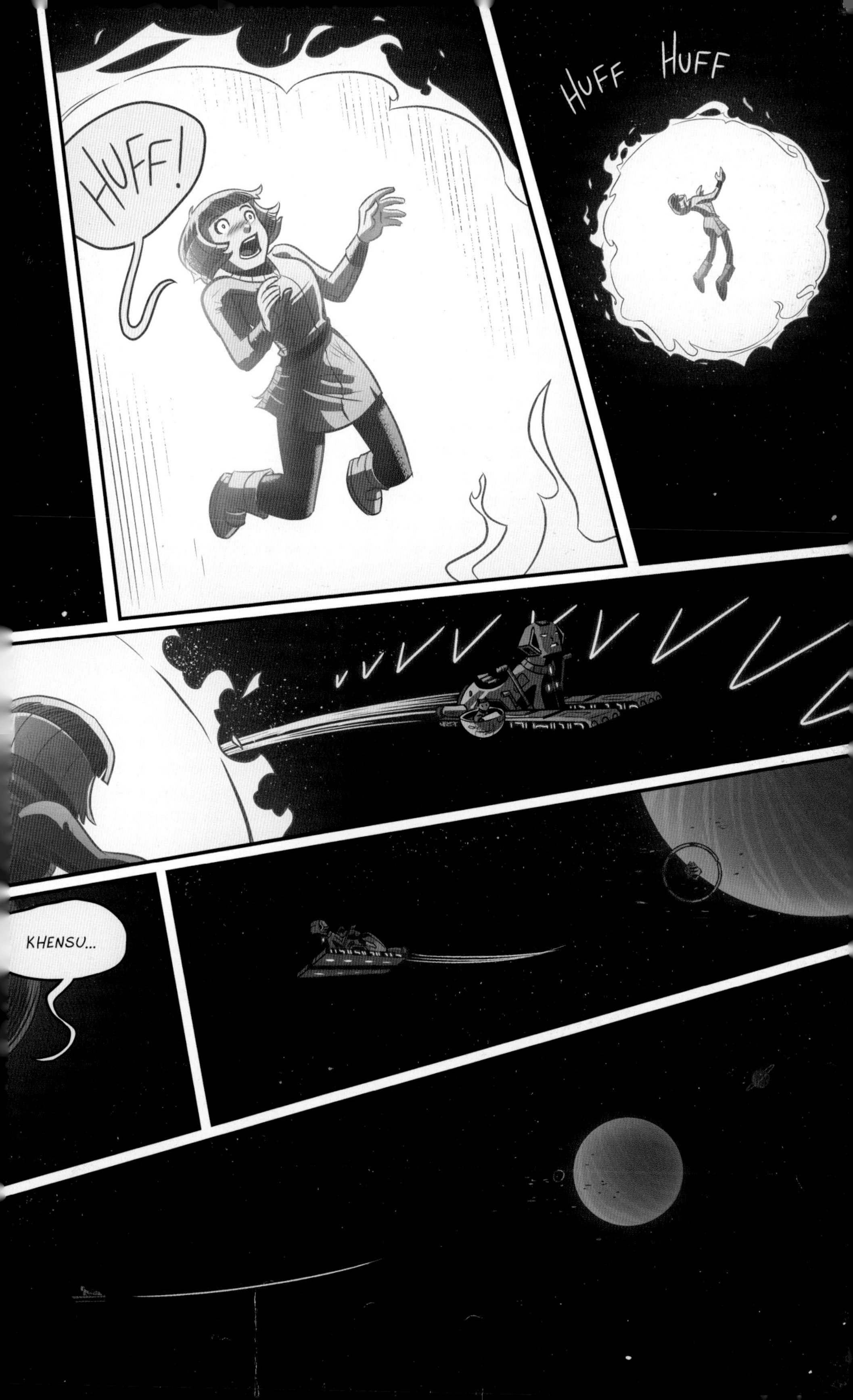

HUFF!
HUFF HUFF
KHENSU...

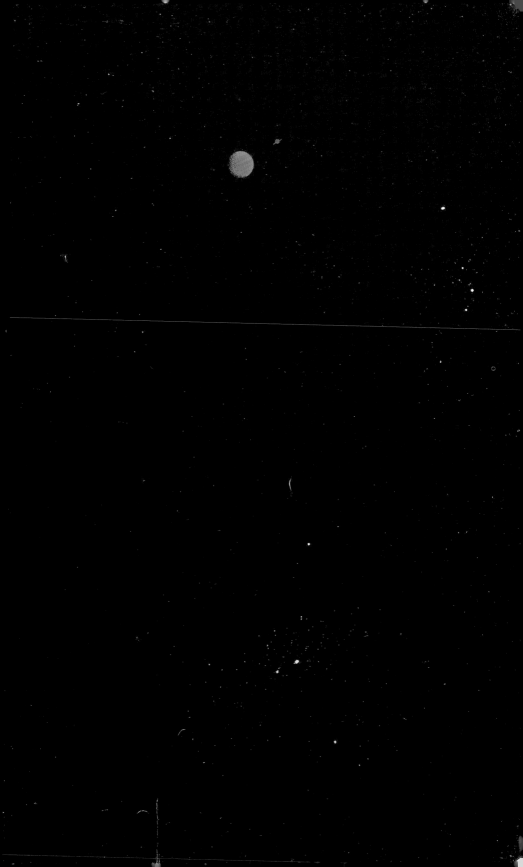

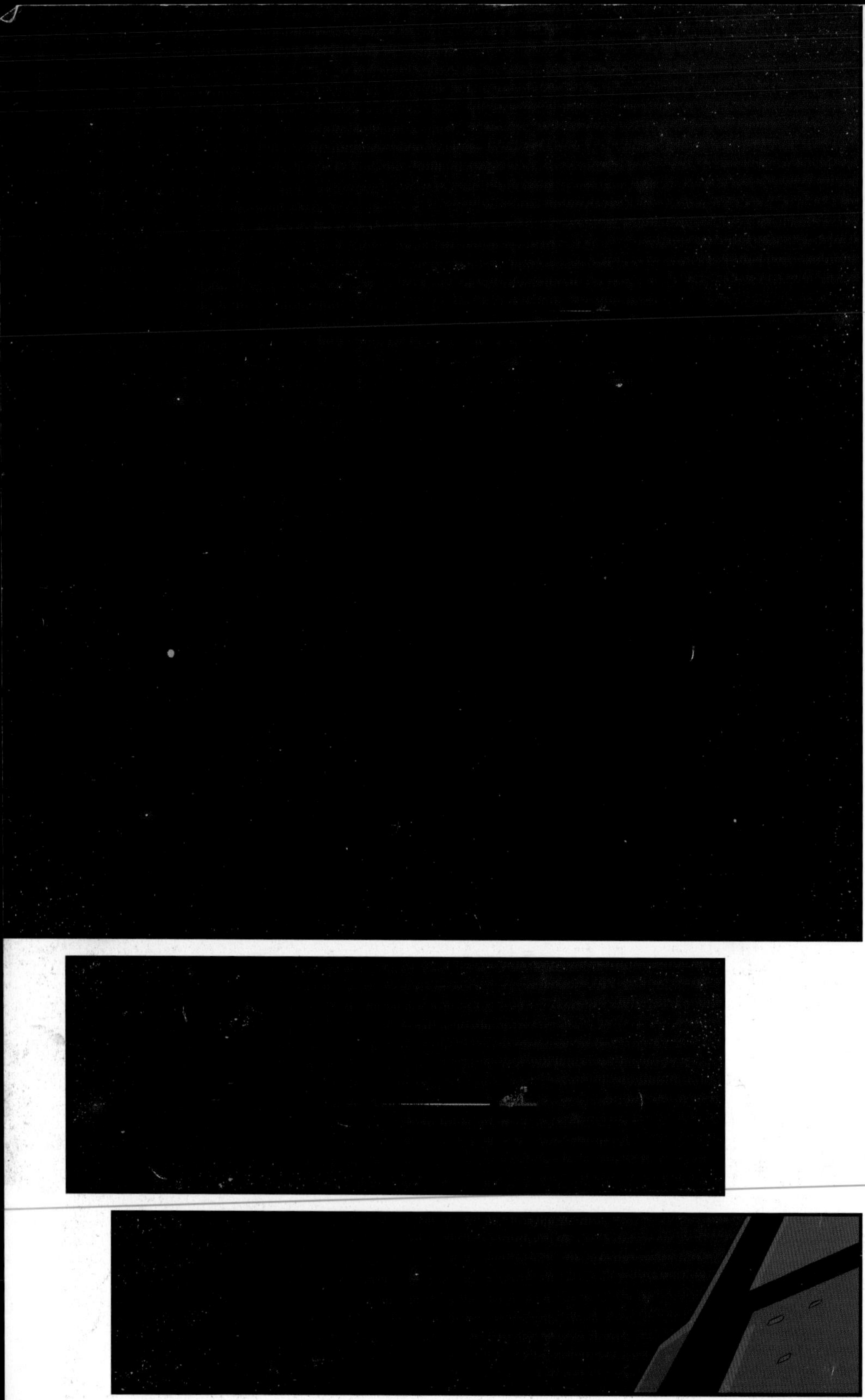

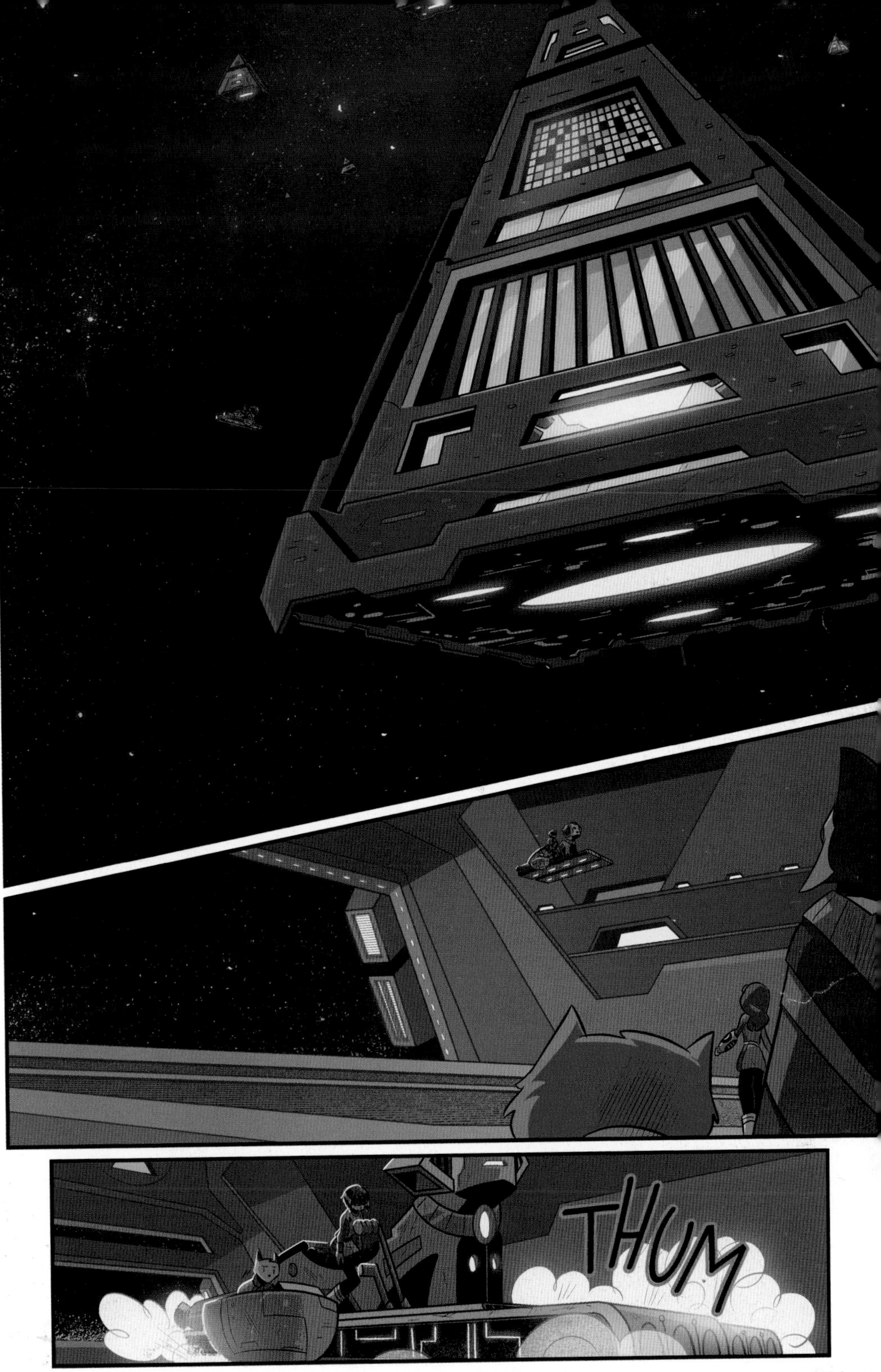
THUM

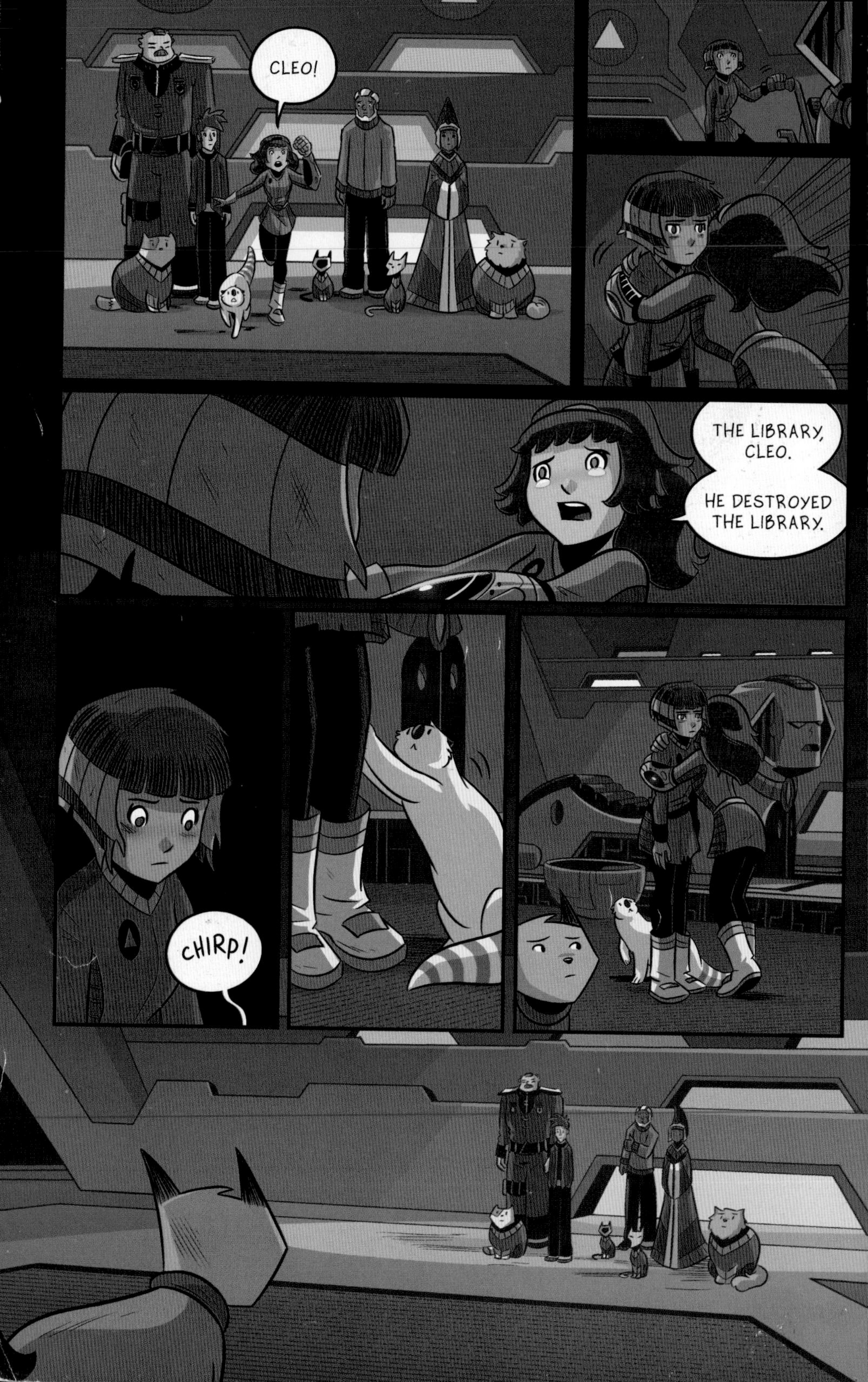
CLEO!
THE LIBRARY, CLEO.
HE DESTROYED THE LIBRARY.
CHIRP!

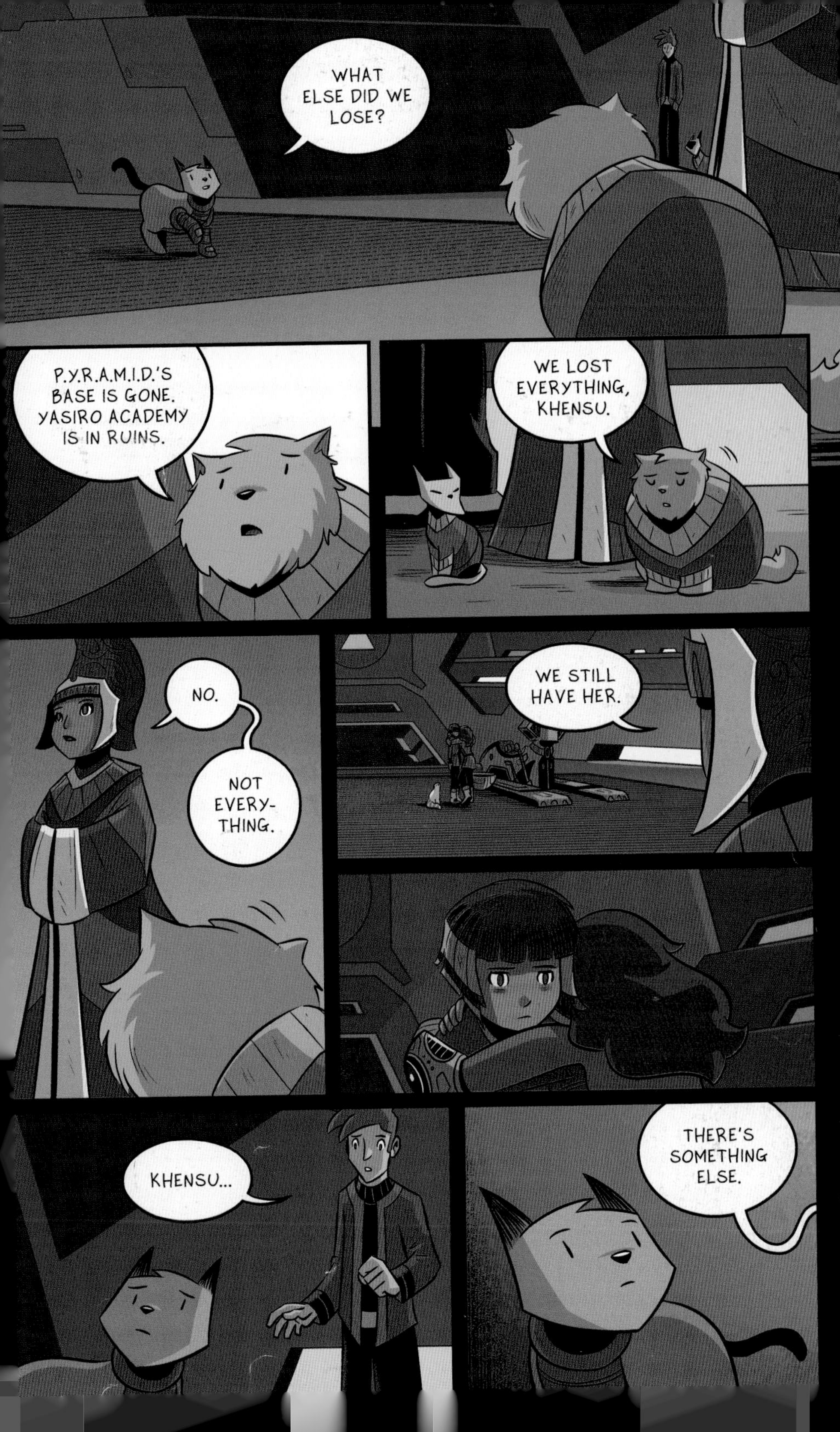
WHAT ELSE DID WE LOSE?
P.Y.R.A.M.I.D.'S BASE IS GONE. YASIRO ACADEMY IS IN RUINS.
WE LOST EVERYTHING, KHENSU.
NO.
NOT EVERY-THING.
WE STILL HAVE HER.
KHENSU...
THERE'S SOMETHING ELSE.

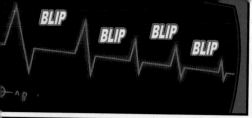

BLIP BLIP BLIP BLIP

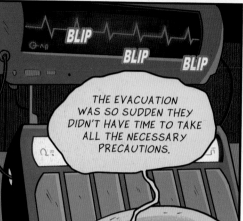

BLIP BLIP BLIP

THE EVACUATION WAS SO SUDDEN THEY DIDN'T HAVE TIME TO TAKE ALL THE NECESSARY PRECAUTIONS.

THE HOLDING CELLS.

THEY COLLAPSED.

IT'S OKAY. YOU DON'T HAVE TO--

BLIP

BLIP

I DIDN'T KILL TALIBATH. KHENSU. YOU NEED TO KNOW I WOULD NEVER...

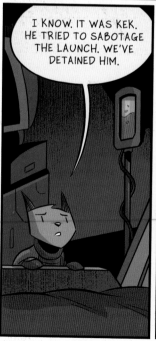

I KNOW. IT WAS KEK. HE TRIED TO SABOTAGE THE LAUNCH. WE'VE DETAINED HIM.

MY CONCERN WAS ALWAYS FOR THE SAFETY OF AILUROS. THE AGREEMENT WAS CLEOPATRA IN EXCHANGE FOR OUR SECURITY.

I SHOULD HAVE KNOWN BETTER. I SHOULD HAVE...

I'M SORRY I LET YOU DOWN. I'M SORRY I DIDN'T TREAT YOU LIKE A SON.

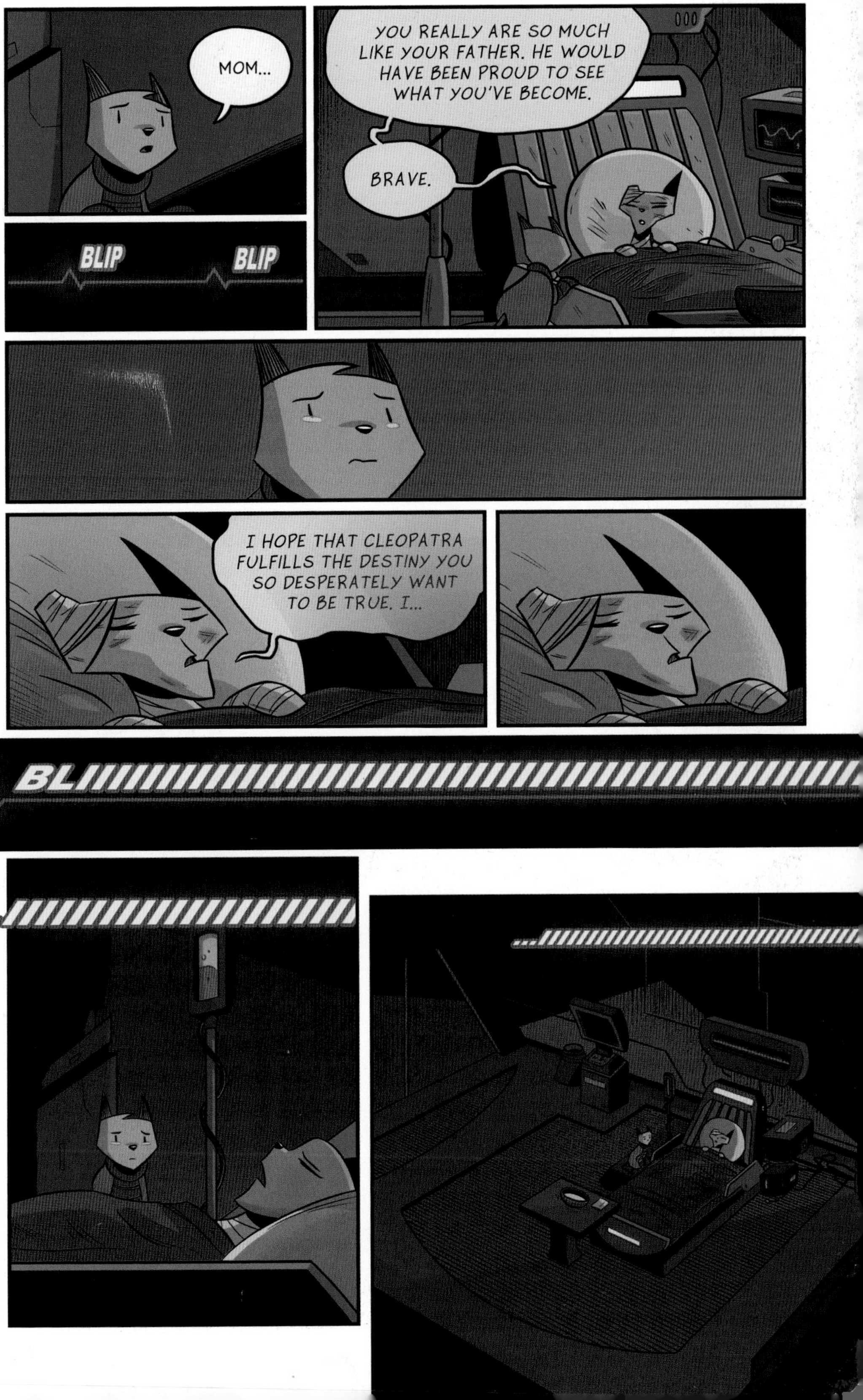
MOM...
YOU REALLY ARE SO MUCH LIKE YOUR FATHER. HE WOULD HAVE BEEN PROUD TO SEE WHAT YOU'VE BECOME.
BRAVE.
BLIP
BLIP
I HOPE THAT CLEOPATRA FULFILLS THE DESTINY YOU SO DESPERATELY WANT TO BE TRUE. I...
BLIIIIIIIIIIIIIIIIIIIIIIIIIIIIII
IIIIIIIIIIIIII
...IIIIIIIIIIIIIIIIIIIIIIIIIIIIII

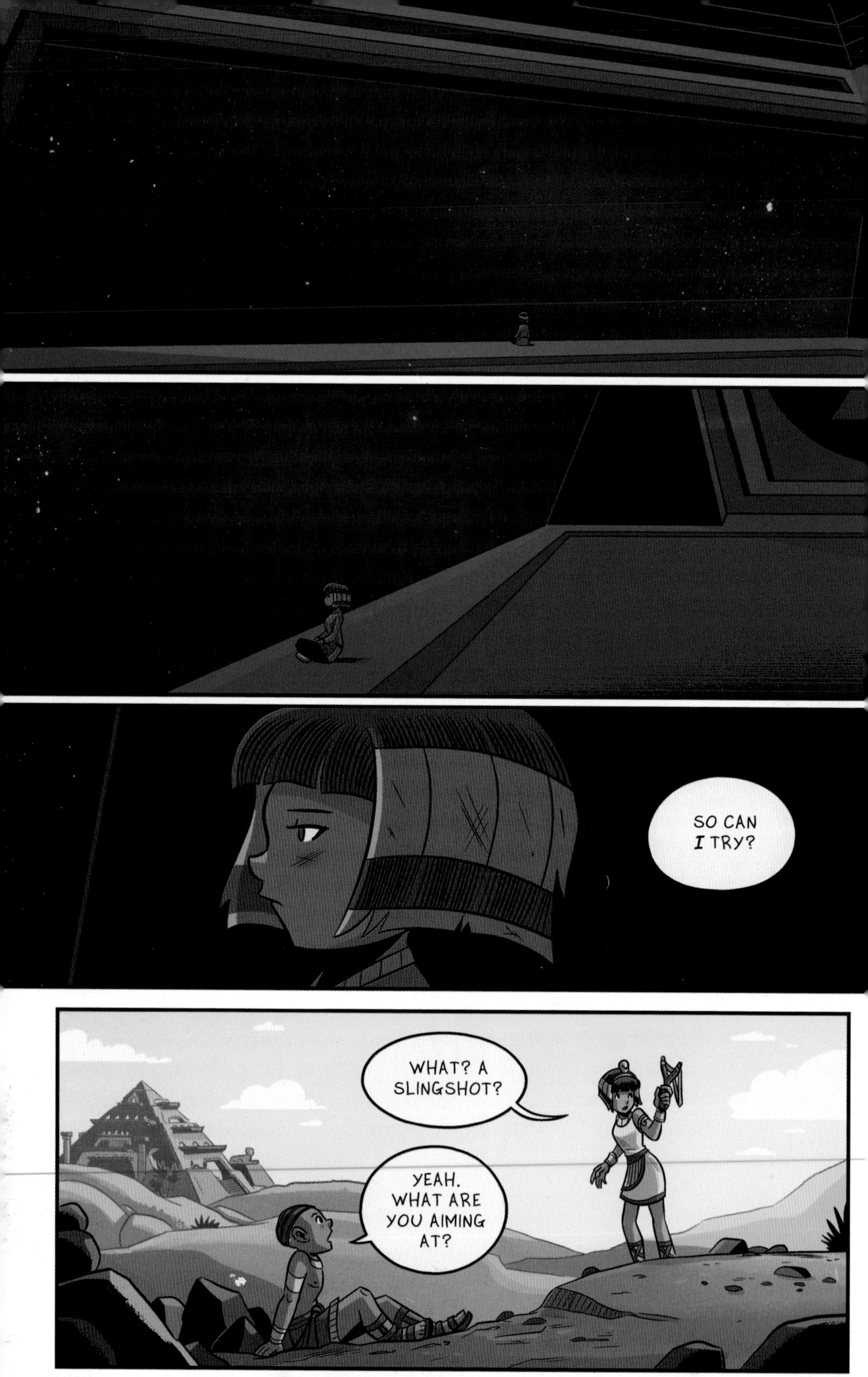
SO CAN *I* TRY?
WHAT? A SLINGSHOT?
YEAH. WHAT ARE YOU AIMING AT?

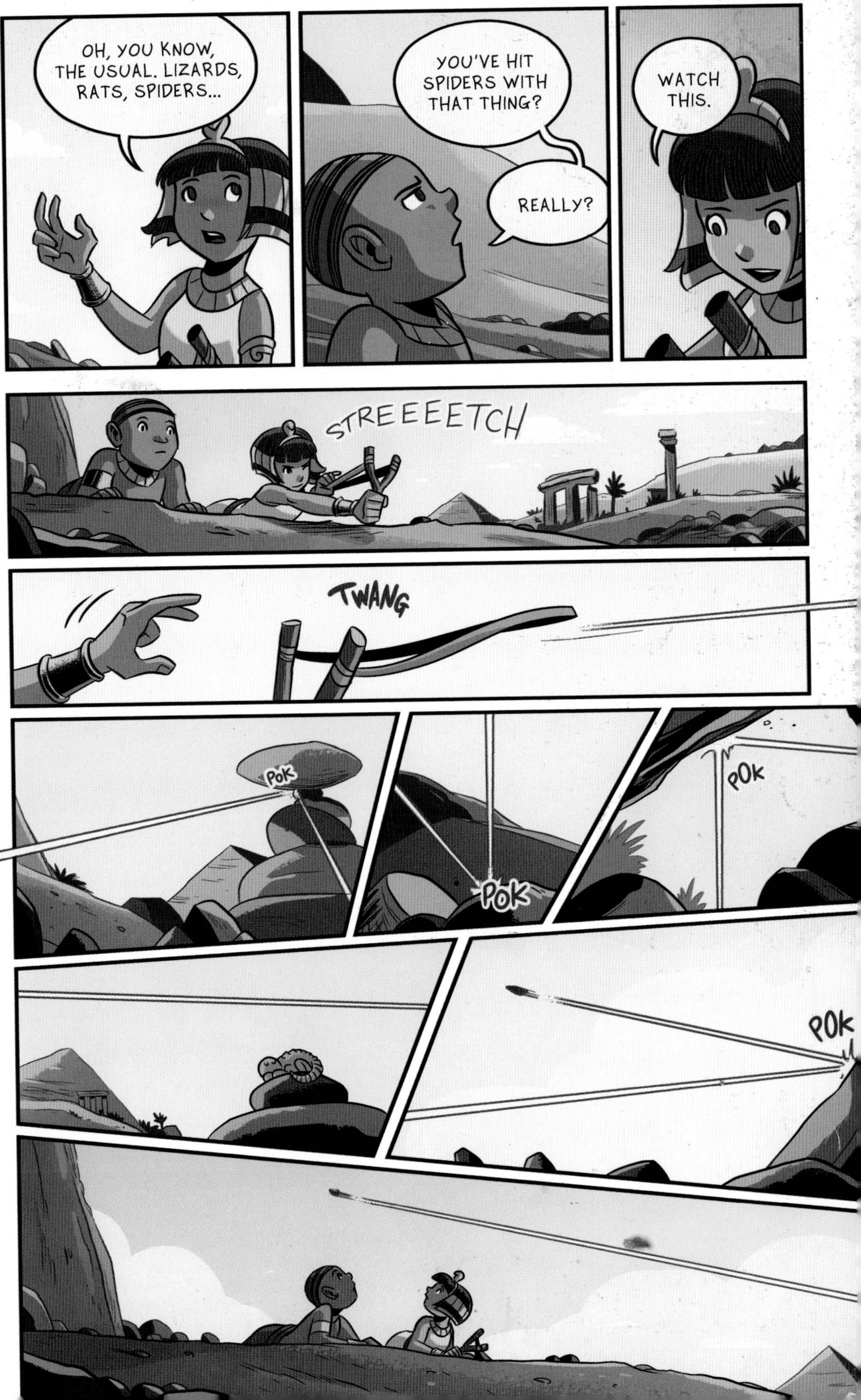
OH, YOU KNOW, THE USUAL. LIZARDS, RATS, SPIDERS...
YOU'VE HIT SPIDERS WITH THAT THING?
REALLY?
WATCH THIS.
STREEEETCH
TWANG
POK
POK
POK
POK

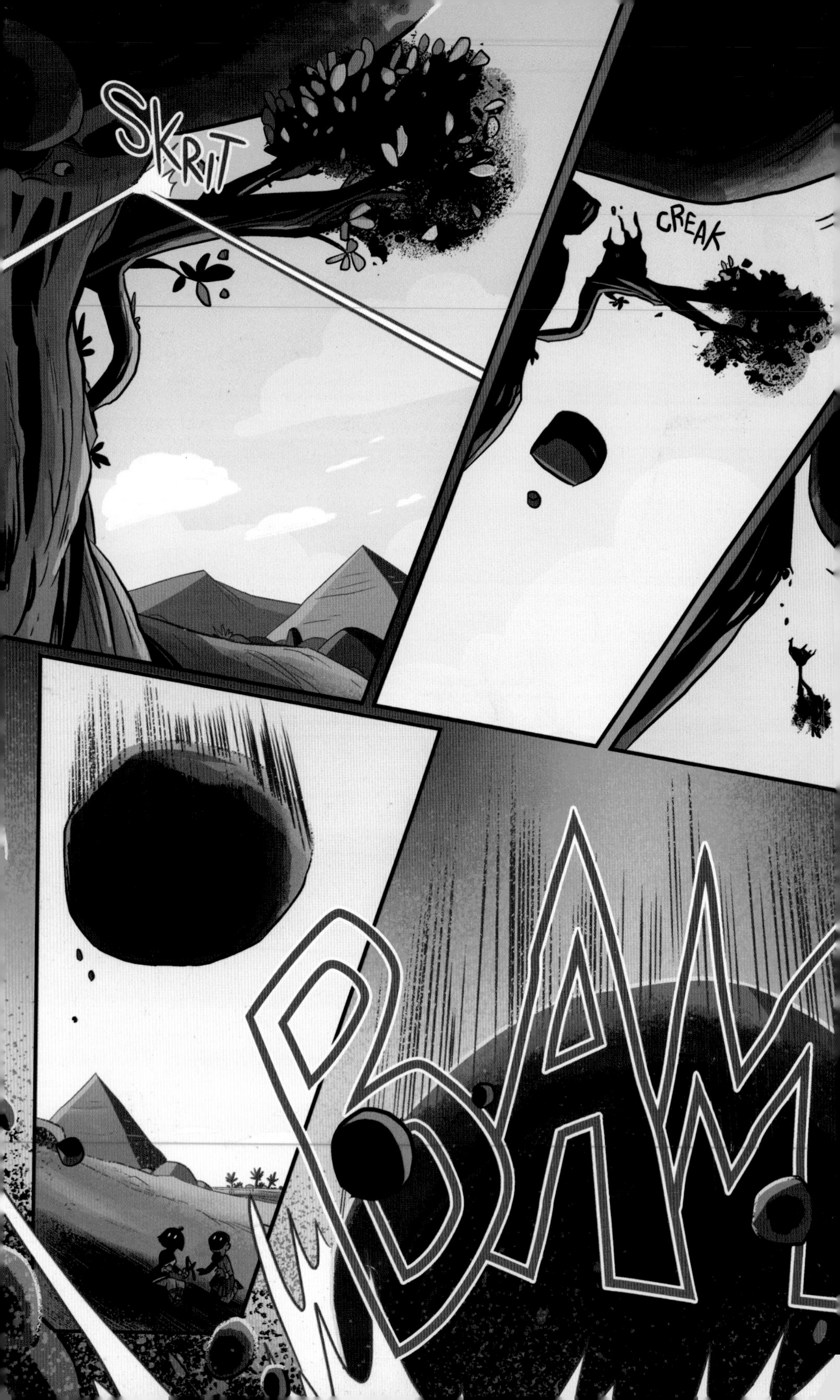
SKRIT
CREAK
BAM

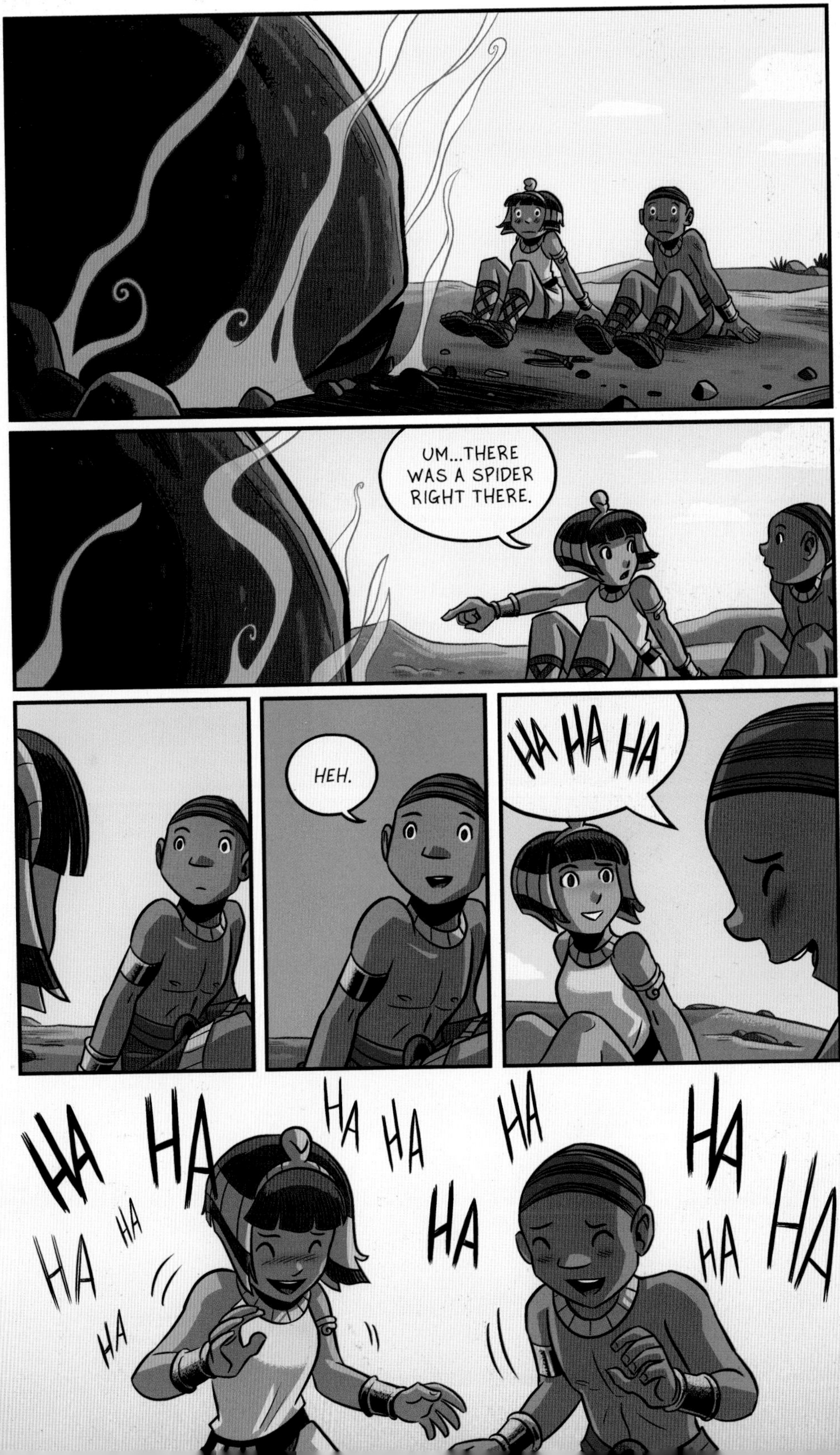
UM...THERE WAS A SPIDER RIGHT THERE.
HEH.
HA HA HA
HA HA HA HA HA HA HA HA HA HA HA HA HA HA

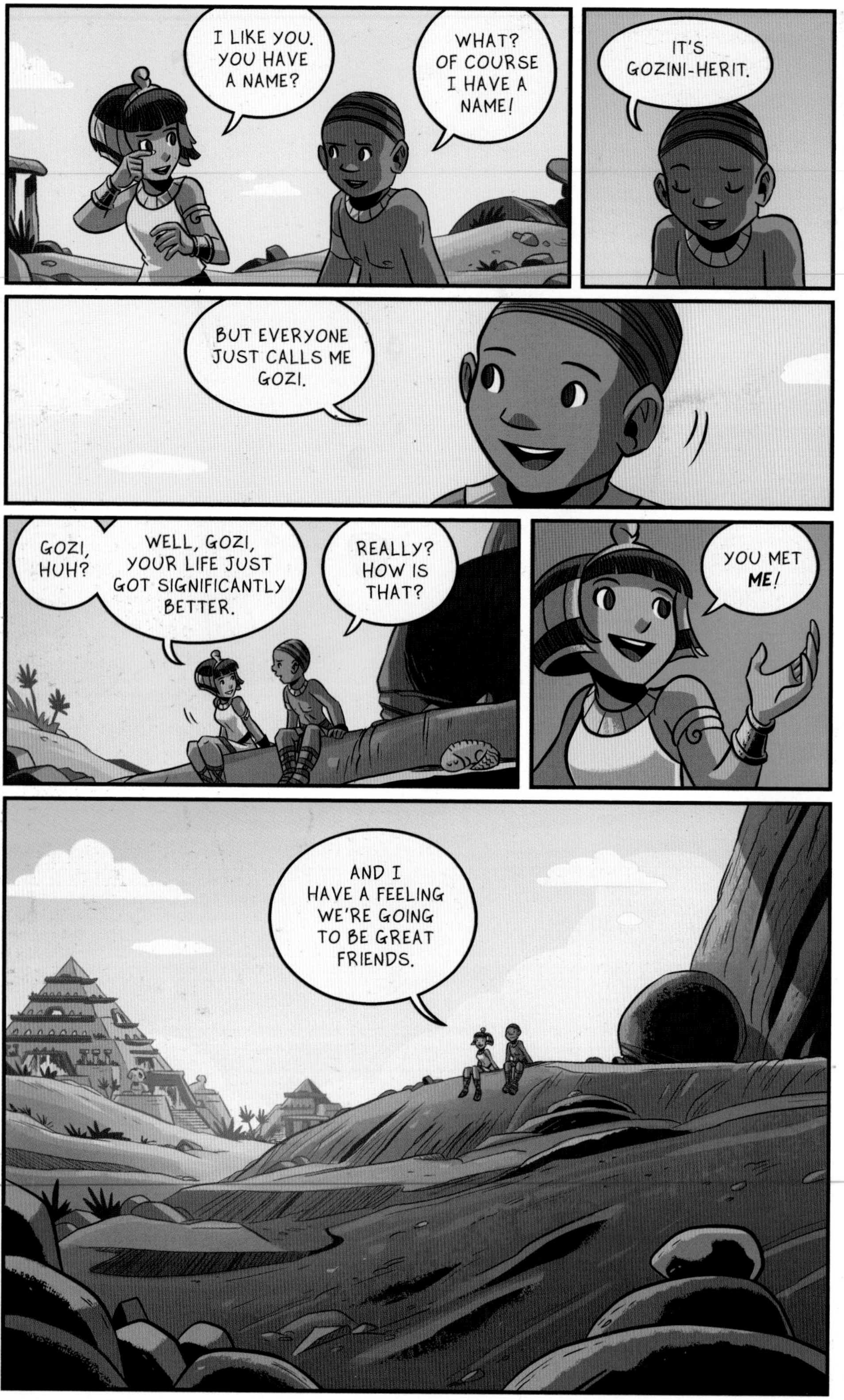
I LIKE YOU. YOU HAVE A NAME?
WHAT? OF COURSE I HAVE A NAME!
IT'S GOZINI-HERIT.
BUT EVERYONE JUST CALLS ME GOZI.
GOZI, HUH?
WELL, GOZI, YOUR LIFE JUST GOT SIGNIFICANTLY BETTER.
REALLY? HOW IS THAT?
YOU MET **ME**!
AND I HAVE A FEELING WE'RE GOING TO BE GREAT FRIENDS.

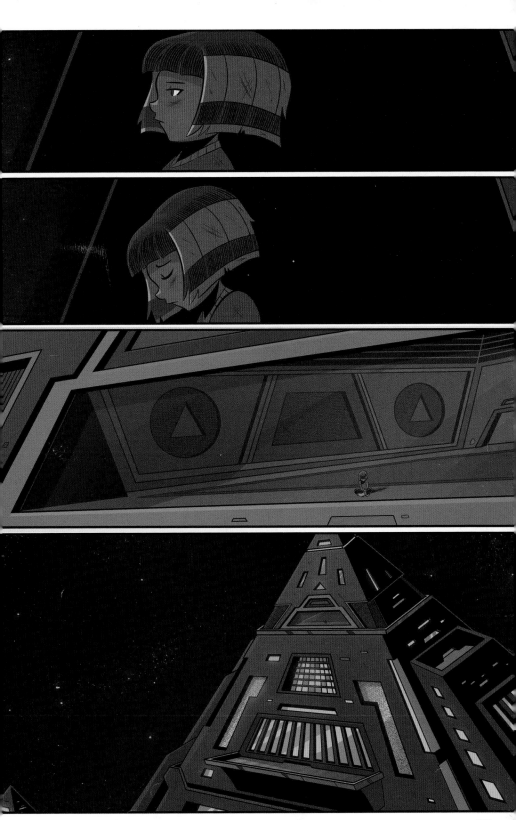

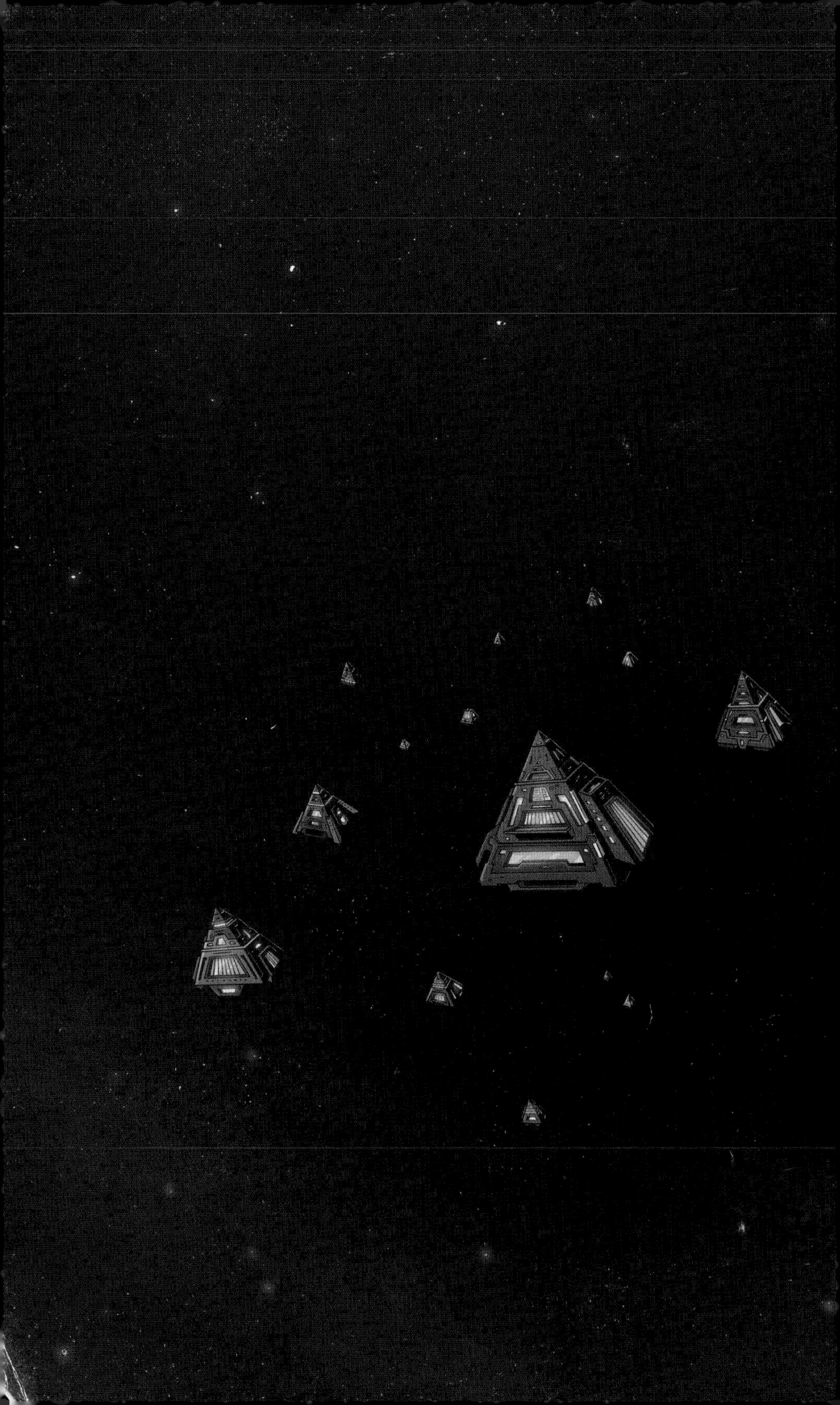

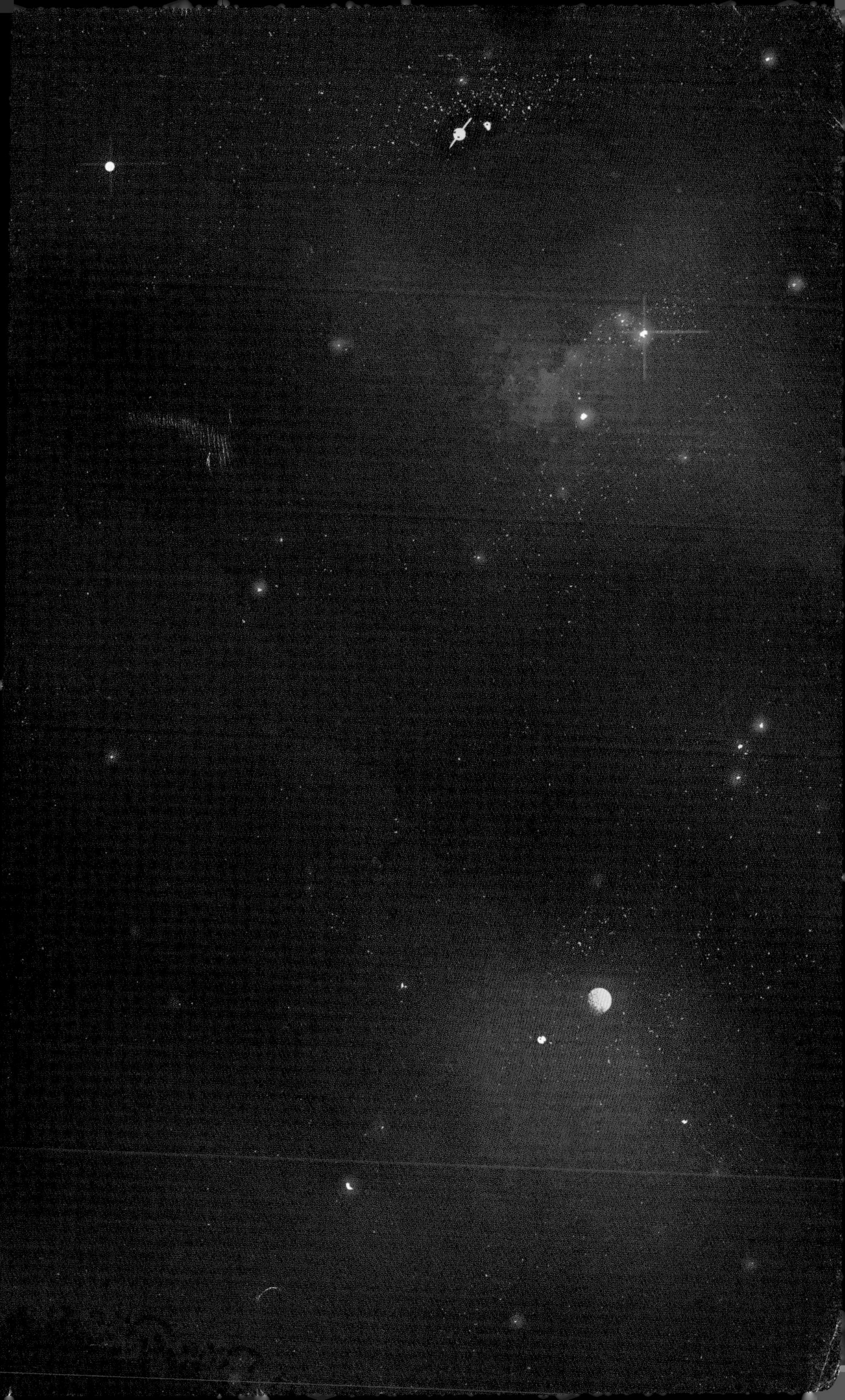

SPECIAL THANKS TO:

My beautiful, loving wife, Jen. Apologies for all the spoilers.

My two boys, Oliver and Orion. I promise to try to fit a dinosaur into the next book.

My cat, Misty, for the gentle purrs and company. The clawing at my leg while I'm working I could do without, but the purring has been aces.

The rest of my *super* supportive friends and family. I'm continually blessed to have so many of you in my life.

Cassandra Pelham Fulton and David Saylor for keeping this series steering in the right direction, Phil Falco for making it look so good, and all the other wonderful folks at Scholastic for the amazing work you've put into it. One more book to go!

My wonderful agent, Judy Hansen. I hope you like dinosaurs.

My incredible team of color flatters: Mary Bellamy, Kate Carleton, Lee Cherolis, Dan Conner, Josh Dykstra, Patricia Krmpotich, and Rachel Polk. I couldn't have gotten this book done on time (well, close to on time) without you.

Christ, for helping with the tough stuff. The easy stuff, too, I suppose.

And last but not least, the artists around the world crafting stories and music. I would be completely directionless if not for your inspiration and melodies.

EXTRA SPECIAL THANKS TO:

All the teachers, librarians, booksellers, parents, and readers out there who have supported Cleopatra in Space and/or given me high fives. CONTINUE TO BE AWESOME!

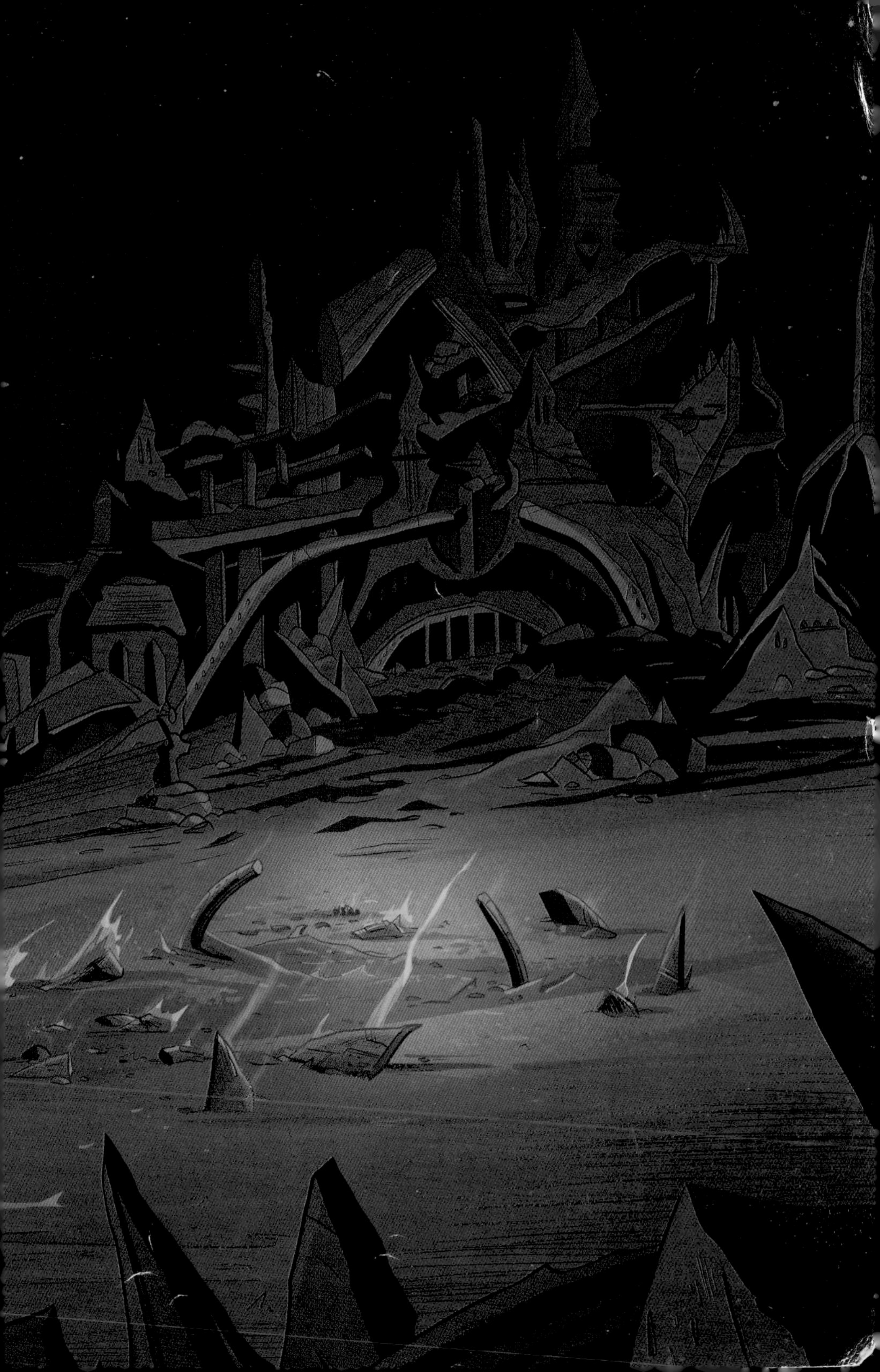

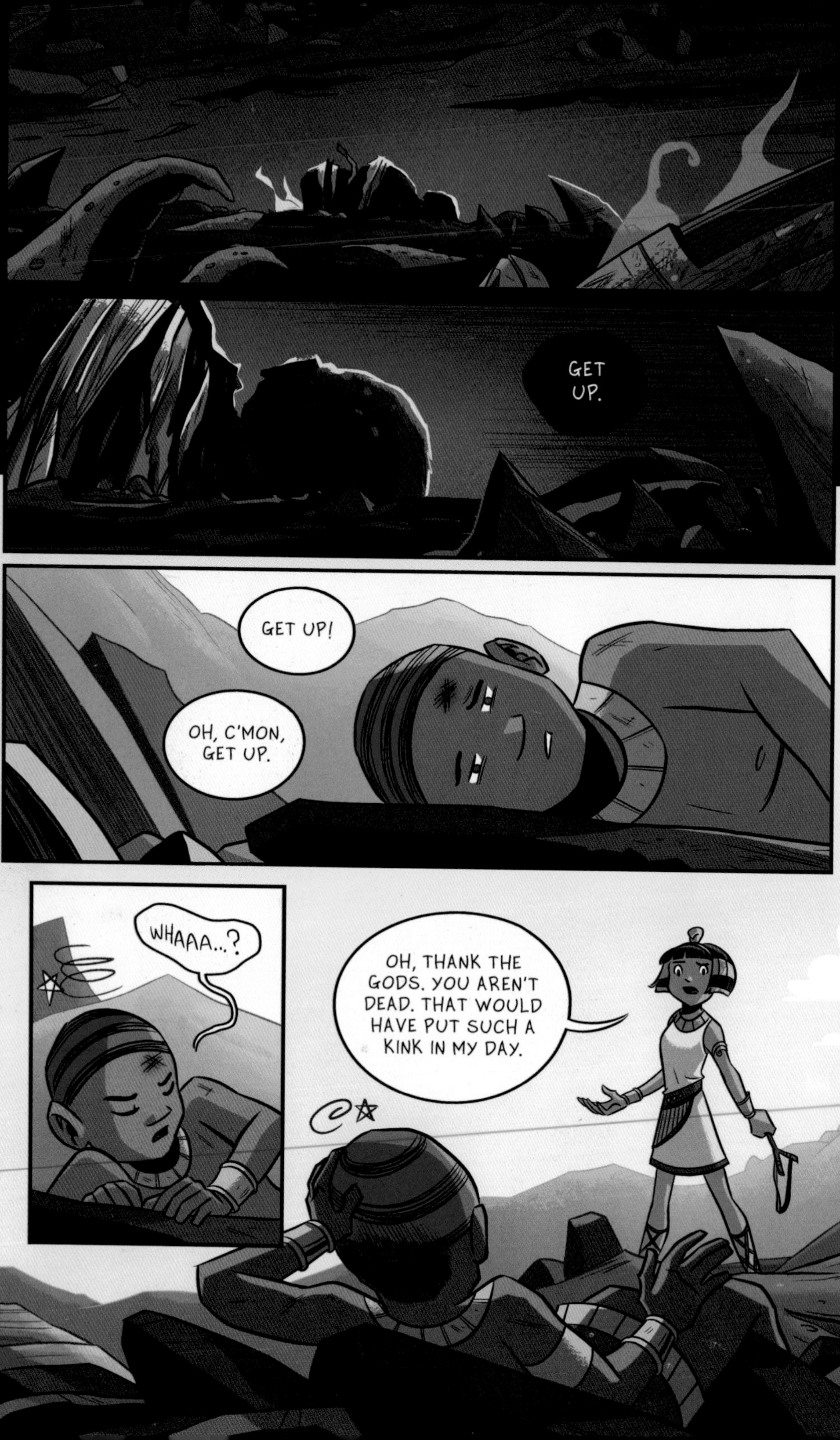
GET UP.
GET UP!
OH, C'MON, GET UP.
WHAAA...?
OH, THANK THE GODS. YOU AREN'T DEAD. THAT WOULD HAVE PUT SUCH A KINK IN MY DAY.

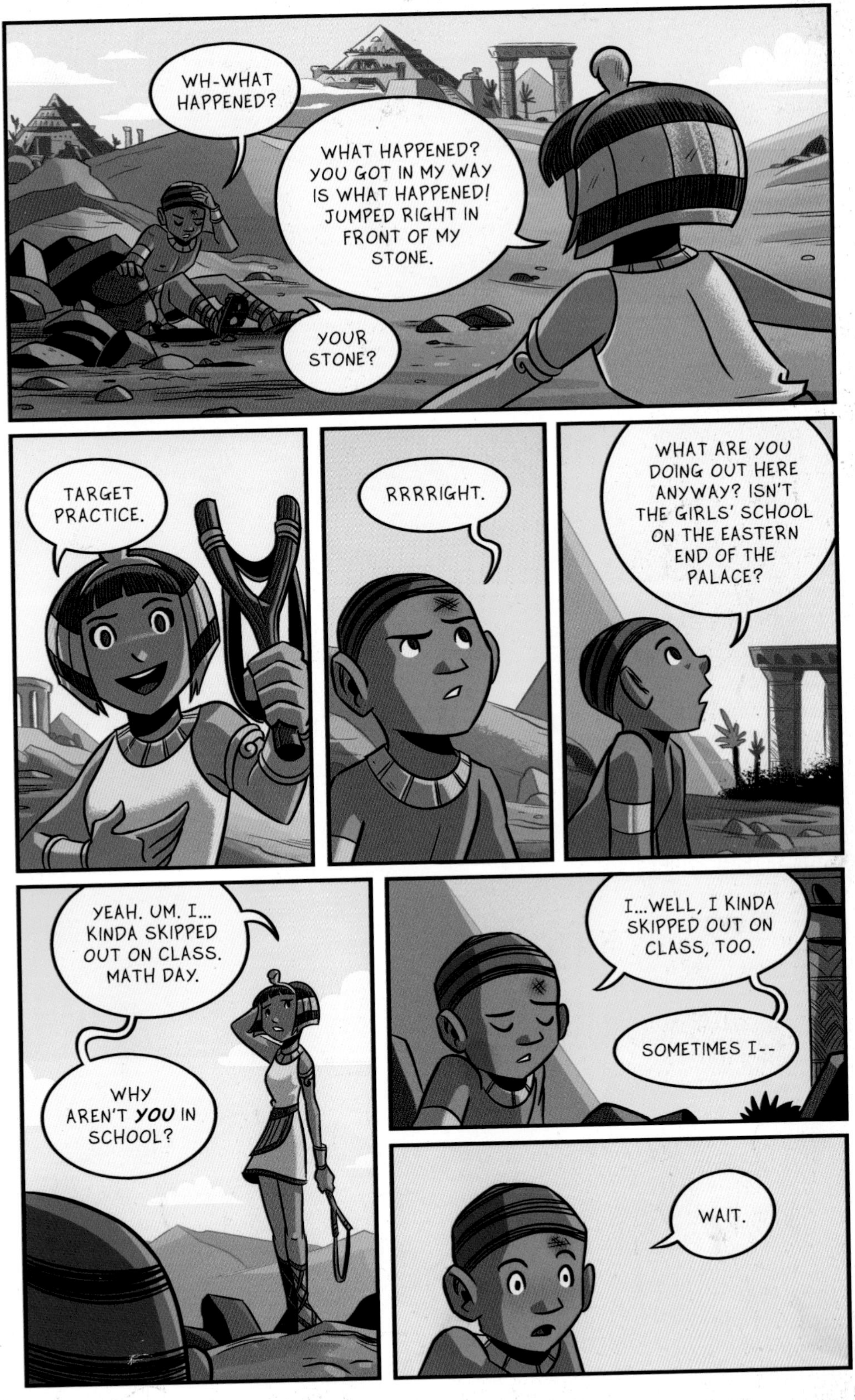
WH-WHAT HAPPENED?
WHAT HAPPENED? YOU GOT IN MY WAY IS WHAT HAPPENED! JUMPED RIGHT IN FRONT OF MY STONE.
YOUR STONE?
TARGET PRACTICE.
RRRRIGHT.
WHAT ARE YOU DOING OUT HERE ANYWAY? ISN'T THE GIRLS' SCHOOL ON THE EASTERN END OF THE PALACE?
YEAH. UM. I... KINDA SKIPPED OUT ON CLASS. MATH DAY.
WHY AREN'T *YOU* IN SCHOOL?
I...WELL, I KINDA SKIPPED OUT ON CLASS, TOO.
SOMETIMES I--
WAIT.

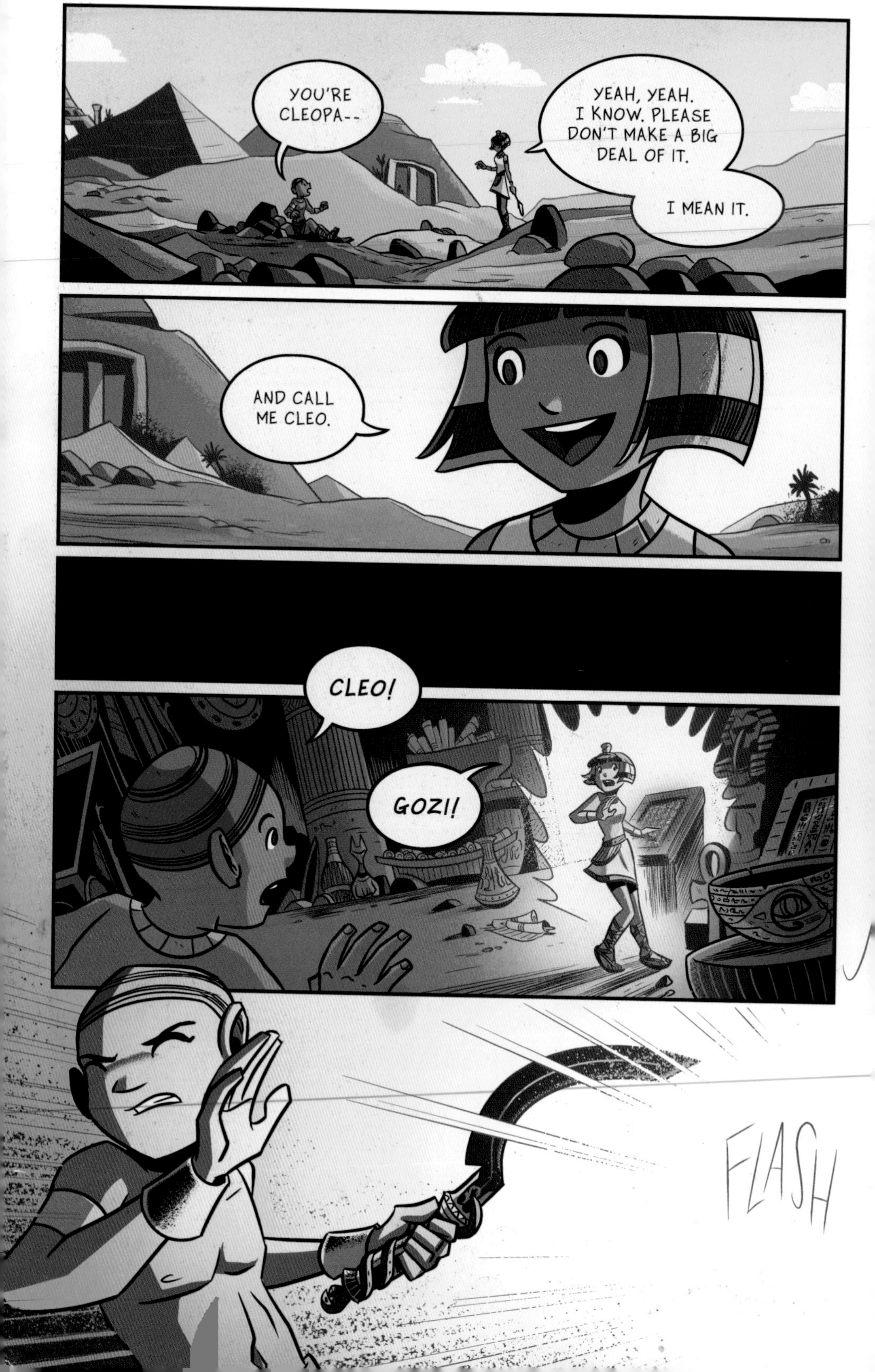
YOU'RE CLEOPA--
YEAH, YEAH. I KNOW. PLEASE DON'T MAKE A BIG DEAL OF IT.
I MEAN IT.
AND CALL ME CLEO.
CLEO!
GOZI!
FLASH

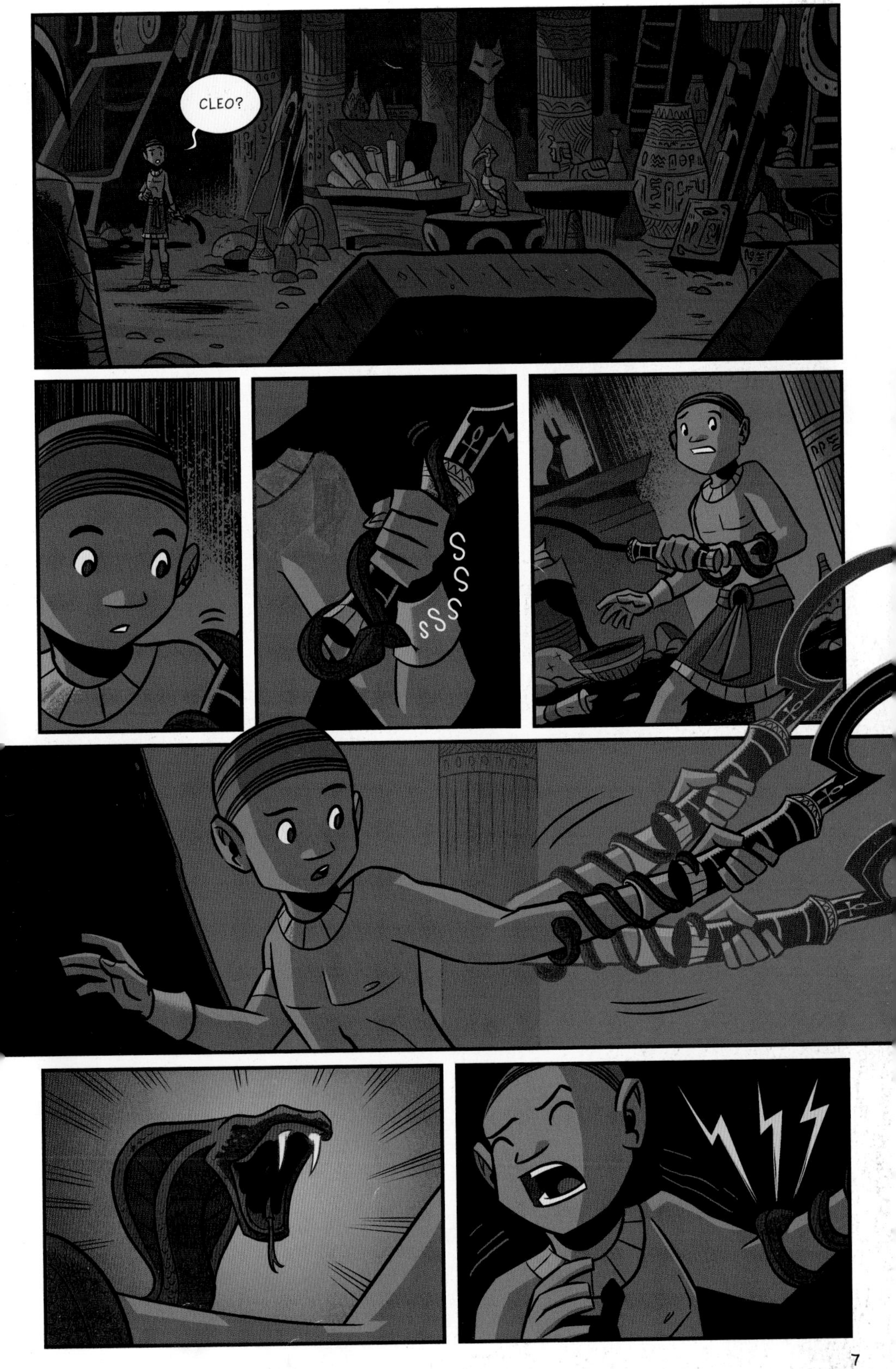
CLEO?
SSSSSS

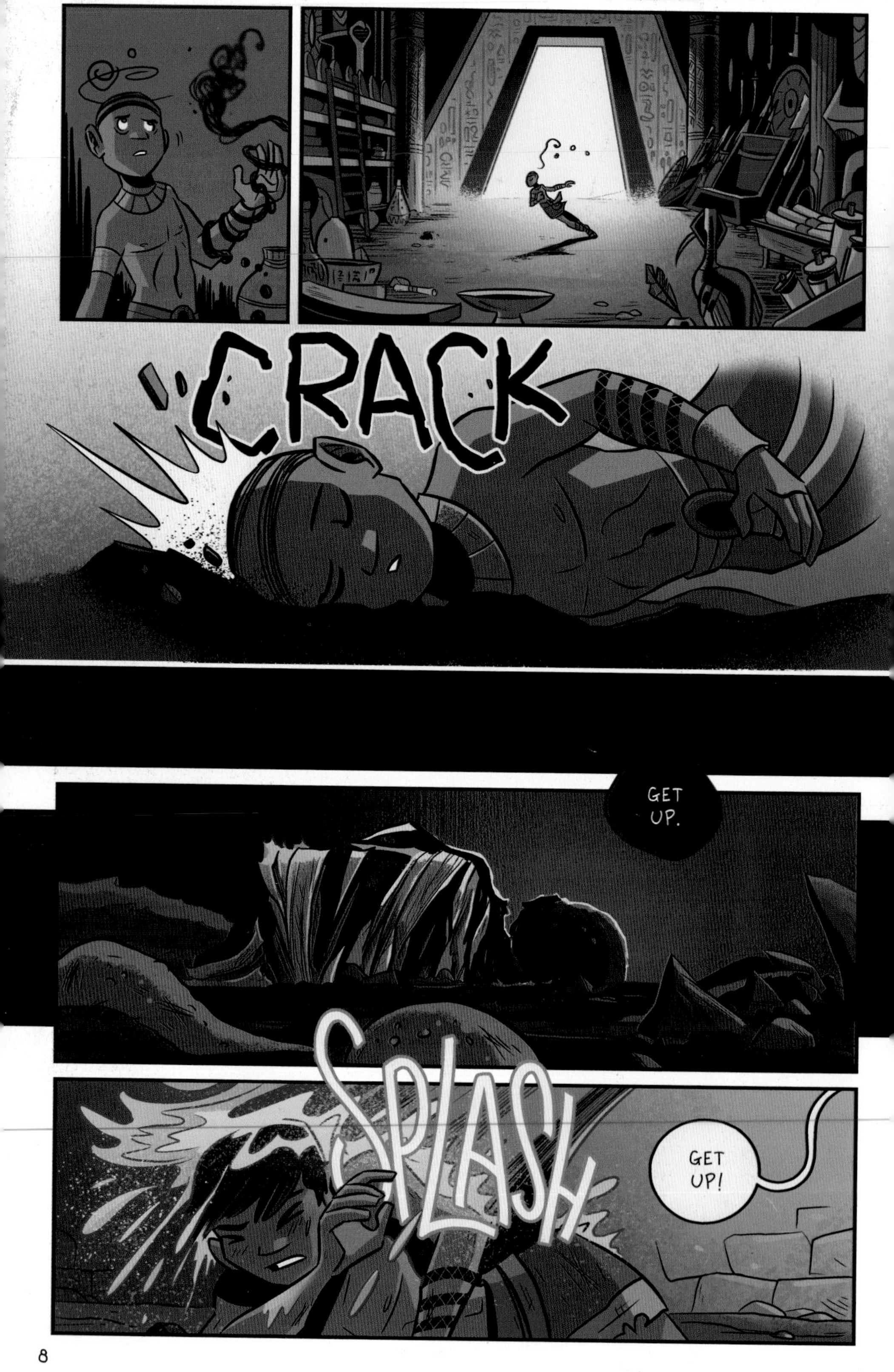
CRACK
GET UP.
SPLASH
GET UP!

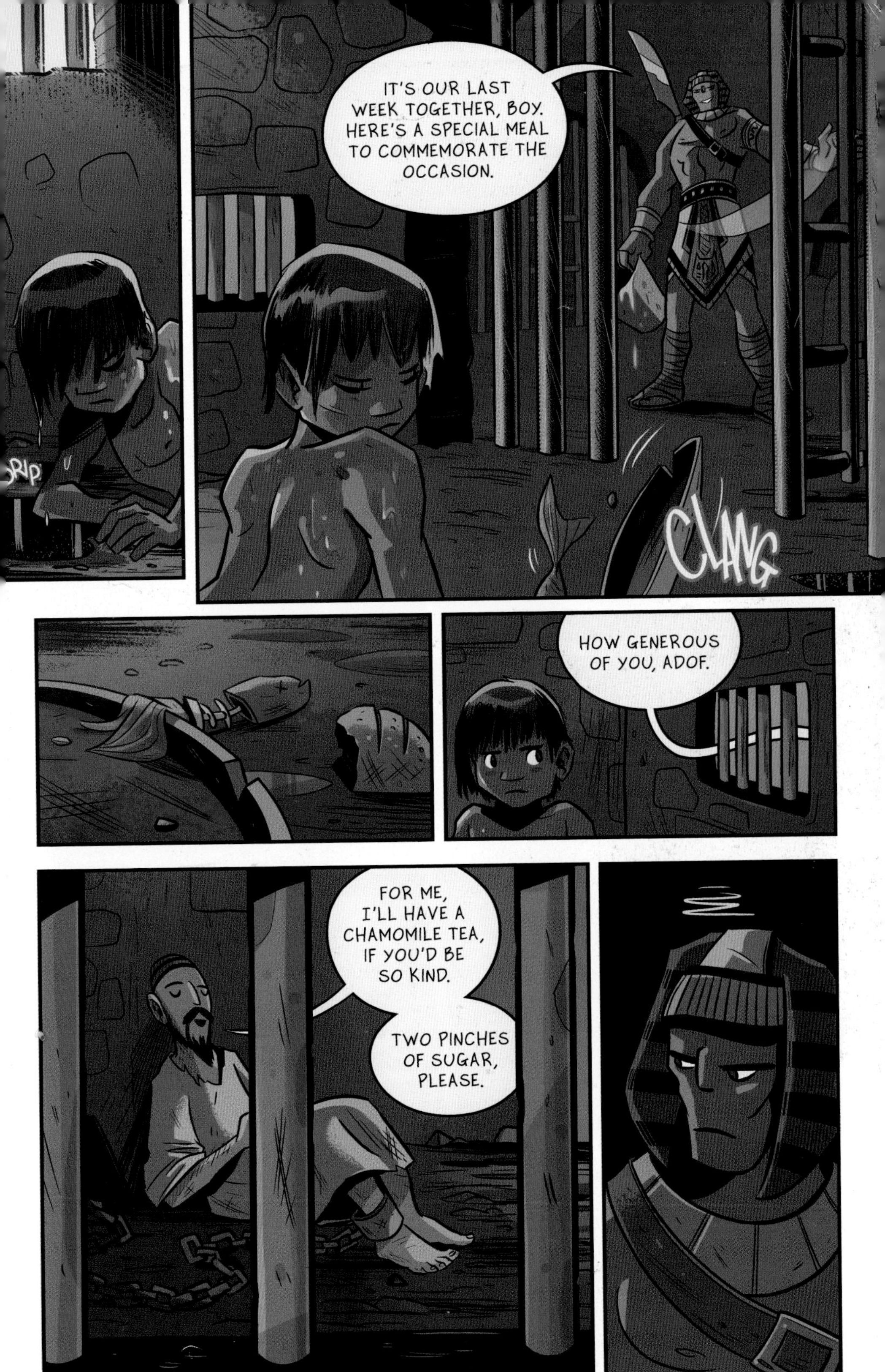
DRIP
IT'S OUR LAST WEEK TOGETHER, BOY. HERE'S A SPECIAL MEAL TO COMMEMORATE THE OCCASION.
CLANG
HOW GENEROUS OF YOU, ADOF.
FOR ME, I'LL HAVE A CHAMOMILE TEA, IF YOU'D BE SO KIND.
TWO PINCHES OF SUGAR, PLEASE.

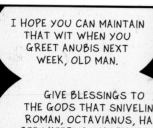

I HOPE YOU CAN MAINTAIN THAT WIT WHEN YOU GREET ANUBIS NEXT WEEK, OLD MAN.

GIVE BLESSINGS TO THE GODS THAT SNIVELING ROMAN, OCTAVIANUS, HAS BEEN KEEPING THE PHARAOH SO OCCUPIED THIS YEAR OR HE PROBABLY WOULD HAVE ORDERED YOUR DEATHS MONTHS AGO.

YES, HOW FORTUNATE FOR US THAT WE'VE BEEN GRANTED THE PLEASURE OF YOUR POLITE COMPANY INSTEAD. I THANK THE GODS EVERY DAY.

WELL DONE.

YOU JUST WON YOURSELF ANOTHER DAY WITHOUT FOOD.

GOOD FORTUNE CONTINUES TO SHINE UPON US!

TWO DAYS!

YOU ONLY AGITATE THEM, BAKARI.

MAYBE IF YOU WERE LESS COMPLACENT, WE'D AT LEAST HAVE GOTTEN FRESH BREAD IN HERE THESE PAST TWO YEARS.

CRACK

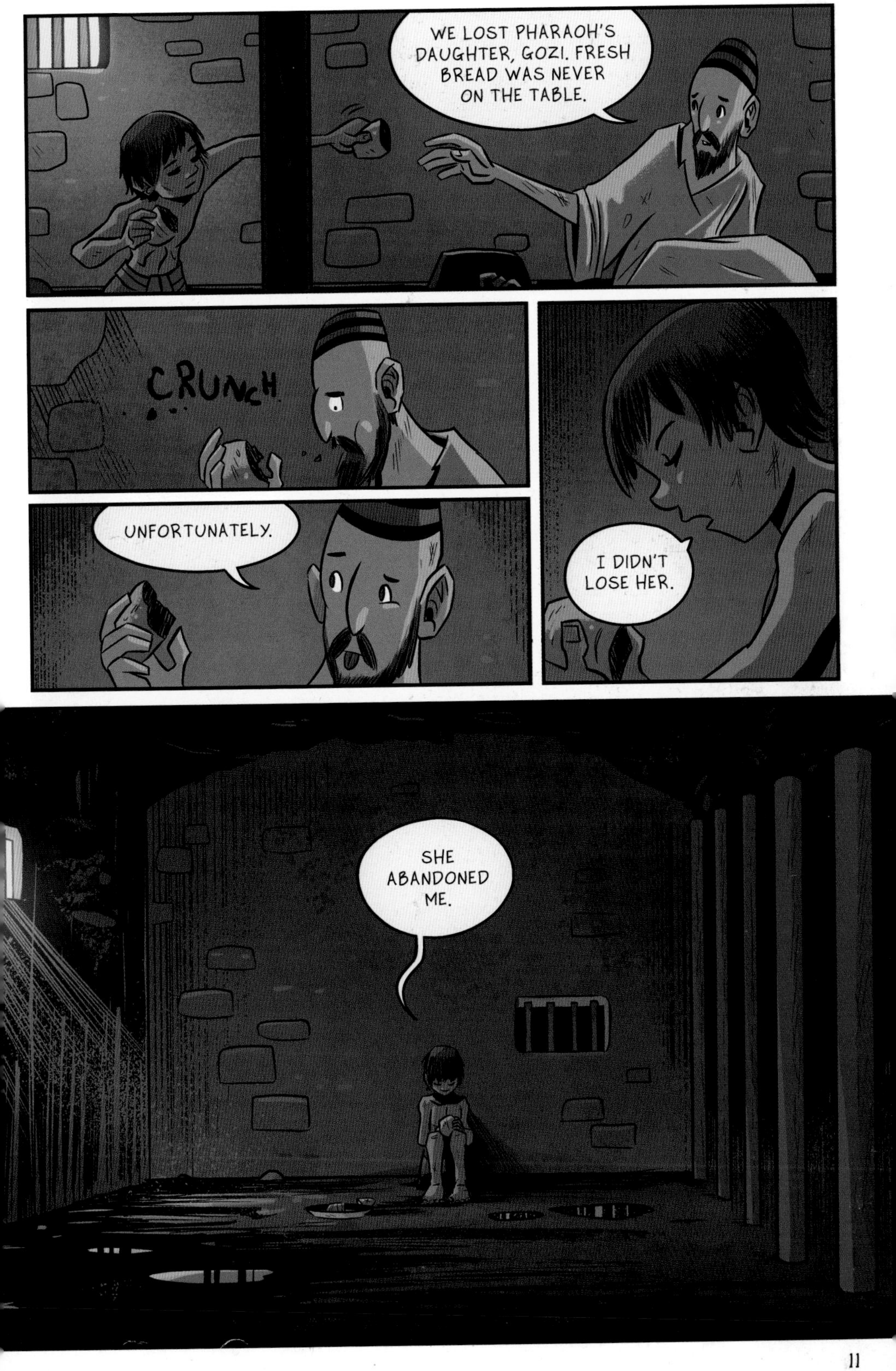
WE LOST PHARAOH'S DAUGHTER, GOZI. FRESH BREAD WAS NEVER ON THE TABLE.
CRUNCH
UNFORTUNATELY.
I DIDN'T LOSE HER.
SHE ABANDONED ME.

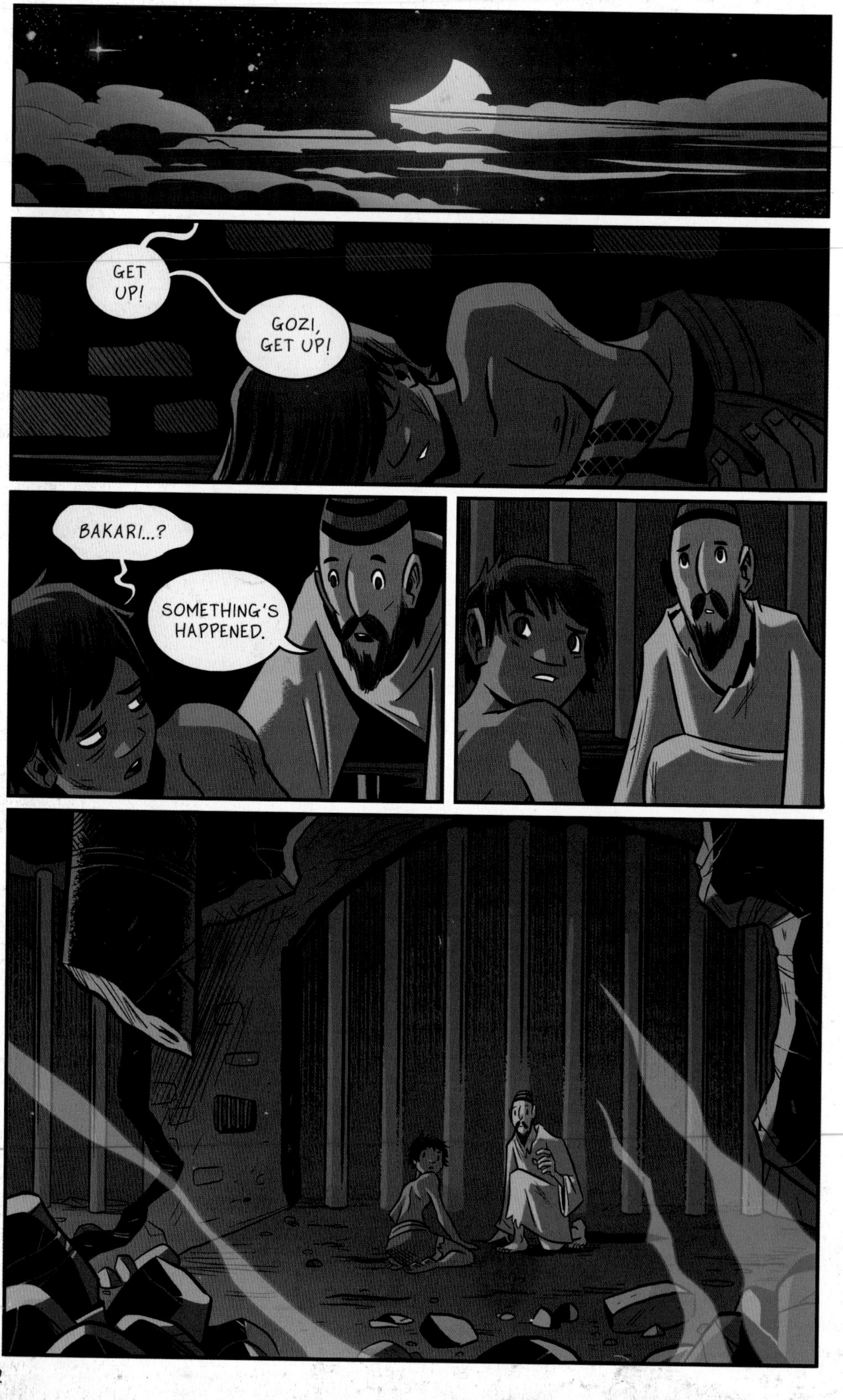
GET UP!
GOZI, GET UP!
BAKARI...?
SOMETHING'S HAPPENED.

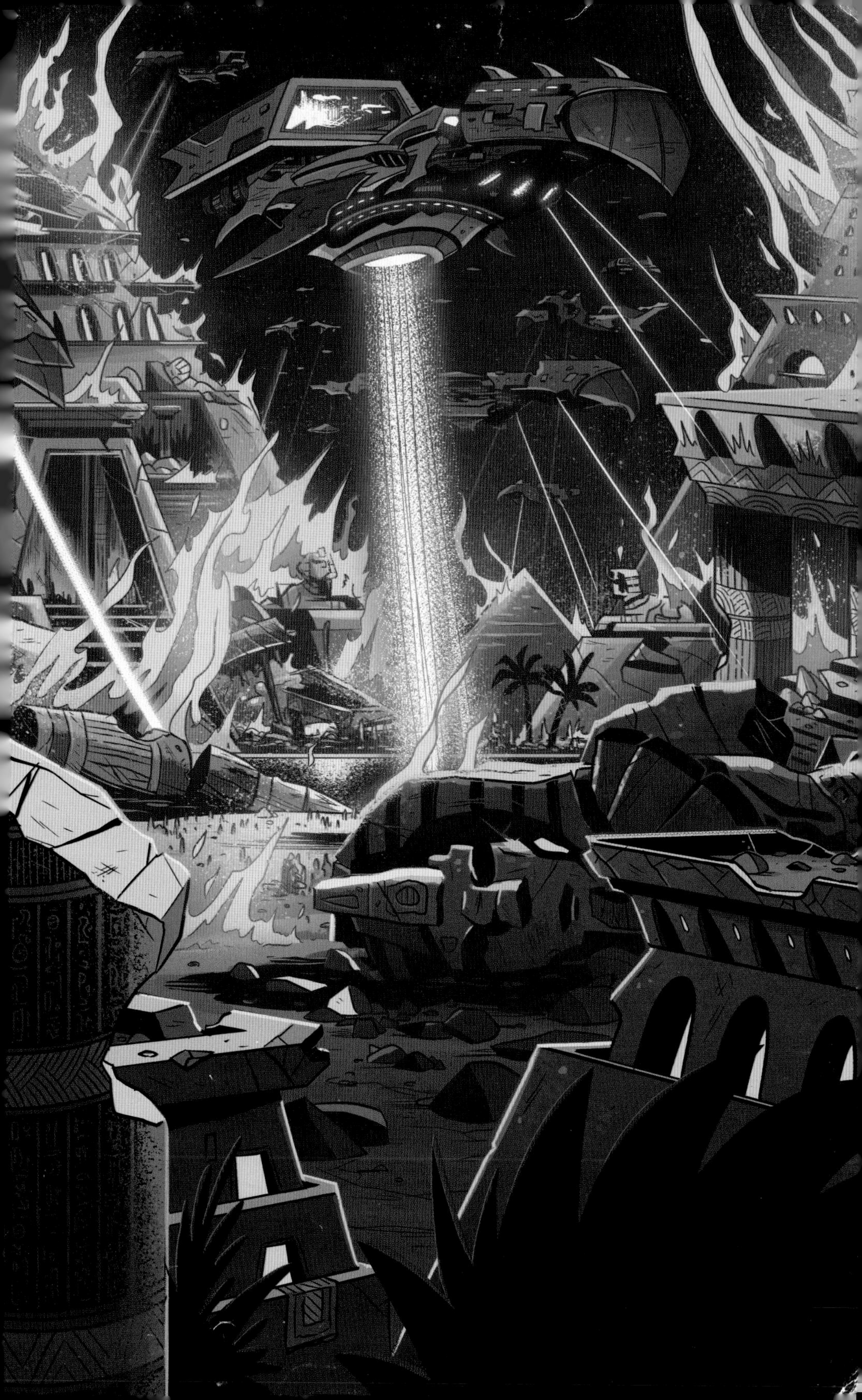

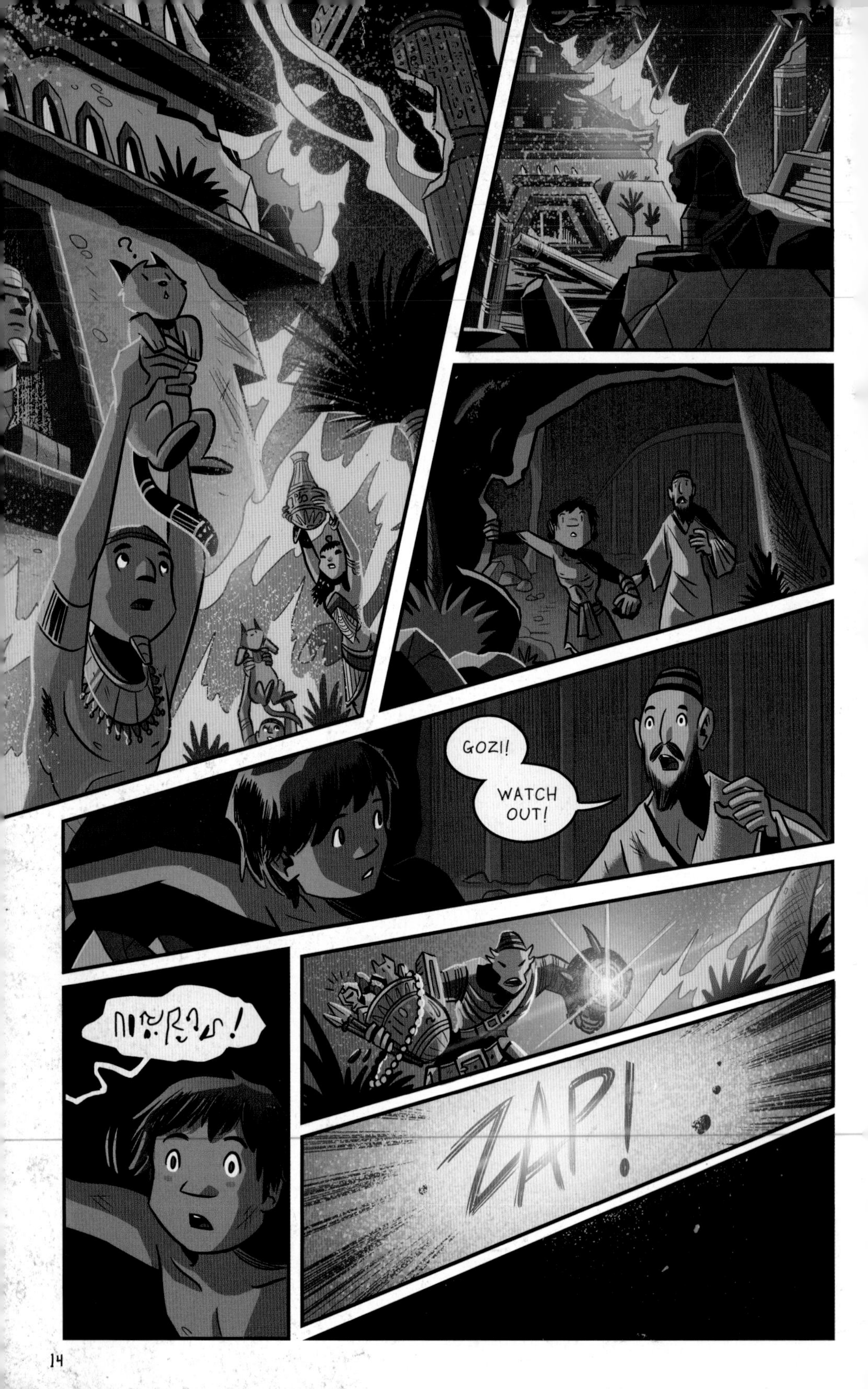
?
GOZI!
WATCH OUT!
ZAP!

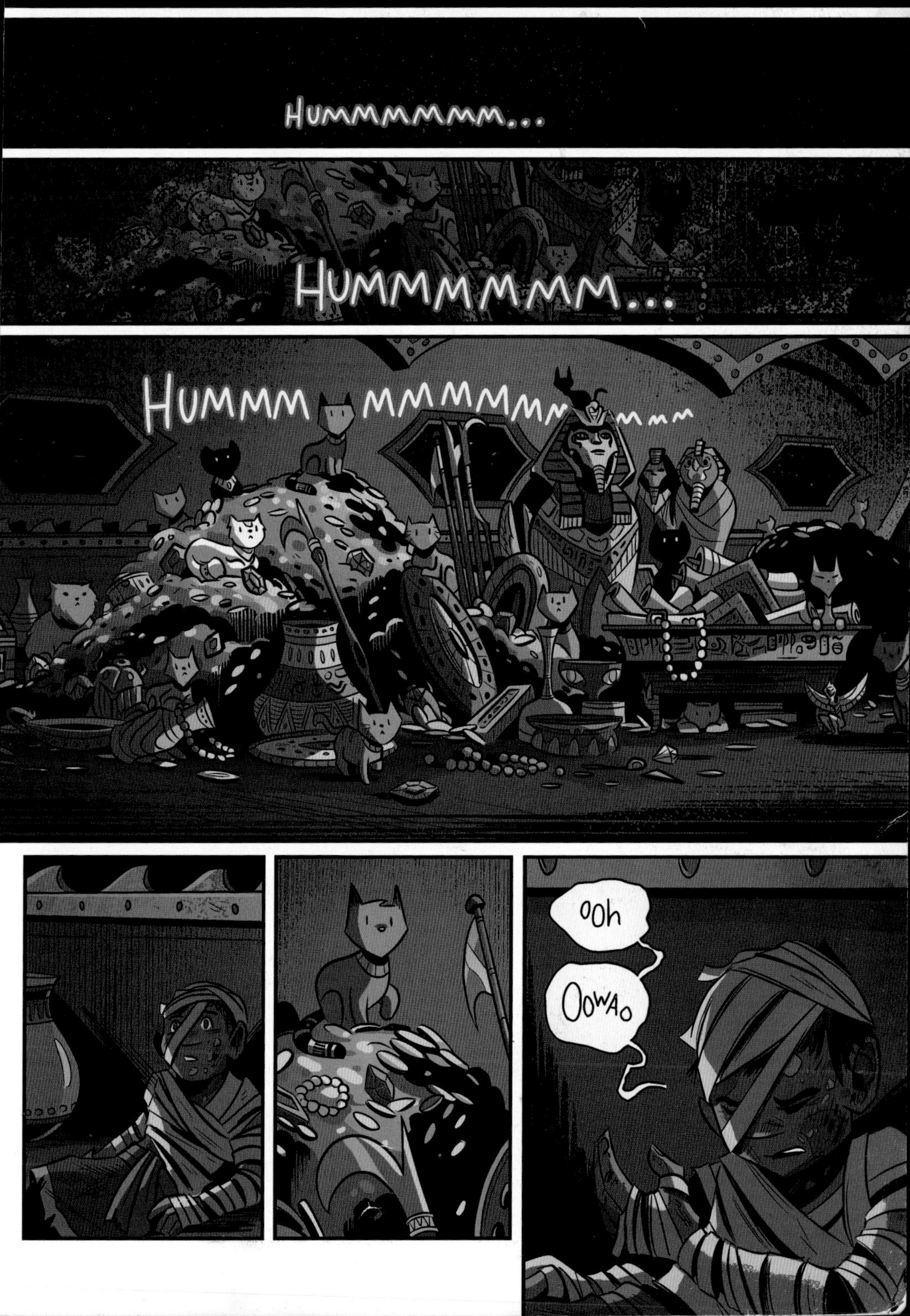
HUMMMMMMM...
HUMMMMMMM...
HUMMM MMMMMMmmm
OOh
OOWAO

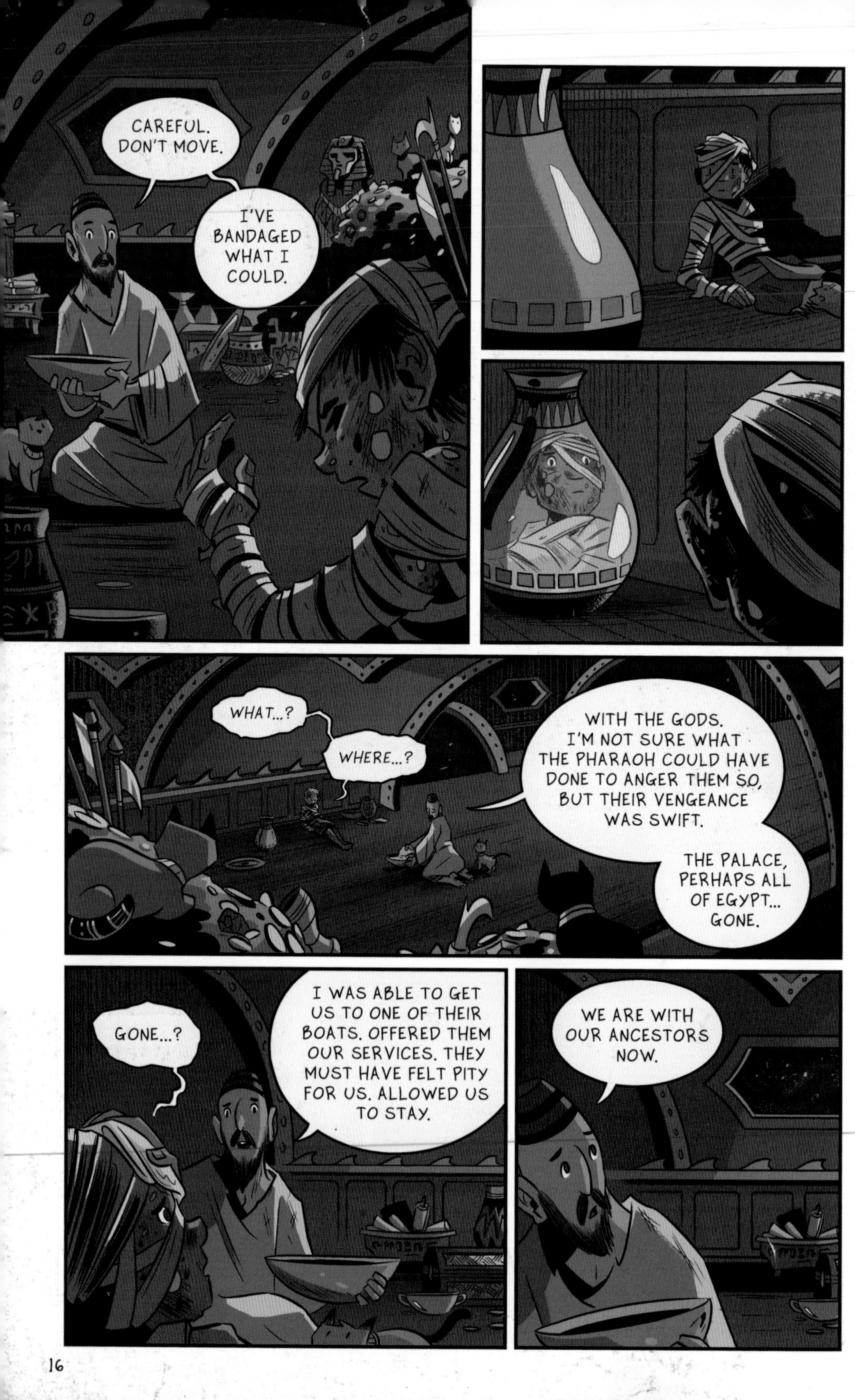
CAREFUL. DON'T MOVE.
I'VE BANDAGED WHAT I COULD.
WHAT...?
WHERE...?
WITH THE GODS. I'M NOT SURE WHAT THE PHARAOH COULD HAVE DONE TO ANGER THEM SO, BUT THEIR VENGEANCE WAS SWIFT.
THE PALACE, PERHAPS ALL OF EGYPT... GONE.
GONE...?
I WAS ABLE TO GET US TO ONE OF THEIR BOATS. OFFERED THEM OUR SERVICES. THEY MUST HAVE FELT PITY FOR US. ALLOWED US TO STAY.
WE ARE WITH OUR ANCESTORS NOW.

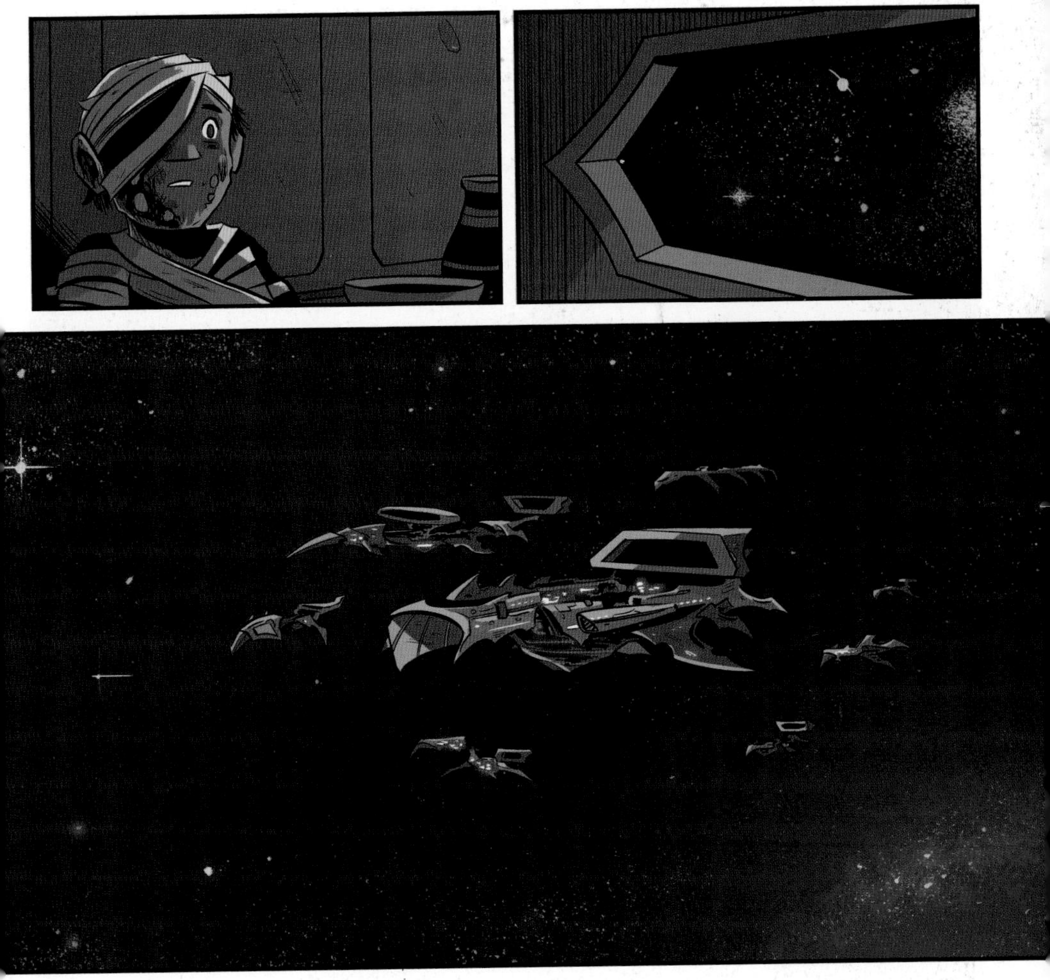

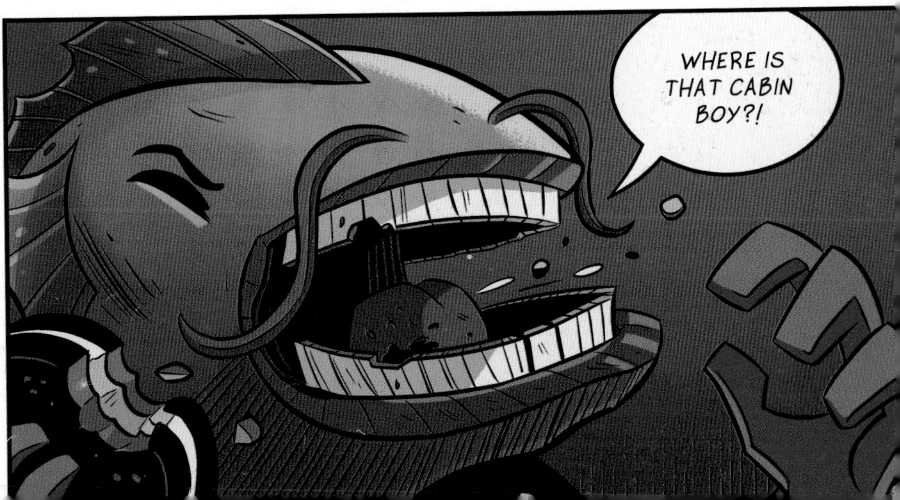
WHERE IS THAT CABIN BOY?!

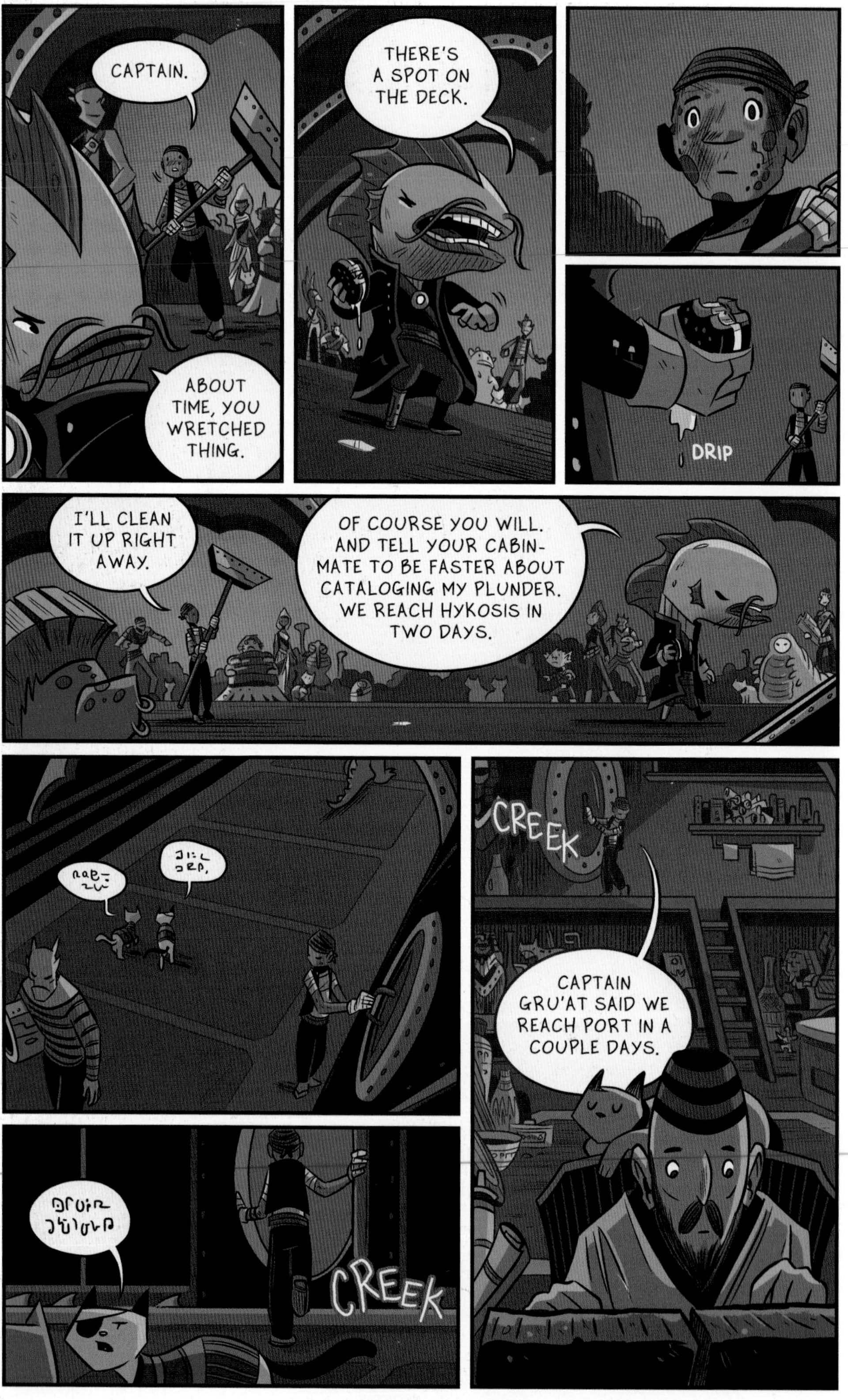
CAPTAIN.
ABOUT TIME, YOU WRETCHED THING.
THERE'S A SPOT ON THE DECK.
DRIP
I'LL CLEAN IT UP RIGHT AWAY.
OF COURSE YOU WILL. AND TELL YOUR CABIN-MATE TO BE FASTER ABOUT CATALOGING MY PLUNDER. WE REACH HYKOSIS IN TWO DAYS.
CREEK
CAPTAIN GRU'AT SAID WE REACH PORT IN A COUPLE DAYS.
CREEK

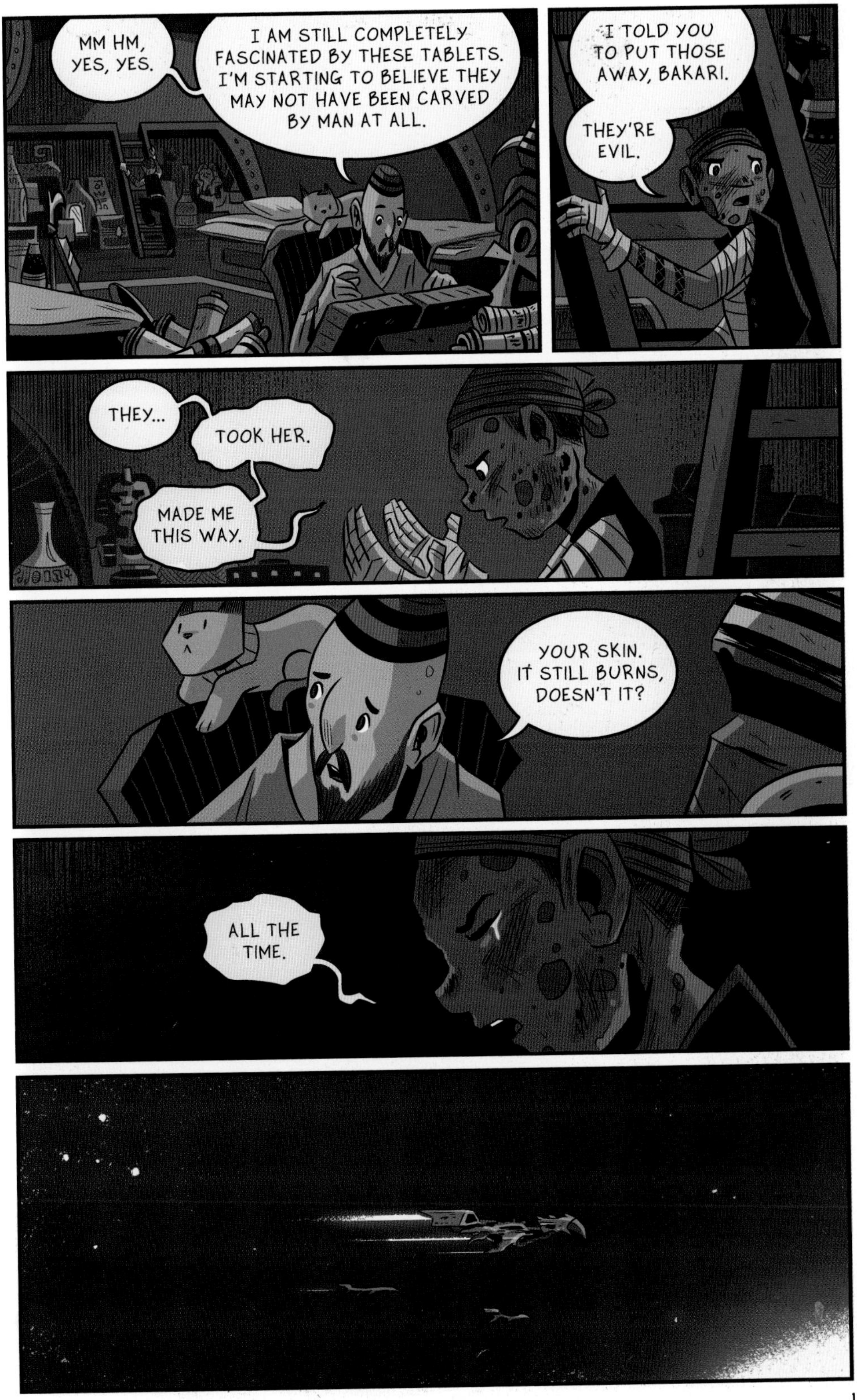
MM HM, YES, YES.
I AM STILL COMPLETELY FASCINATED BY THESE TABLETS. I'M STARTING TO BELIEVE THEY MAY NOT HAVE BEEN CARVED BY MAN AT ALL.
I TOLD YOU TO PUT THOSE AWAY, BAKARI.
THEY'RE EVIL.
THEY...
TOOK HER.
MADE ME THIS WAY.
YOUR SKIN. IT STILL BURNS, DOESN'T IT?
ALL THE TIME.

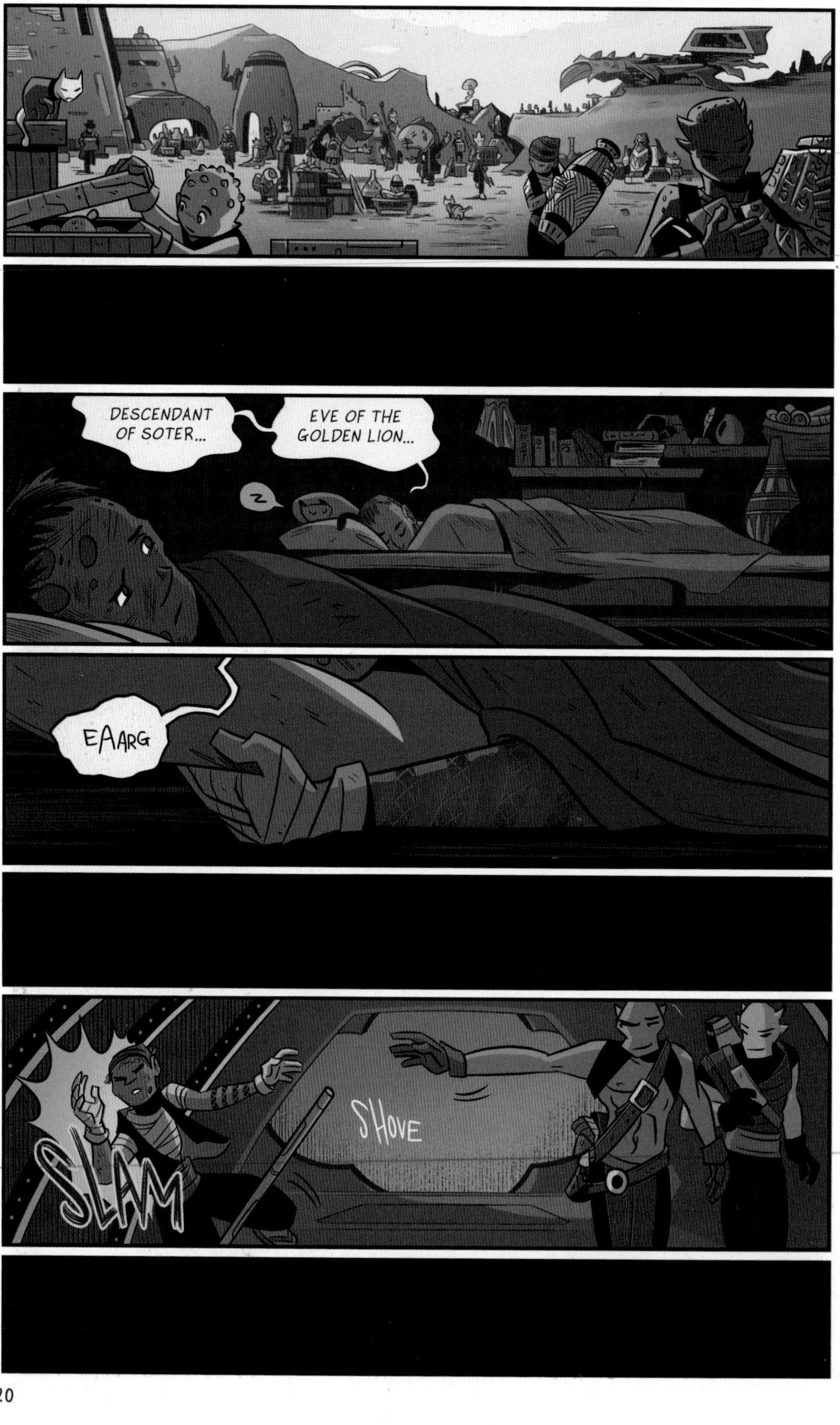
DESCENDANT OF SOTER...
EVE OF THE GOLDEN LION...
Z
EAARG
SLAM
SHOVE

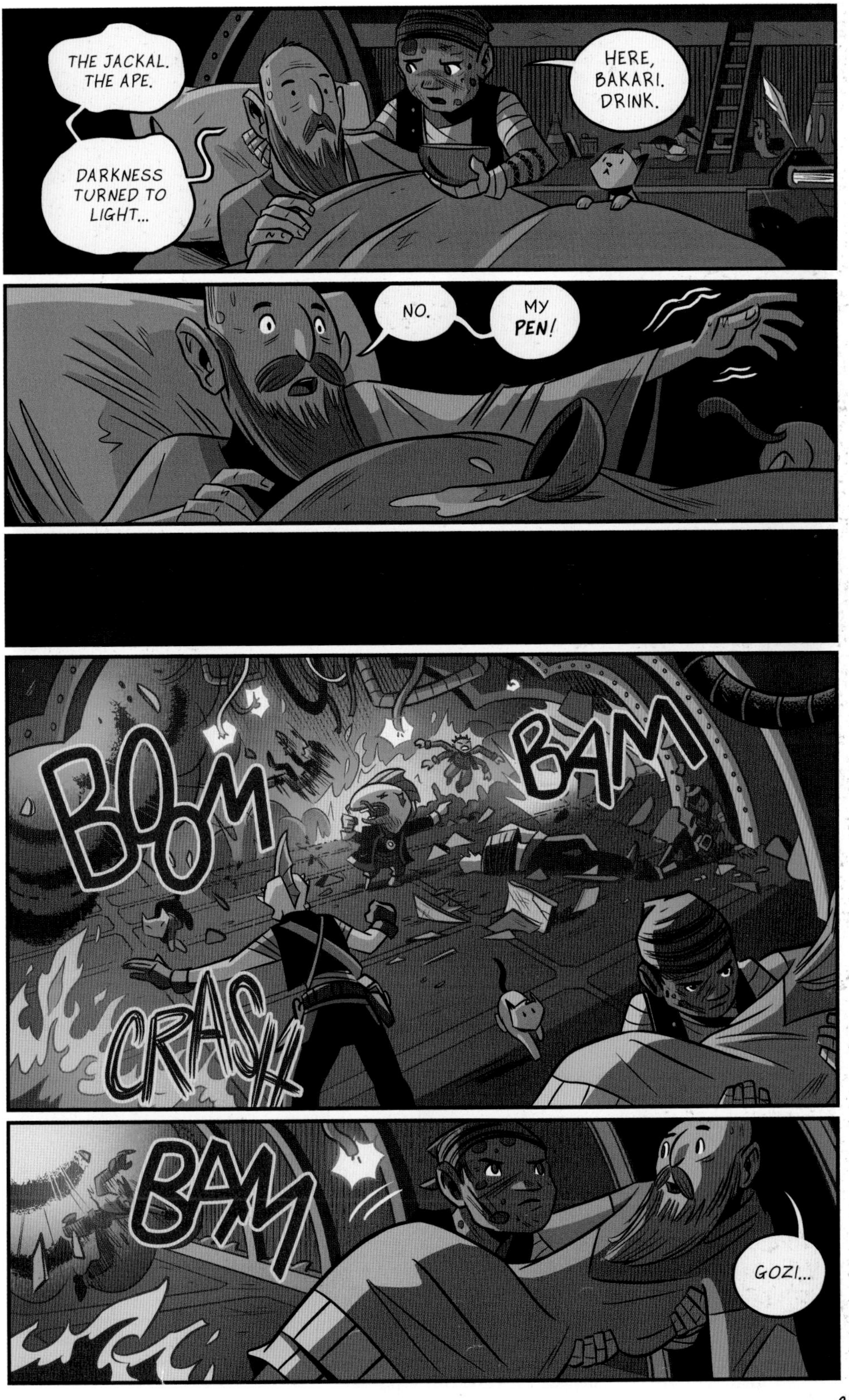
THE JACKAL. THE APE.
DARKNESS TURNED TO LIGHT...
HERE, BAKARI. DRINK.
NO.
MY PEN!
BOOM
BAM
CRASH
BAM
GOZI...

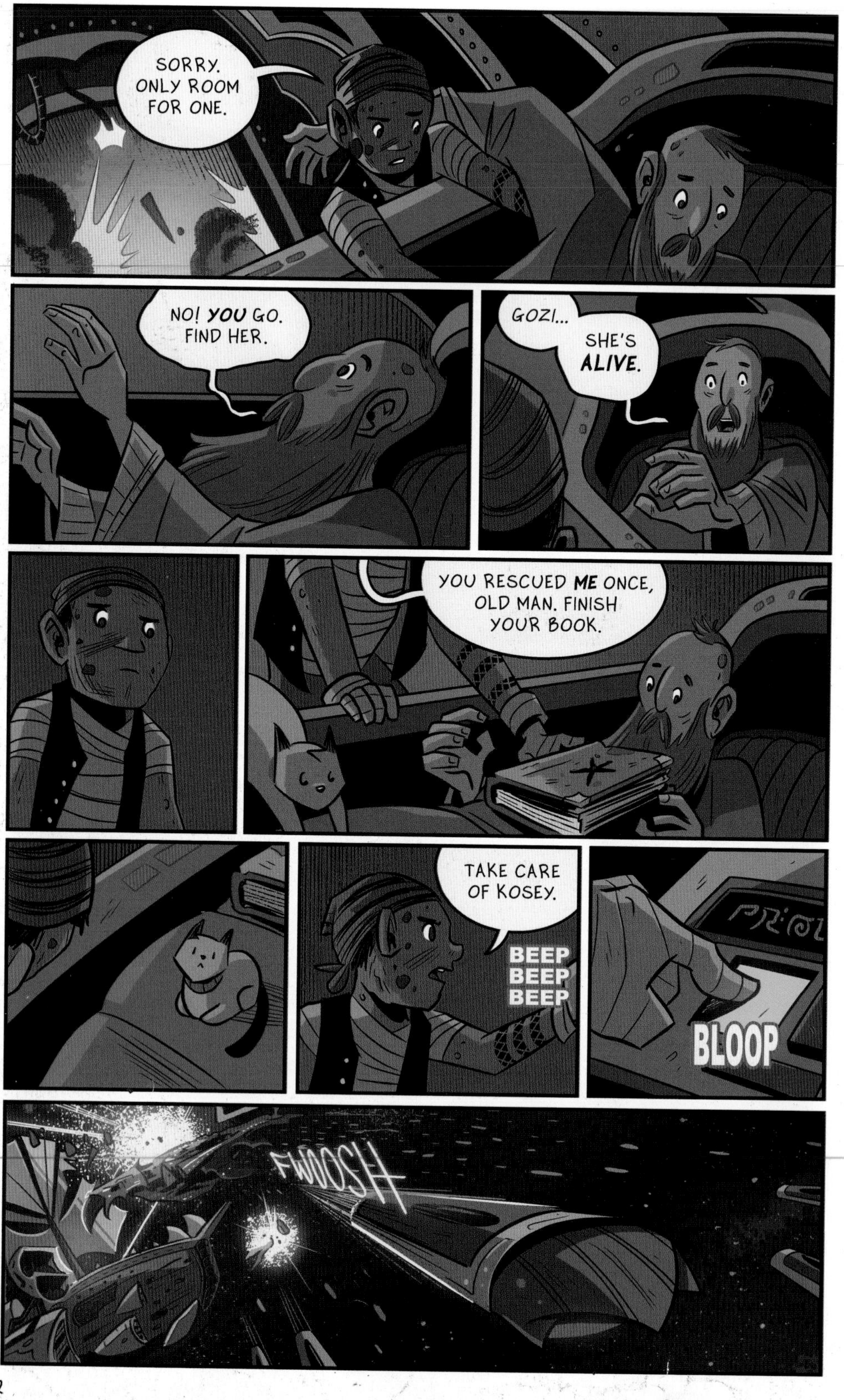
SORRY. ONLY ROOM FOR ONE.
NO! YOU GO. FIND HER.
GOZI...
SHE'S ALIVE.
YOU RESCUED ME ONCE, OLD MAN. FINISH YOUR BOOK.
TAKE CARE OF KOSEY.
BEEP BEEP BEEP
BLOOP
FWOOSH

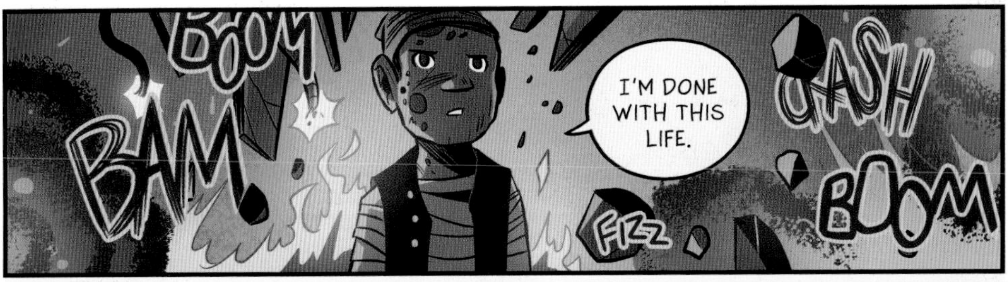
BOOM
BAM
I'M DONE WITH THIS LIFE.
CRASH
FIZZ
BOOM

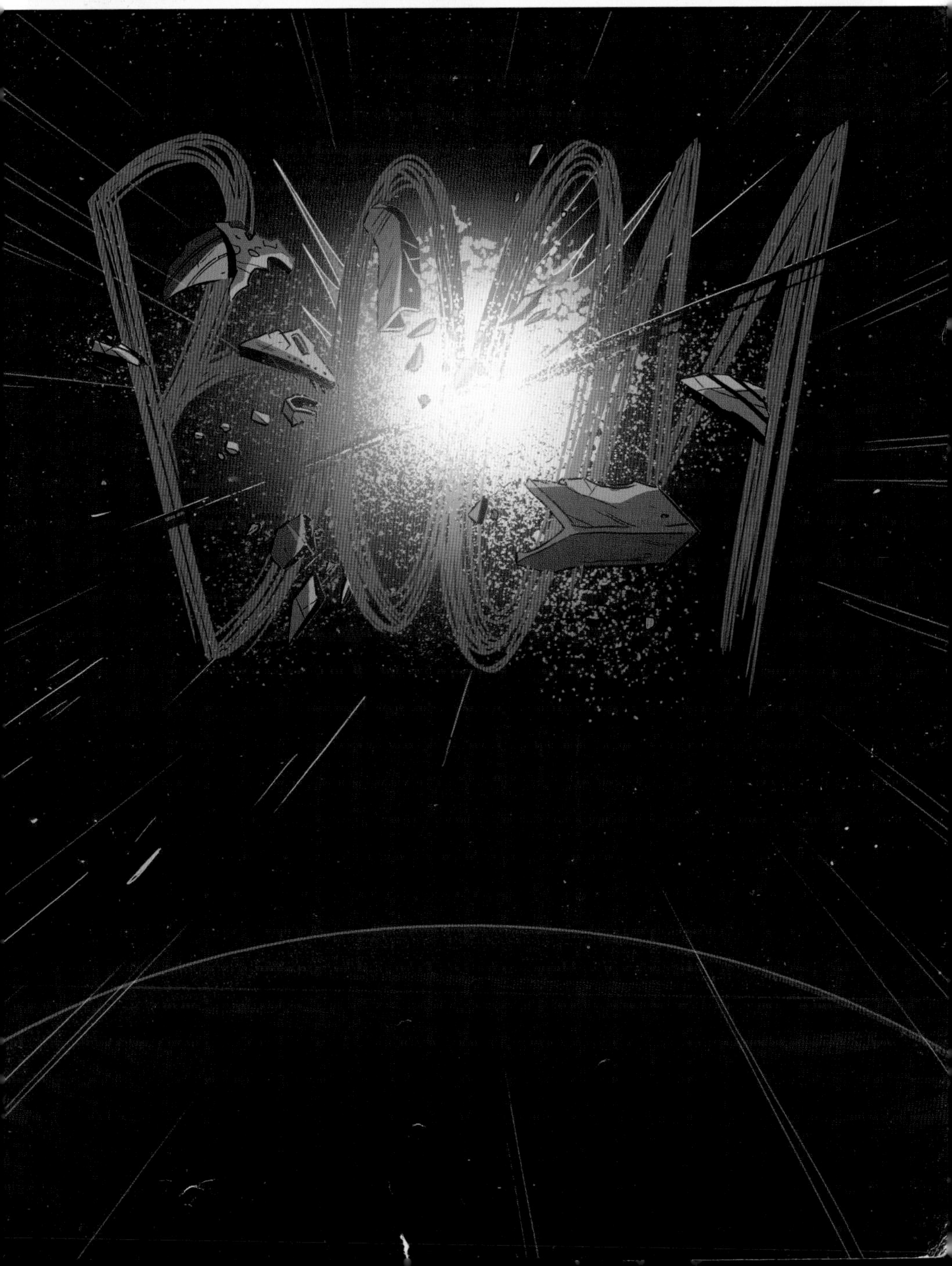
BOOM

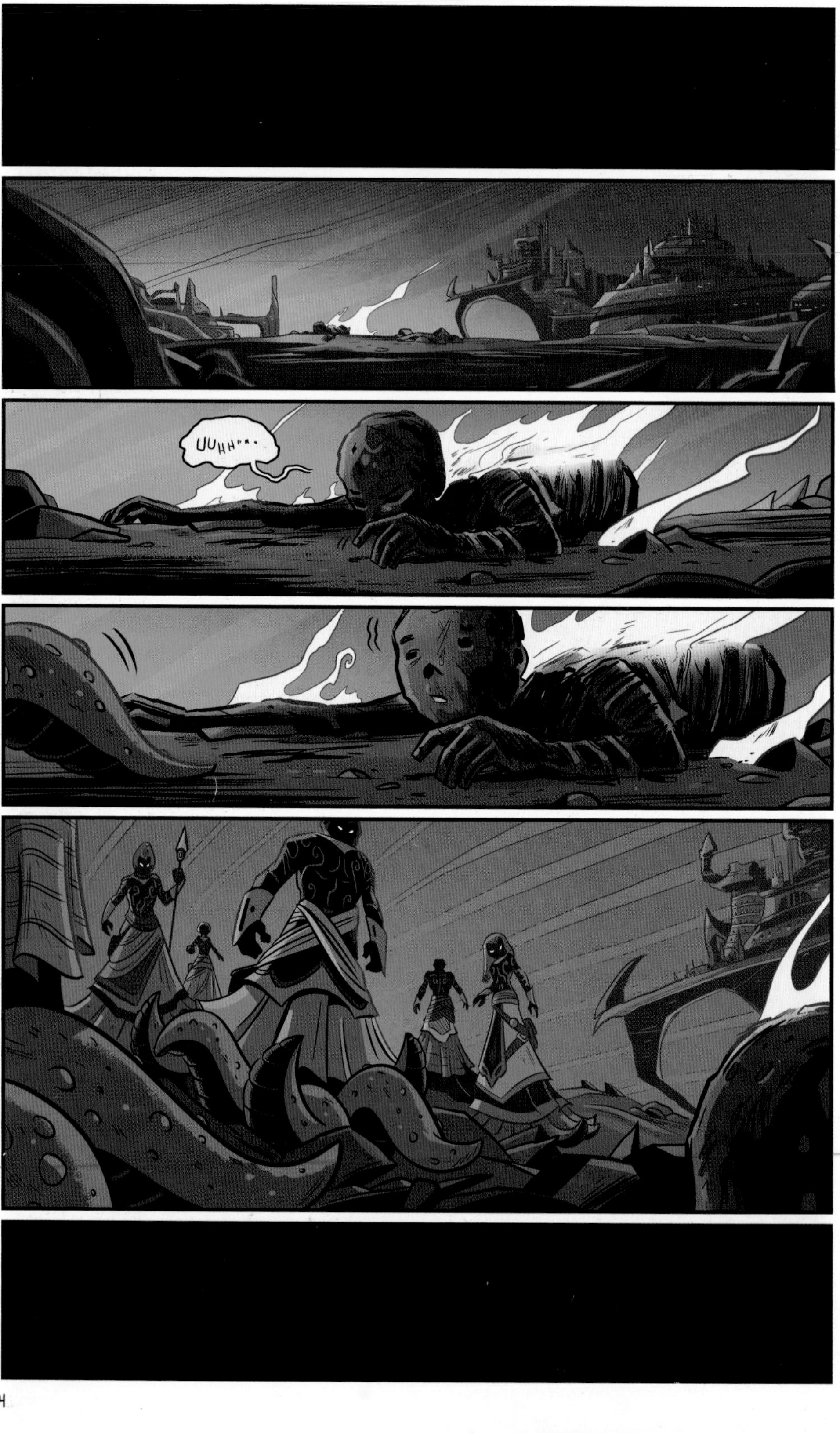
UUHH...

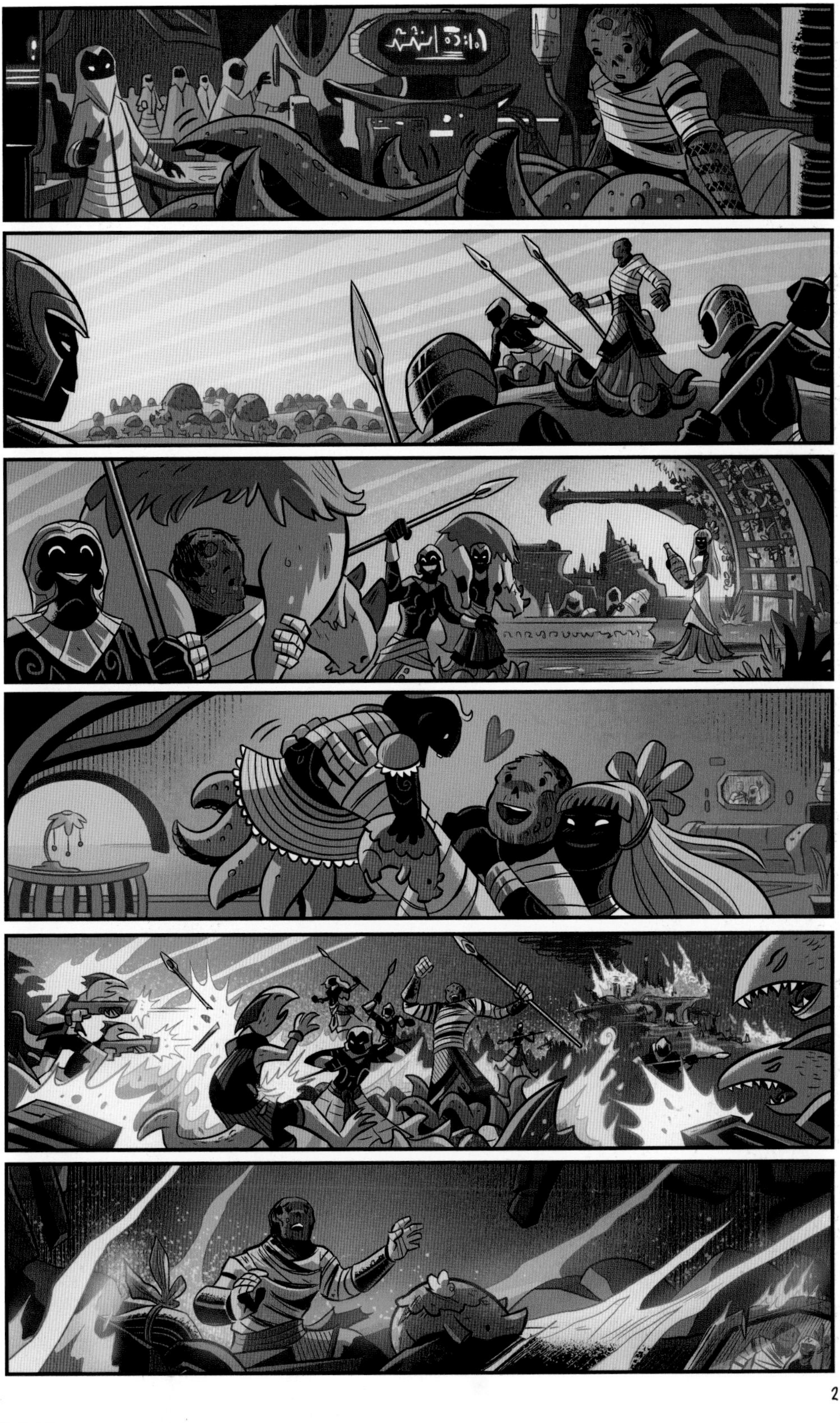

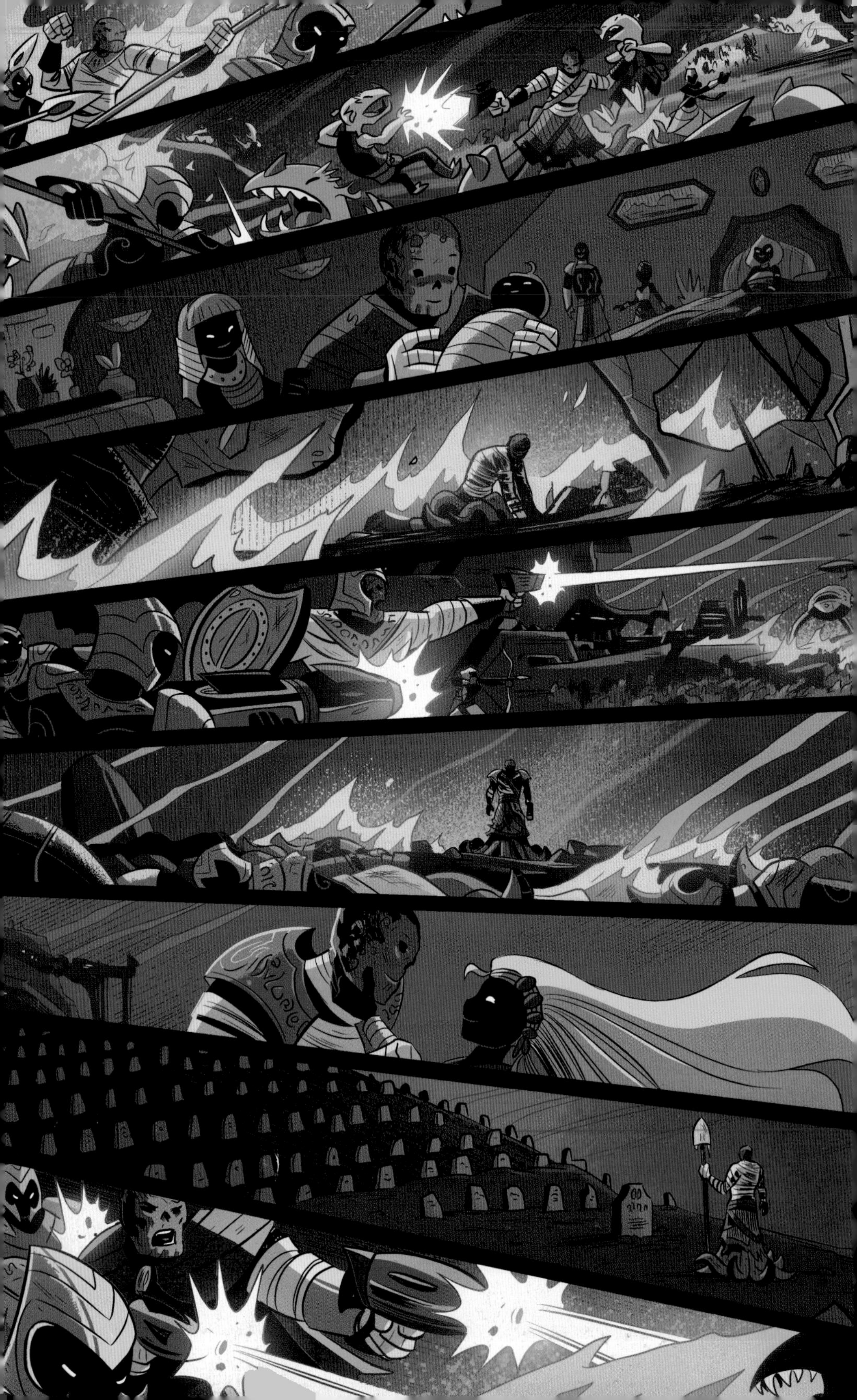

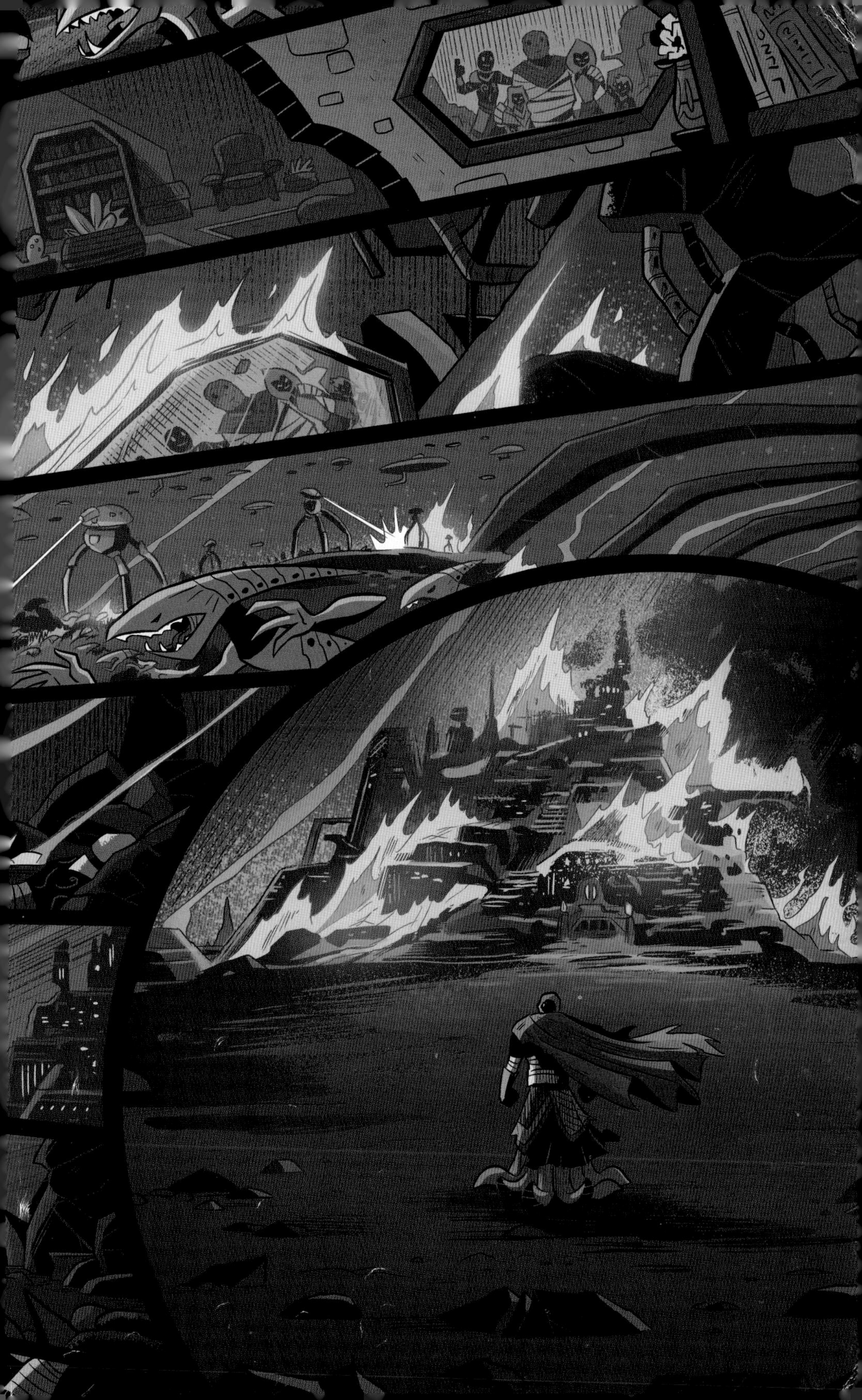

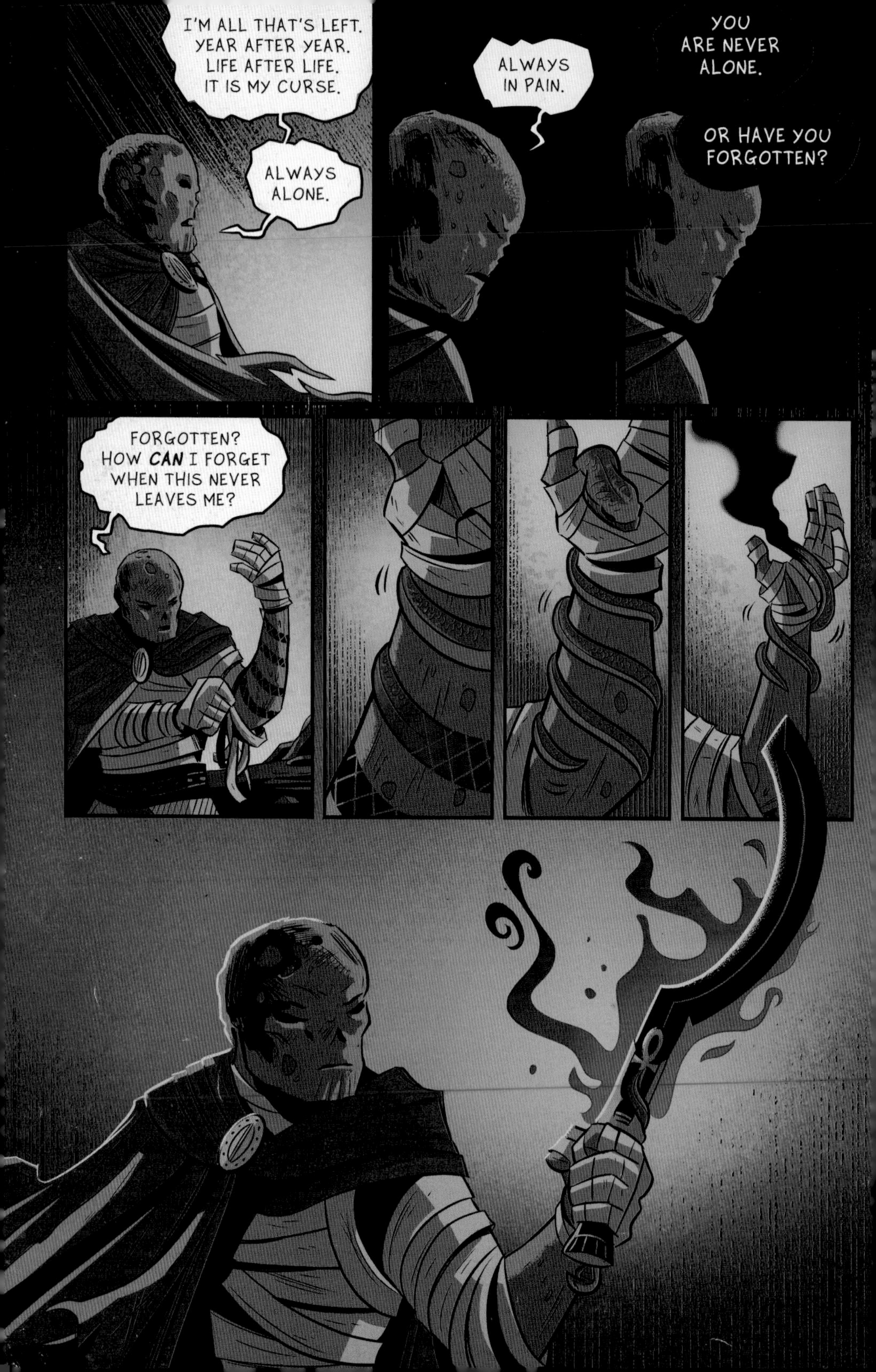

I'M ALL THAT'S LEFT. YEAR AFTER YEAR. LIFE AFTER LIFE. IT IS MY CURSE.
ALWAYS ALONE.
ALWAYS IN PAIN.
YOU ARE NEVER ALONE.
OR HAVE YOU FORGOTTEN?
FORGOTTEN? HOW **CAN** I FORGET WHEN THIS NEVER LEAVES ME?

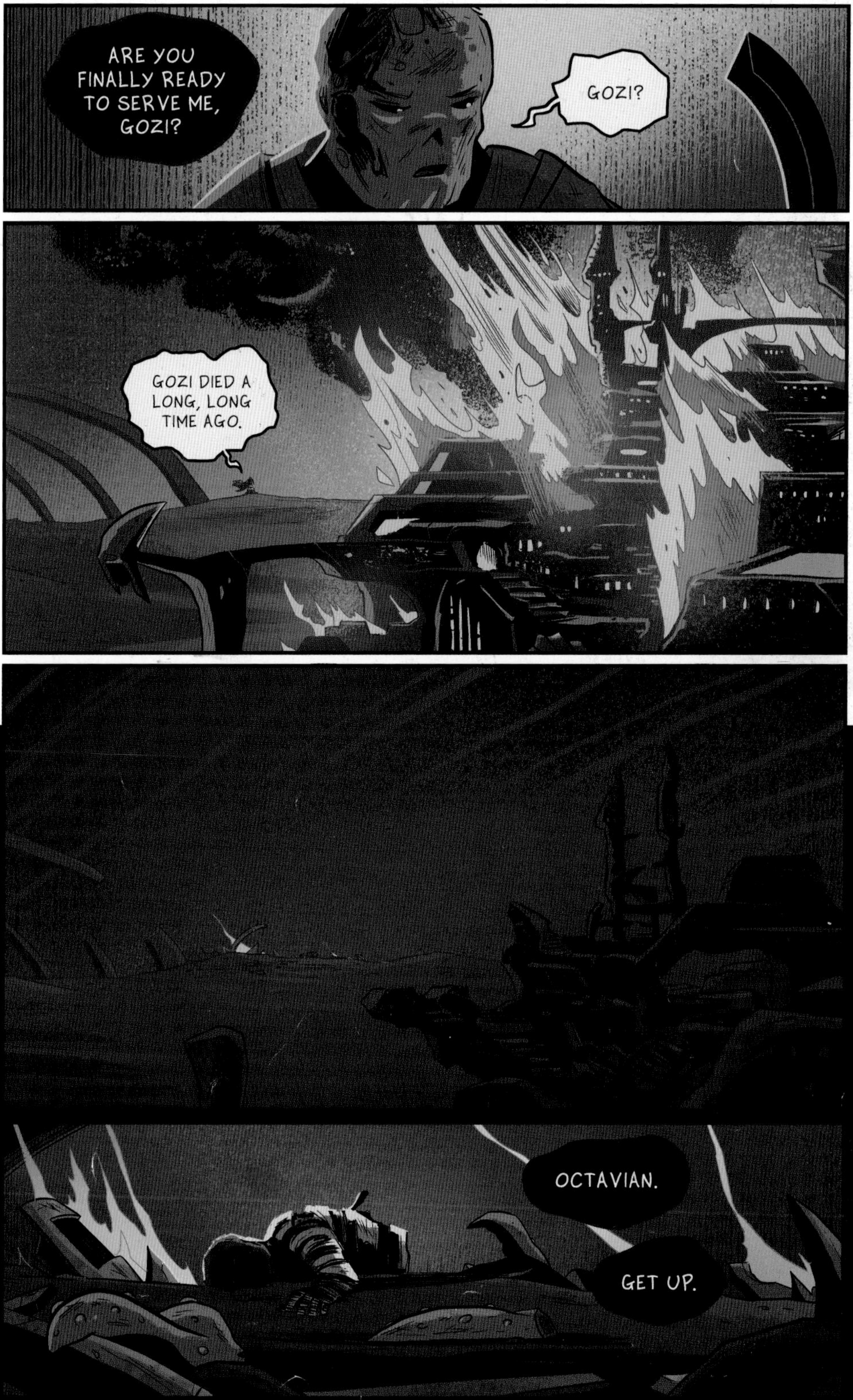
ARE YOU FINALLY READY TO SERVE ME, GOZI?
GOZI?
GOZI DIED A LONG, LONG TIME AGO.
OCTAVIAN.
GET UP.

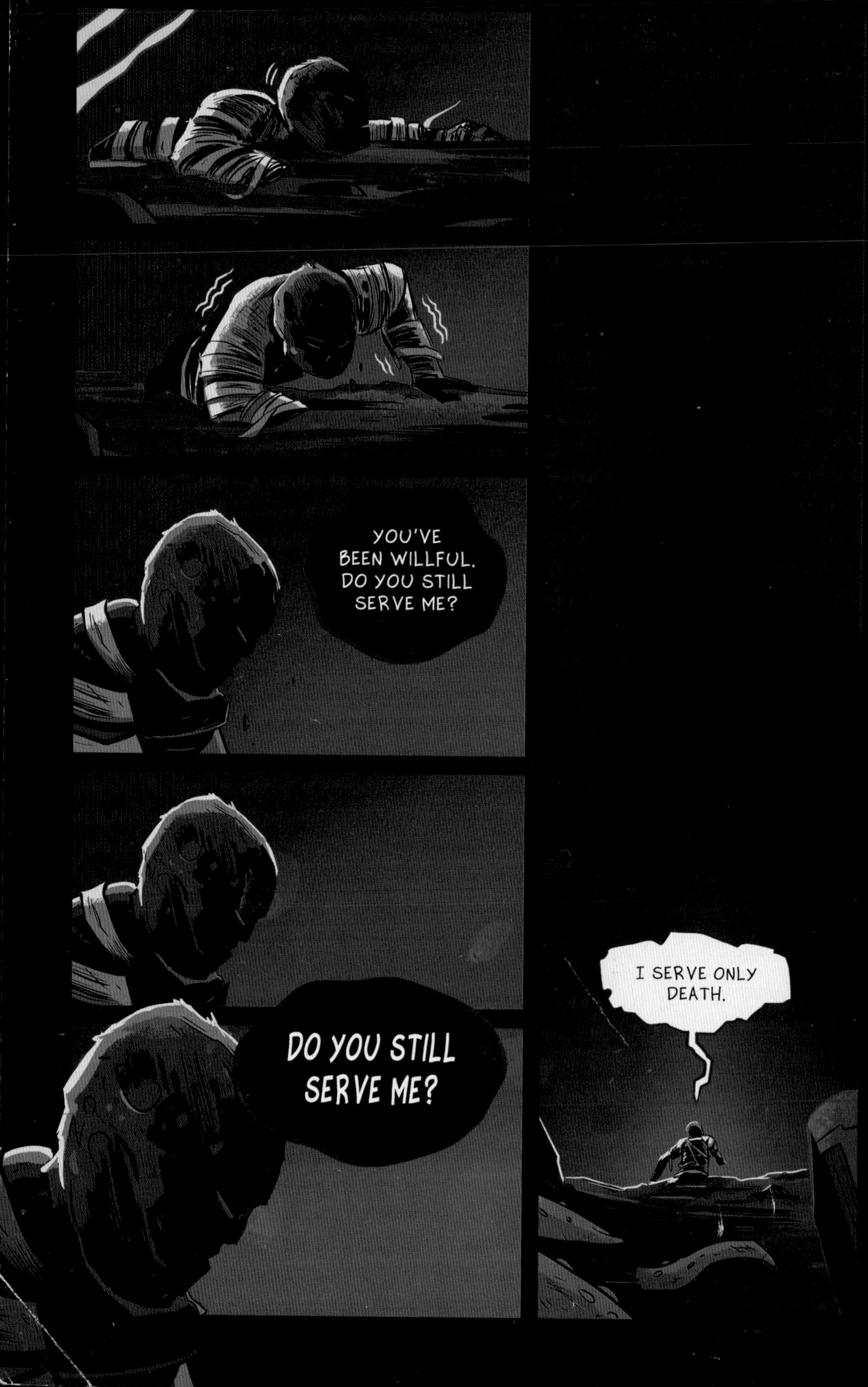
YOU'VE BEEN WILLFUL. DO YOU STILL SERVE ME?
DO YOU STILL SERVE ME?
I SERVE ONLY DEATH.

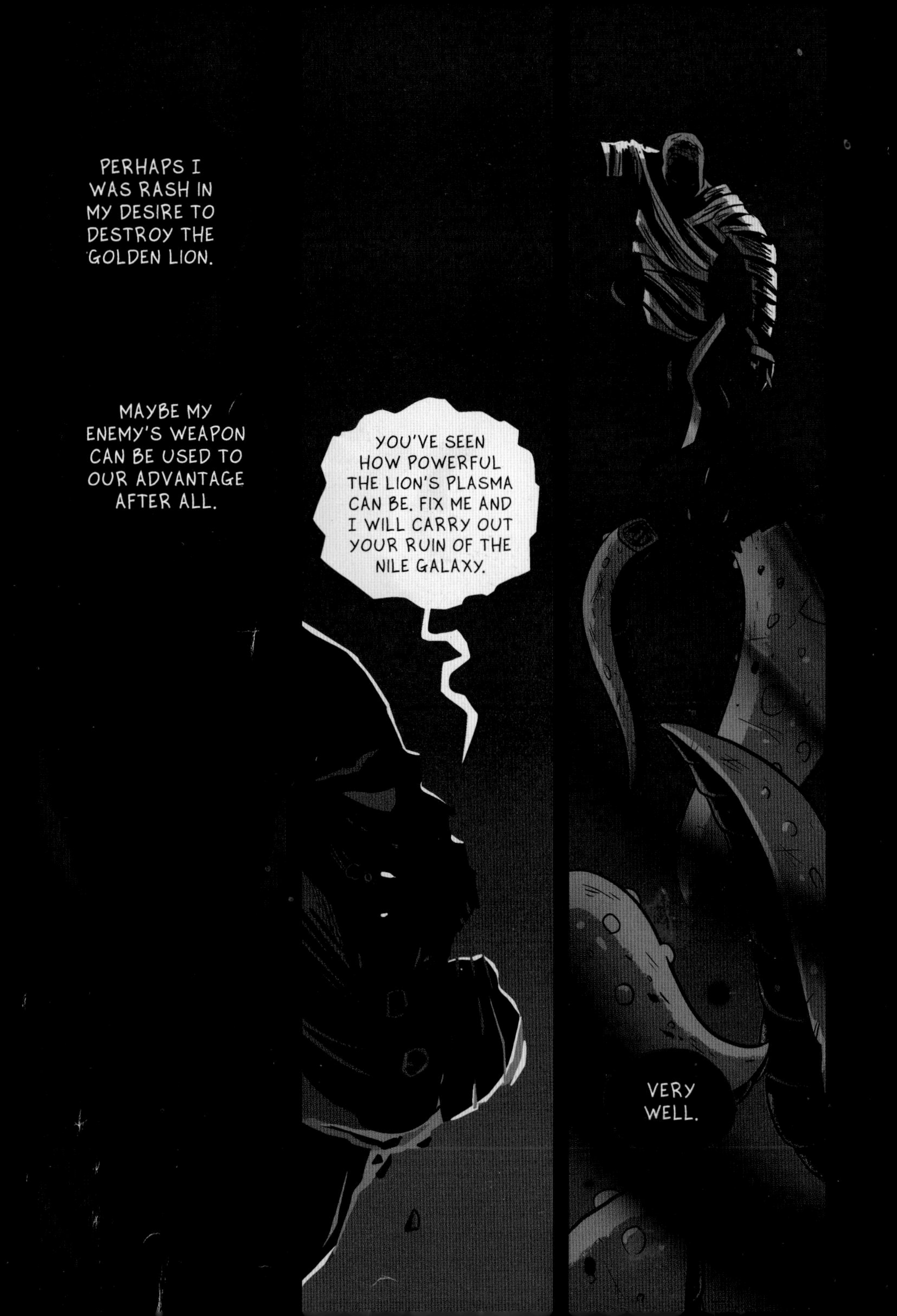
PERHAPS I WAS RASH IN MY DESIRE TO DESTROY THE GOLDEN LION.
MAYBE MY ENEMY'S WEAPON CAN BE USED TO OUR ADVANTAGE AFTER ALL.
YOU'VE SEEN HOW POWERFUL THE LION'S PLASMA CAN BE. FIX ME AND I WILL CARRY OUT YOUR RUIN OF THE NILE GALAXY.
VERY WELL.

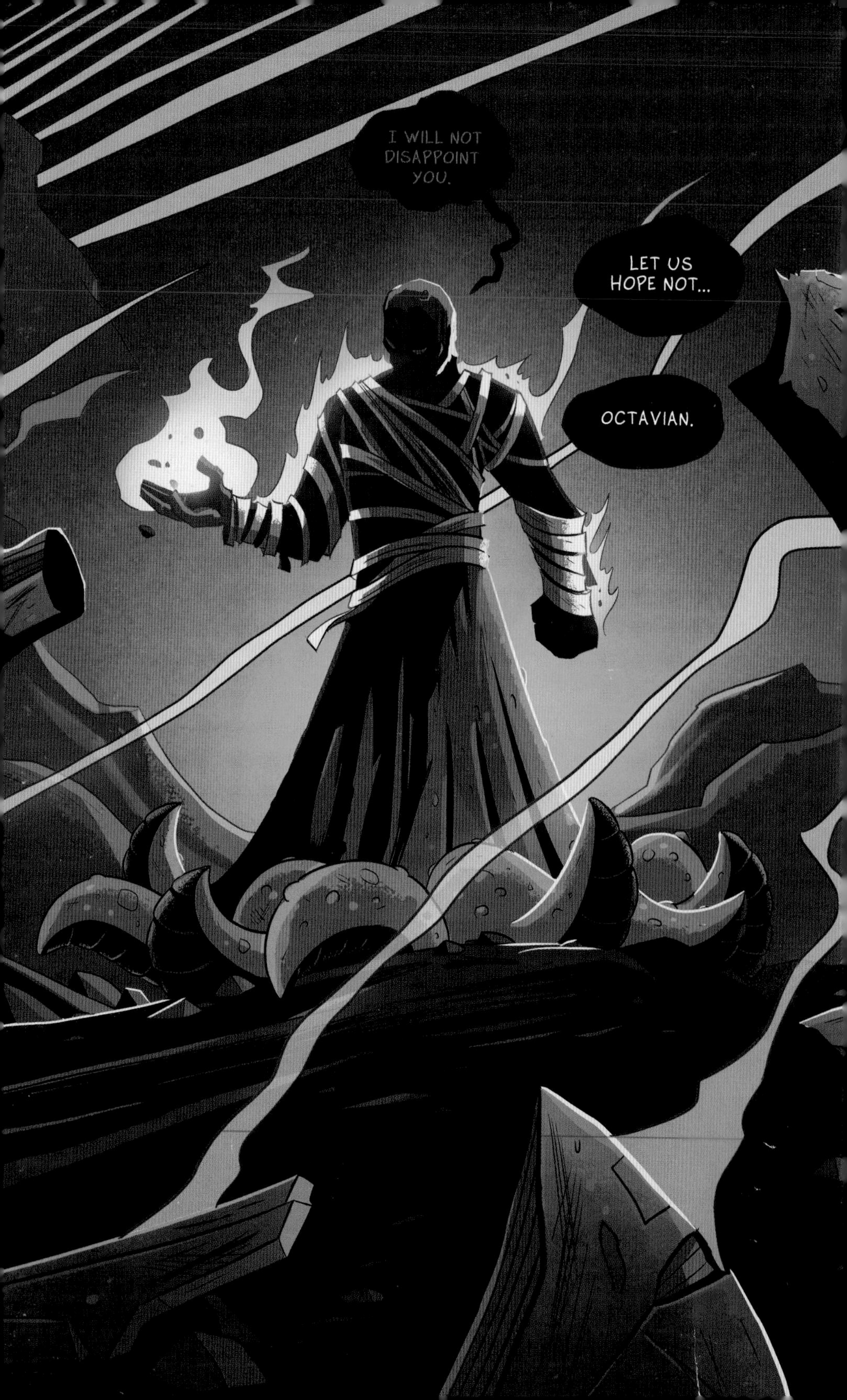
I WILL NOT DISAPPOINT YOU.
LET US HOPE NOT...
OCTAVIAN.

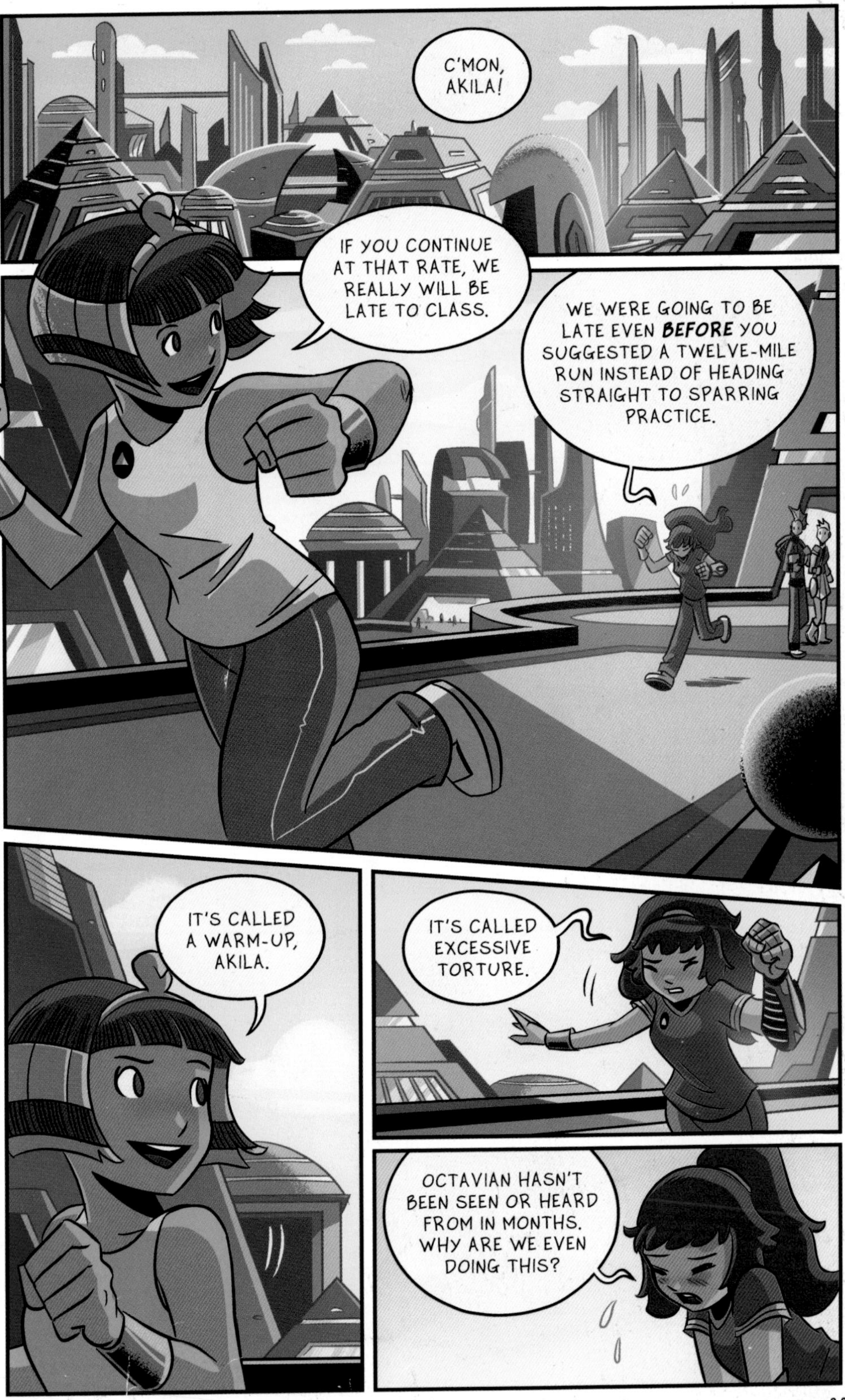
C'MON, AKILA!
IF YOU CONTINUE AT THAT RATE, WE REALLY WILL BE LATE TO CLASS.
WE WERE GOING TO BE LATE EVEN **BEFORE** YOU SUGGESTED A TWELVE-MILE RUN INSTEAD OF HEADING STRAIGHT TO SPARRING PRACTICE.
IT'S CALLED A WARM-UP, AKILA.
IT'S CALLED EXCESSIVE TORTURE.
OCTAVIAN HASN'T BEEN SEEN OR HEARD FROM IN MONTHS. WHY ARE WE EVEN DOING THIS?

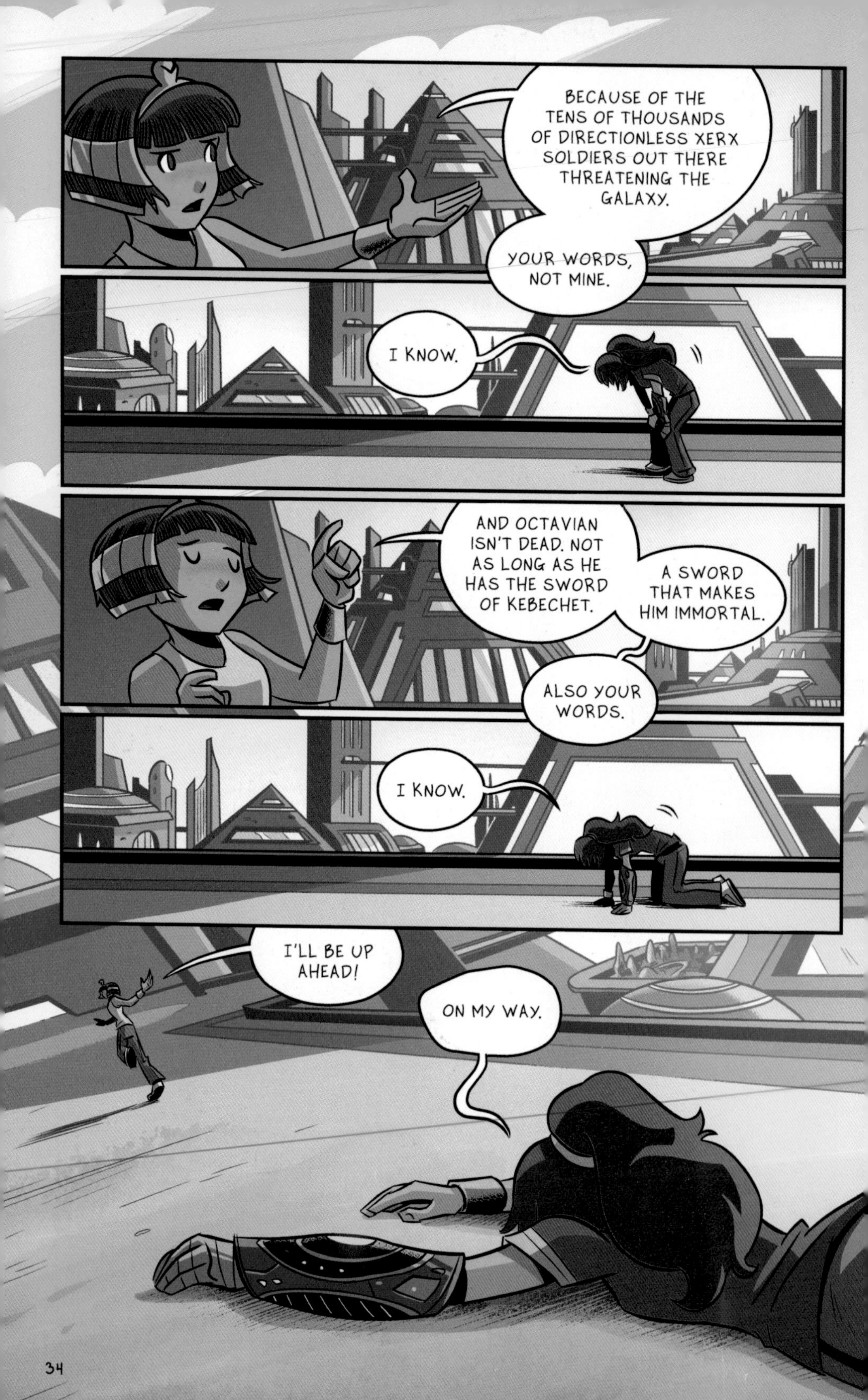
BECAUSE OF THE TENS OF THOUSANDS OF DIRECTIONLESS XERX SOLDIERS OUT THERE THREATENING THE GALAXY.
YOUR WORDS, NOT MINE.
I KNOW.
AND OCTAVIAN ISN'T DEAD. NOT AS LONG AS HE HAS THE SWORD OF KEBECHET.
A SWORD THAT MAKES HIM IMMORTAL.
ALSO YOUR WORDS.
I KNOW.
I'LL BE UP AHEAD!
ON MY WAY.

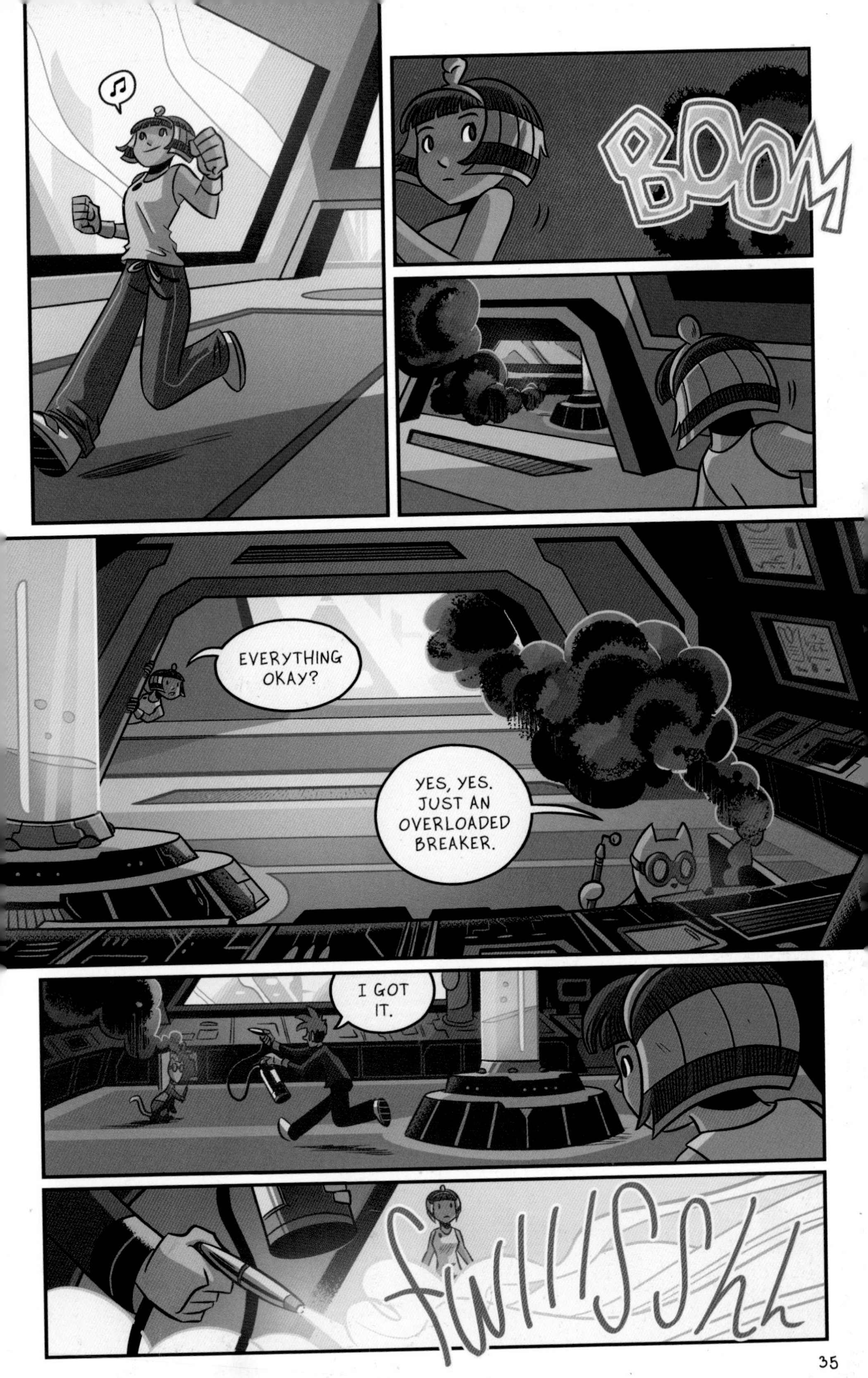

♫
BOOM
EVERYTHING OKAY?
YES, YES. JUST AN OVERLOADED BREAKER.
I GOT IT.
FWIIISShh

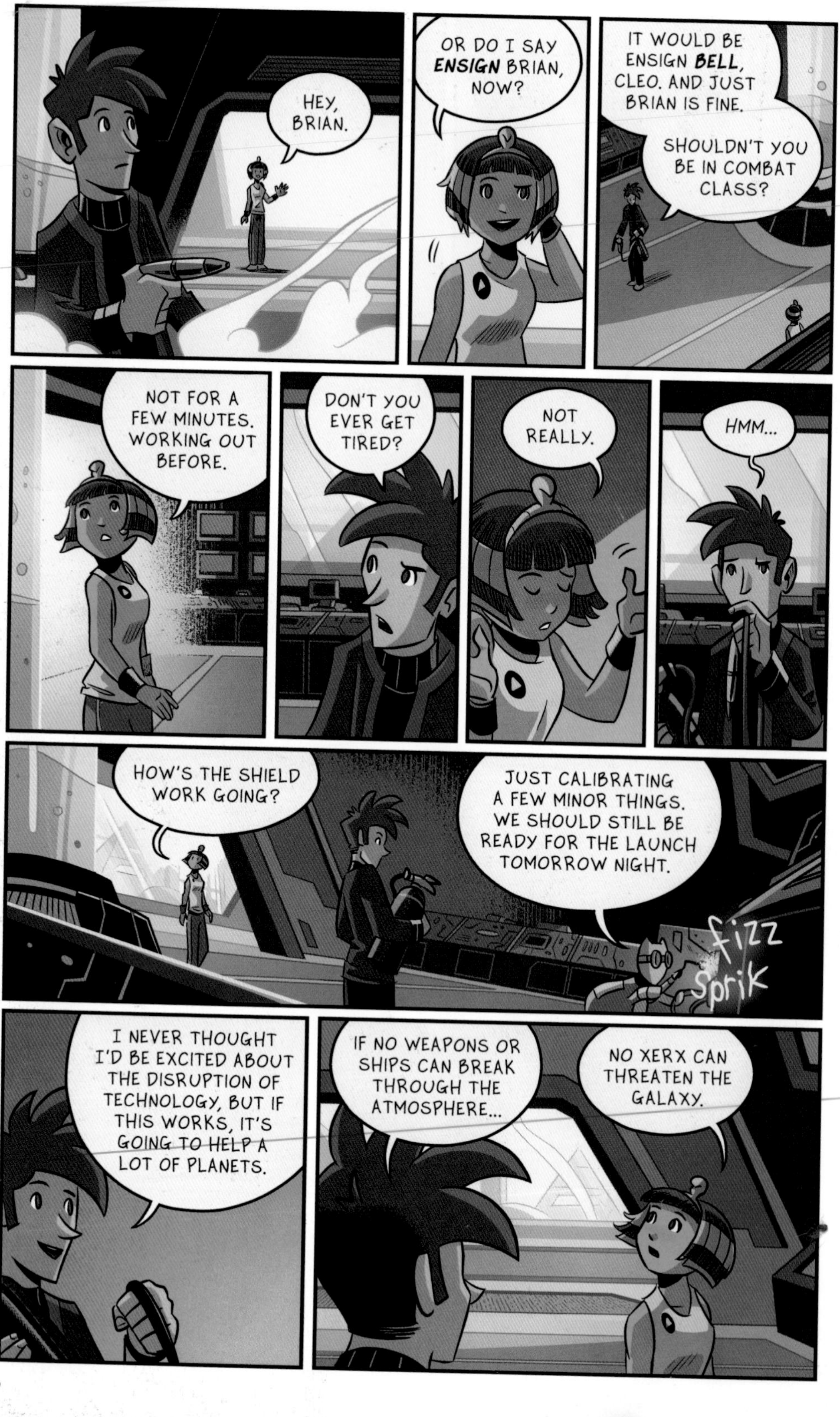
HEY, BRIAN.
OR DO I SAY **ENSIGN** BRIAN, NOW?
IT WOULD BE ENSIGN **BELL**, CLEO. AND JUST BRIAN IS FINE.
SHOULDN'T YOU BE IN COMBAT CLASS?
NOT FOR A FEW MINUTES. WORKING OUT BEFORE.
DON'T YOU EVER GET TIRED?
NOT REALLY.
HMM...
HOW'S THE SHIELD WORK GOING?
JUST CALIBRATING A FEW MINOR THINGS. WE SHOULD STILL BE READY FOR THE LAUNCH TOMORROW NIGHT.
fizz
Sprik
I NEVER THOUGHT I'D BE EXCITED ABOUT THE DISRUPTION OF TECHNOLOGY, BUT IF THIS WORKS, IT'S GOING TO HELP A LOT OF PLANETS.
IF NO WEAPONS OR SHIPS CAN BREAK THROUGH THE ATMOSPHERE...
NO XERX CAN THREATEN THE GALAXY.

AND WITH STILL NO SIGN OF OCTAVIAN, YOU MIGHT FINALLY BE ABLE TO RETURN TO YOUR OWN TIME, CLEOPATRA.

YEAH...

MAKING SURE THE SHIELD FUNCTIONS PROPERLY IS MAINLY JUST A MATTER OF BALANCING THE CORRECT FREQUENCIES BETWEEN CADA'DUUN'S AND OUR TECHNOLOGY. SOMETIMES THEY DON'T GET ALONG.

FWOOOSH

FWITISSH

WE ARE OPTIMISTIC.

SSSSS

RIGHT.

LAST... TIME... I... LISTEN... TO... YOU.

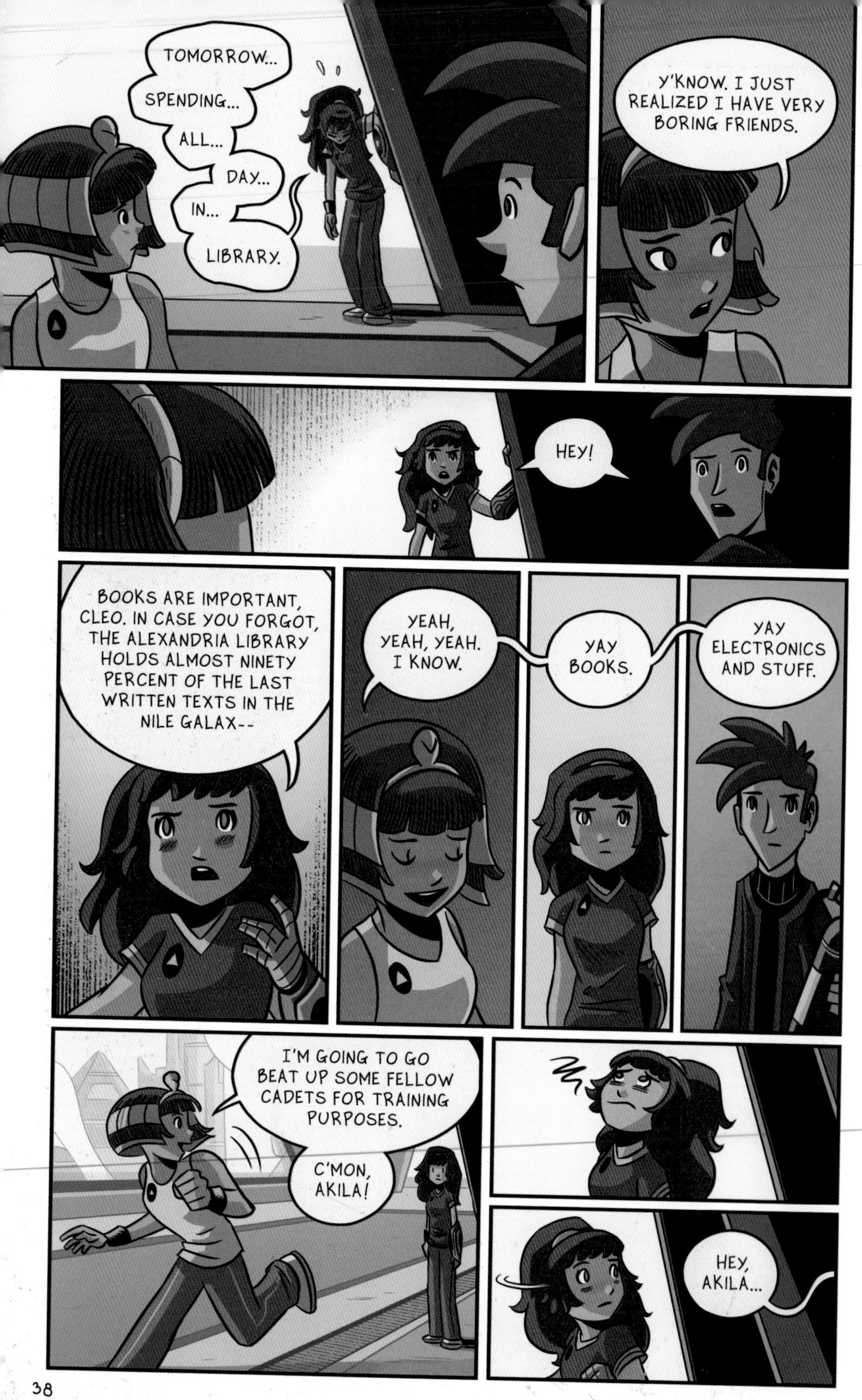
TOMORROW...
SPENDING...
ALL...
DAY...
IN...
LIBRARY.
Y'KNOW. I JUST REALIZED I HAVE VERY BORING FRIENDS.
HEY!
BOOKS ARE IMPORTANT, CLEO. IN CASE YOU FORGOT, THE ALEXANDRIA LIBRARY HOLDS ALMOST NINETY PERCENT OF THE LAST WRITTEN TEXTS IN THE NILE GALAX--
YEAH, YEAH, YEAH. I KNOW.
YAY BOOKS.
YAY ELECTRONICS AND STUFF.
I'M GOING TO GO BEAT UP SOME FELLOW CADETS FOR TRAINING PURPOSES.
C'MON, AKILA!
HEY, AKILA...

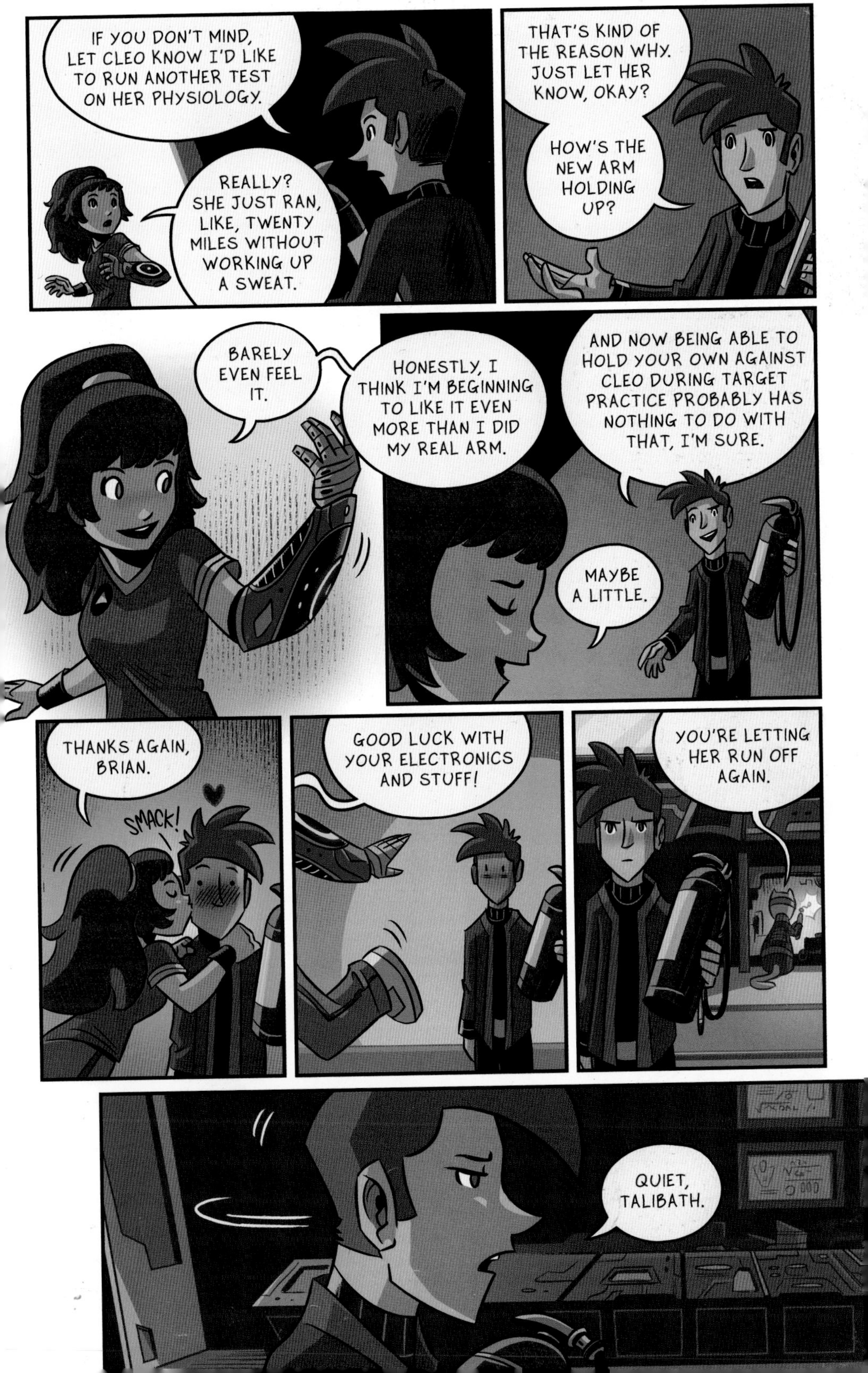
IF YOU DON'T MIND, LET CLEO KNOW I'D LIKE TO RUN ANOTHER TEST ON HER PHYSIOLOGY.
REALLY? SHE JUST RAN, LIKE, TWENTY MILES WITHOUT WORKING UP A SWEAT.
THAT'S KIND OF THE REASON WHY. JUST LET HER KNOW, OKAY?
HOW'S THE NEW ARM HOLDING UP?
BARELY EVEN FEEL IT.
HONESTLY, I THINK I'M BEGINNING TO LIKE IT EVEN MORE THAN I DID MY REAL ARM.
AND NOW BEING ABLE TO HOLD YOUR OWN AGAINST CLEO DURING TARGET PRACTICE PROBABLY HAS NOTHING TO DO WITH THAT, I'M SURE.
MAYBE A LITTLE.
THANKS AGAIN, BRIAN.
SMACK!
GOOD LUCK WITH YOUR ELECTRONICS AND STUFF!
YOU'RE LETTING HER RUN OFF AGAIN.
QUIET, TALIBATH.

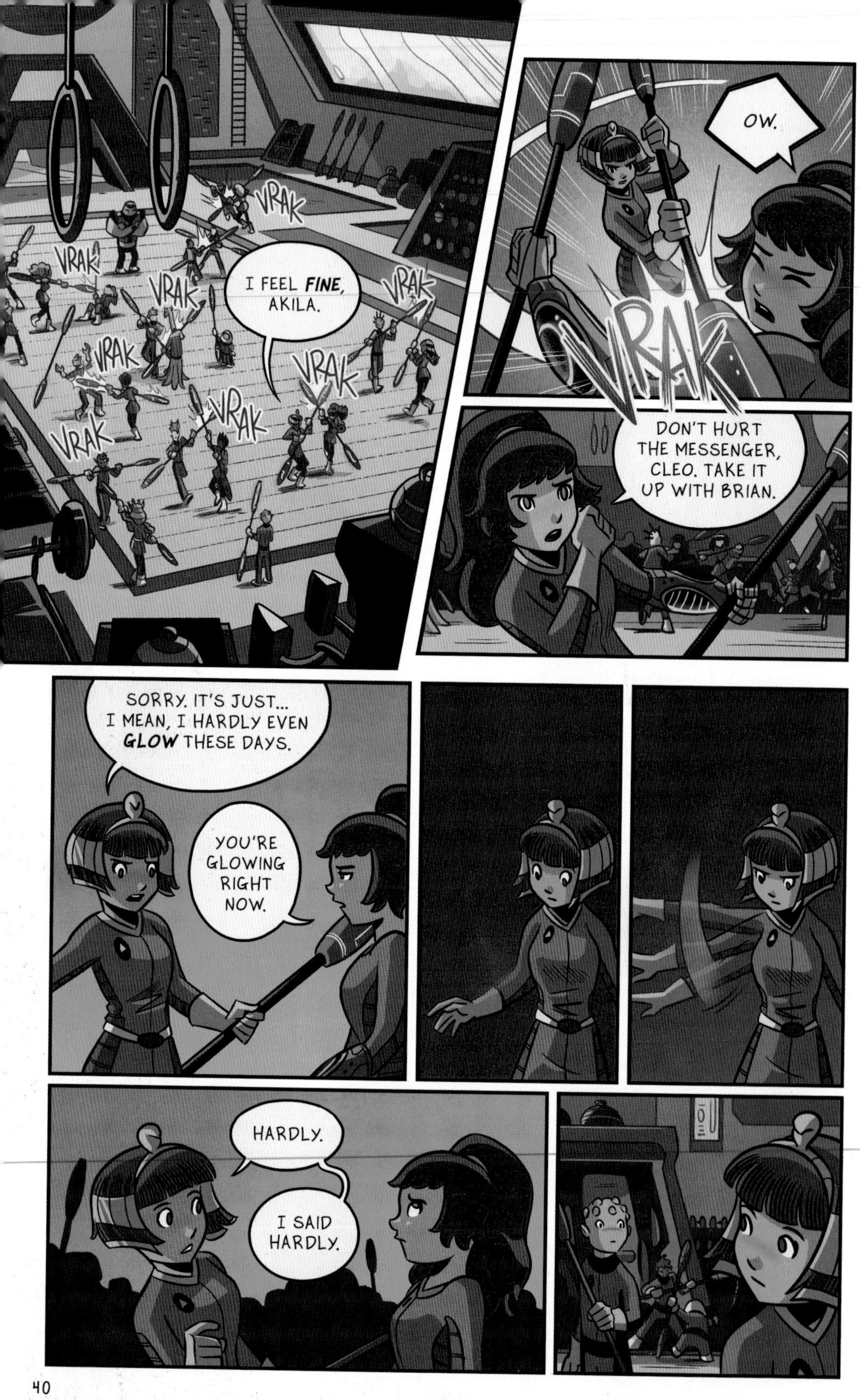
VRAK
VRAK
VRAK
VRAK
VRAK
VRAK
VRAK
VRAK
I FEEL **FINE**, AKILA.
OW.
VRAK
DON'T HURT THE MESSENGER, CLEO. TAKE IT UP WITH BRIAN.
SORRY. IT'S JUST... I MEAN, I HARDLY EVEN **GLOW** THESE DAYS.
YOU'RE GLOWING RIGHT NOW.
HARDLY.
I SAID HARDLY.

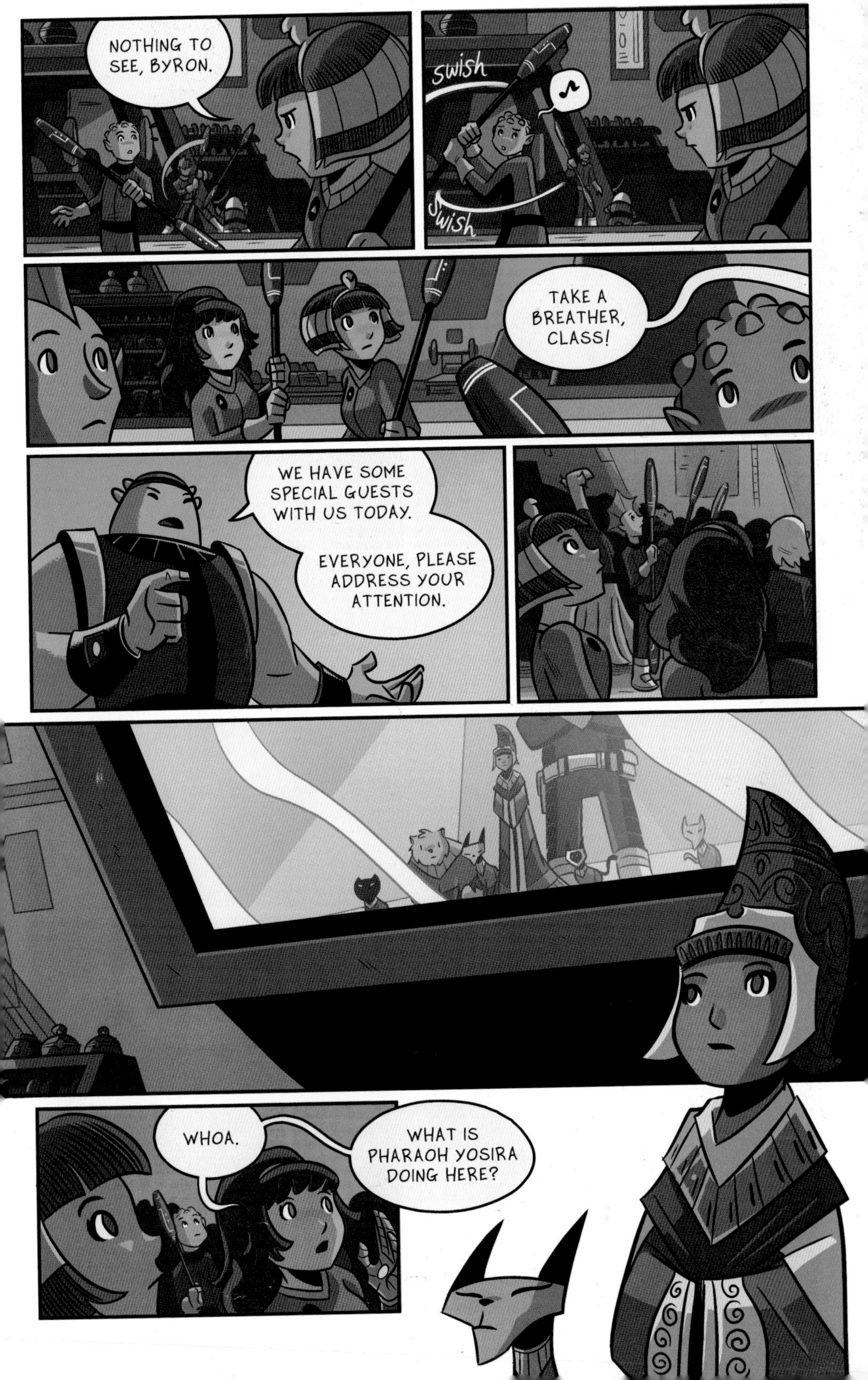
NOTHING TO SEE, BYRON.
SWISH
♪
SWISH
TAKE A BREATHER, CLASS!
WE HAVE SOME SPECIAL GUESTS WITH US TODAY.
EVERYONE, PLEASE ADDRESS YOUR ATTENTION.
WHOA.
WHAT IS PHARAOH YOSIRA DOING HERE?

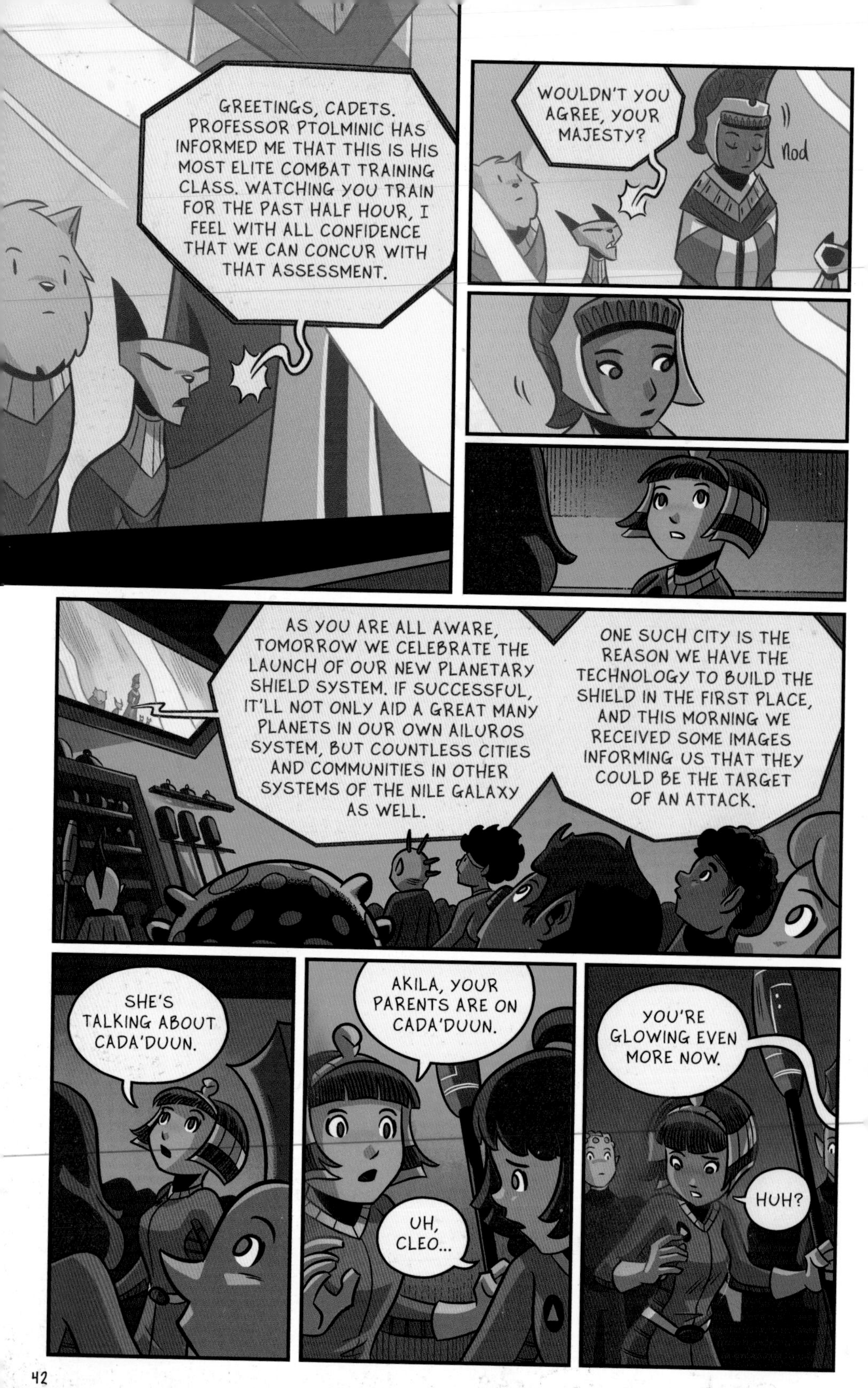
GREETINGS, CADETS. PROFESSOR PTOLMINIC HAS INFORMED ME THAT THIS IS HIS MOST ELITE COMBAT TRAINING CLASS. WATCHING YOU TRAIN FOR THE PAST HALF HOUR, I FEEL WITH ALL CONFIDENCE THAT WE CAN CONCUR WITH THAT ASSESSMENT.
WOULDN'T YOU AGREE, YOUR MAJESTY?
Nod
AS YOU ARE ALL AWARE, TOMORROW WE CELEBRATE THE LAUNCH OF OUR NEW PLANETARY SHIELD SYSTEM. IF SUCCESSFUL, IT'LL NOT ONLY AID A GREAT MANY PLANETS IN OUR OWN AILUROS SYSTEM, BUT COUNTLESS CITIES AND COMMUNITIES IN OTHER SYSTEMS OF THE NILE GALAXY AS WELL.
ONE SUCH CITY IS THE REASON WE HAVE THE TECHNOLOGY TO BUILD THE SHIELD IN THE FIRST PLACE, AND THIS MORNING WE RECEIVED SOME IMAGES INFORMING US THAT THEY COULD BE THE TARGET OF AN ATTACK.
SHE'S TALKING ABOUT CADA'DUUN.
AKILA, YOUR PARENTS ARE ON CADA'DUUN.
UH, CLEO...
YOU'RE GLOWING EVEN MORE NOW.
HUH?

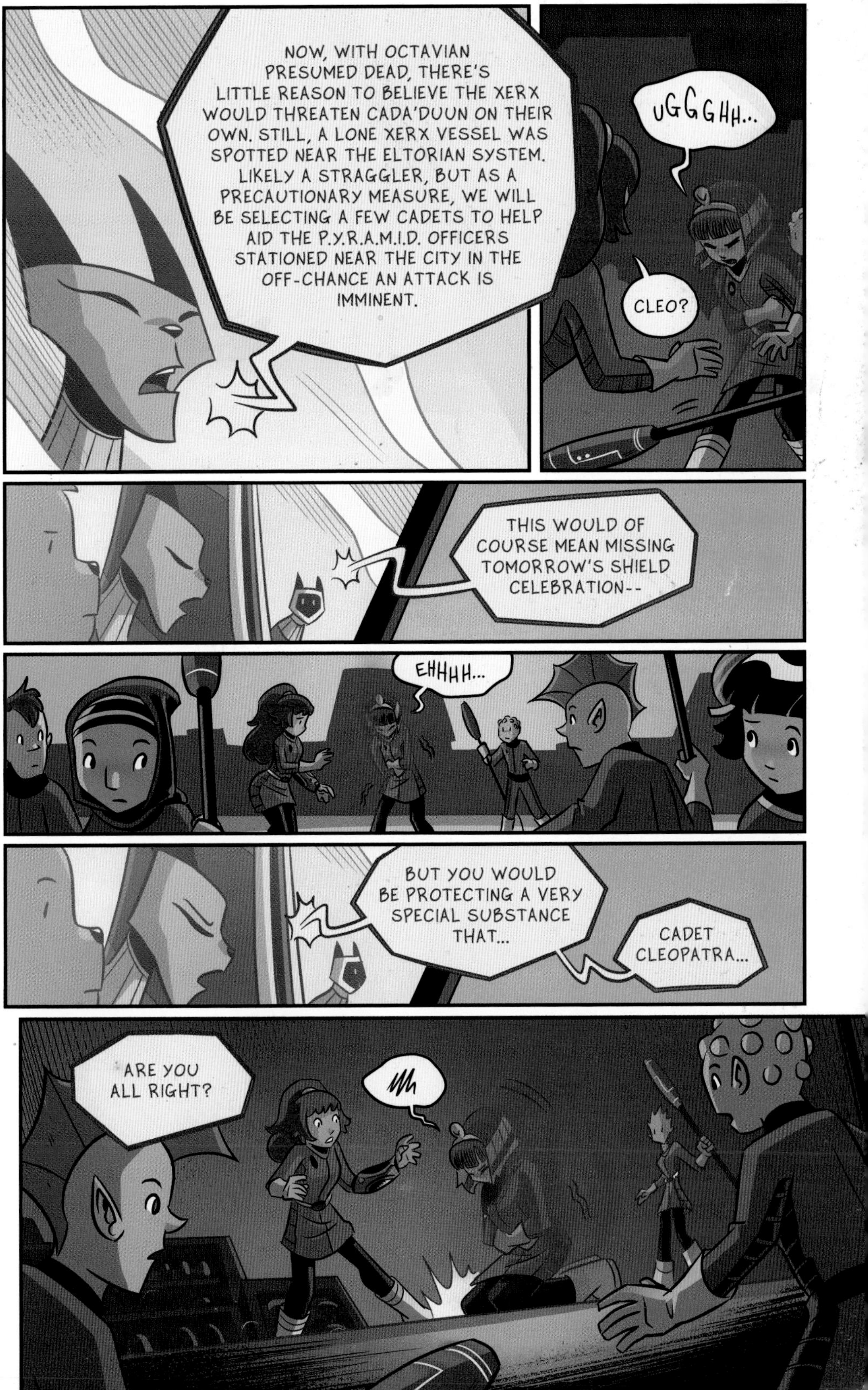
NOW, WITH OCTAVIAN PRESUMED DEAD, THERE'S LITTLE REASON TO BELIEVE THE XERX WOULD THREATEN CADA'DUUN ON THEIR OWN. STILL, A LONE XERX VESSEL WAS SPOTTED NEAR THE ELTORIAN SYSTEM. LIKELY A STRAGGLER, BUT AS A PRECAUTIONARY MEASURE, WE WILL BE SELECTING A FEW CADETS TO HELP AID THE P.Y.R.A.M.I.D. OFFICERS STATIONED NEAR THE CITY IN THE OFF-CHANCE AN ATTACK IS IMMINENT.
UGGGHH...
CLEO?
THIS WOULD OF COURSE MEAN MISSING TOMORROW'S SHIELD CELEBRATION--
EHHHH...
BUT YOU WOULD BE PROTECTING A VERY SPECIAL SUBSTANCE THAT...
CADET CLEOPATRA...
ARE YOU ALL RIGHT?

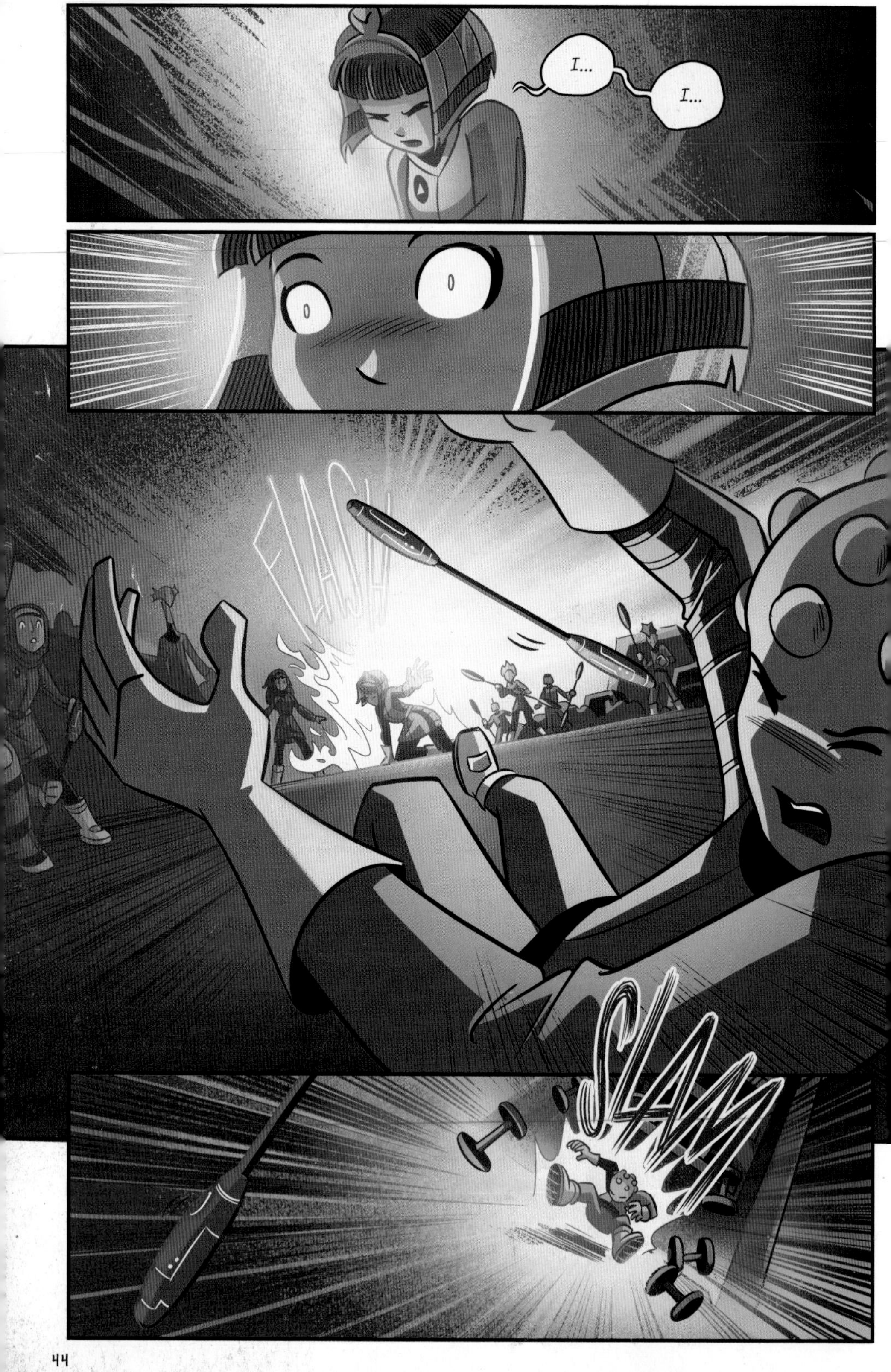
I...
I...
FLASH
SLAM

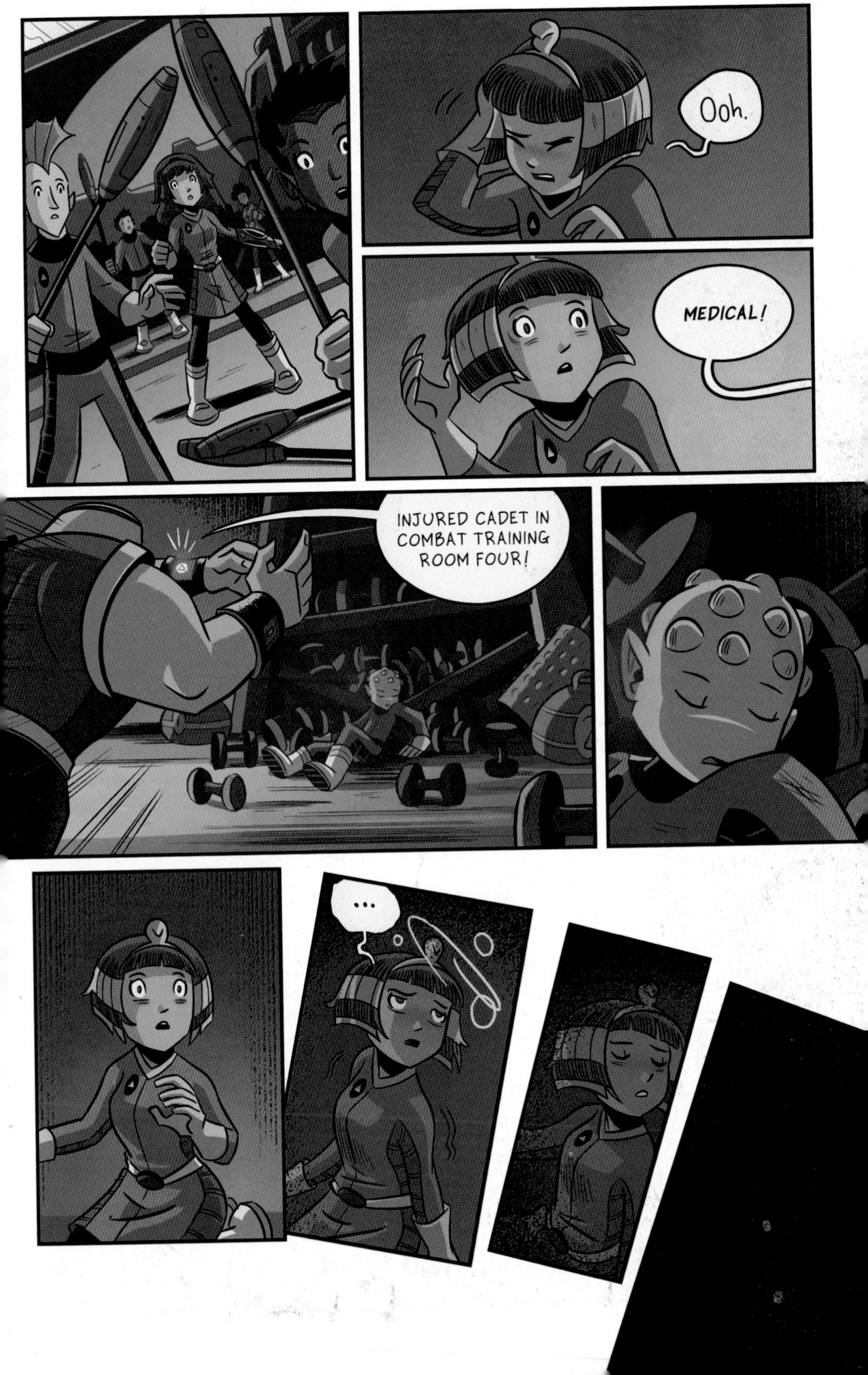
Ooh.
MEDICAL!
INJURED CADET IN COMBAT TRAINING ROOM FOUR!
...

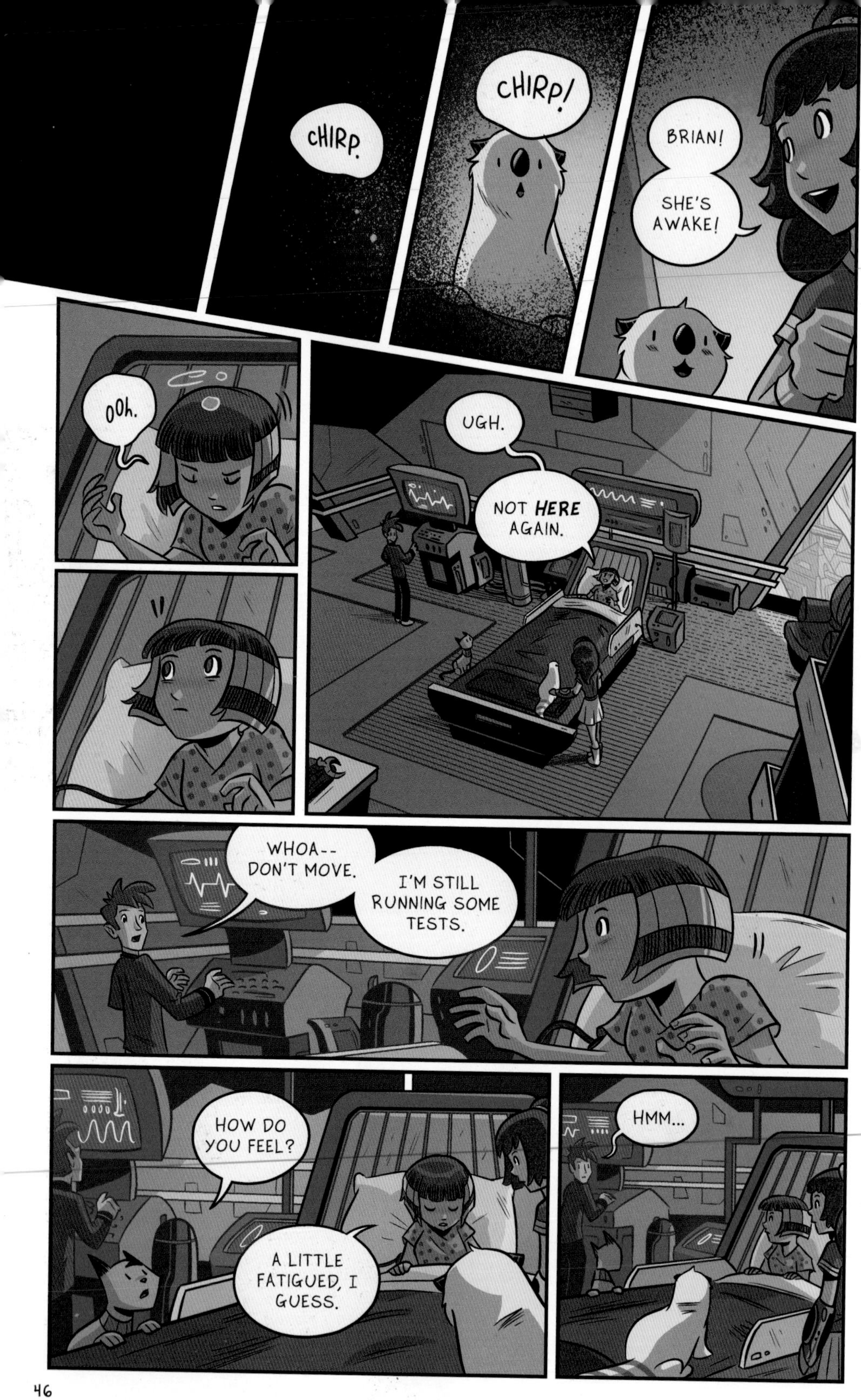
CHIRP.
CHIRP!
BRIAN!
SHE'S AWAKE!
OOH.
UGH.
NOT HERE AGAIN.
WHOA-- DON'T MOVE.
I'M STILL RUNNING SOME TESTS.
HOW DO YOU FEEL?
A LITTLE FATIGUED, I GUESS.
HMM...

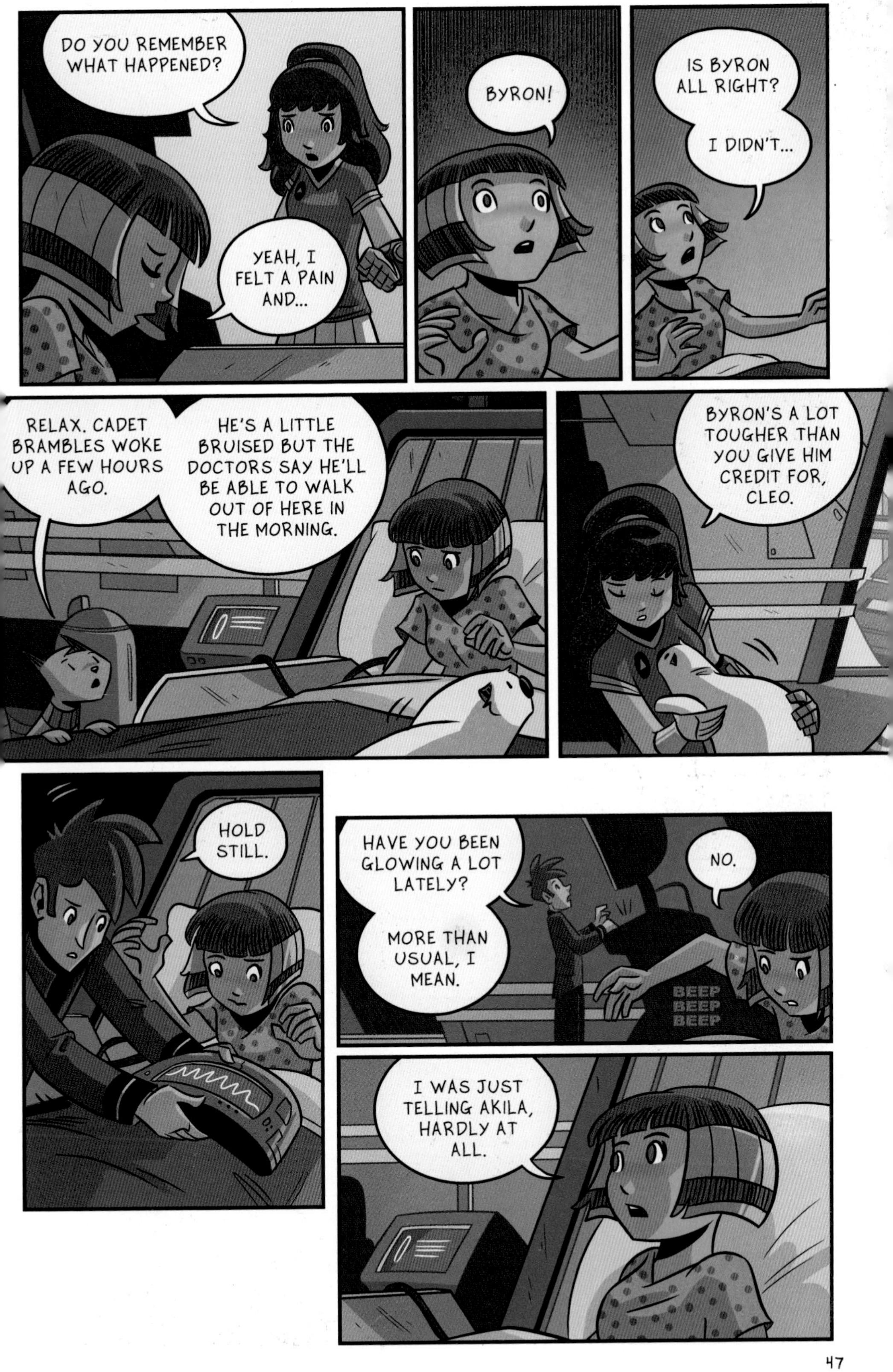
DO YOU REMEMBER WHAT HAPPENED?
YEAH, I FELT A PAIN AND...
BYRON!
IS BYRON ALL RIGHT?
I DIDN'T...
RELAX. CADET BRAMBLES WOKE UP A FEW HOURS AGO.
HE'S A LITTLE BRUISED BUT THE DOCTORS SAY HE'LL BE ABLE TO WALK OUT OF HERE IN THE MORNING.
BYRON'S A LOT TOUGHER THAN YOU GIVE HIM CREDIT FOR, CLEO.
HOLD STILL.
HAVE YOU BEEN GLOWING A LOT LATELY?
MORE THAN USUAL, I MEAN.
NO.
BEEP BEEP BEEP
I WAS JUST TELLING AKILA, HARDLY AT ALL.

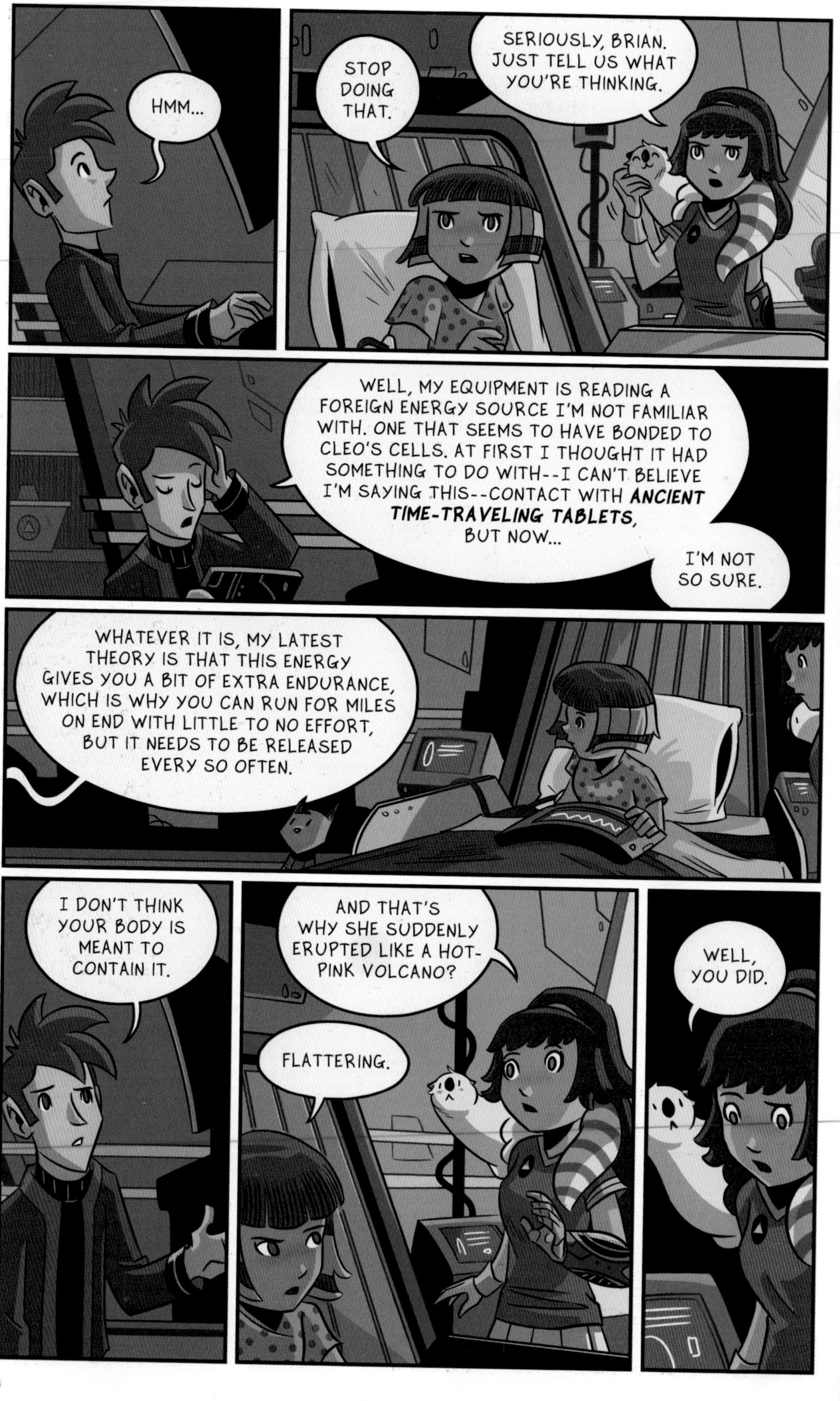
HMM...
STOP DOING THAT.
SERIOUSLY, BRIAN. JUST TELL US WHAT YOU'RE THINKING.
WELL, MY EQUIPMENT IS READING A FOREIGN ENERGY SOURCE I'M NOT FAMILIAR WITH. ONE THAT SEEMS TO HAVE BONDED TO CLEO'S CELLS. AT FIRST I THOUGHT IT HAD SOMETHING TO DO WITH--I CAN'T BELIEVE I'M SAYING THIS--CONTACT WITH **ANCIENT TIME-TRAVELING TABLETS,** BUT NOW...
I'M NOT SO SURE.
WHATEVER IT IS, MY LATEST THEORY IS THAT THIS ENERGY GIVES YOU A BIT OF EXTRA ENDURANCE, WHICH IS WHY YOU CAN RUN FOR MILES ON END WITH LITTLE TO NO EFFORT, BUT IT NEEDS TO BE RELEASED EVERY SO OFTEN.
I DON'T THINK YOUR BODY IS MEANT TO CONTAIN IT.
AND THAT'S WHY SHE SUDDENLY ERUPTED LIKE A HOT-PINK VOLCANO?
FLATTERING.
WELL, YOU DID.

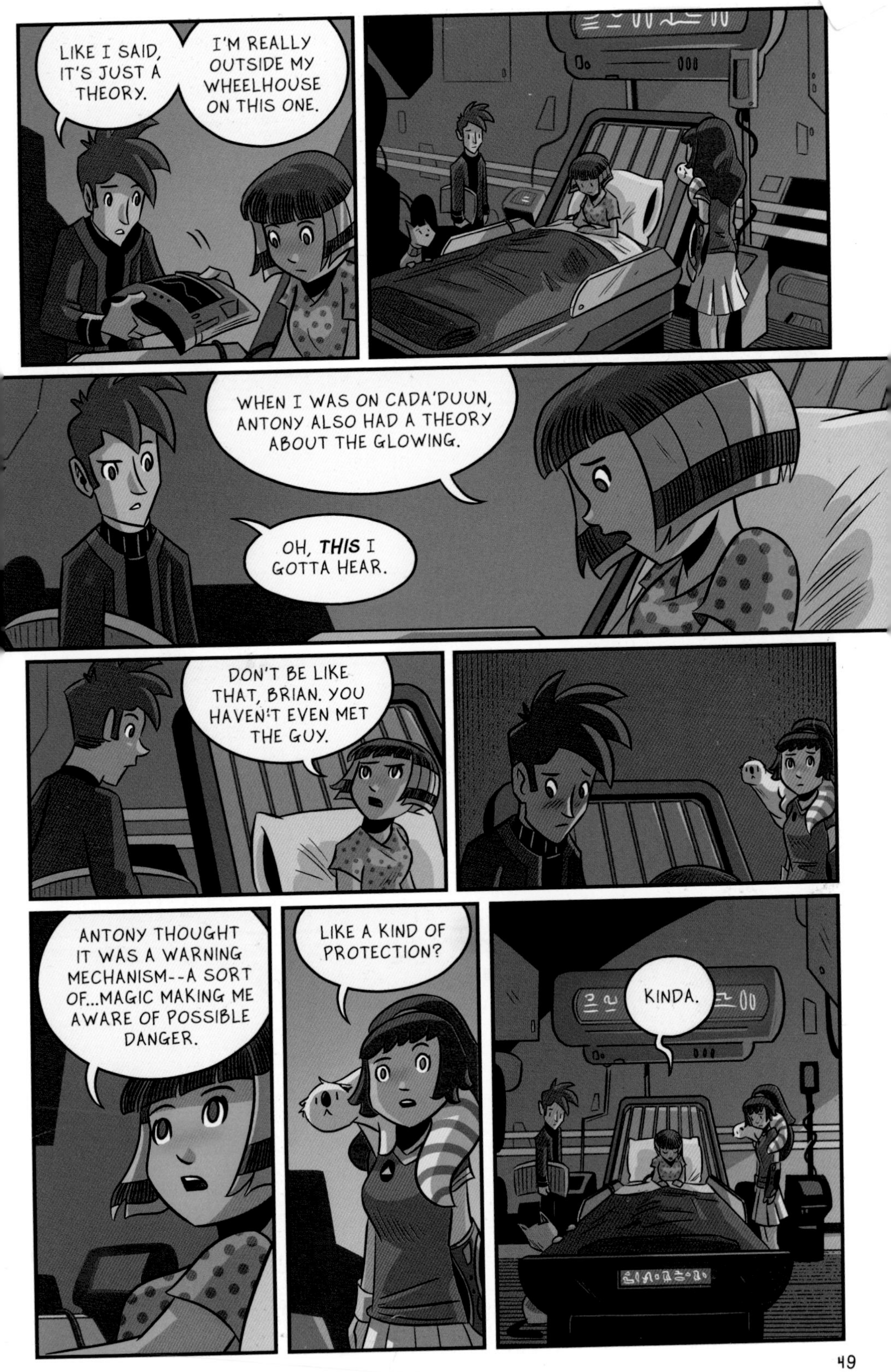

LIKE I SAID, IT'S JUST A THEORY.
I'M REALLY OUTSIDE MY WHEELHOUSE ON THIS ONE.
WHEN I WAS ON CADA'DUUN, ANTONY ALSO HAD A THEORY ABOUT THE GLOWING.
OH, **THIS** I GOTTA HEAR.
DON'T BE LIKE THAT, BRIAN. YOU HAVEN'T EVEN MET THE GUY.
ANTONY THOUGHT IT WAS A WARNING MECHANISM--A SORT OF...MAGIC MAKING ME AWARE OF POSSIBLE DANGER.
LIKE A KIND OF PROTECTION?
KINDA.

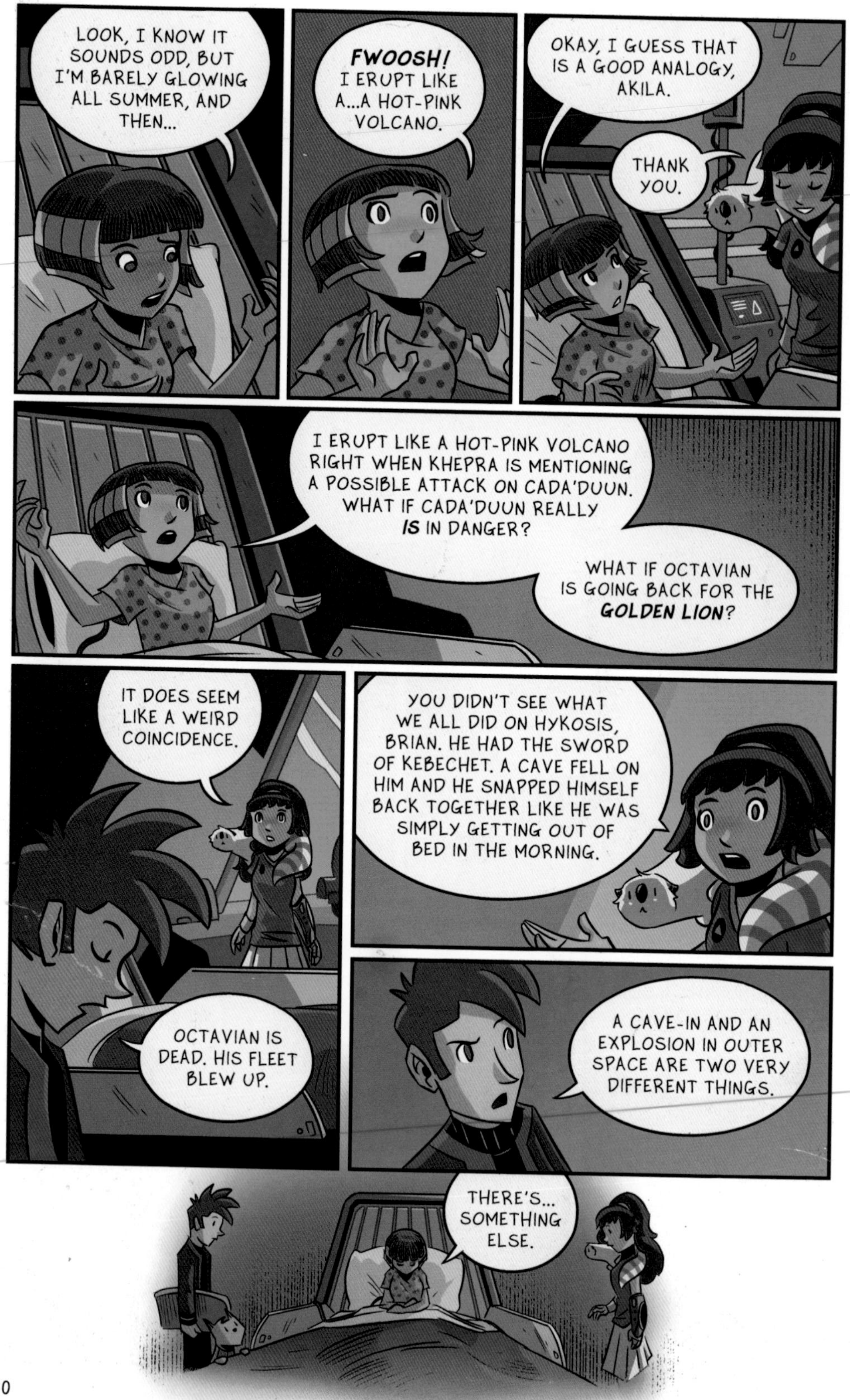
LOOK, I KNOW IT SOUNDS ODD, BUT I'M BARELY GLOWING ALL SUMMER, AND THEN...
FWOOSH! I ERUPT LIKE A...A HOT-PINK VOLCANO.
OKAY, I GUESS THAT IS A GOOD ANALOGY, AKILA.
THANK YOU.
I ERUPT LIKE A HOT-PINK VOLCANO RIGHT WHEN KHEPRA IS MENTIONING A POSSIBLE ATTACK ON CADA'DUUN. WHAT IF CADA'DUUN REALLY IS IN DANGER?
WHAT IF OCTAVIAN IS GOING BACK FOR THE GOLDEN LION?
IT DOES SEEM LIKE A WEIRD COINCIDENCE.
OCTAVIAN IS DEAD. HIS FLEET BLEW UP.
YOU DIDN'T SEE WHAT WE ALL DID ON HYKOSIS, BRIAN. HE HAD THE SWORD OF KEBECHET. A CAVE FELL ON HIM AND HE SNAPPED HIMSELF BACK TOGETHER LIKE HE WAS SIMPLY GETTING OUT OF BED IN THE MORNING.
A CAVE-IN AND AN EXPLOSION IN OUTER SPACE ARE TWO VERY DIFFERENT THINGS.
THERE'S... SOMETHING ELSE.

ON CADA'DUUN...

I...

WELL, I DIED.

YOU **WHAT?**

I...DIED. I WAS FIGHTING THIS BOUNTY HUNTER WHO WAS TRYING TO DESTROY THE GOLDEN LION.

ALTHOUGH NOW I THINK HE WAS WORKING FOR OCTAVIAN.

HE WAS BETTER THAN ME. HE IMPALED ME.

RIGHT HERE.

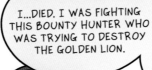

IT WAS DARK FOR A WHILE. COLD. BUT...I WOKE UP. FULLY HEALED.

I WAS GLOWING WHEN IT HAPPENED.

I'M SORRY, KHENSU. I SHOULD HAVE TOLD YOU BACK ON CADA'DUUN. WE SAID NO MORE LIES, BUT YOU GAVE ME THAT SINCERE APOLOGY ON HOW MUCH FAITH YOU HAD IN ME.

I DIDN'T KNOW HOW TO TELL YOU.

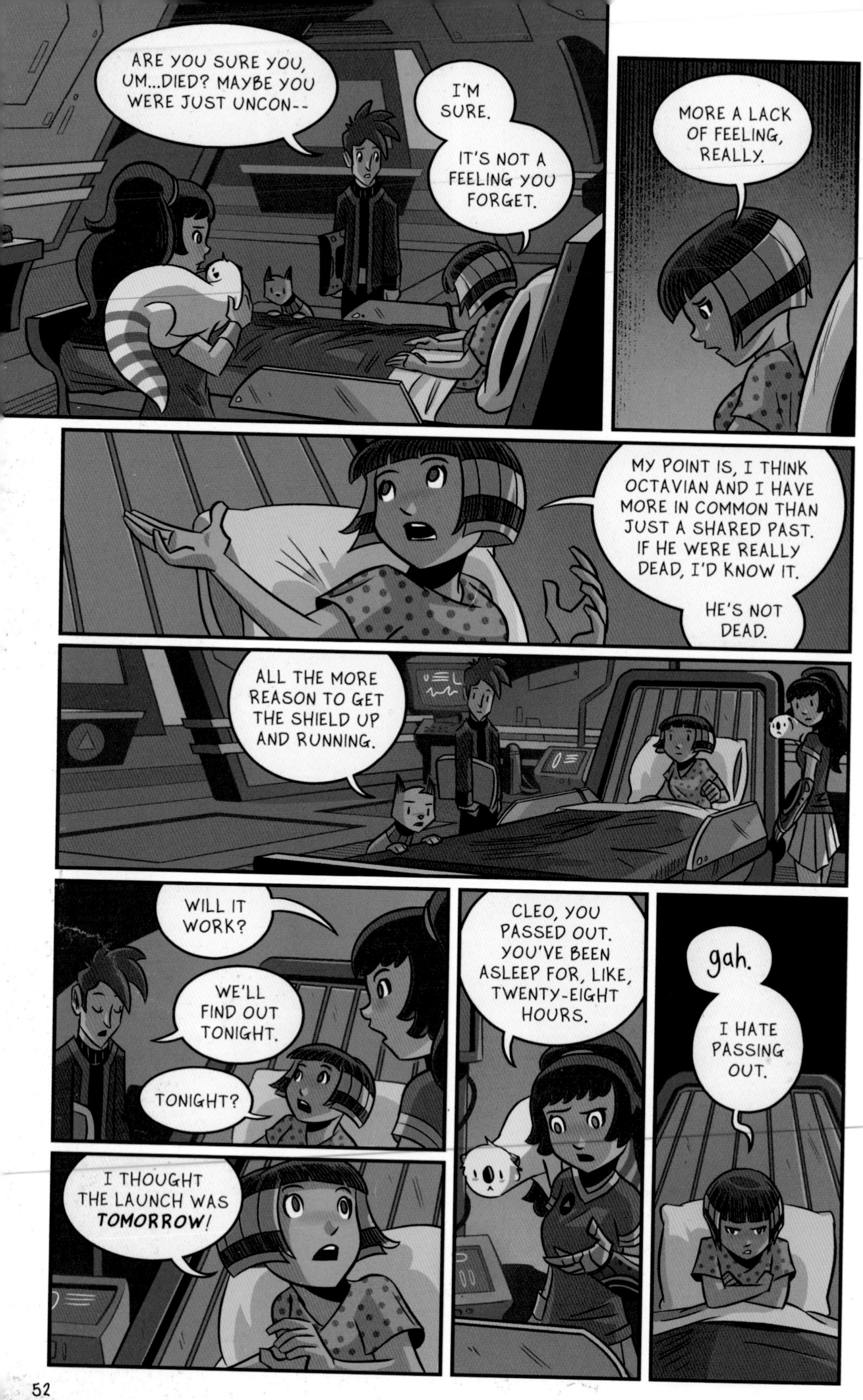
ARE YOU SURE YOU, UM...DIED? MAYBE YOU WERE JUST UNCON--
I'M SURE.
IT'S NOT A FEELING YOU FORGET.
MORE A LACK OF FEELING, REALLY.
MY POINT IS, I THINK OCTAVIAN AND I HAVE MORE IN COMMON THAN JUST A SHARED PAST. IF HE WERE REALLY DEAD, I'D KNOW IT.
HE'S NOT DEAD.
ALL THE MORE REASON TO GET THE SHIELD UP AND RUNNING.
WILL IT WORK?
WE'LL FIND OUT TONIGHT.
TONIGHT?
I THOUGHT THE LAUNCH WAS **TOMORROW**!
CLEO, YOU PASSED OUT. YOU'VE BEEN ASLEEP FOR, LIKE, TWENTY-EIGHT HOURS.
gah.
I HATE PASSING OUT.

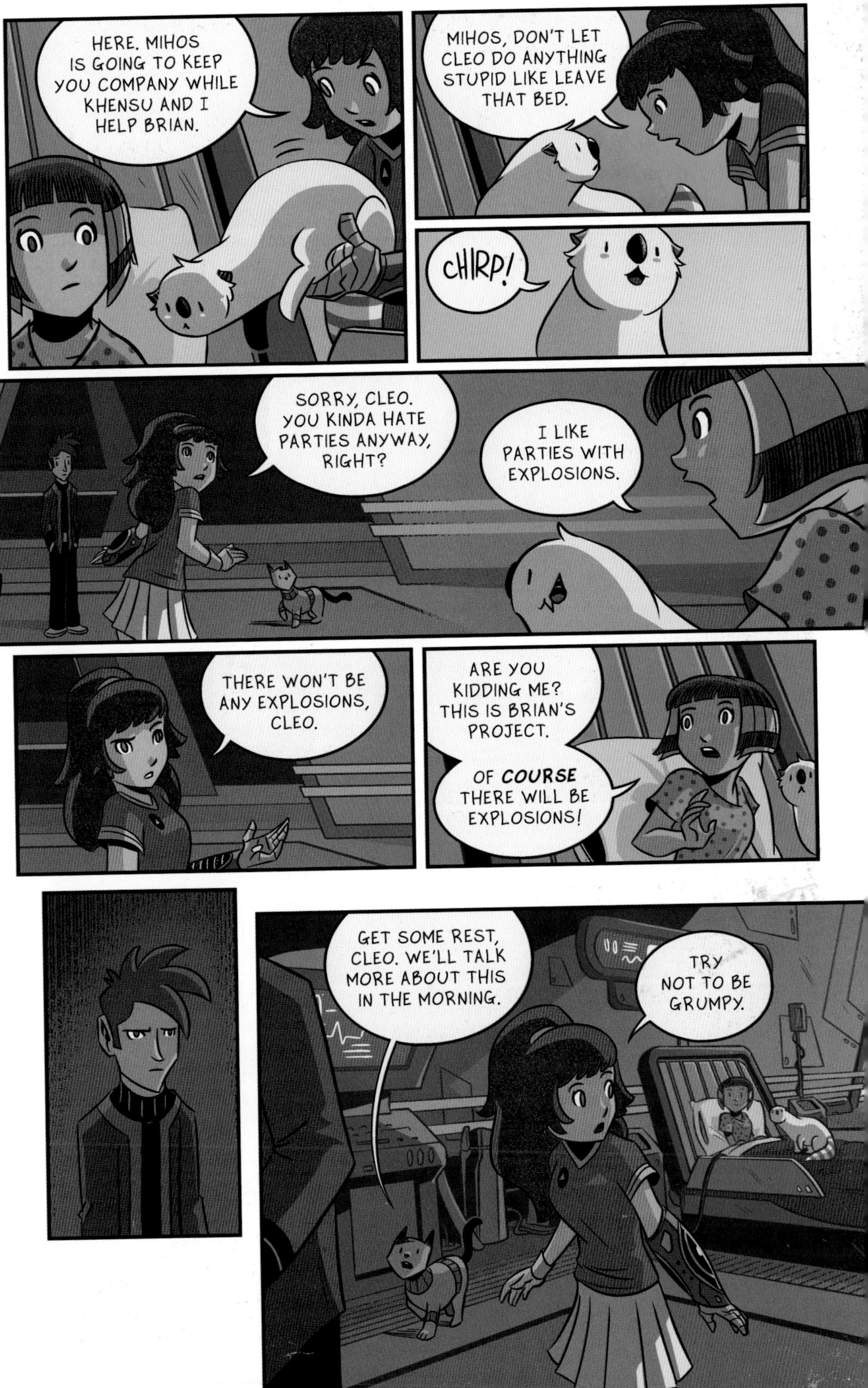
HERE. MIHOS IS GOING TO KEEP YOU COMPANY WHILE KHENSU AND I HELP BRIAN.
MIHOS, DON'T LET CLEO DO ANYTHING STUPID LIKE LEAVE THAT BED.
CHIRP!
SORRY, CLEO. YOU KINDA HATE PARTIES ANYWAY, RIGHT?
I LIKE PARTIES WITH EXPLOSIONS.
THERE WON'T BE ANY EXPLOSIONS, CLEO.
ARE YOU KIDDING ME? THIS IS BRIAN'S PROJECT.
OF COURSE THERE WILL BE EXPLOSIONS!
GET SOME REST, CLEO. WE'LL TALK MORE ABOUT THIS IN THE MORNING.
TRY NOT TO BE GRUMPY.

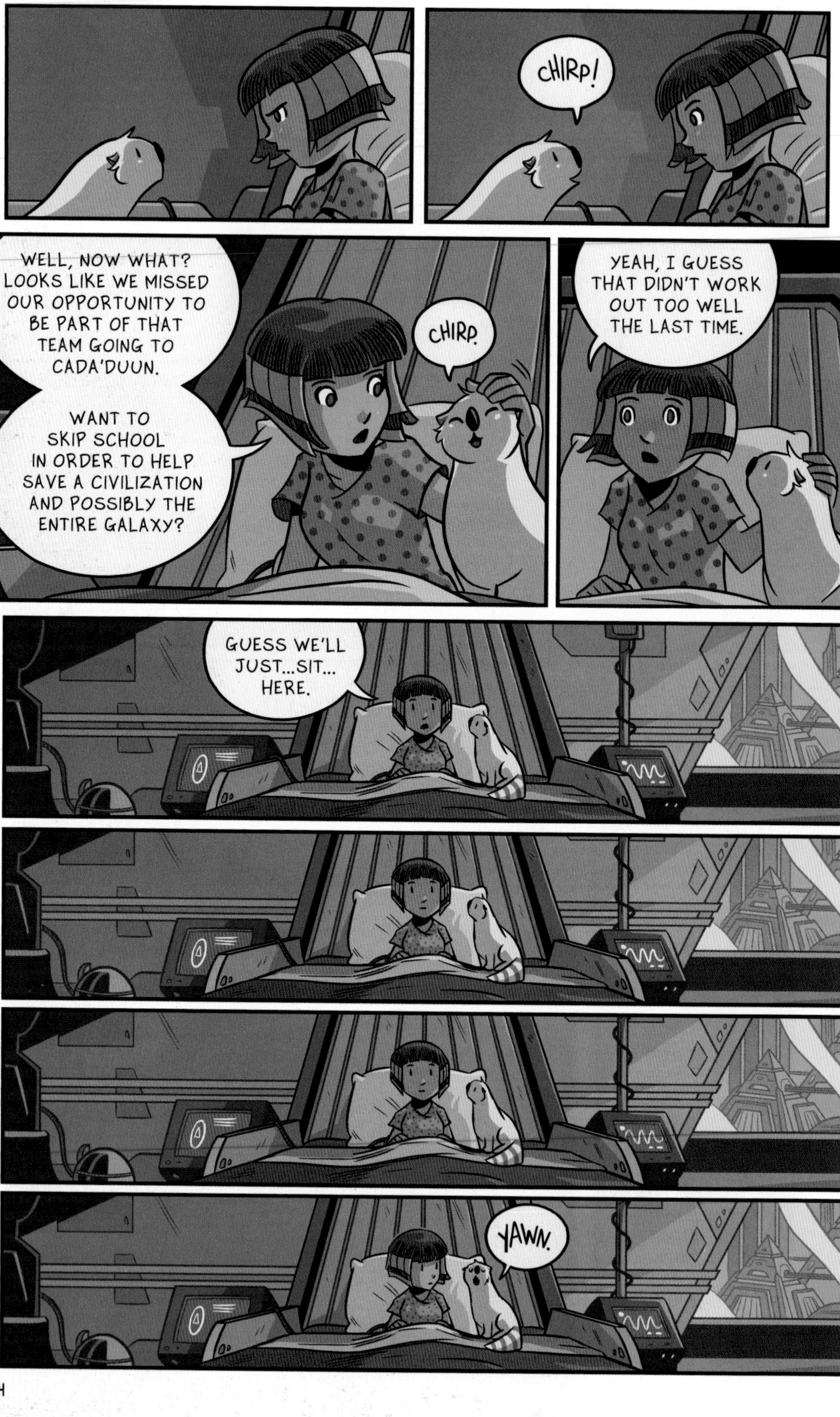

CHIRP!

WELL, NOW WHAT? LOOKS LIKE WE MISSED OUR OPPORTUNITY TO BE PART OF THAT TEAM GOING TO CADA'DUUN.

WANT TO SKIP SCHOOL IN ORDER TO HELP SAVE A CIVILIZATION AND POSSIBLY THE ENTIRE GALAXY?

CHIRP.

YEAH, I GUESS THAT DIDN'T WORK OUT TOO WELL THE LAST TIME.

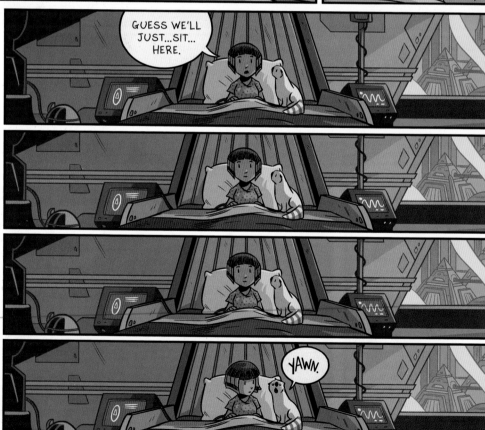

GUESS WE'LL JUST...SIT... HERE.

YAWN.

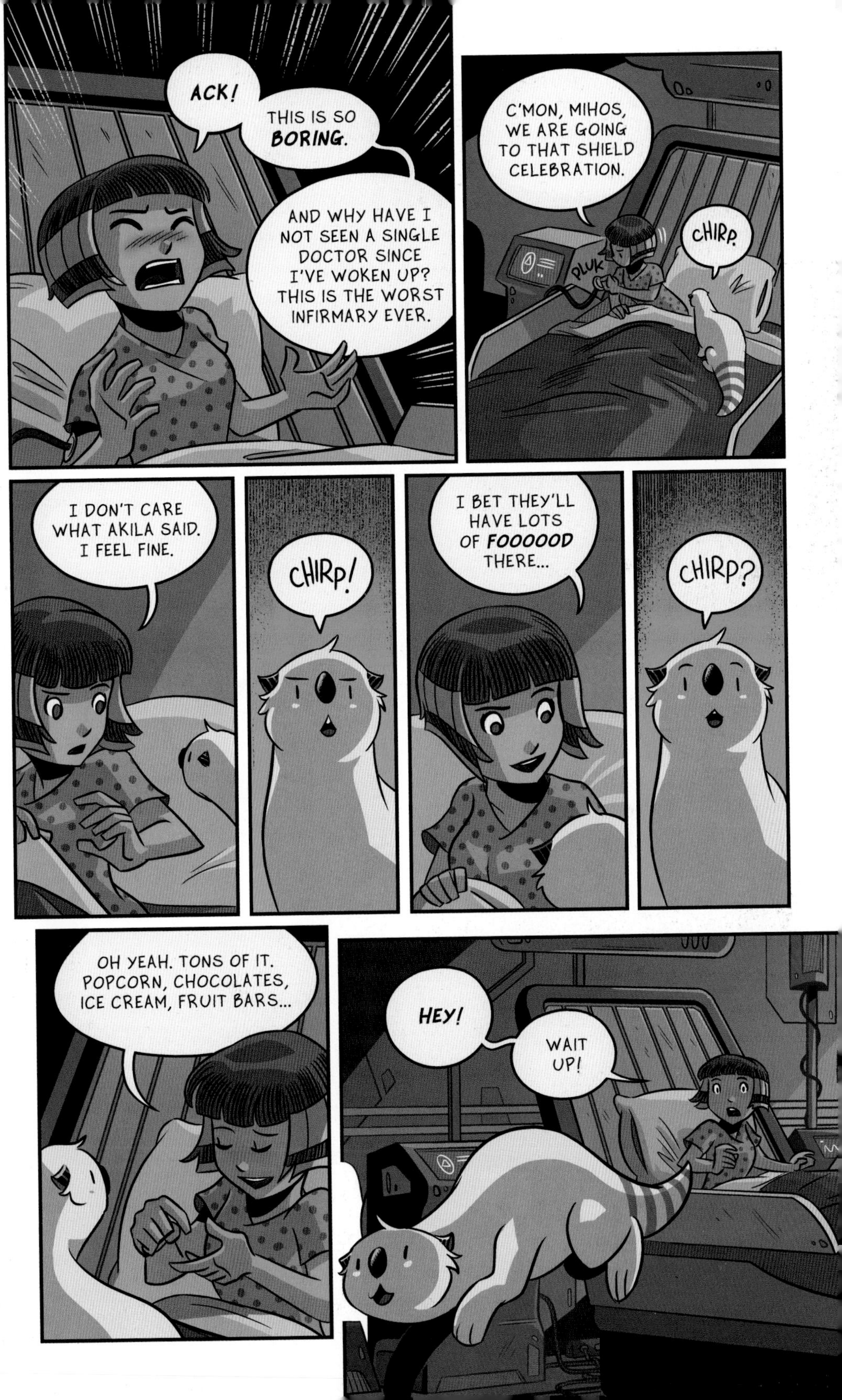
ACK!
THIS IS SO BORING.
AND WHY HAVE I NOT SEEN A SINGLE DOCTOR SINCE I'VE WOKEN UP? THIS IS THE WORST INFIRMARY EVER.
C'MON, MIHOS, WE ARE GOING TO THAT SHIELD CELEBRATION.
PLUK
CHIRP.
I DON'T CARE WHAT AKILA SAID. I FEEL FINE.
CHIRP!
I BET THEY'LL HAVE LOTS OF FOOOOOD THERE...
CHIRP?
OH YEAH. TONS OF IT. POPCORN, CHOCOLATES, ICE CREAM, FRUIT BARS...
HEY!
WAIT UP!

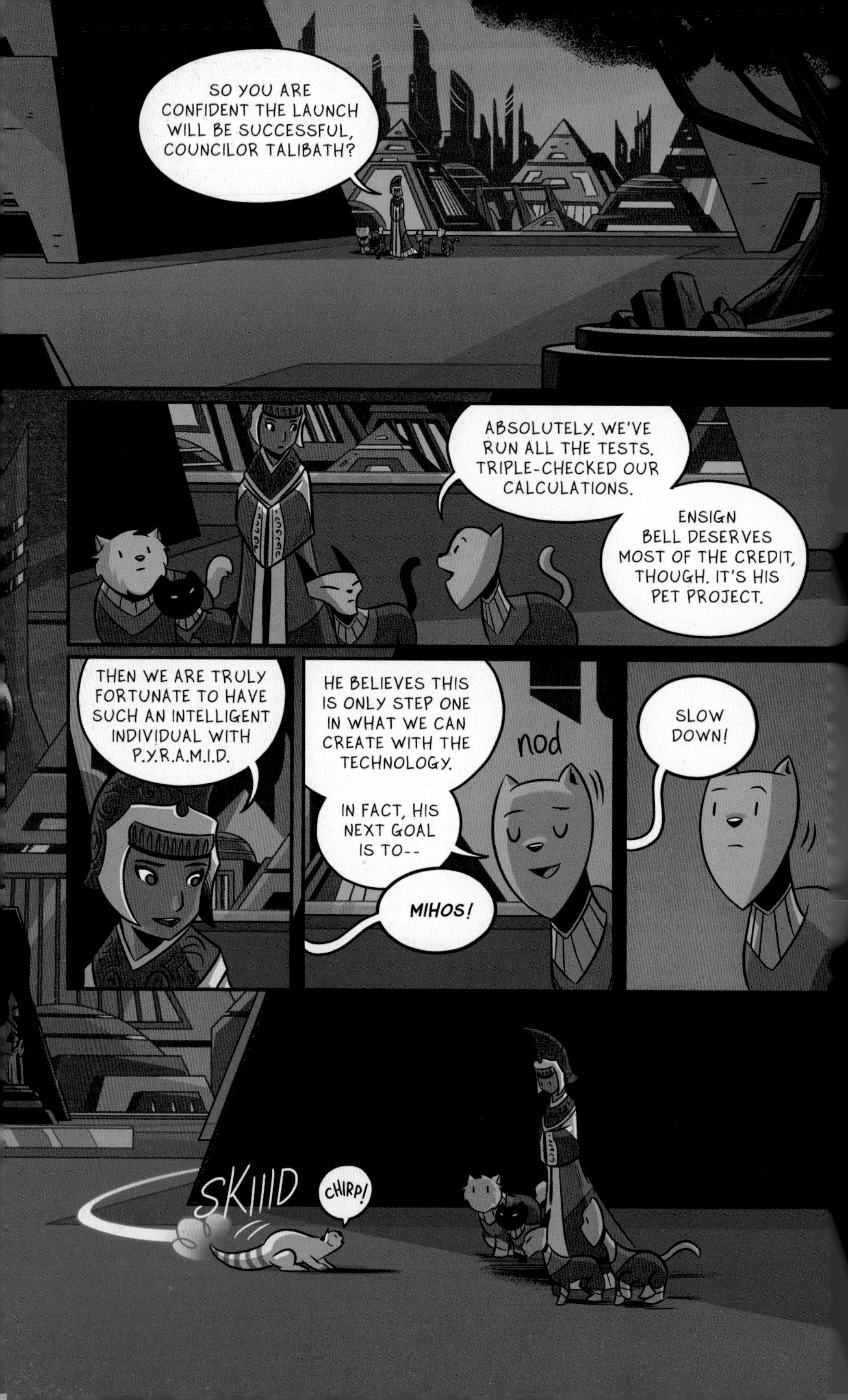
SO YOU ARE CONFIDENT THE LAUNCH WILL BE SUCCESSFUL, COUNCILOR TALIBATH?
ABSOLUTELY. WE'VE RUN ALL THE TESTS. TRIPLE-CHECKED OUR CALCULATIONS.
ENSIGN BELL DESERVES MOST OF THE CREDIT, THOUGH. IT'S HIS PET PROJECT.
THEN WE ARE TRULY FORTUNATE TO HAVE SUCH AN INTELLIGENT INDIVIDUAL WITH P.Y.R.A.M.I.D.
HE BELIEVES THIS IS ONLY STEP ONE IN WHAT WE CAN CREATE WITH THE TECHNOLOGY.
IN FACT, HIS NEXT GOAL IS TO--
MIHOS!
nod
SLOW DOWN!
SKIIID
CHIRP!

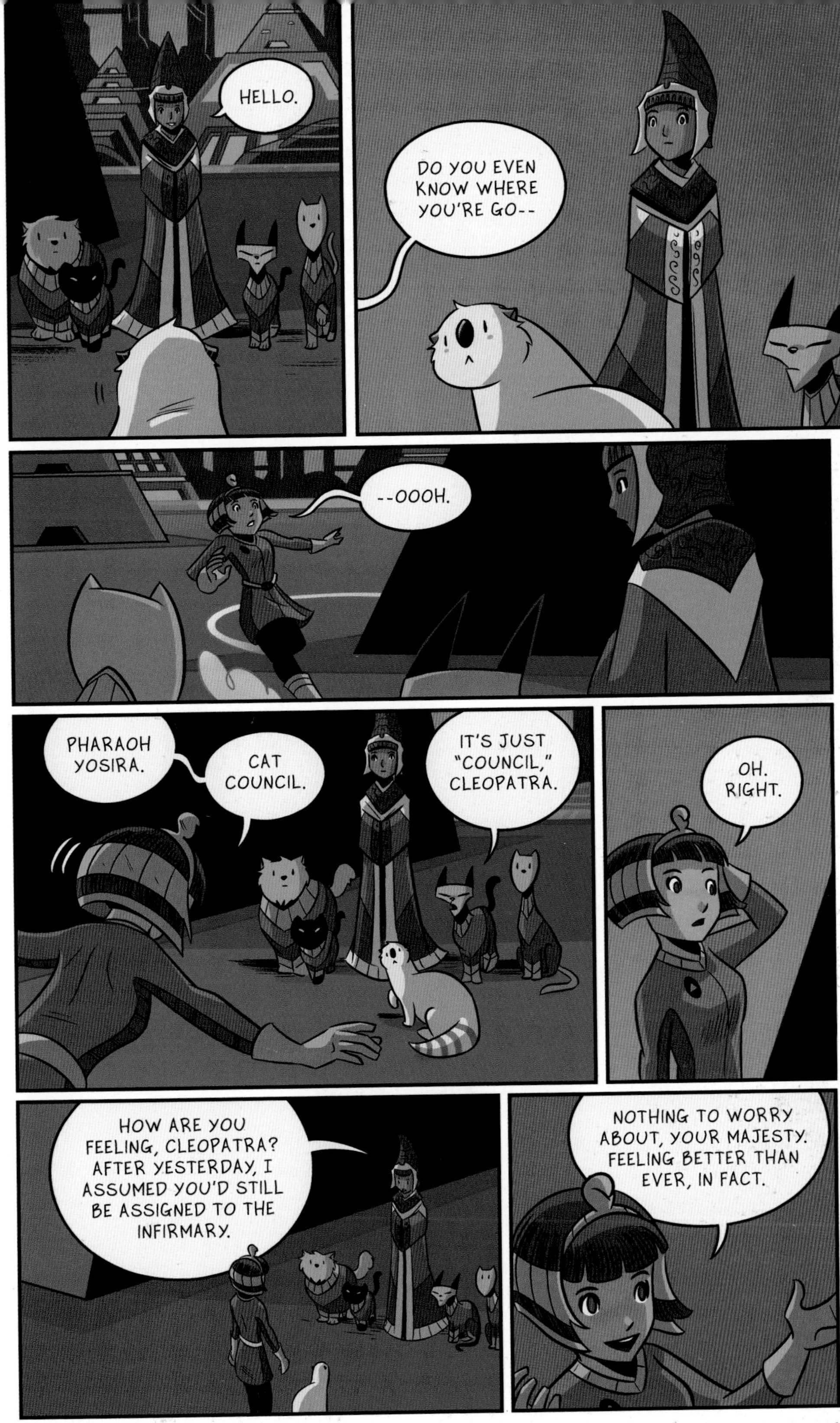
HELLO.
DO YOU EVEN KNOW WHERE YOU'RE GO--
--OOOH.
PHARAOH YOSIRA.
CAT COUNCIL.
IT'S JUST "COUNCIL," CLEOPATRA.
OH. RIGHT.
HOW ARE YOU FEELING, CLEOPATRA? AFTER YESTERDAY, I ASSUMED YOU'D STILL BE ASSIGNED TO THE INFIRMARY.
NOTHING TO WORRY ABOUT, YOUR MAJESTY. FEELING BETTER THAN EVER, IN FACT.

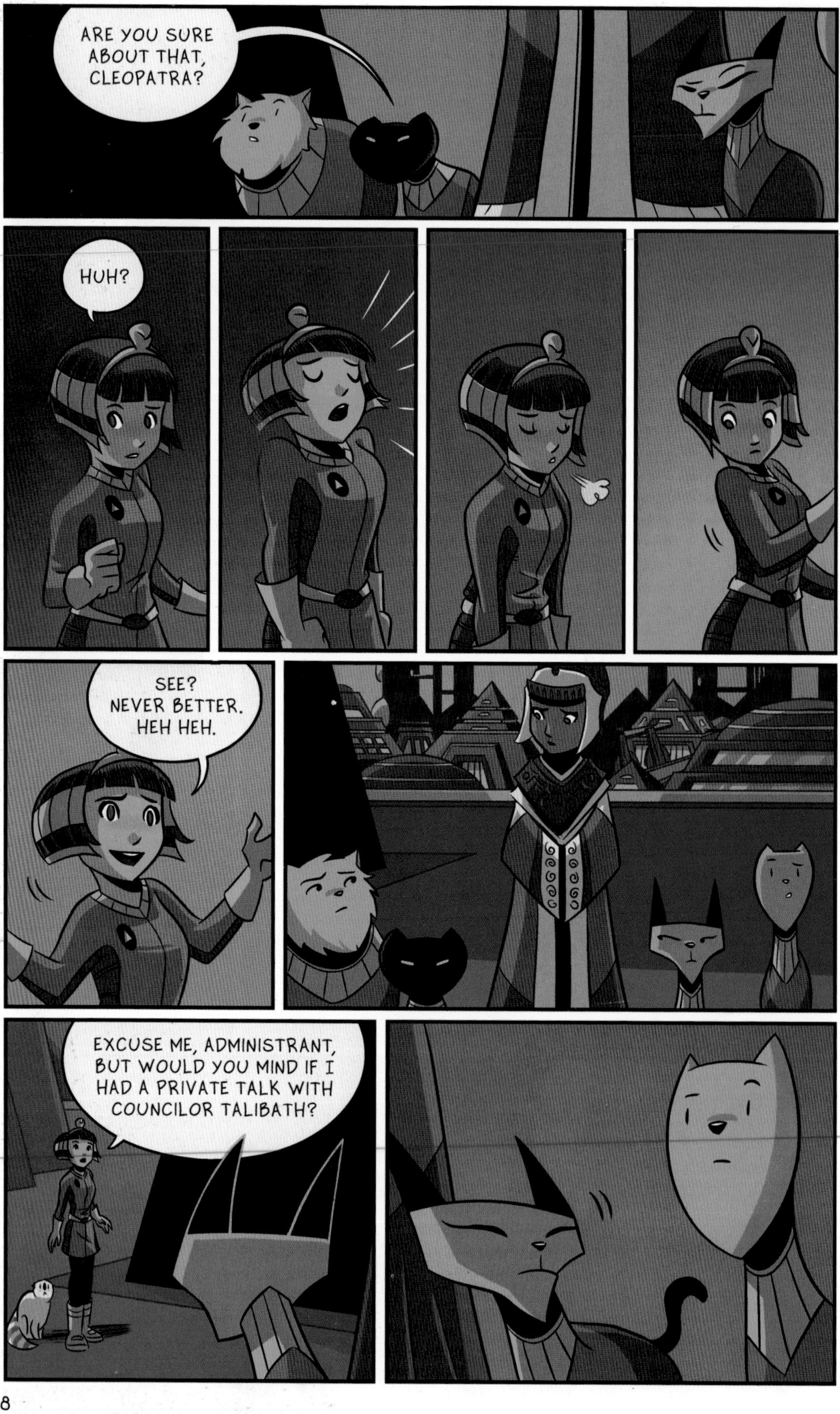
ARE YOU SURE ABOUT THAT, CLEOPATRA?
HUH?
SEE? NEVER BETTER. HEH HEH.
EXCUSE ME, ADMINISTRANT, BUT WOULD YOU MIND IF I HAD A PRIVATE TALK WITH COUNCILOR TALIBATH?

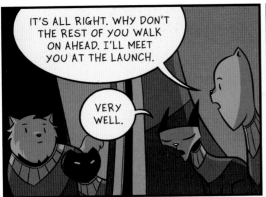

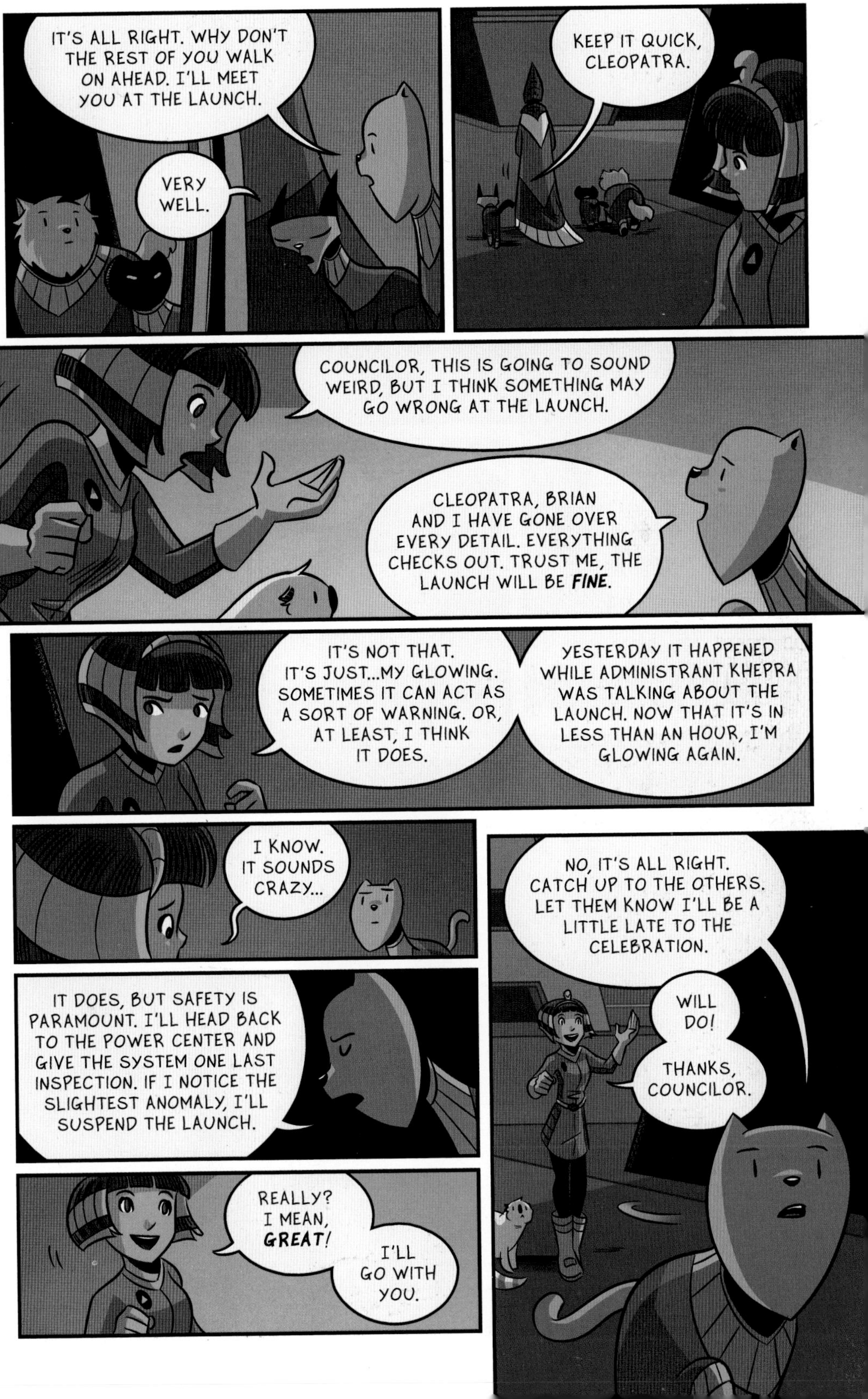

IT'S ALL RIGHT. WHY DON'T THE REST OF YOU WALK ON AHEAD. I'LL MEET YOU AT THE LAUNCH.

VERY WELL.

KEEP IT QUICK, CLEOPATRA.

COUNCILOR, THIS IS GOING TO SOUND WEIRD, BUT I THINK SOMETHING MAY GO WRONG AT THE LAUNCH.

CLEOPATRA, BRIAN AND I HAVE GONE OVER EVERY DETAIL. EVERYTHING CHECKS OUT. TRUST ME, THE LAUNCH WILL BE *FINE*.

IT'S NOT THAT. IT'S JUST...MY GLOWING. SOMETIMES IT CAN ACT AS A SORT OF WARNING. OR, AT LEAST, I THINK IT DOES.

YESTERDAY IT HAPPENED WHILE ADMINISTRANT KHEPRA WAS TALKING ABOUT THE LAUNCH. NOW THAT IT'S IN LESS THAN AN HOUR, I'M GLOWING AGAIN.

I KNOW. IT SOUNDS CRAZY...

IT DOES, BUT SAFETY IS PARAMOUNT. I'LL HEAD BACK TO THE POWER CENTER AND GIVE THE SYSTEM ONE LAST INSPECTION. IF I NOTICE THE SLIGHTEST ANOMALY, I'LL SUSPEND THE LAUNCH.

NO, IT'S ALL RIGHT. CATCH UP TO THE OTHERS. LET THEM KNOW I'LL BE A LITTLE LATE TO THE CELEBRATION.

WILL DO!

THANKS, COUNCILOR.

REALLY? I MEAN, **GREAT!**

I'LL GO WITH YOU.

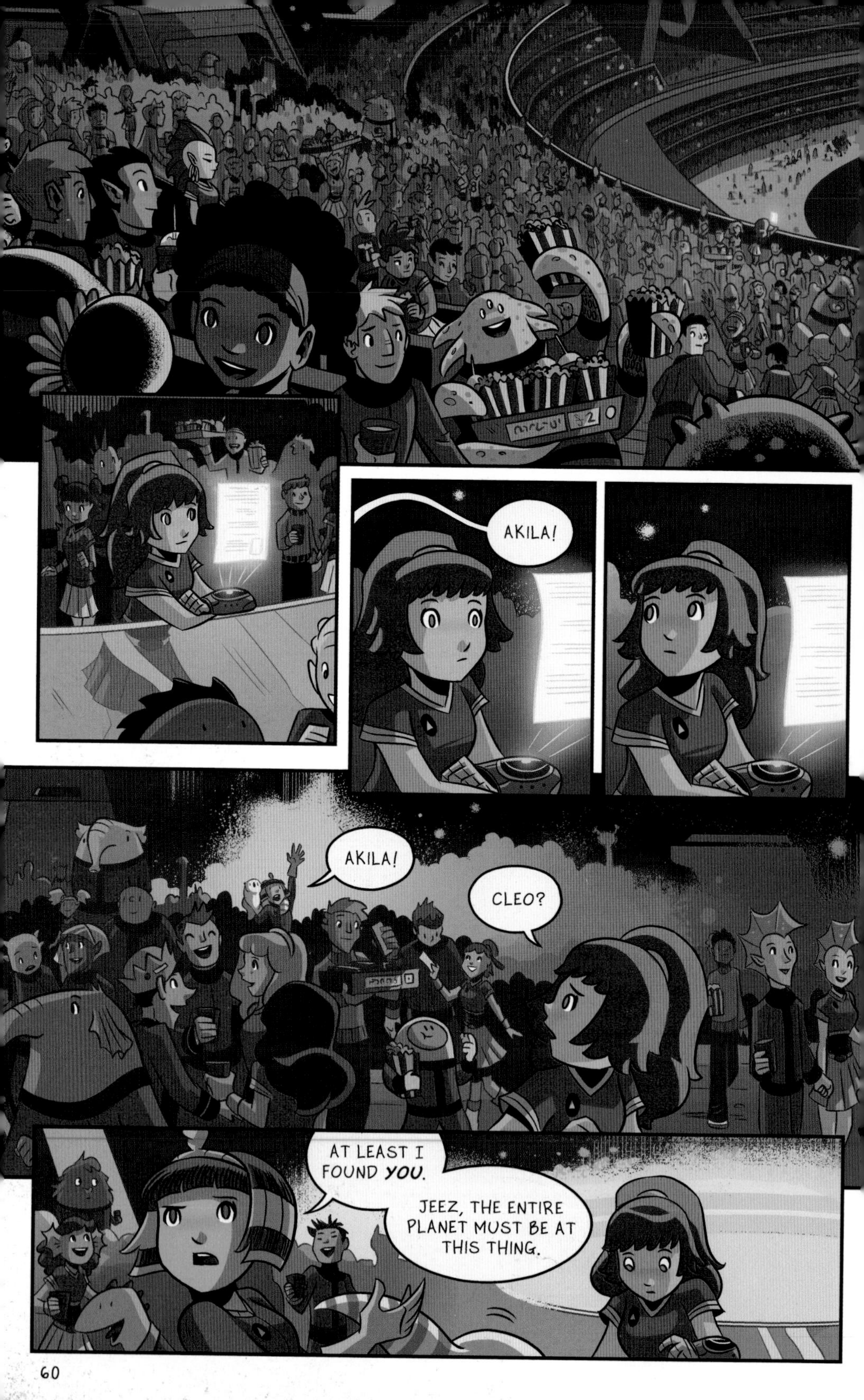
AKILA!
AKILA!
CLEO?
AT LEAST I FOUND *YOU*.
JEEZ, THE ENTIRE PLANET MUST BE AT THIS THING.

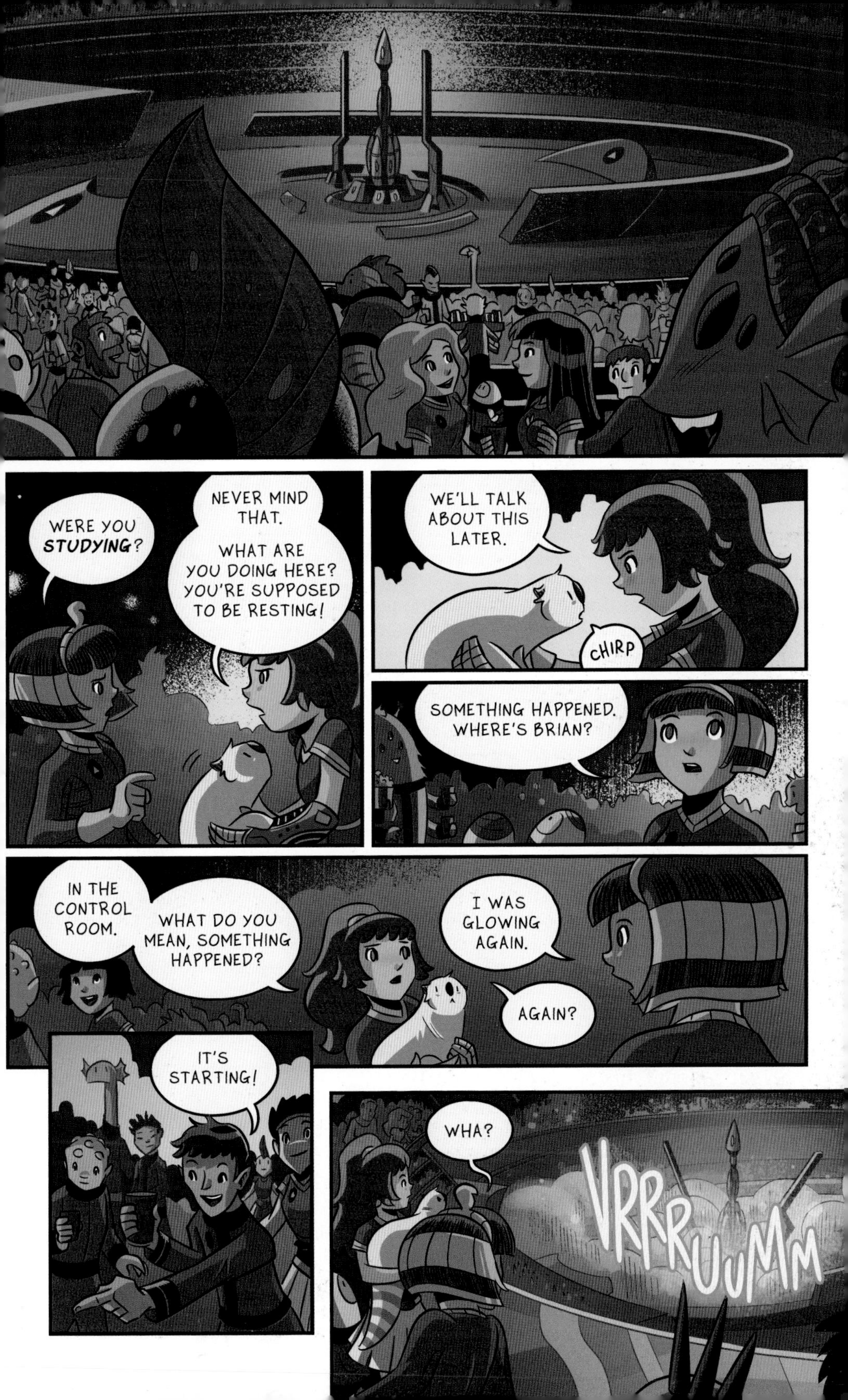
WERE YOU STUDYING?
NEVER MIND THAT.
WHAT ARE YOU DOING HERE? YOU'RE SUPPOSED TO BE RESTING!
WE'LL TALK ABOUT THIS LATER.
CHIRP
SOMETHING HAPPENED. WHERE'S BRIAN?
IN THE CONTROL ROOM.
WHAT DO YOU MEAN, SOMETHING HAPPENED?
I WAS GLOWING AGAIN.
AGAIN?
IT'S STARTING!
WHA?
VRRRUUMM

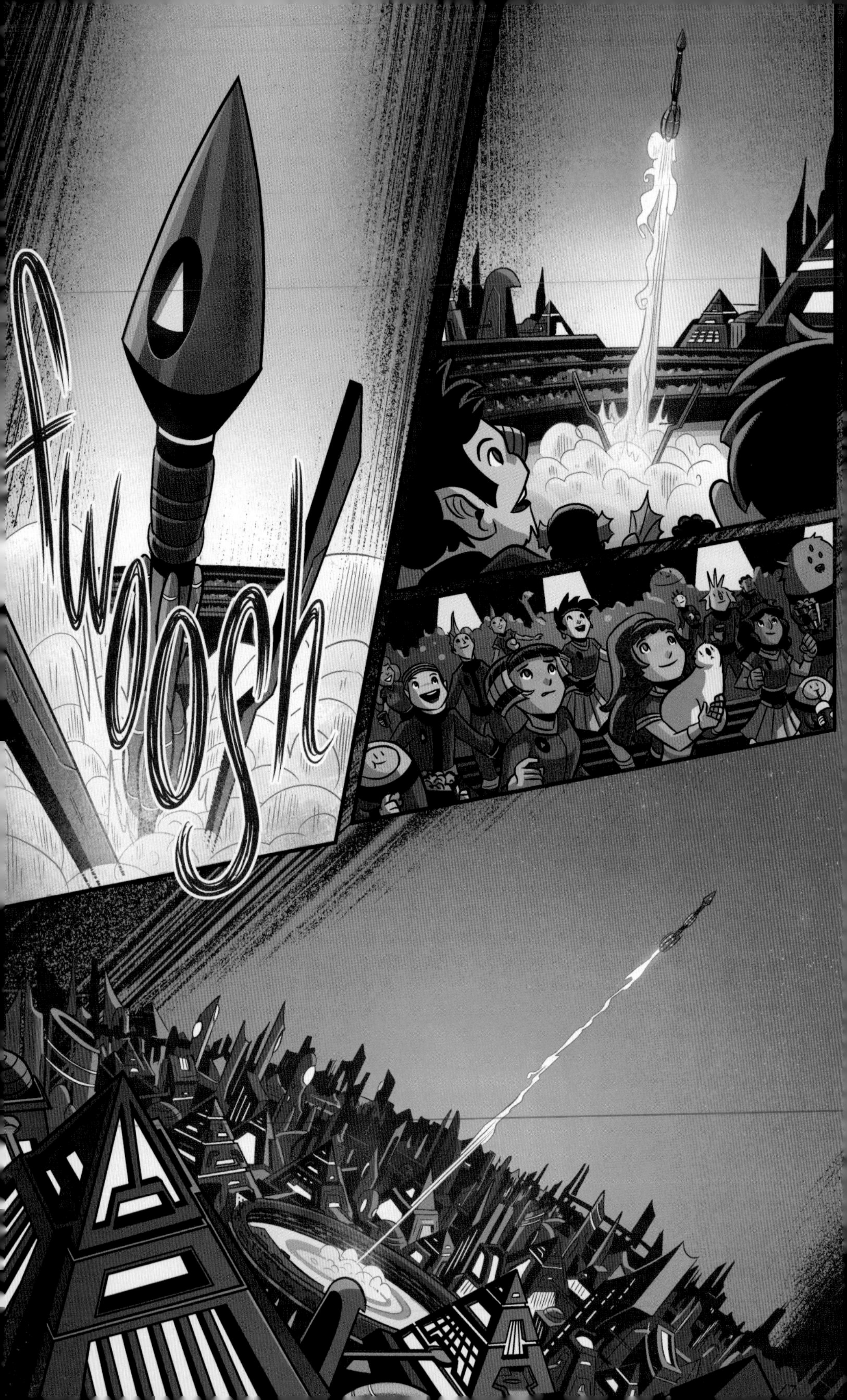
fwoosh

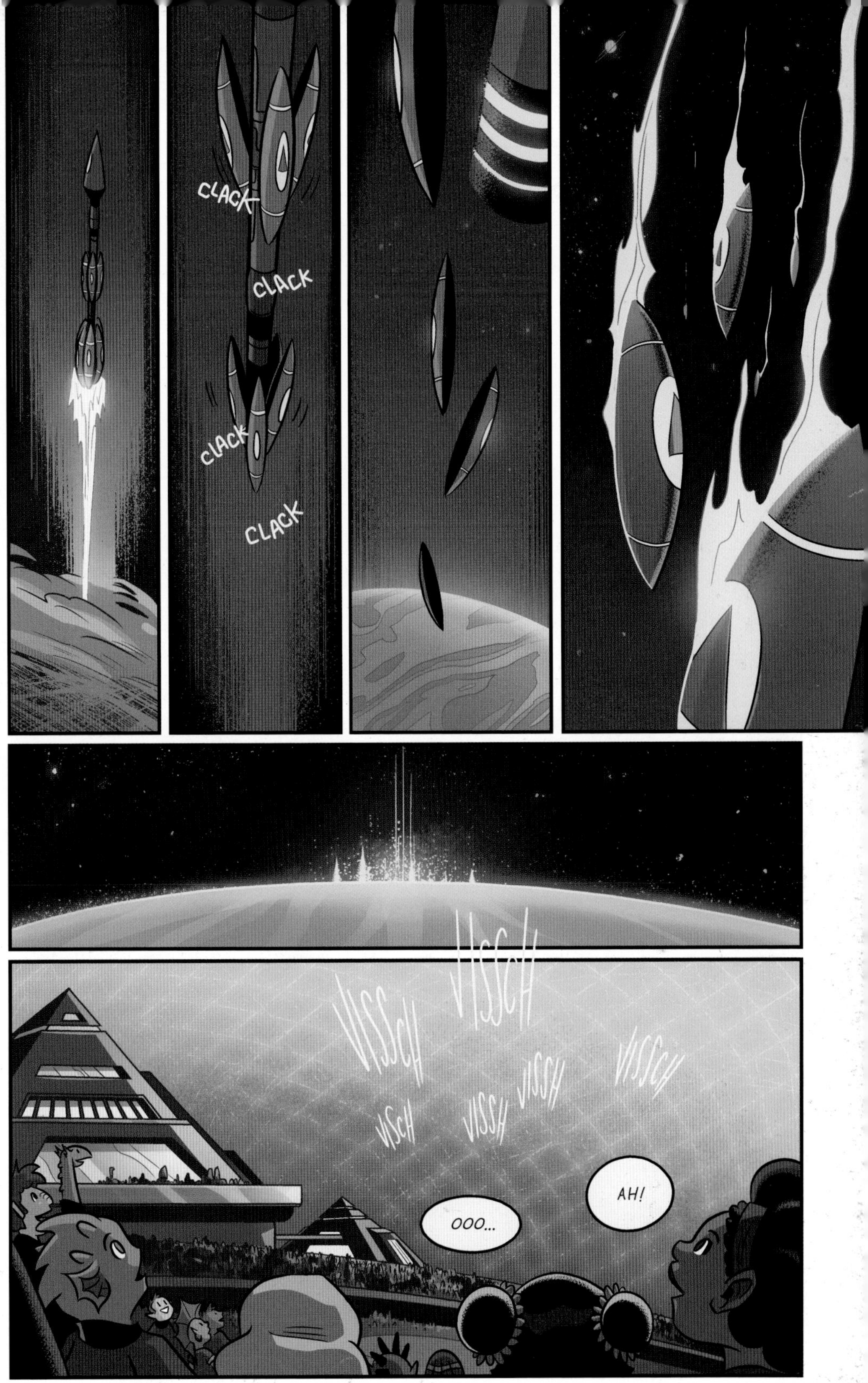
CLACK
CLACK
CLACK
CLACK
VISSCH
VISSCH
VISCH
VISSH
VISSH
VISSCH
OOO...
AH!

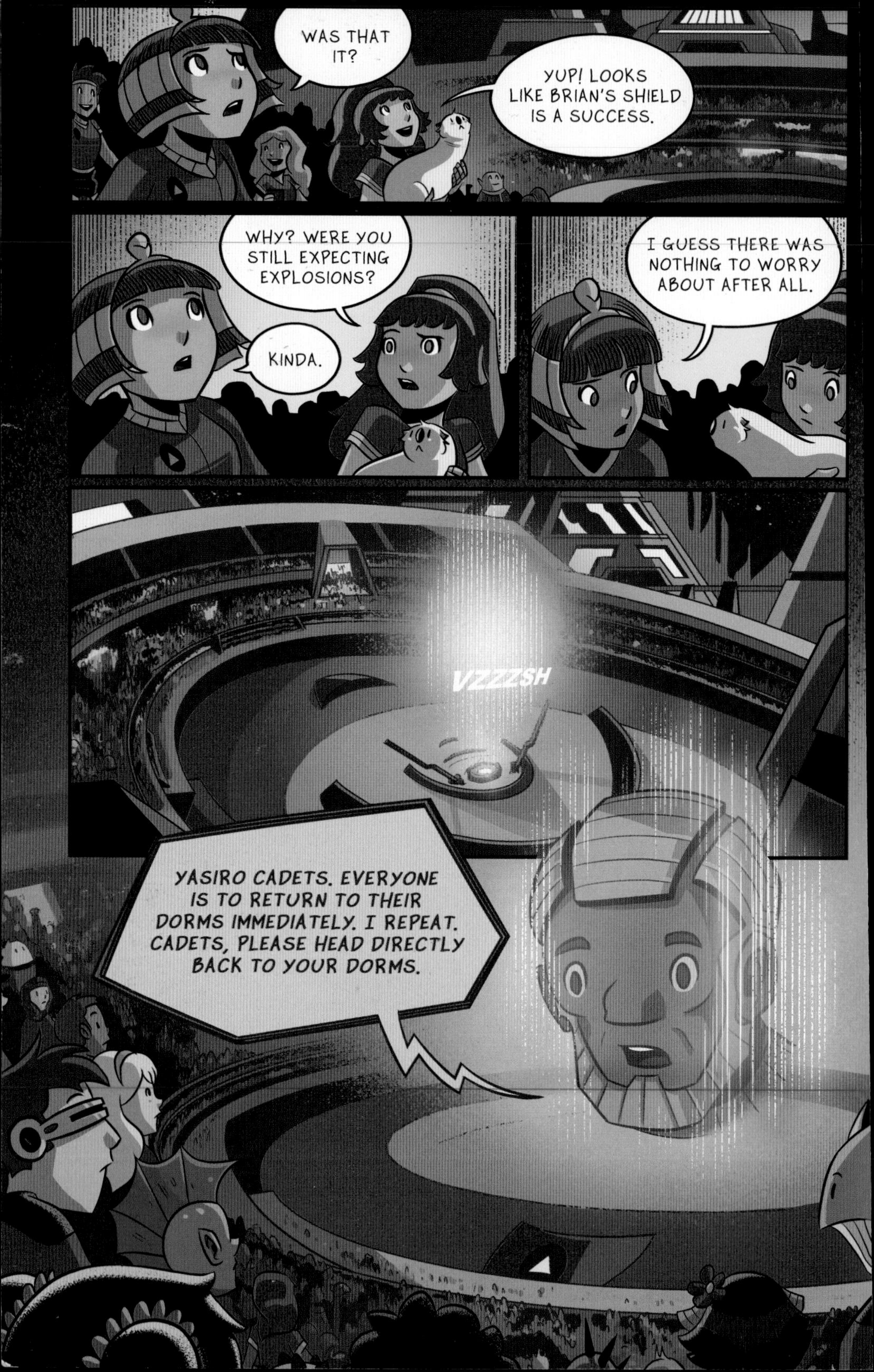
WAS THAT IT?
YUP! LOOKS LIKE BRIAN'S SHIELD IS A SUCCESS.
WHY? WERE YOU STILL EXPECTING EXPLOSIONS?
KINDA.
I GUESS THERE WAS NOTHING TO WORRY ABOUT AFTER ALL.
VZZZSH
YASIRO CADETS. EVERYONE IS TO RETURN TO THEIR DORMS IMMEDIATELY. I REPEAT. CADETS, PLEASE HEAD DIRECTLY BACK TO YOUR DORMS.

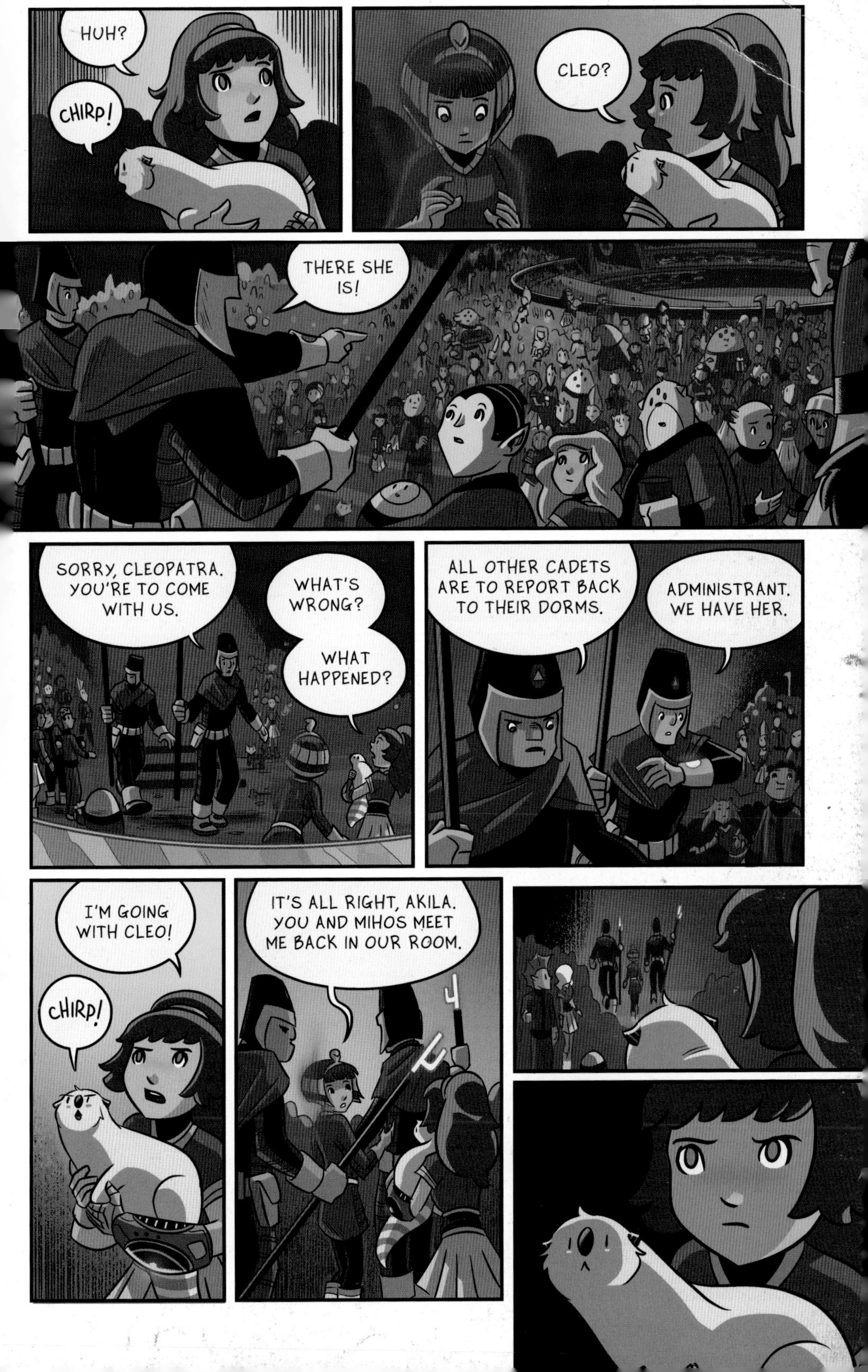
HUH?
CHIRP!
CLEO?
THERE SHE IS!
SORRY, CLEOPATRA. YOU'RE TO COME WITH US.
WHAT'S WRONG?
WHAT HAPPENED?
ALL OTHER CADETS ARE TO REPORT BACK TO THEIR DORMS.
ADMINISTRANT. WE HAVE HER.
I'M GOING WITH CLEO!
CHIRP!
IT'S ALL RIGHT, AKILA. YOU AND MIHOS MEET ME BACK IN OUR ROOM.

HERE SHE IS, ADMINISTRANT.

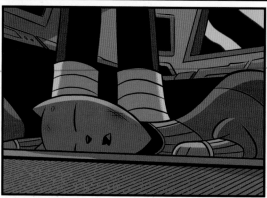

TALIBATH?

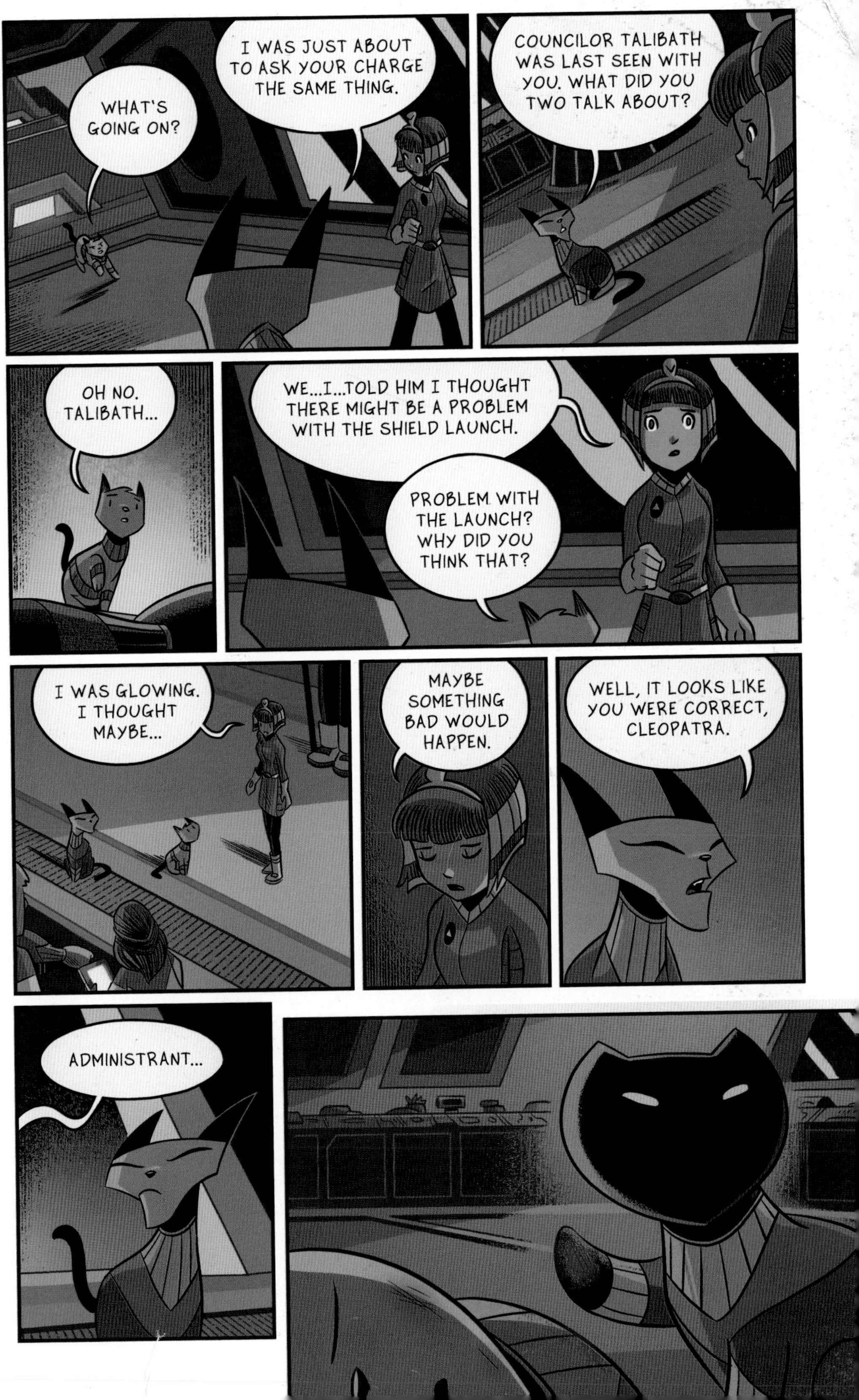
WHAT'S GOING ON?
I WAS JUST ABOUT TO ASK YOUR CHARGE THE SAME THING.
COUNCILOR TALIBATH WAS LAST SEEN WITH YOU. WHAT DID YOU TWO TALK ABOUT?
OH NO. TALIBATH...
WE...I...TOLD HIM I THOUGHT THERE MIGHT BE A PROBLEM WITH THE SHIELD LAUNCH.
PROBLEM WITH THE LAUNCH? WHY DID YOU THINK THAT?
I WAS GLOWING. I THOUGHT MAYBE...
MAYBE SOMETHING BAD WOULD HAPPEN.
WELL, IT LOOKS LIKE YOU WERE CORRECT, CLEOPATRA.
ADMINISTRANT...

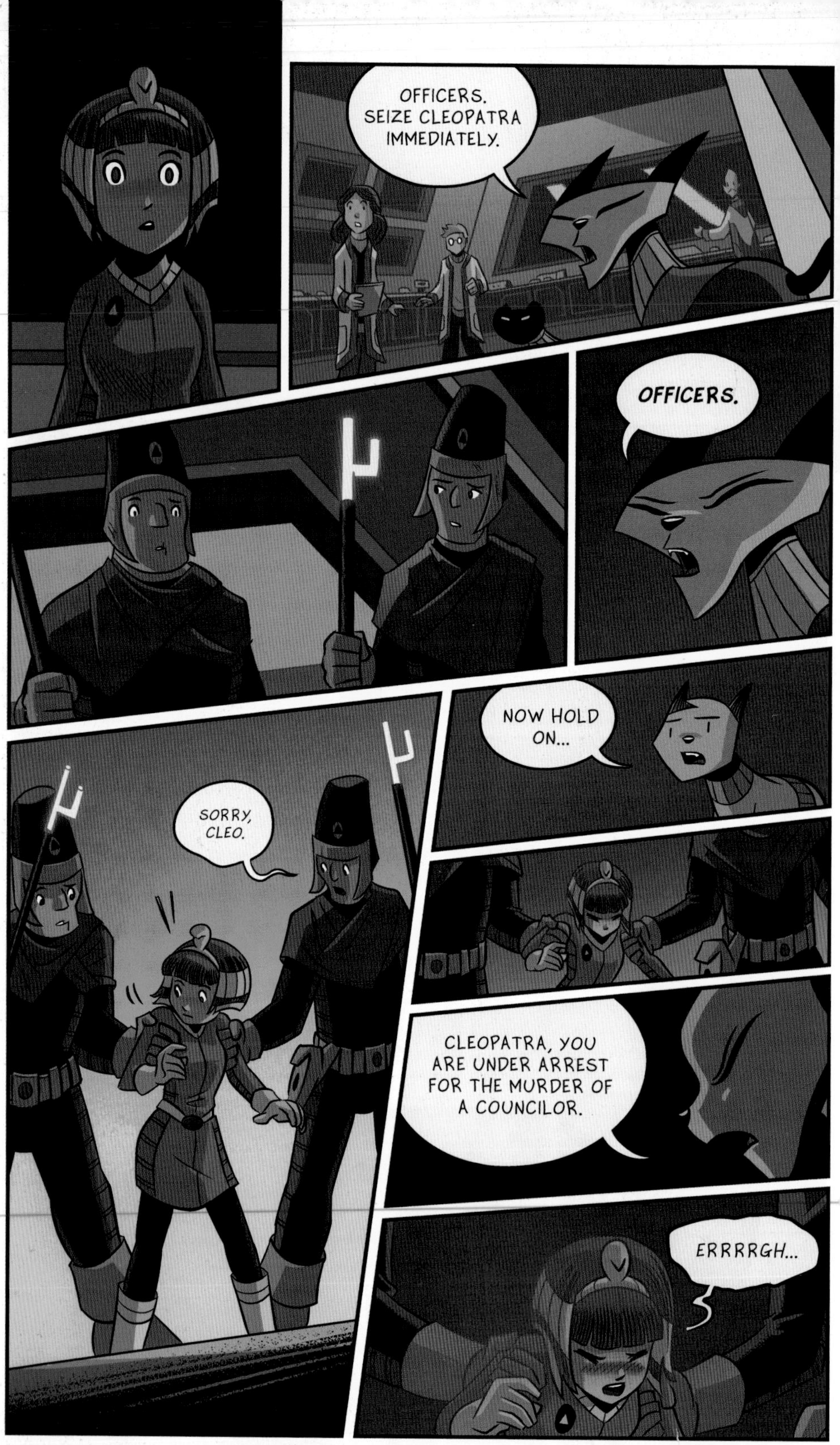
OFFICERS. SEIZE CLEOPATRA IMMEDIATELY.
OFFICERS.
NOW HOLD ON...
SORRY, CLEO.
CLEOPATRA, YOU ARE UNDER ARREST FOR THE MURDER OF A COUNCILOR.
ERRRRGH...

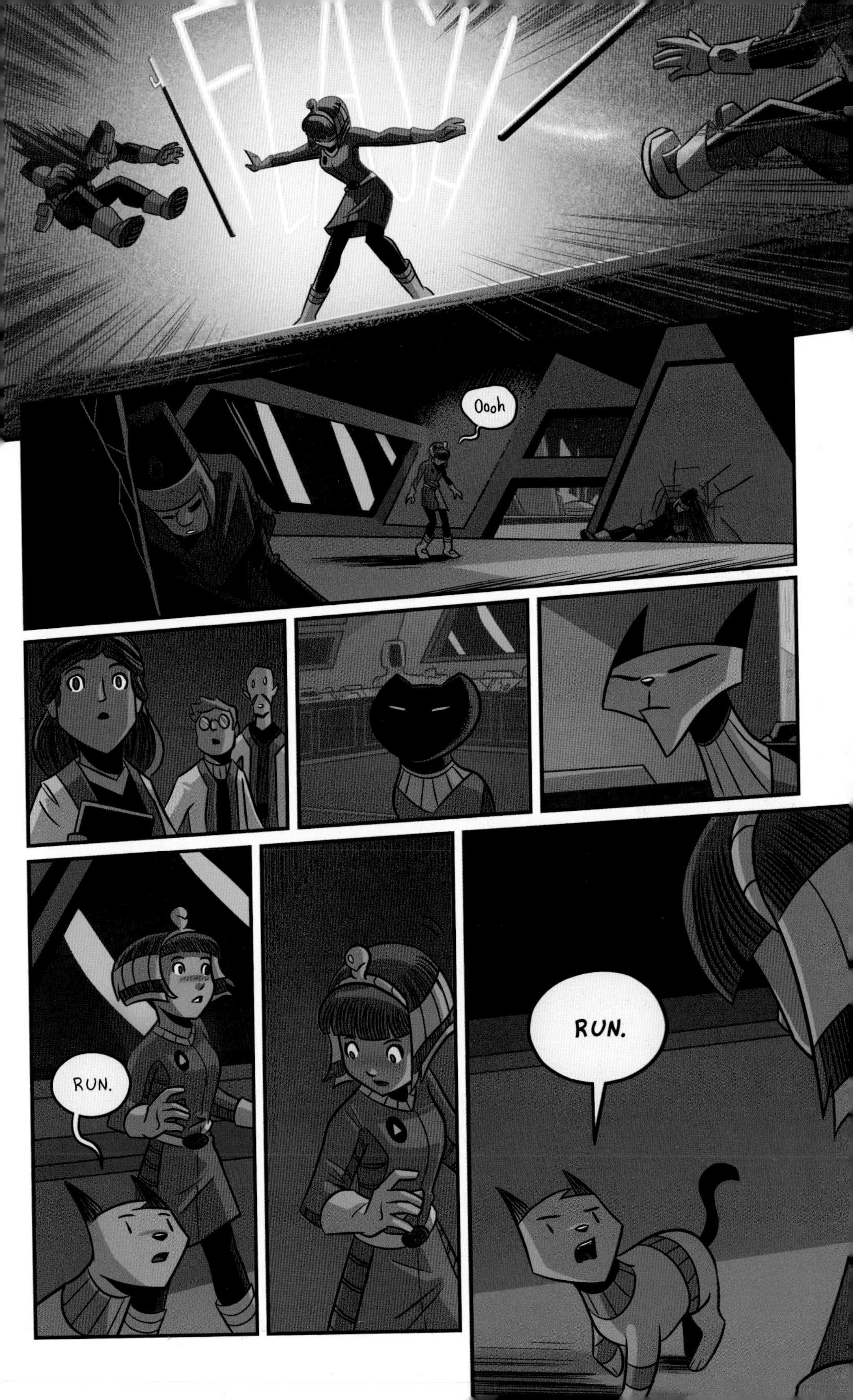
FLASH
Oooh
RUN.
RUN.

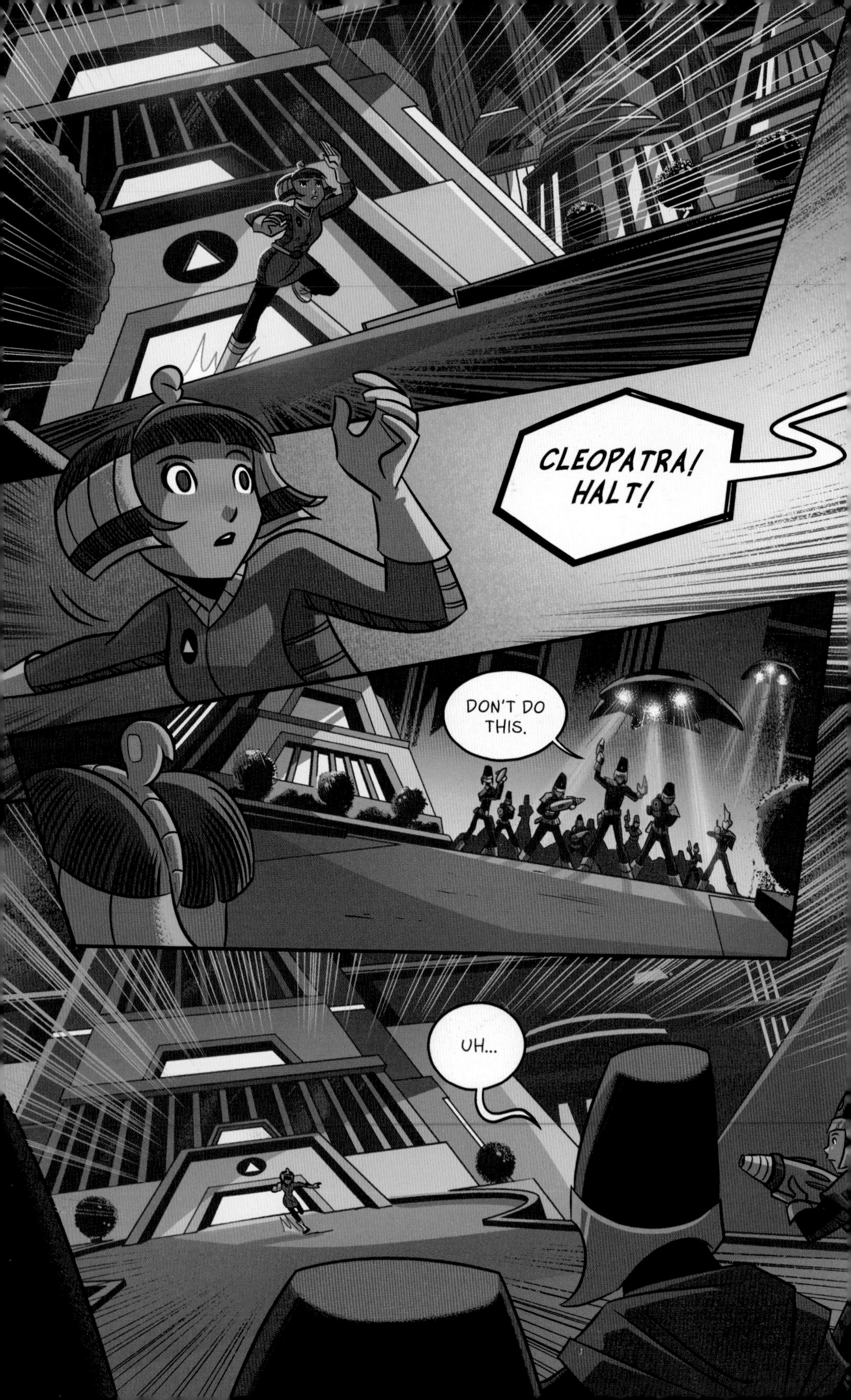
CLEOPATRA! HALT!
DON'T DO THIS.
UH...

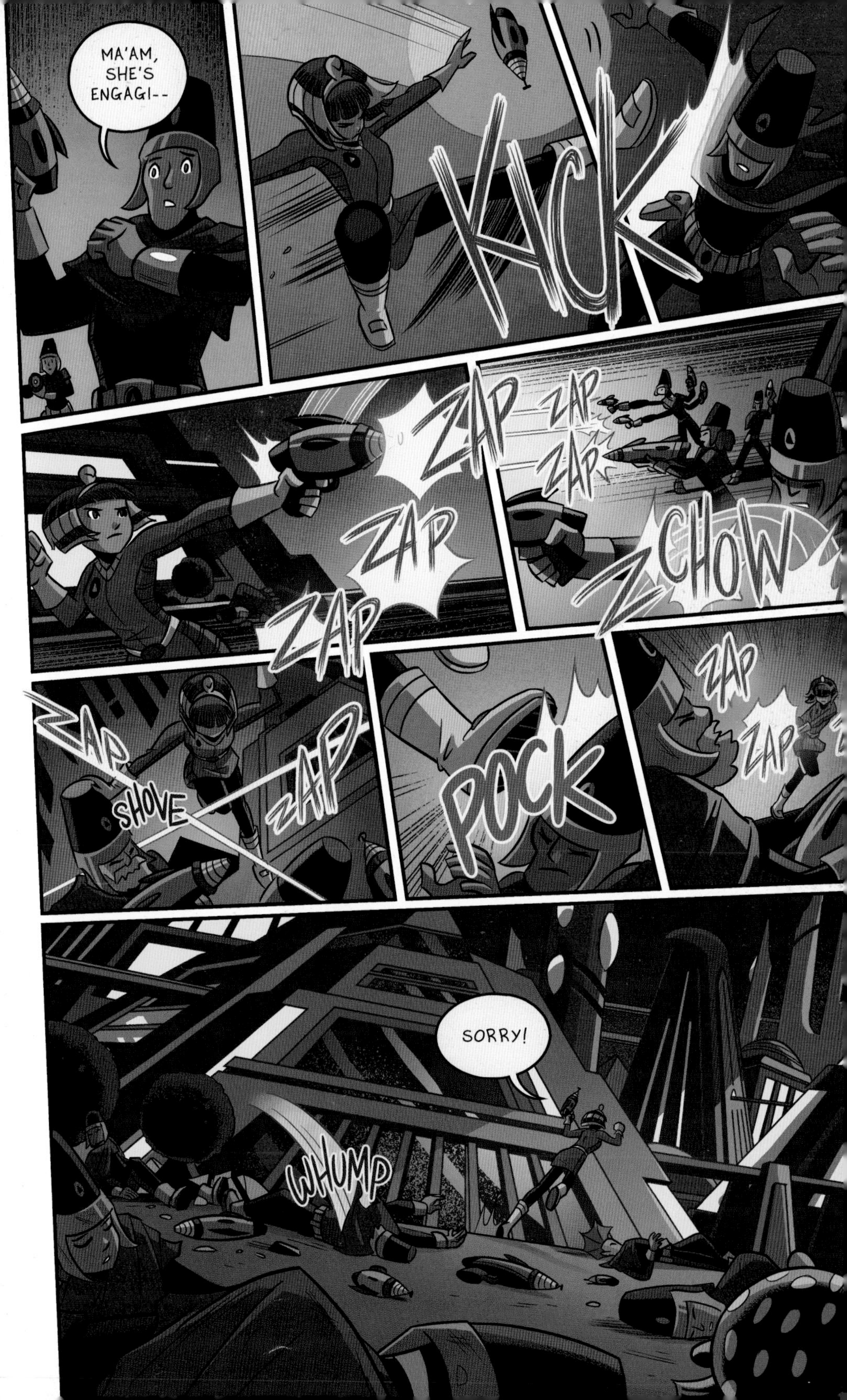
MA'AM, SHE'S ENGAGI--
KICK
ZAP
ZAP
ZAP
ZAP
ZAP
ZCHOW
ZAP
SHOVE
ZAP
POCK
ZAP
ZAP
SORRY!
WHUMP

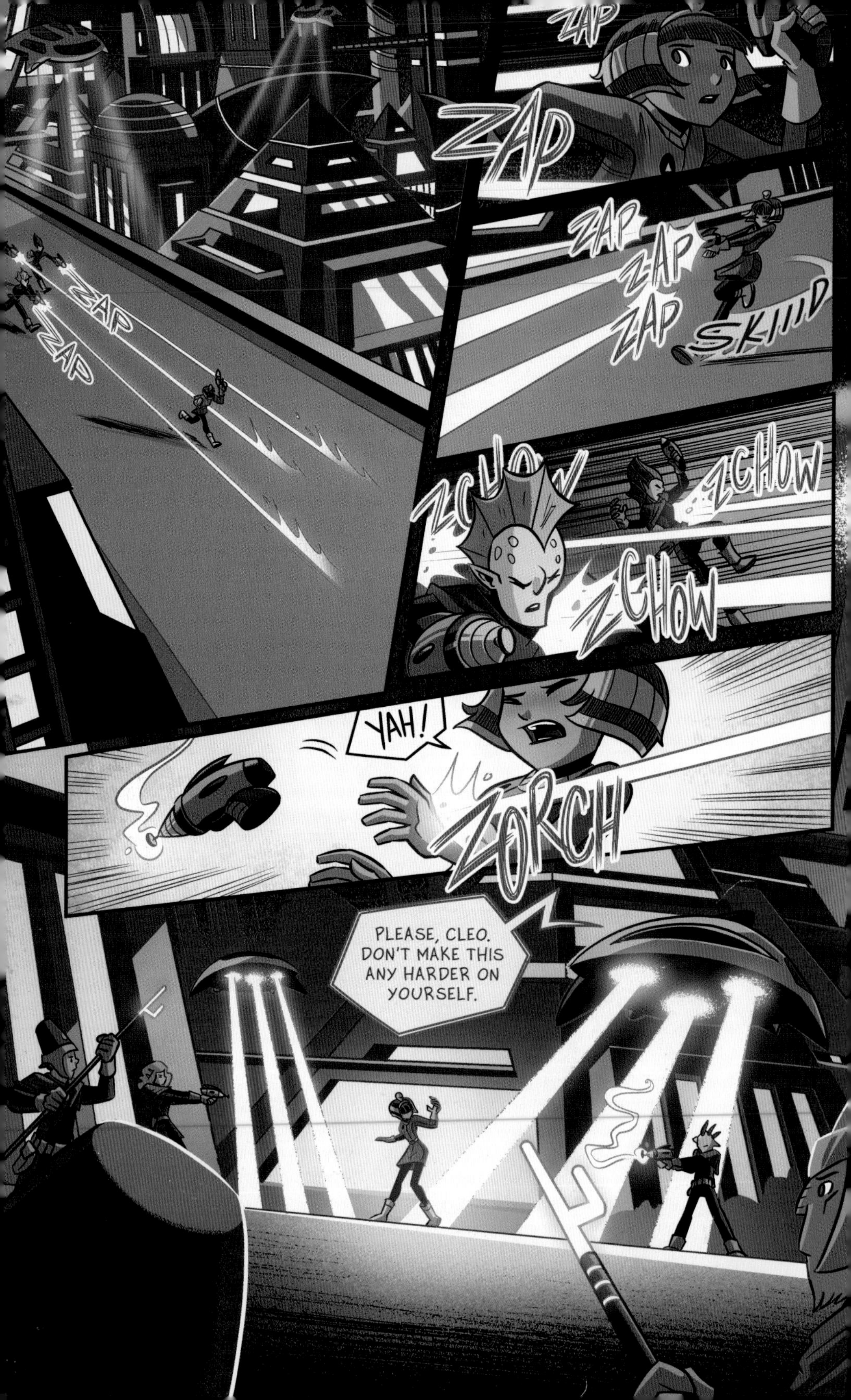
ZAP
ZAP
ZAP
ZAP
ZAP
ZAP
ZAP
SKIIID
ZCHOW
ZCHOW
ZCHOW
YAH!
ZORCH
PLEASE, CLEO. DON'T MAKE THIS ANY HARDER ON YOURSELF.

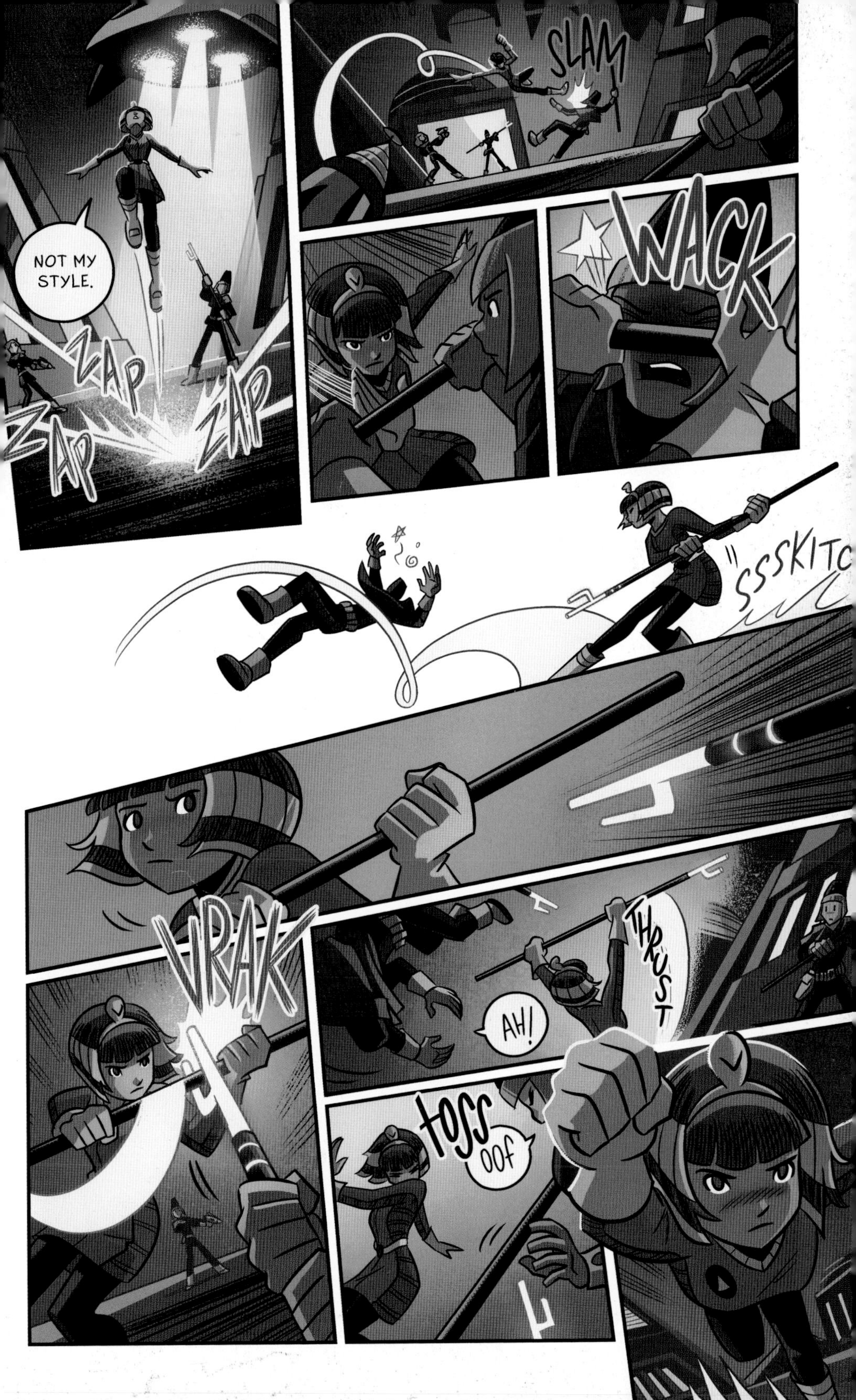
NOT MY STYLE.
ZAP
ZAP
ZAP
SLAM
WACK
SSSKITCH
VRAK
THRUST
AH!
TOSS
OOF

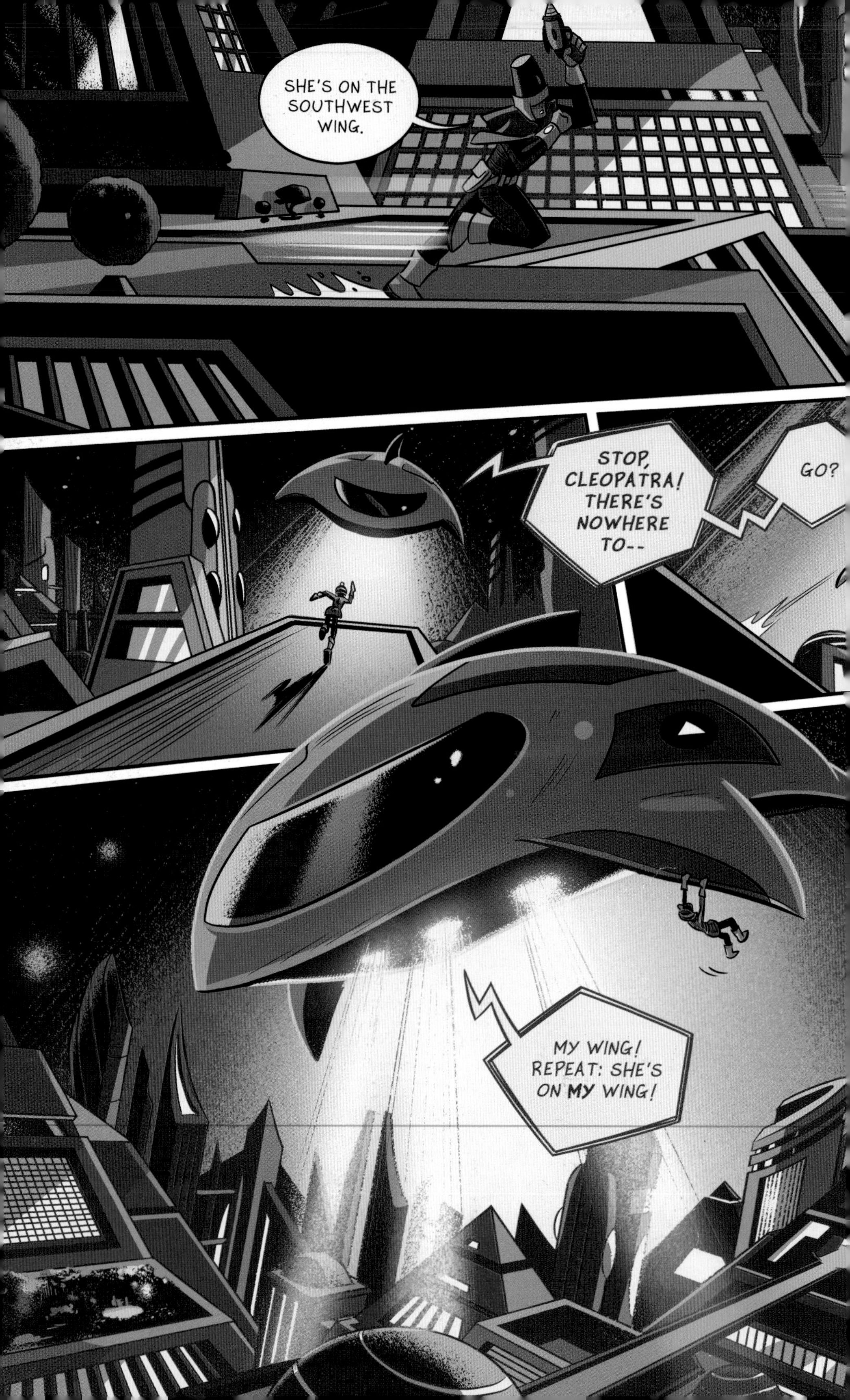
SHE'S ON THE SOUTHWEST WING.
STOP, CLEOPATRA! THERE'S NOWHERE TO--
GO?
MY WING! REPEAT: SHE'S ON MY WING!

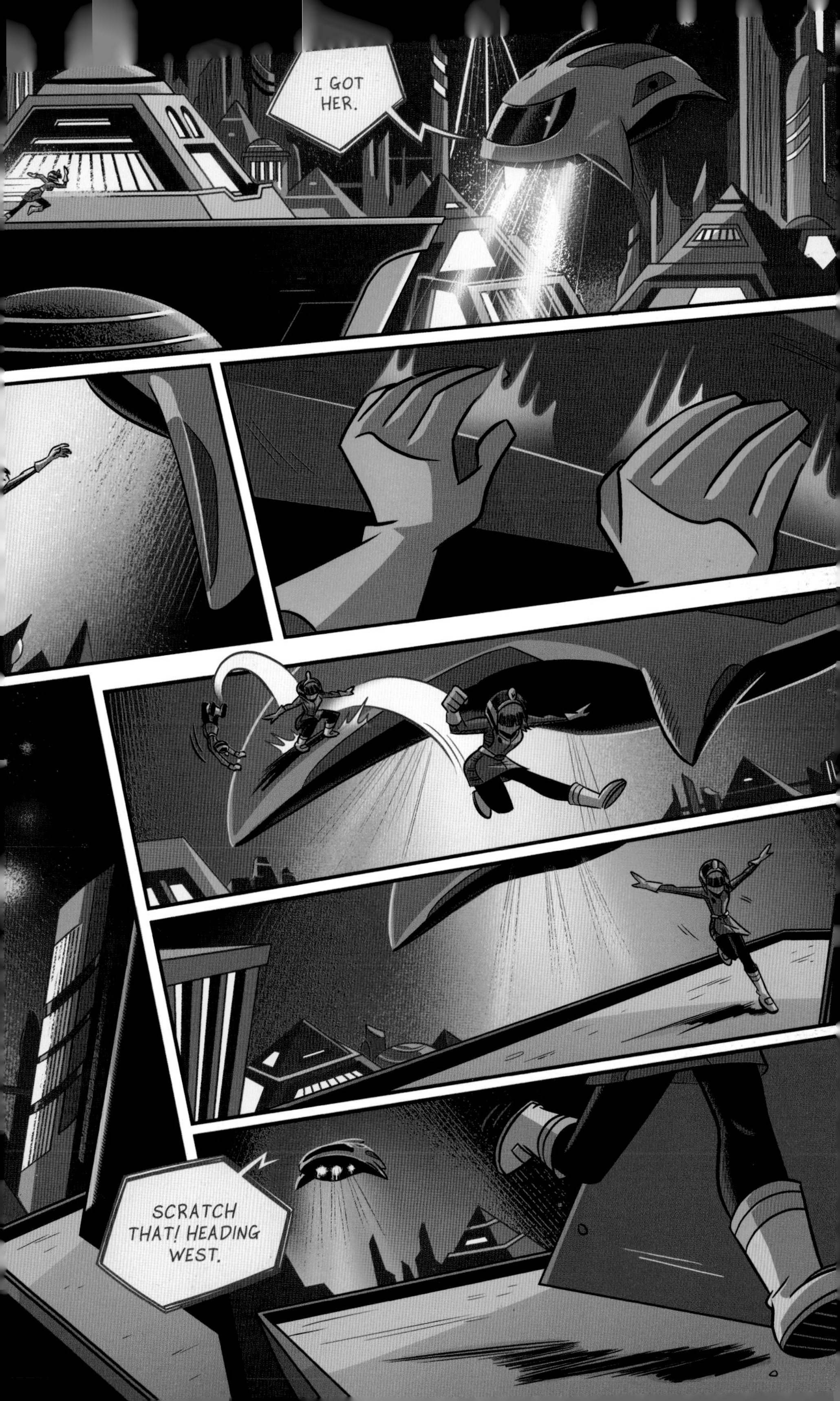
I GOT HER.
SCRATCH THAT! HEADING WEST.

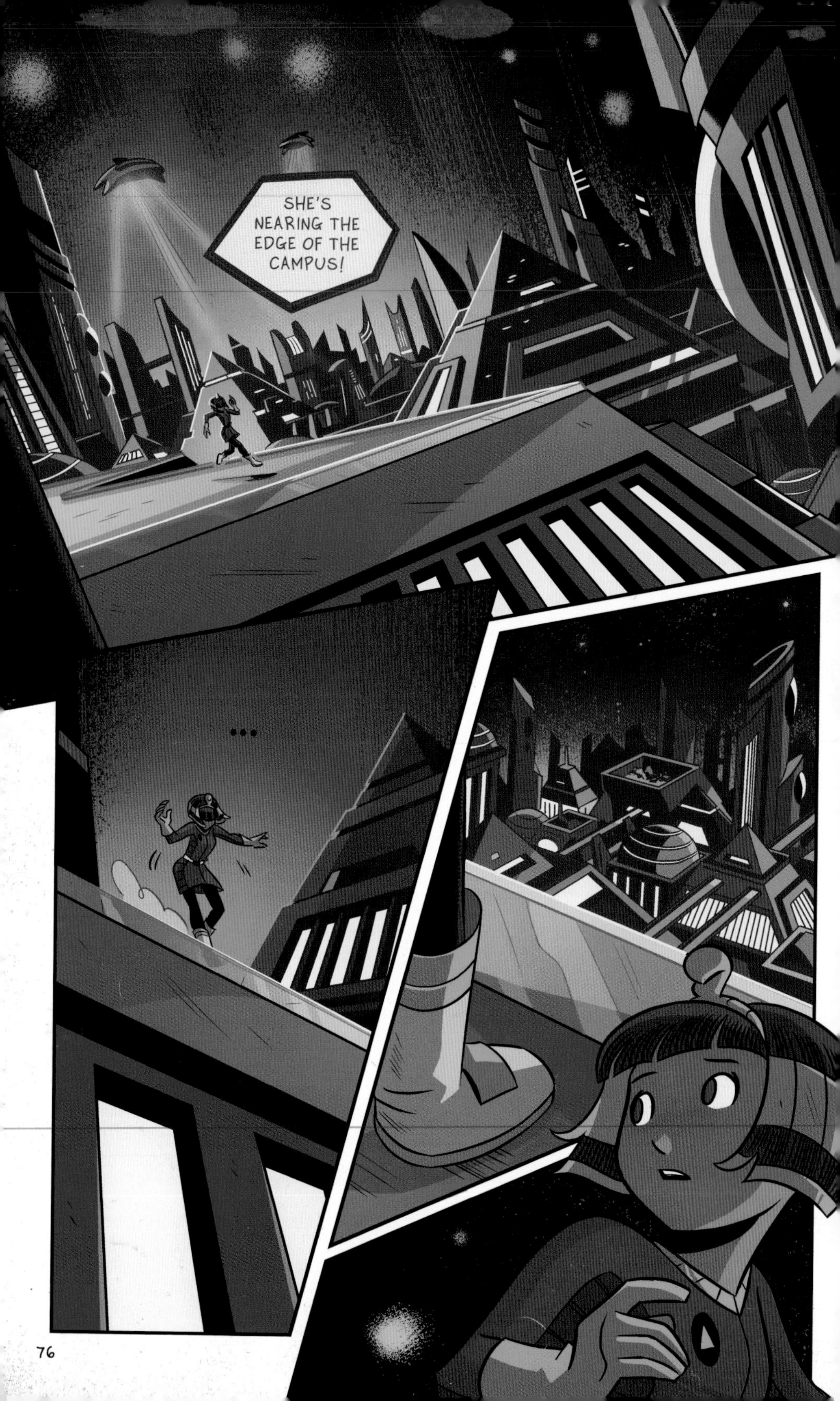

SHE'S NEARING THE EDGE OF THE CAMPUS!
...

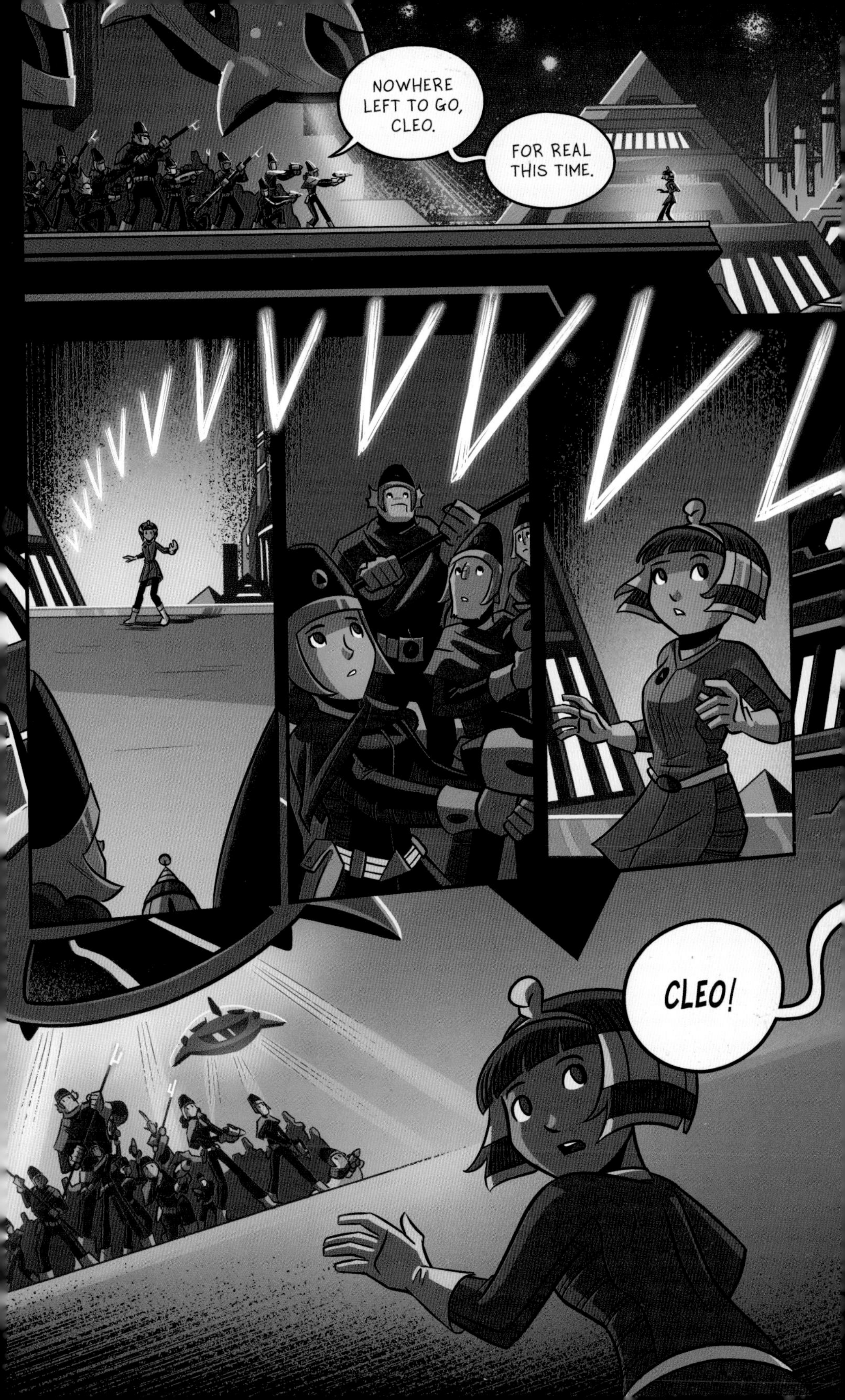
NOWHERE LEFT TO GO, CLEO.
FOR REAL THIS TIME.
CLEO!

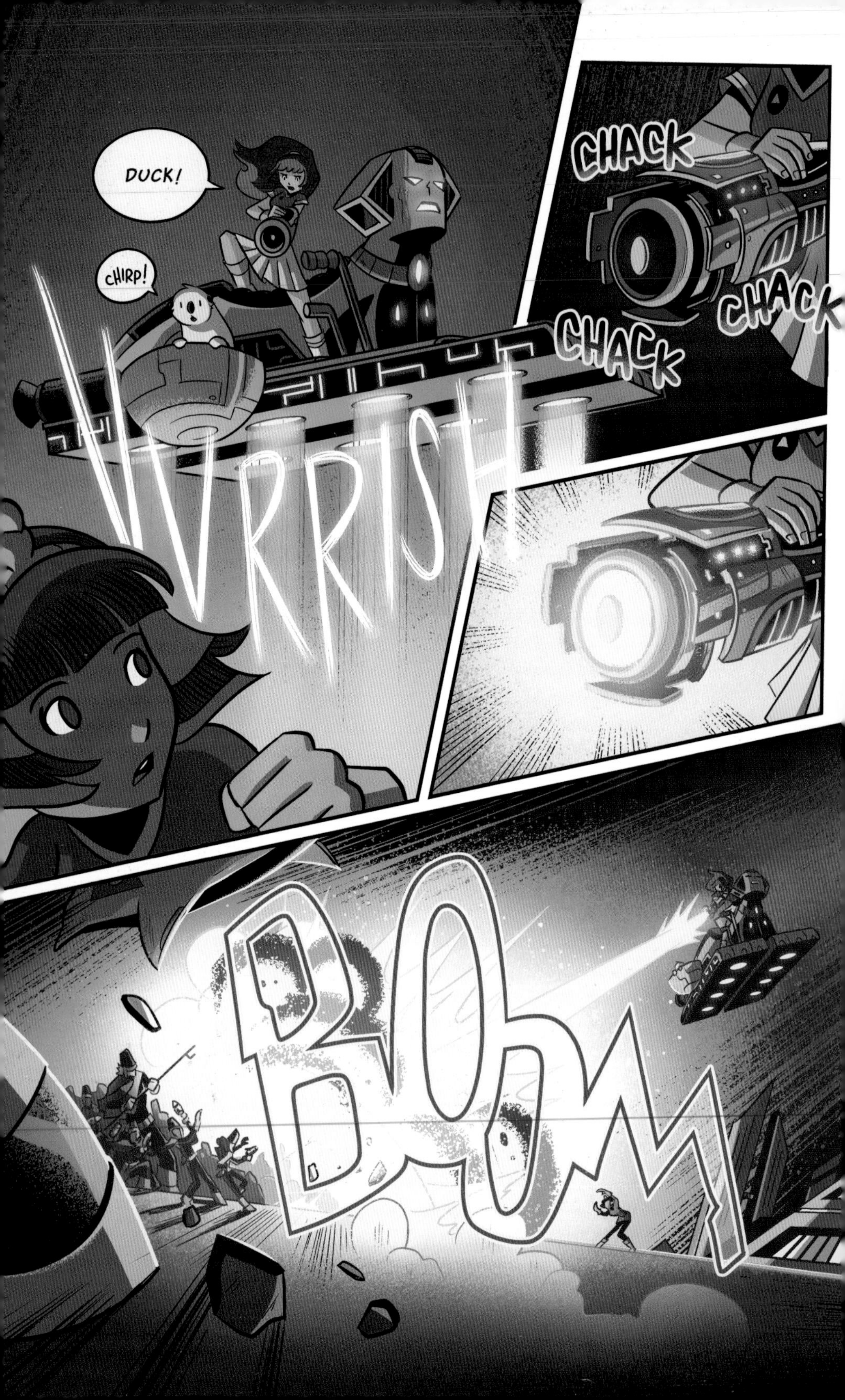
DUCK!
CHIRP!
CHACK
CHACK
CHACK
VVRRISH
BOOM

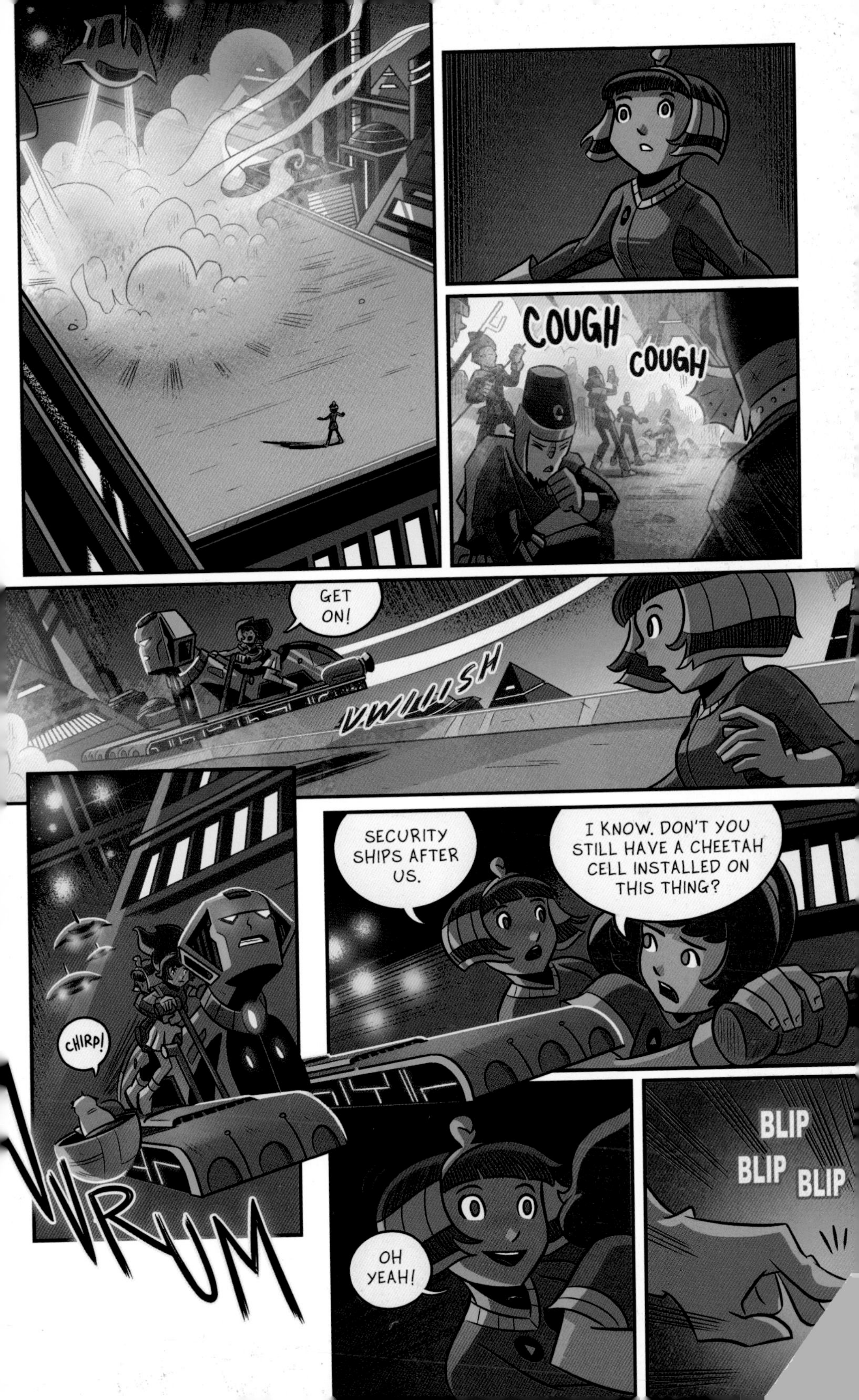

COUGH
COUGH
GET ON!
VWIIISH
SECURITY SHIPS AFTER US.
I KNOW. DON'T YOU STILL HAVE A CHEETAH CELL INSTALLED ON THIS THING?
CHIRP!
VRUM
OH YEAH!
BLIP
BLIP
BLIP

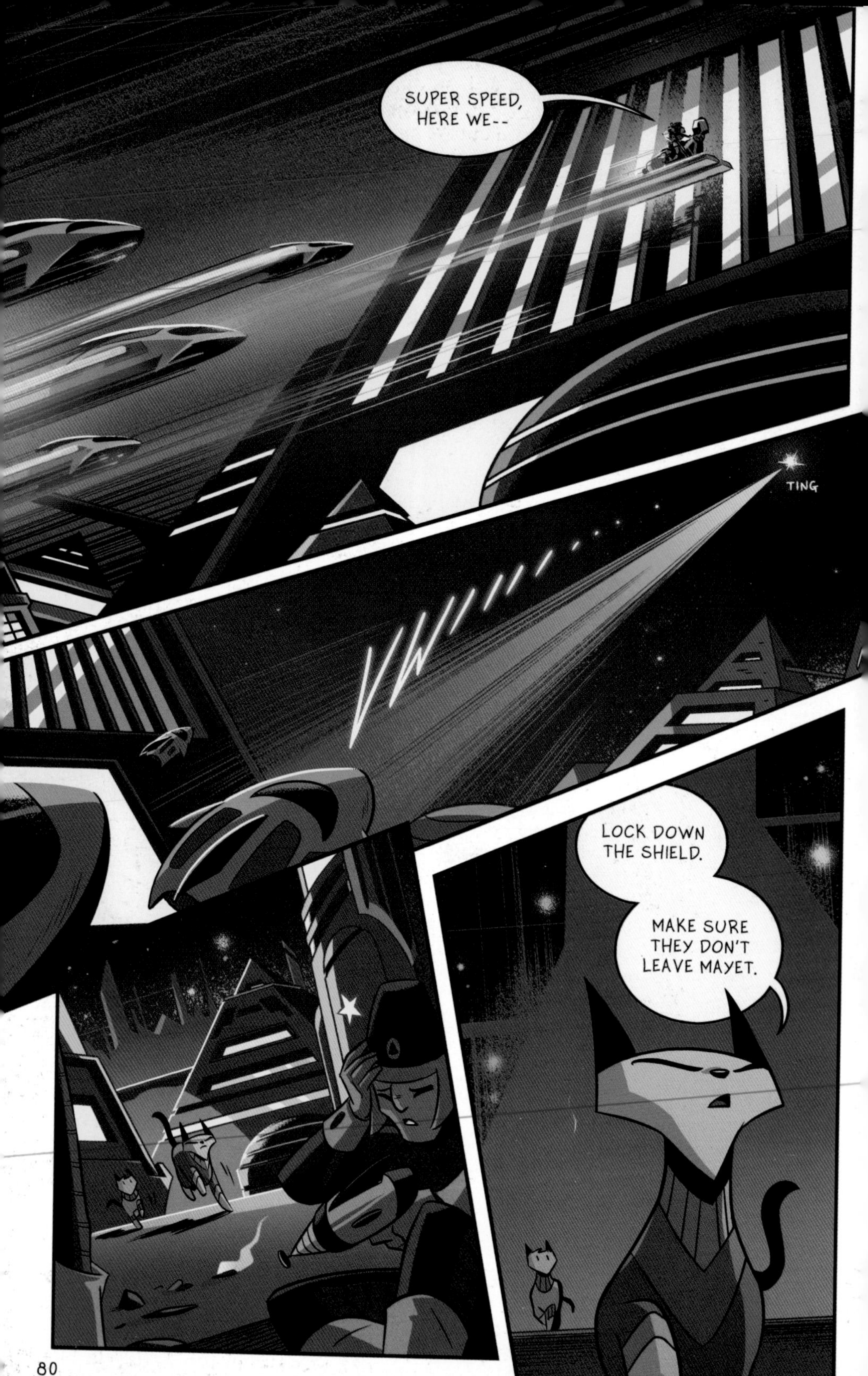
SUPER SPEED, HERE WE--
TING
LOCK DOWN THE SHIELD.
MAKE SURE THEY DON'T LEAVE MAYET.

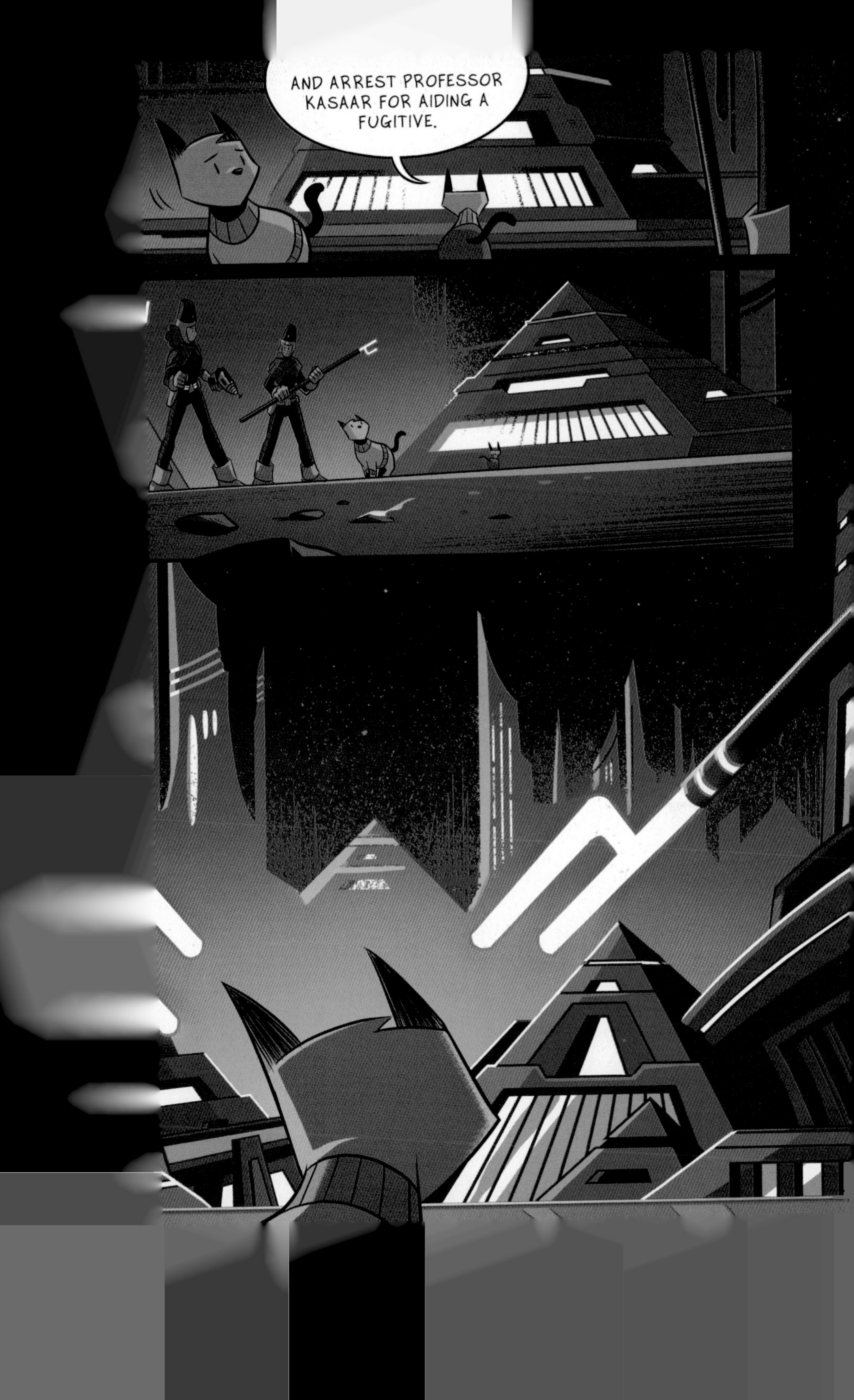
AND ARREST PROFESSOR KASAAR FOR AIDING A FUGITIVE.

CHAPTER TWO

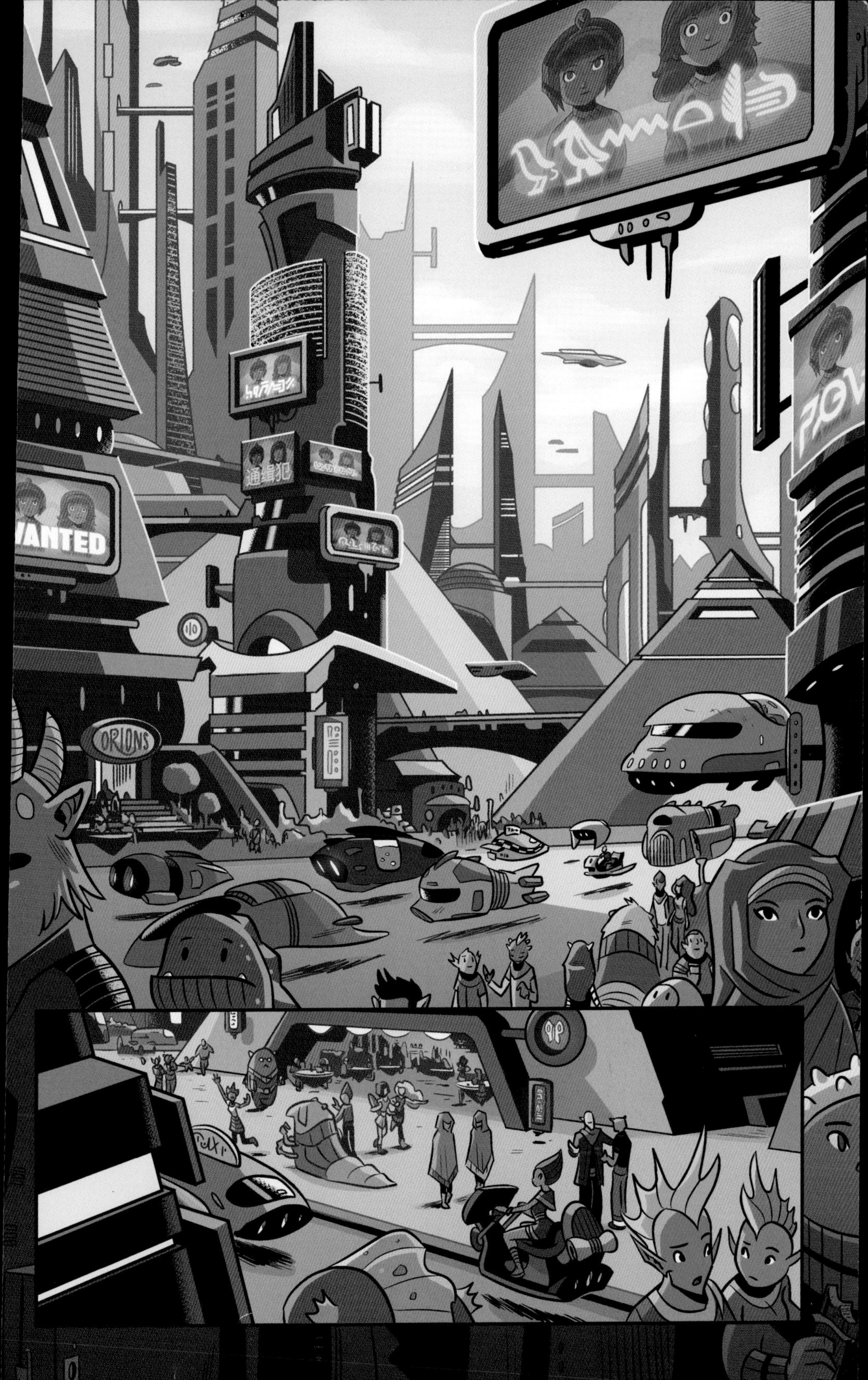
通缉犯
ORIONS

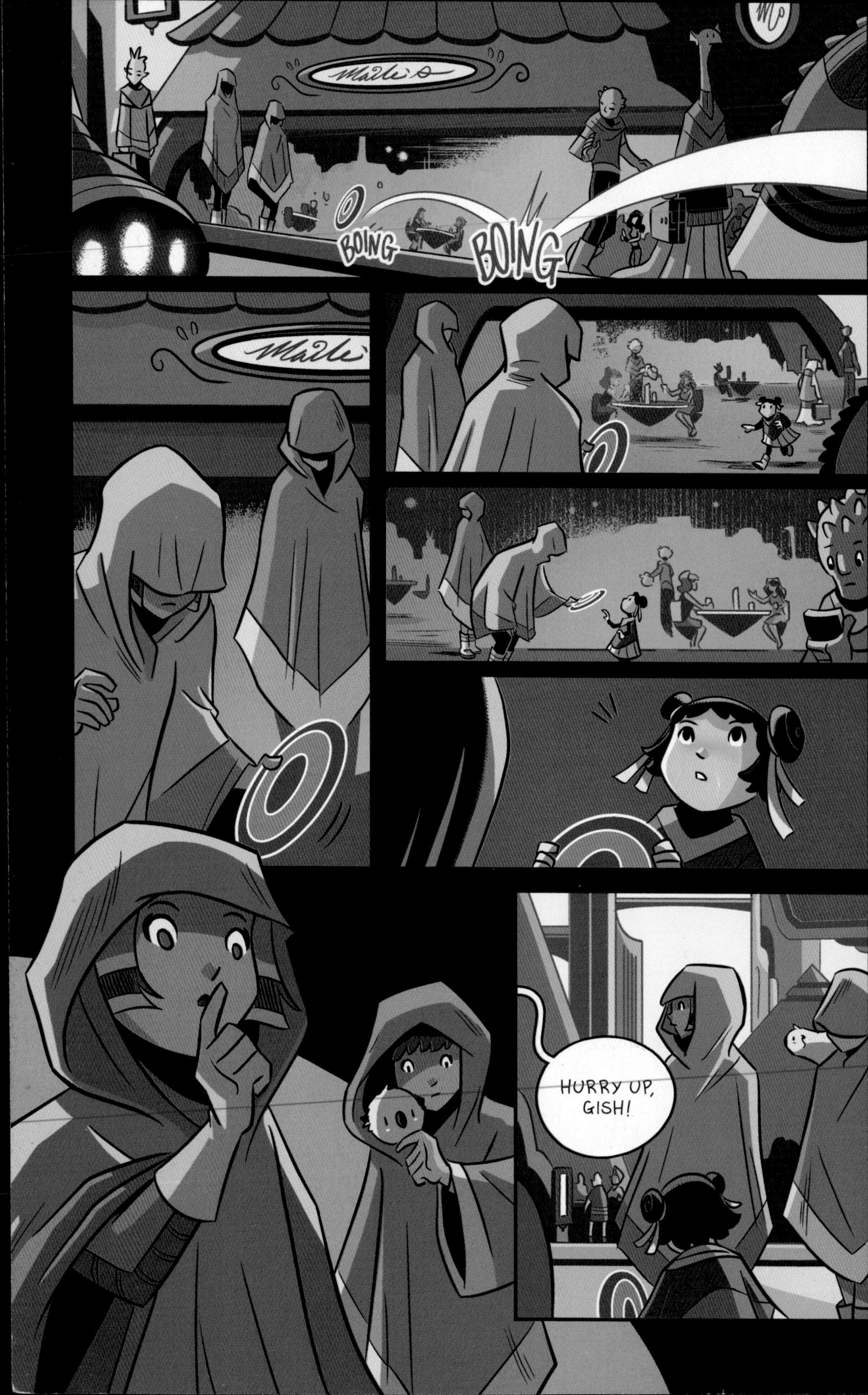
BOING
BOING
HURRY UP, GISH!

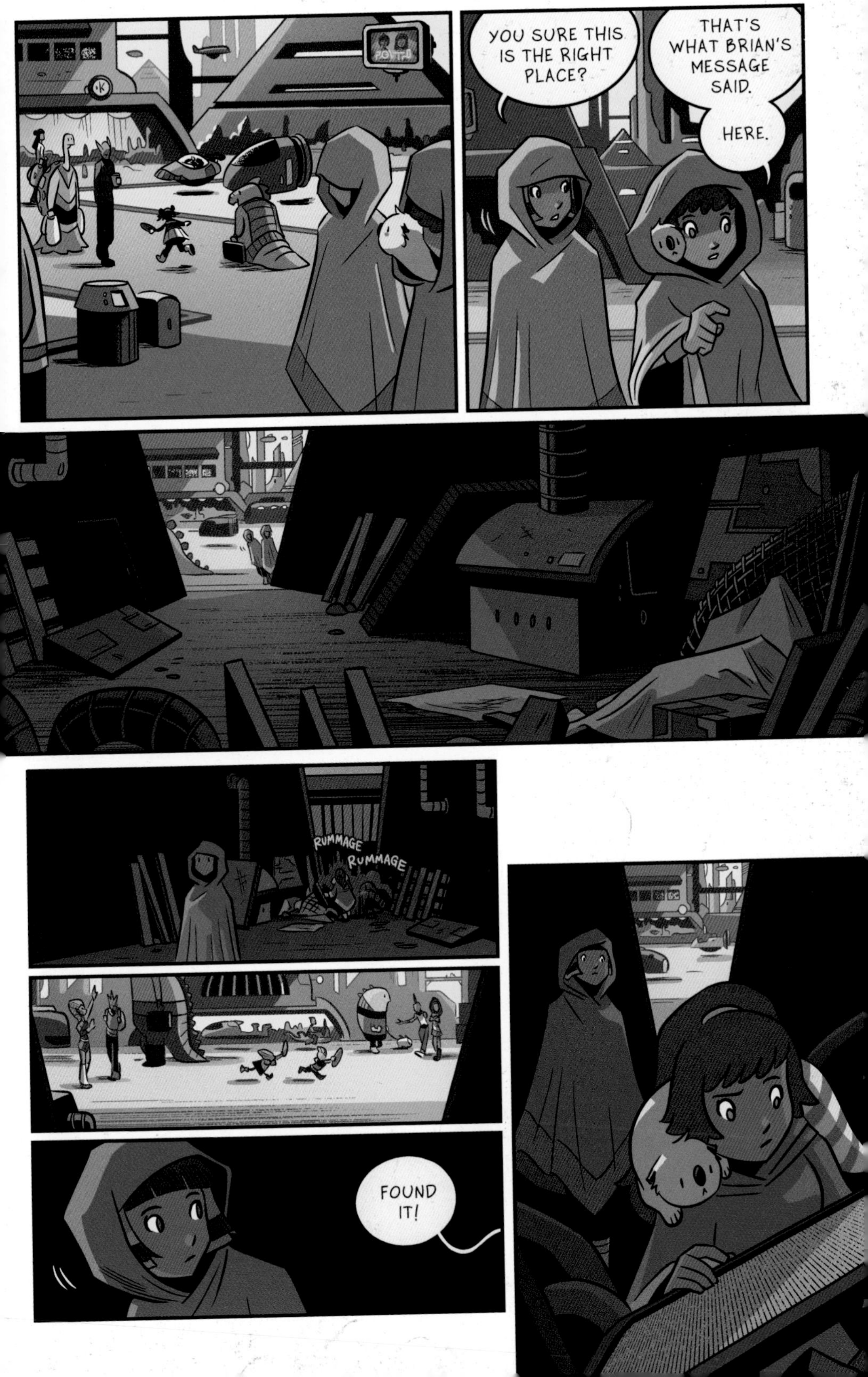
YOU SURE THIS IS THE RIGHT PLACE?
THAT'S WHAT BRIAN'S MESSAGE SAID.
HERE.
RUMMAGE
RUMMAGE
FOUND IT!

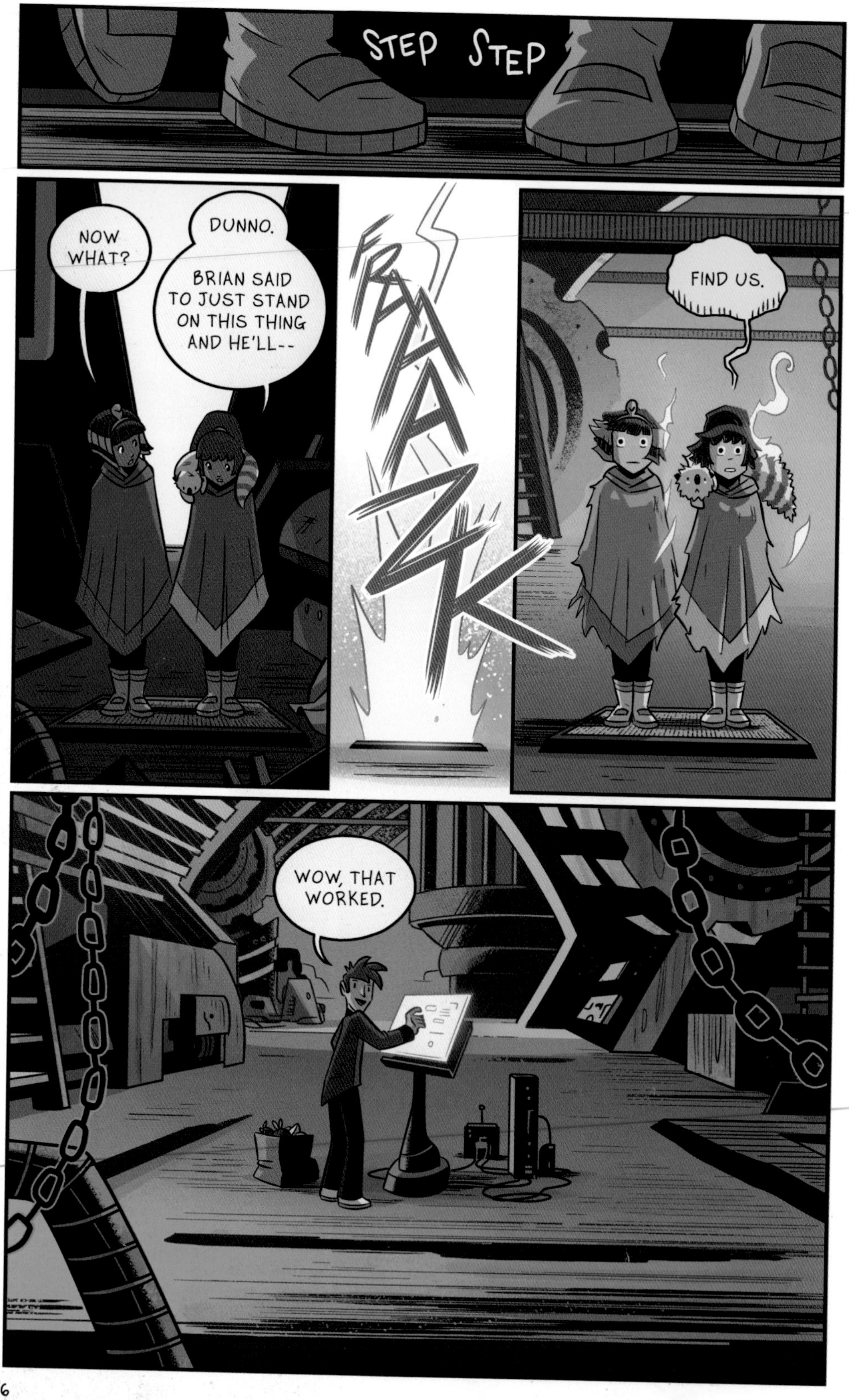
STEP STEP
NOW WHAT?
DUNNO.
BRIAN SAID TO JUST STAND ON THIS THING AND HE'LL--
FRAAAZZK
FIND US.
WOW, THAT WORKED.

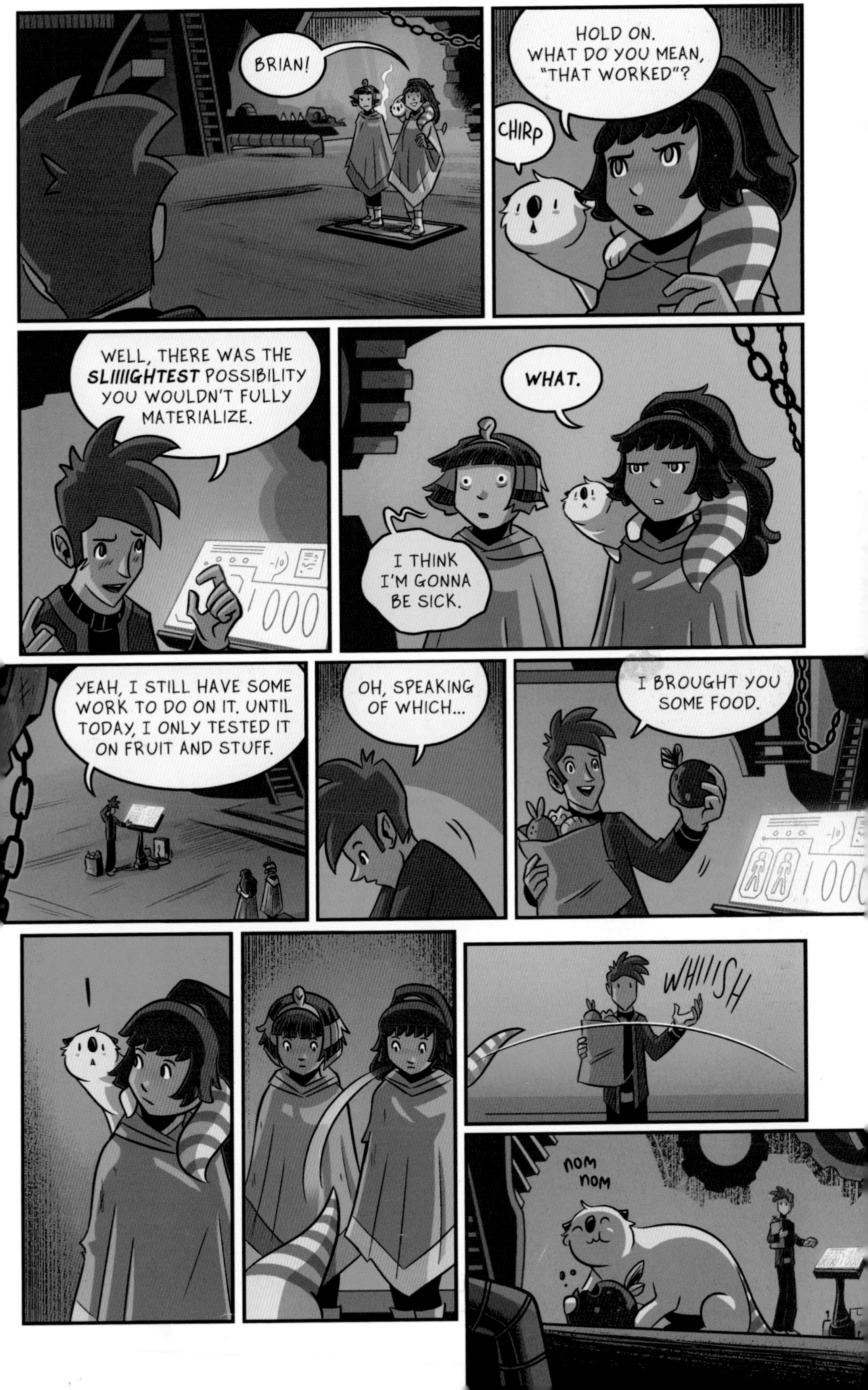
BRIAN!
HOLD ON. WHAT DO YOU MEAN, "THAT WORKED"?
CHIRP
WELL, THERE WAS THE SLIIIIGHTEST POSSIBILITY YOU WOULDN'T FULLY MATERIALIZE.
WHAT.
I THINK I'M GONNA BE SICK.
YEAH, I STILL HAVE SOME WORK TO DO ON IT. UNTIL TODAY, I ONLY TESTED IT ON FRUIT AND STUFF.
OH, SPEAKING OF WHICH...
I BROUGHT YOU SOME FOOD.
WHIIISH
nom nom

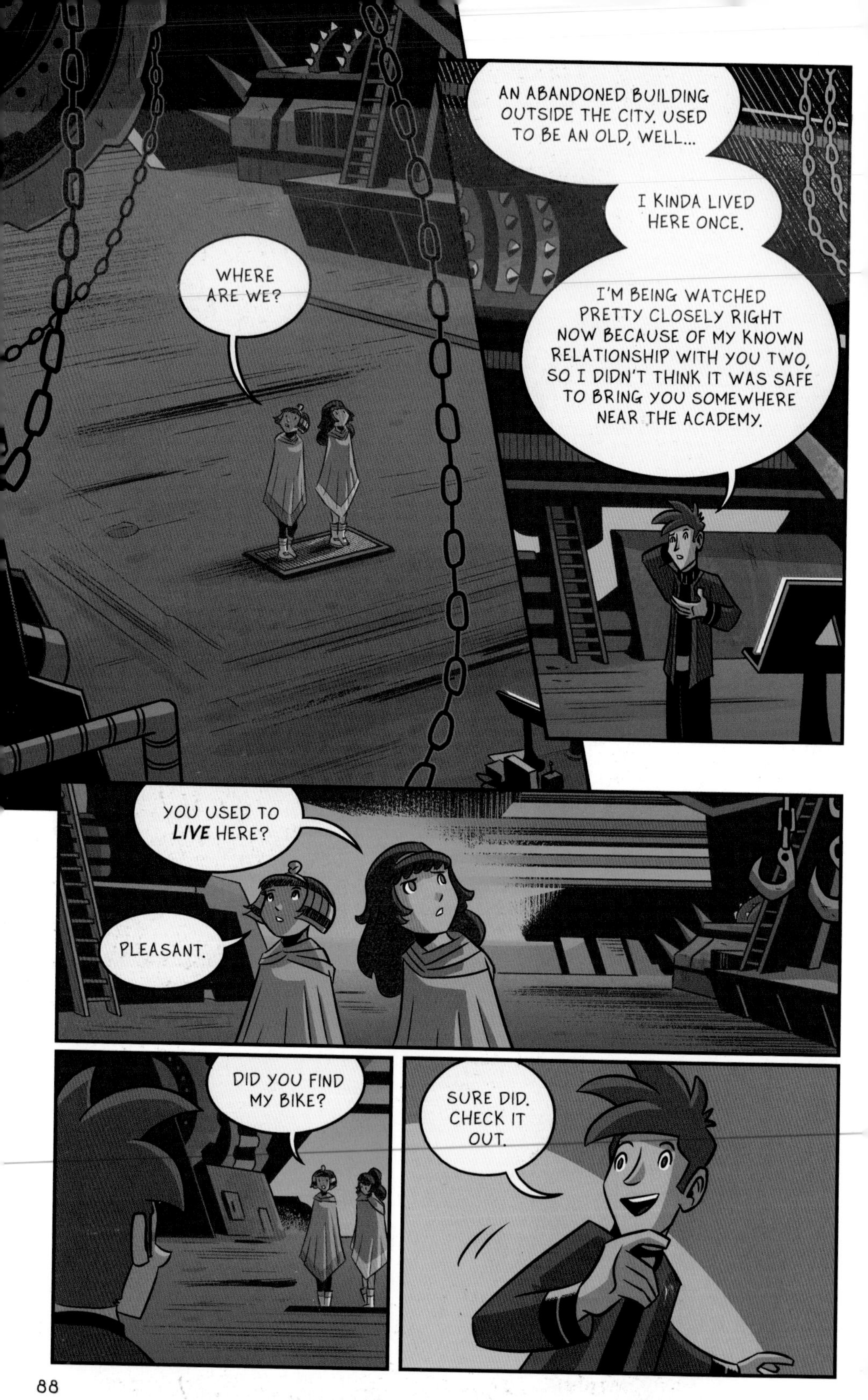
WHERE ARE WE?
AN ABANDONED BUILDING OUTSIDE THE CITY. USED TO BE AN OLD, WELL...
I KINDA LIVED HERE ONCE.
I'M BEING WATCHED PRETTY CLOSELY RIGHT NOW BECAUSE OF MY KNOWN RELATIONSHIP WITH YOU TWO, SO I DIDN'T THINK IT WAS SAFE TO BRING YOU SOMEWHERE NEAR THE ACADEMY.
YOU USED TO **LIVE** HERE?
PLEASANT.
DID YOU FIND MY BIKE?
SURE DID. CHECK IT OUT.

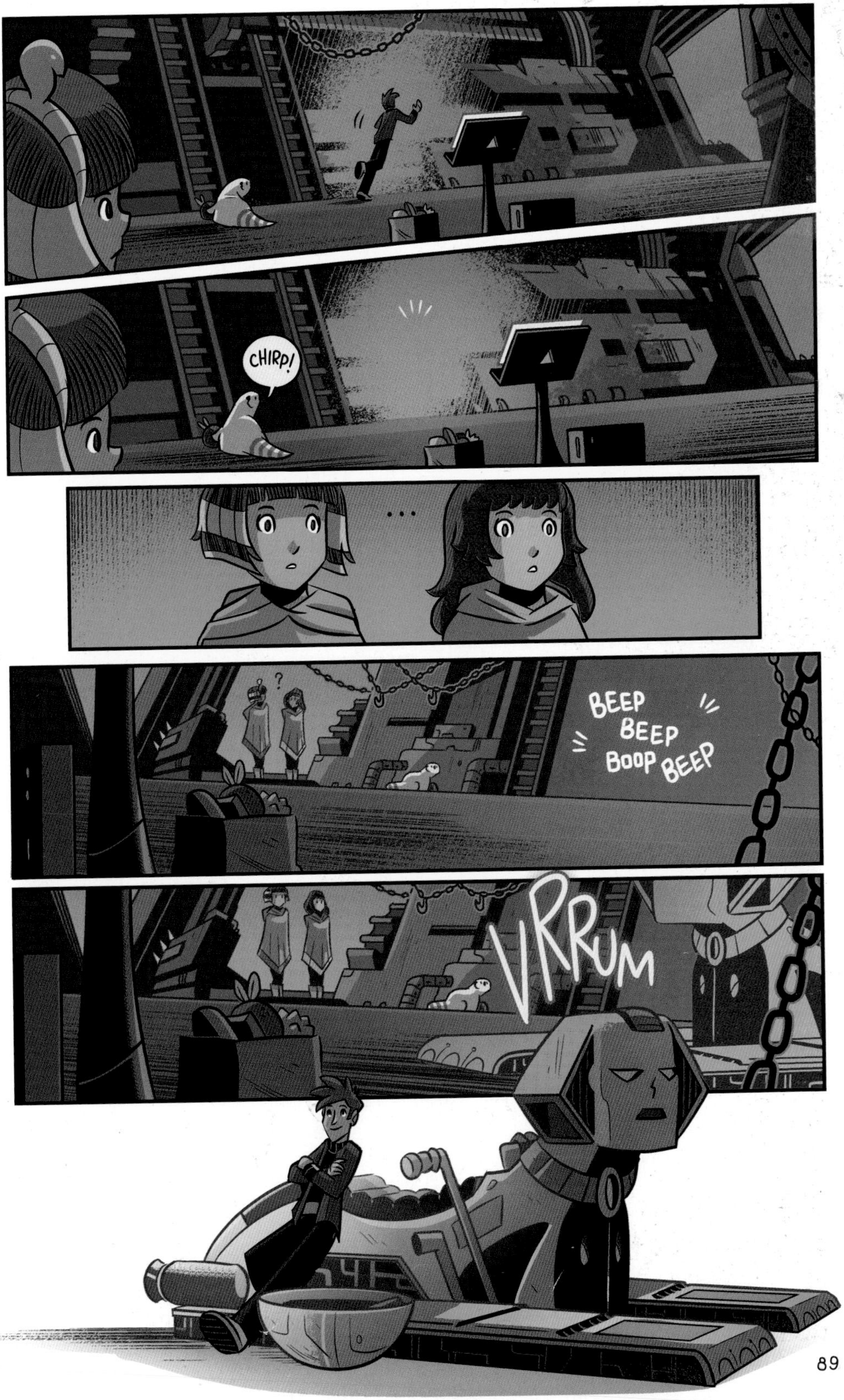
CHIRP!
...
BEEP BEEP BOOP BEEP
VRRUM

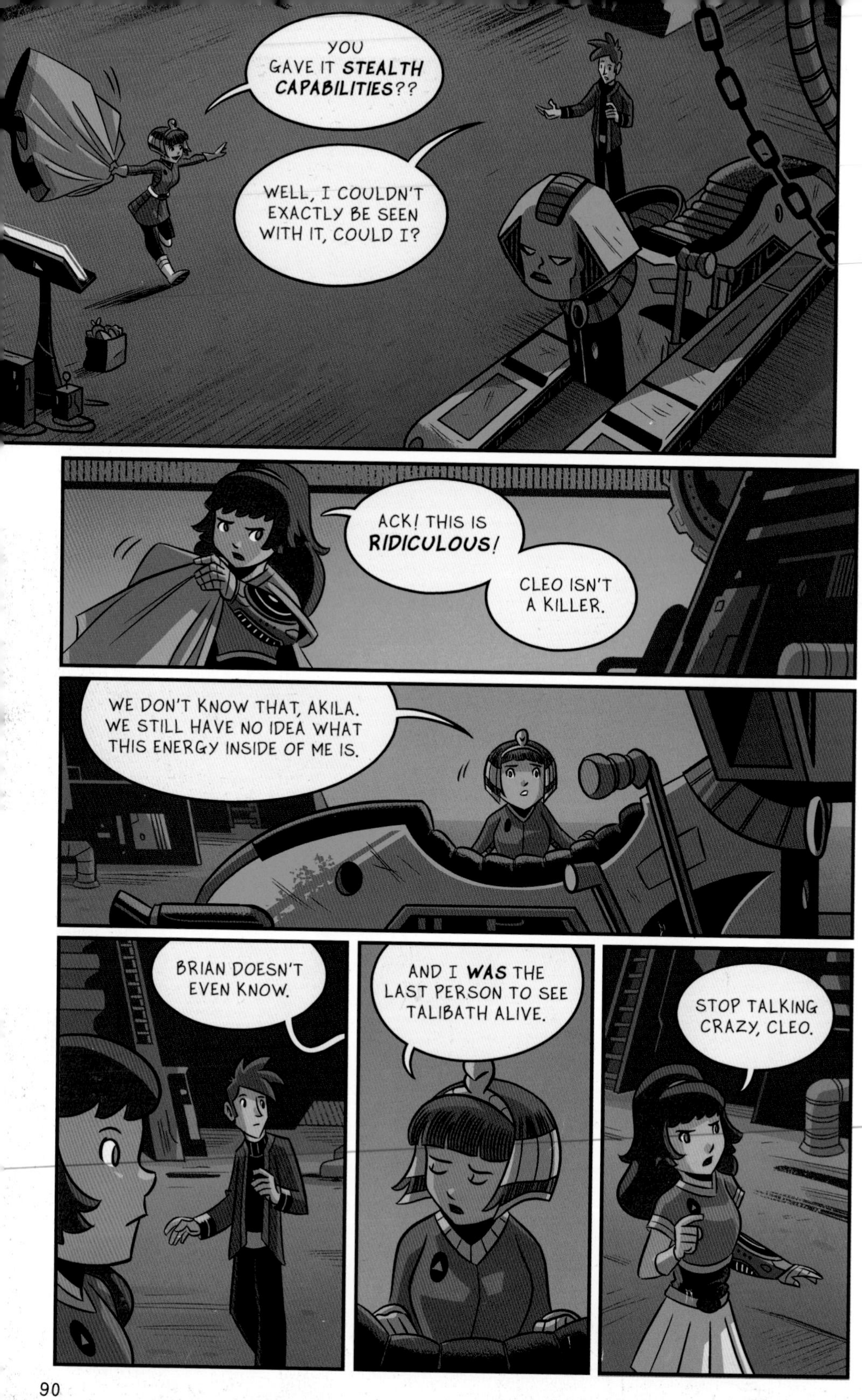
YOU GAVE IT **STEALTH CAPABILITIES**??
WELL, I COULDN'T EXACTLY BE SEEN WITH IT, COULD I?
ACK! THIS IS **RIDICULOUS**!
CLEO ISN'T A KILLER.
WE DON'T KNOW THAT, AKILA. WE STILL HAVE NO IDEA WHAT THIS ENERGY INSIDE OF ME IS.
BRIAN DOESN'T EVEN KNOW.
AND I **WAS** THE LAST PERSON TO SEE TALIBATH ALIVE.
STOP TALKING CRAZY, CLEO.

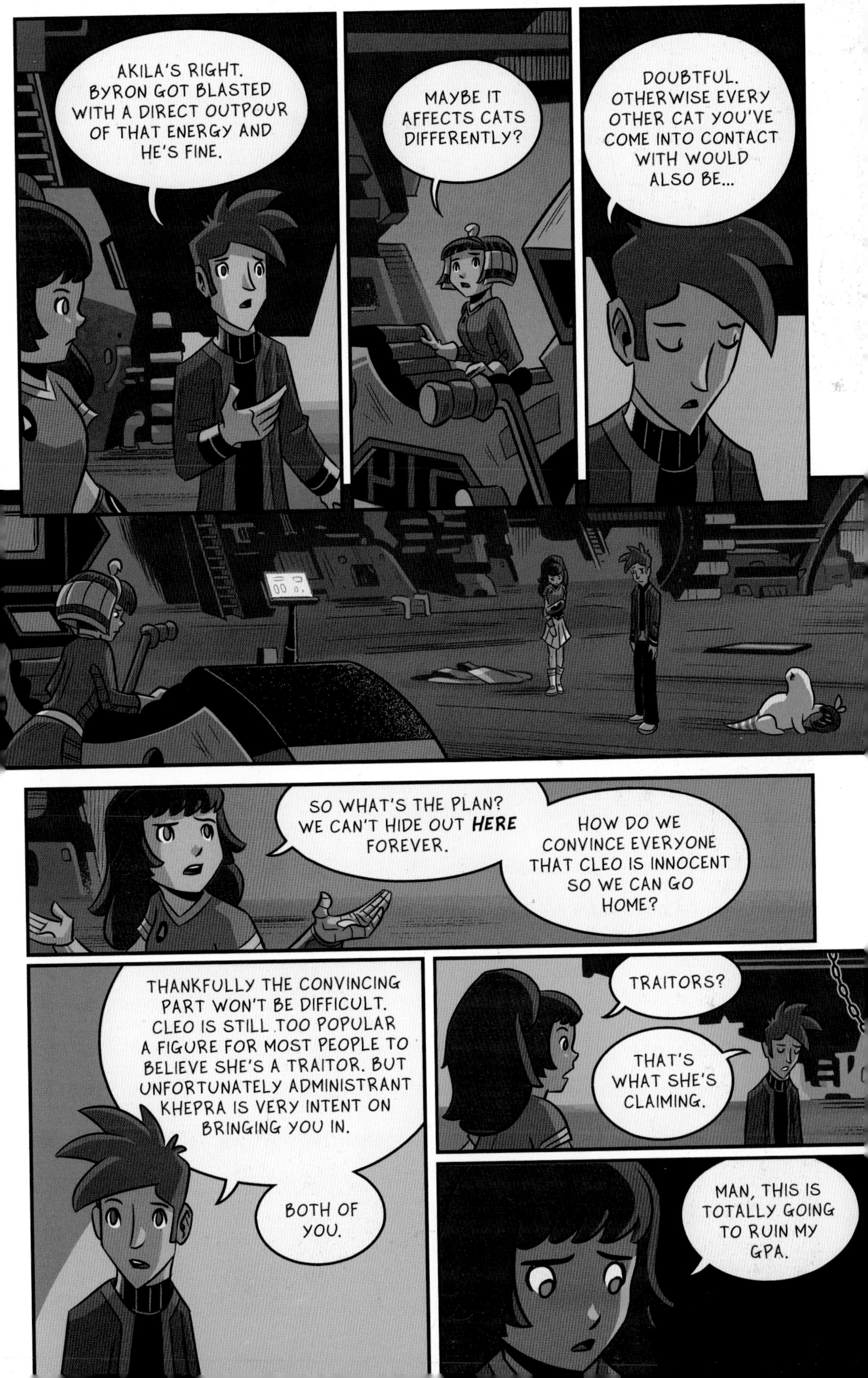
AKILA'S RIGHT. BYRON GOT BLASTED WITH A DIRECT OUTPOUR OF THAT ENERGY AND HE'S FINE.
MAYBE IT AFFECTS CATS DIFFERENTLY?
DOUBTFUL. OTHERWISE EVERY OTHER CAT YOU'VE COME INTO CONTACT WITH WOULD ALSO BE...
SO WHAT'S THE PLAN? WE CAN'T HIDE OUT **HERE** FOREVER.
HOW DO WE CONVINCE EVERYONE THAT CLEO IS INNOCENT SO WE CAN GO HOME?
THANKFULLY THE CONVINCING PART WON'T BE DIFFICULT. CLEO IS STILL TOO POPULAR A FIGURE FOR MOST PEOPLE TO BELIEVE SHE'S A TRAITOR. BUT UNFORTUNATELY ADMINISTRANT KHEPRA IS VERY INTENT ON BRINGING YOU IN.
BOTH OF YOU.
TRAITORS?
THAT'S WHAT SHE'S CLAIMING.
MAN, THIS IS TOTALLY GOING TO RUIN MY GPA.

HMM...

YOU'RE DOING IT AGAIN, BRIAN.

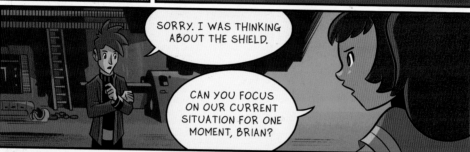

SORRY. I WAS THINKING ABOUT THE SHIELD.

CAN YOU FOCUS ON OUR CURRENT SITUATION FOR ONE MOMENT, BRIAN?

NO--I MEAN, *YES*, I AM. I WAS THINKING ABOUT THE KEY CODES.

munch munch

KEY CODES?

THE SHIELD WAS DESIGNED USING THERMODYNAMIC TECHNOLOGY. ESSENTIALLY, MAYET'S ATMOSPHERE IS WHAT WILL POWER THE GRID INDEFINITELY, SO EVEN IF THE CONTROL CENTER IS COMPROMISED, THE SHIELD WILL REMAIN FUNCTIONAL. IT WAS MEANT AS A SAFEGUARD AGAINST ATTACK.

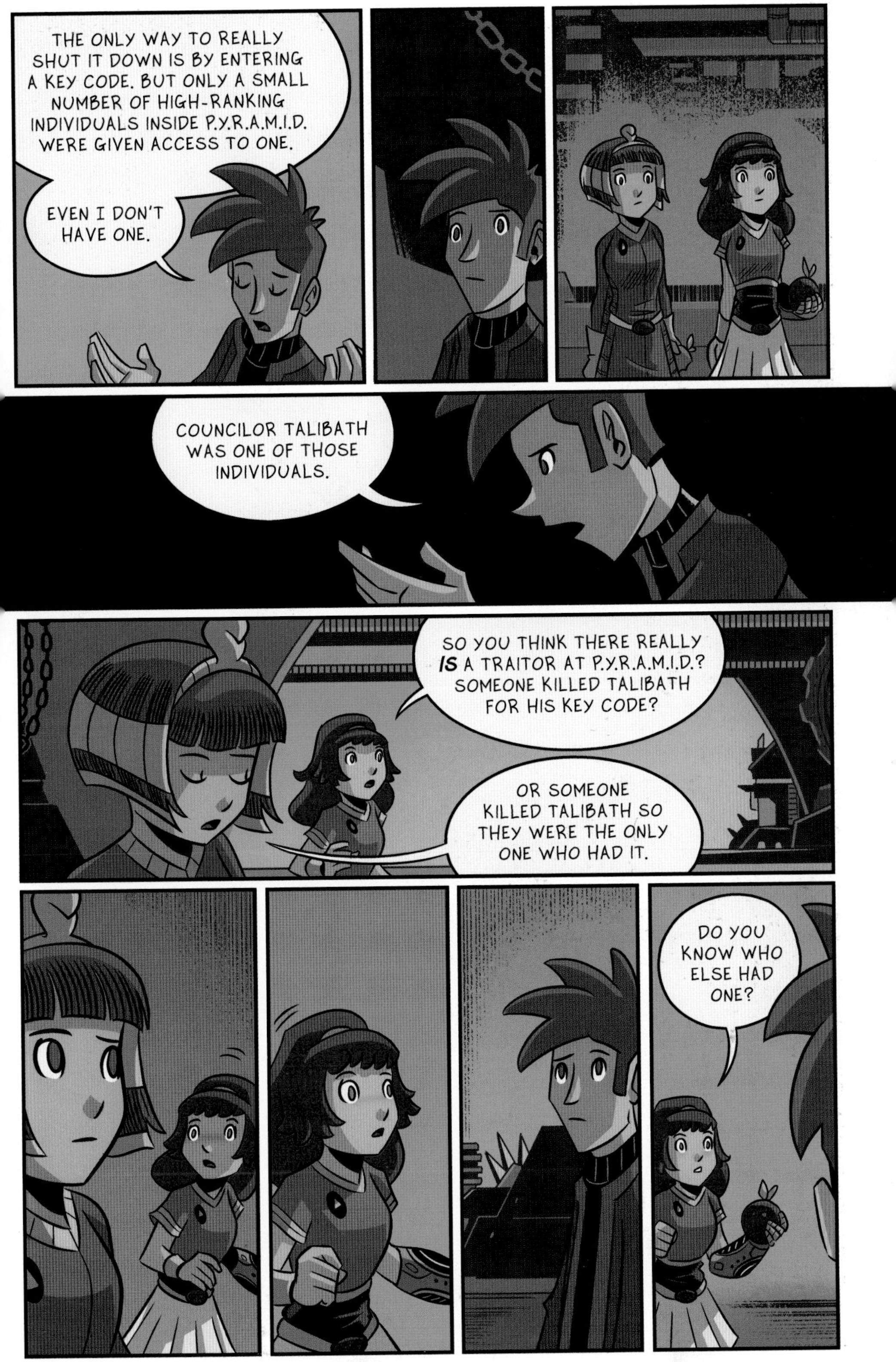
THE ONLY WAY TO REALLY SHUT IT DOWN IS BY ENTERING A KEY CODE. BUT ONLY A SMALL NUMBER OF HIGH-RANKING INDIVIDUALS INSIDE P.Y.R.A.M.I.D. WERE GIVEN ACCESS TO ONE.
EVEN I DON'T HAVE ONE.
COUNCILOR TALIBATH WAS ONE OF THOSE INDIVIDUALS.
SO YOU THINK THERE REALLY **IS** A TRAITOR AT P.Y.R.A.M.I.D.? SOMEONE KILLED TALIBATH FOR HIS KEY CODE?
OR SOMEONE KILLED TALIBATH SO THEY WERE THE ONLY ONE WHO HAD IT.
DO YOU KNOW WHO ELSE HAD ONE?

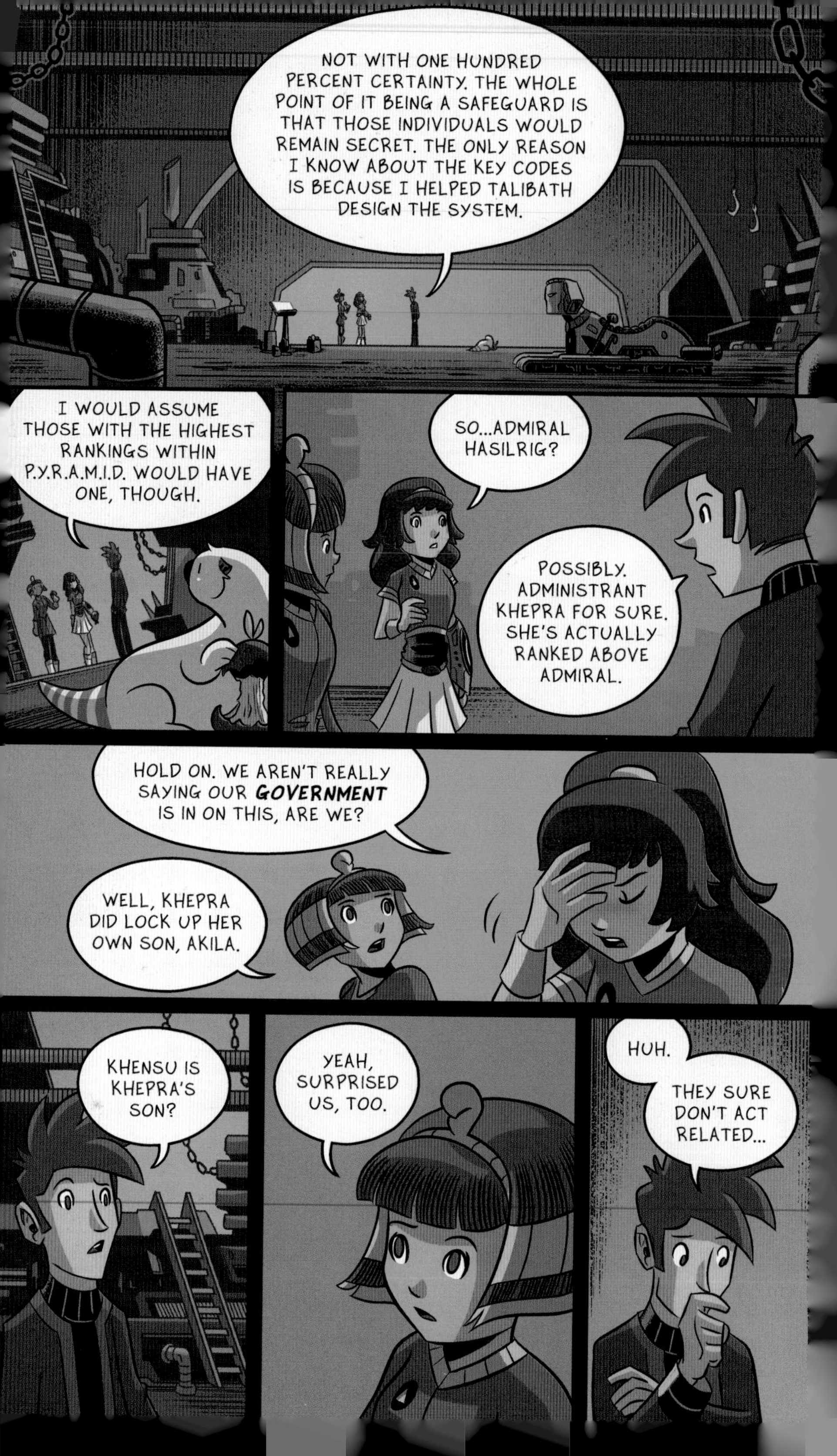
NOT WITH ONE HUNDRED PERCENT CERTAINTY. THE WHOLE POINT OF IT BEING A SAFEGUARD IS THAT THOSE INDIVIDUALS WOULD REMAIN SECRET. THE ONLY REASON I KNOW ABOUT THE KEY CODES IS BECAUSE I HELPED TALIBATH DESIGN THE SYSTEM.
I WOULD ASSUME THOSE WITH THE HIGHEST RANKINGS WITHIN P.Y.R.A.M.I.D. WOULD HAVE ONE, THOUGH.
SO...ADMIRAL HASILRIG?
POSSIBLY. ADMINISTRANT KHEPRA FOR SURE. SHE'S ACTUALLY RANKED ABOVE ADMIRAL.
HOLD ON. WE AREN'T REALLY SAYING OUR **GOVERNMENT** IS IN ON THIS, ARE WE?
WELL, KHEPRA DID LOCK UP HER OWN SON, AKILA.
KHENSU IS KHEPRA'S SON?
YEAH, SURPRISED US, TOO.
HUH.
THEY SURE DON'T ACT RELATED...

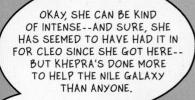

OKAY, SHE CAN BE KIND OF INTENSE--AND SURE, SHE HAS SEEMED TO HAVE HAD IT IN FOR CLEO SINCE SHE GOT HERE-- BUT KHEPRA'S DONE MORE TO HELP THE NILE GALAXY THAN ANYONE.

SHE CERTAINLY WOULDN'T **MURDER** SOMEONE.

HMM...

OH, GREAT. NOW YOU'RE DOING IT.

THE ADMINISTRANT DOESN'T HOLD THE HIGHEST RANK.

THE PHARAOH DOES.

HEY--YOU'RE RIGHT!

PHARAOH YOSIRA IS RANKED ABOVE EVERYONE.

YOU BOTH AREN'T SERIOUSLY IMPLYING THAT PHARAOH YOSIRA IS THE TRAITOR?

OF COURSE NOT. BUT IF SHE HAS A KEY CODE, AND SOMEONE IS GOING AROUND MURDERING THOSE WHO HAVE ONE...

BUT PHARAOH YOSIRA HASN'T TAKEN AN ACTIVE ROLE AT P.Y.R.A.M.I.D. IN ALL THE TIME I'VE BEEN HERE. SHE SEEMS MORE THAN COMFORTABLE LETTING THE COUNCIL HANDLE EVERYTHING.

THERE'S NO WAY SHE HAS A KEY CODE.

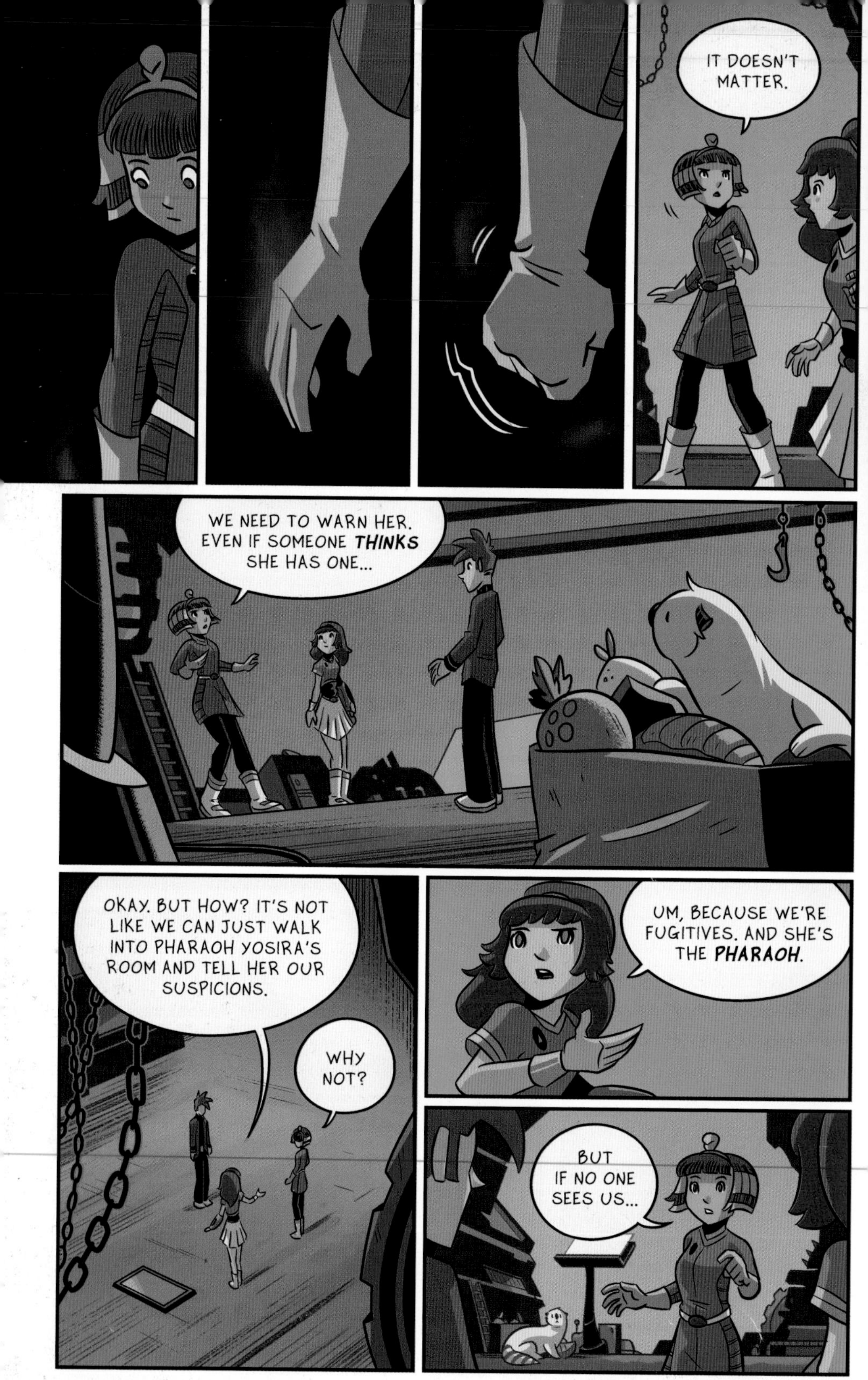
IT DOESN'T MATTER.
WE NEED TO WARN HER. EVEN IF SOMEONE THINKS SHE HAS ONE...
OKAY. BUT HOW? IT'S NOT LIKE WE CAN JUST WALK INTO PHARAOH YOSIRA'S ROOM AND TELL HER OUR SUSPICIONS.
WHY NOT?
UM, BECAUSE WE'RE FUGITIVES. AND SHE'S THE PHARAOH.
BUT IF NO ONE SEES US...

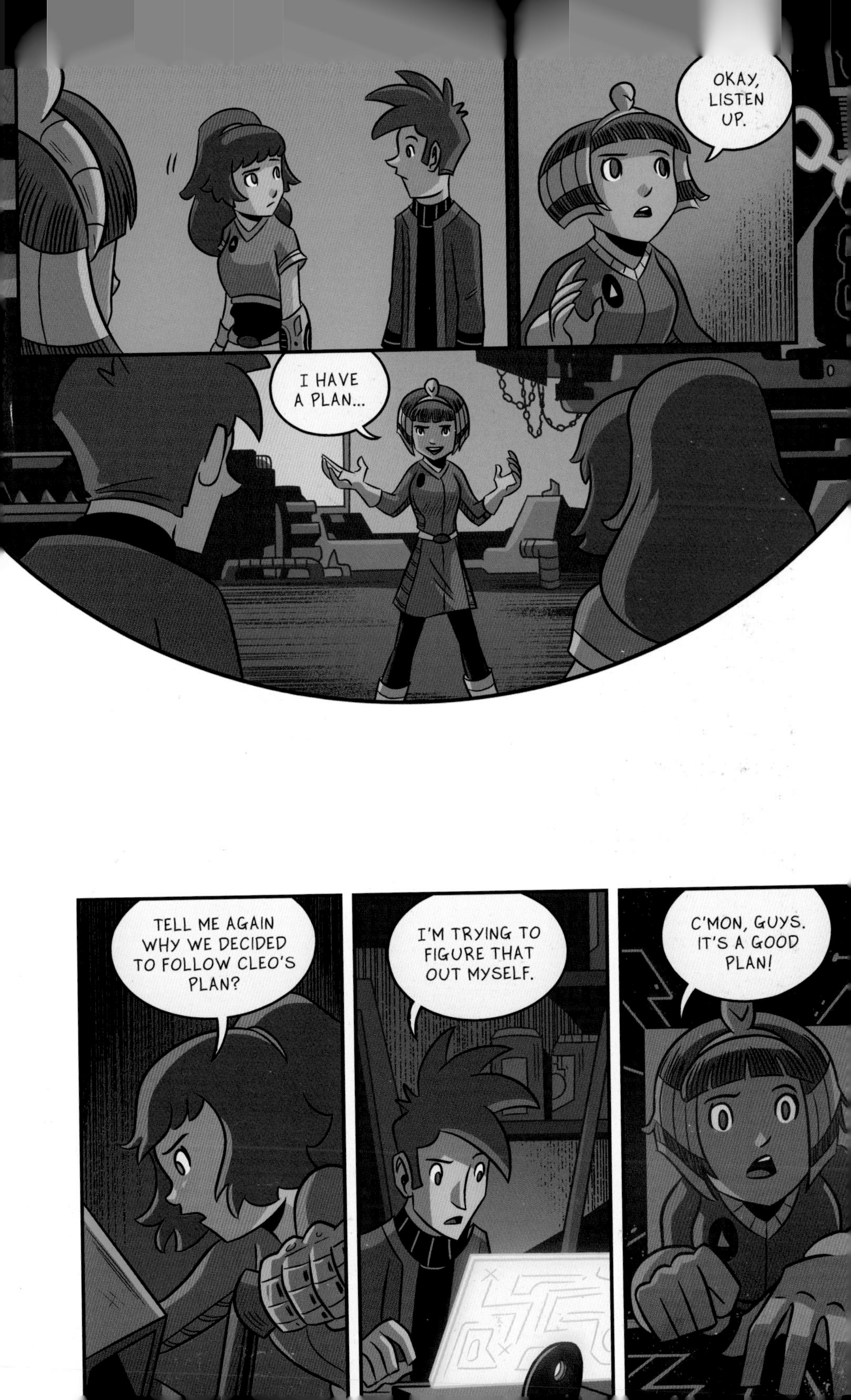
OKAY, LISTEN UP.
I HAVE A PLAN...
TELL ME AGAIN WHY WE DECIDED TO FOLLOW CLEO'S PLAN?
I'M TRYING TO FIGURE THAT OUT MYSELF.
C'MON, GUYS. IT'S A GOOD PLAN!

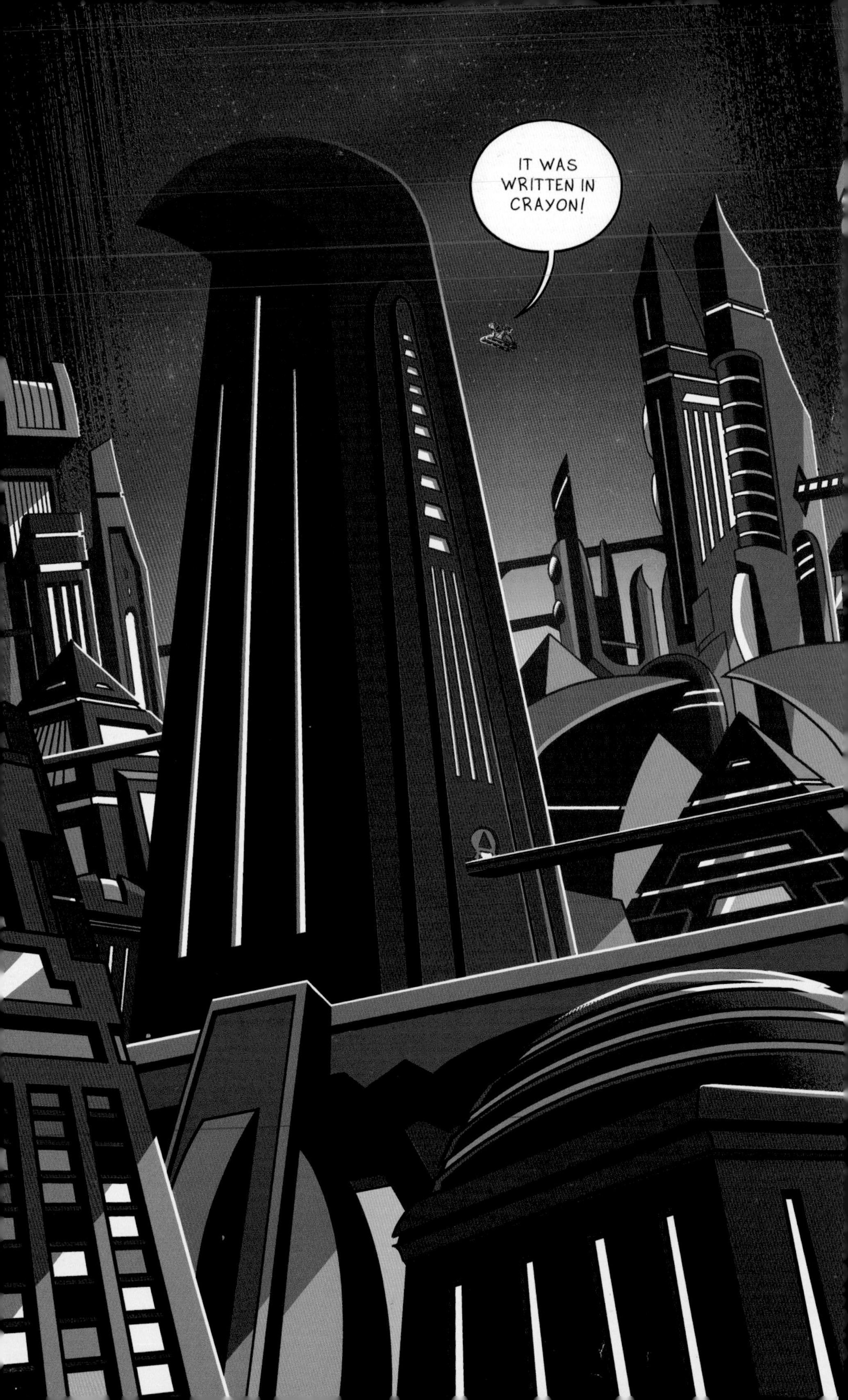
IT WAS WRITTEN IN CRAYON!

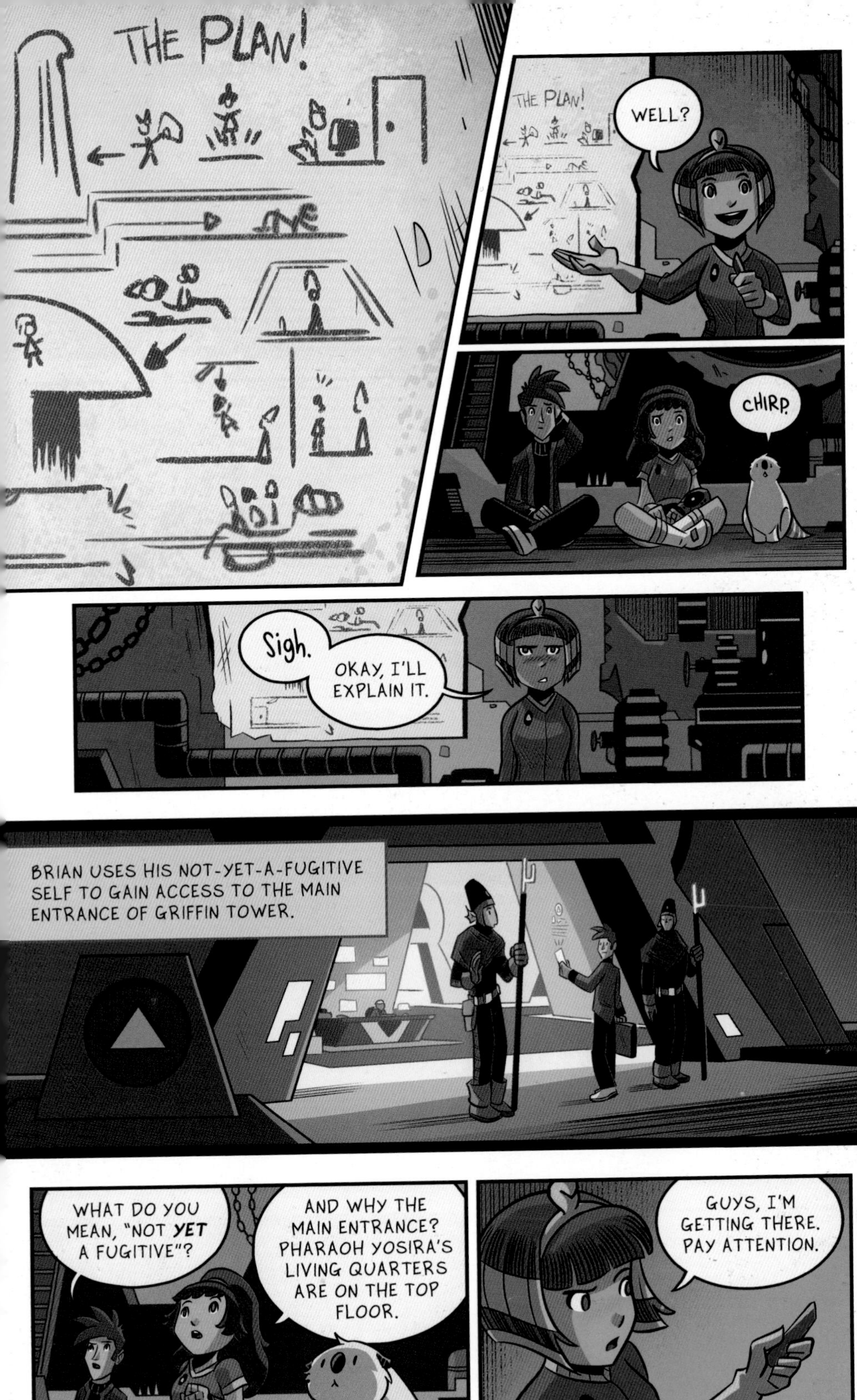
THE PLAN!
THE PLAN!
WELL?
CHIRP.
Sigh.
OKAY, I'LL EXPLAIN IT.
BRIAN USES HIS NOT-YET-A-FUGITIVE SELF TO GAIN ACCESS TO THE MAIN ENTRANCE OF GRIFFIN TOWER.
WHAT DO YOU MEAN, "NOT **YET** A FUGITIVE"?
AND WHY THE MAIN ENTRANCE? PHARAOH YOSIRA'S LIVING QUARTERS ARE ON THE TOP FLOOR.
GUYS, I'M GETTING THERE. PAY ATTENTION.

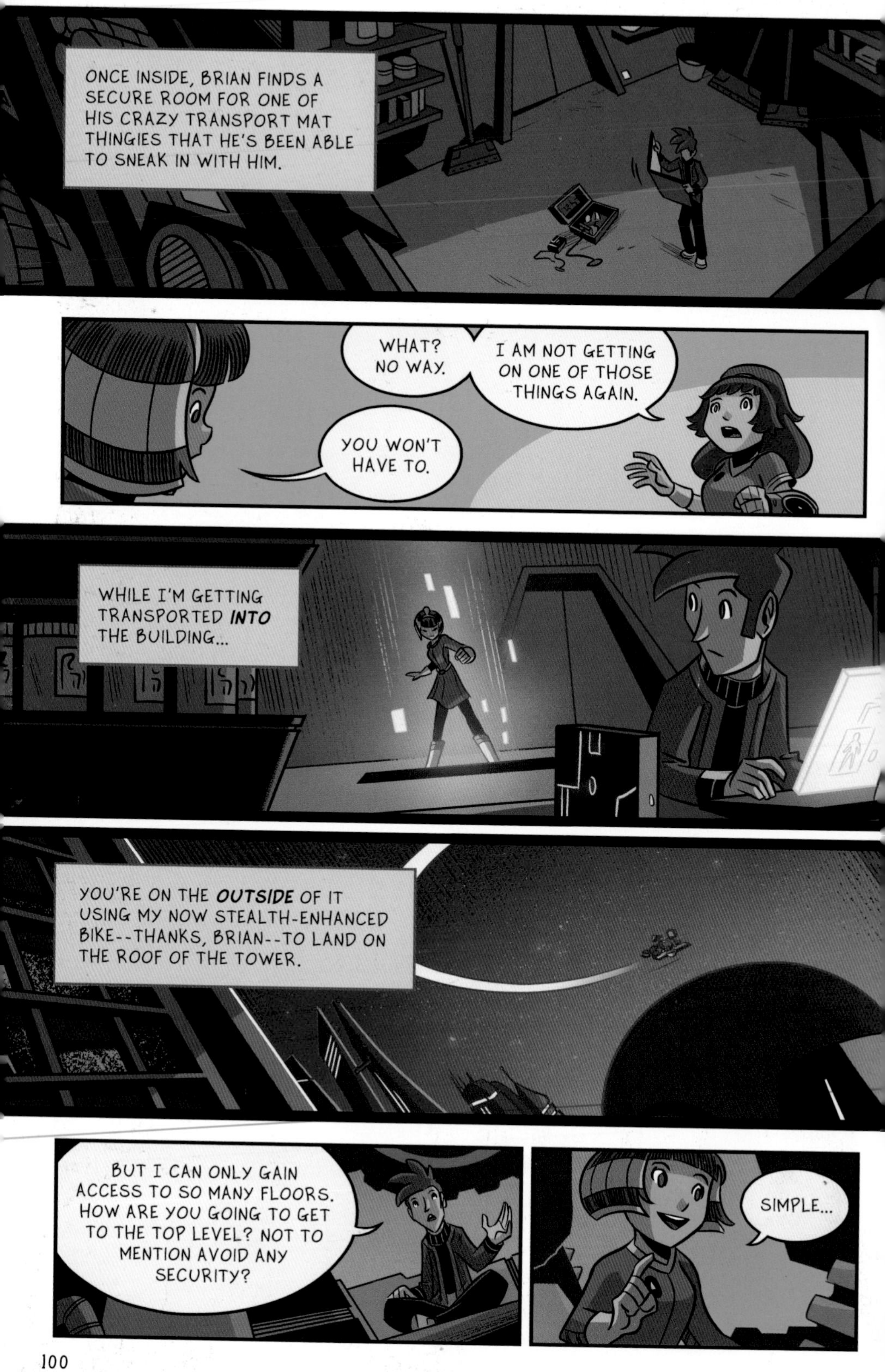
ONCE INSIDE, BRIAN FINDS A SECURE ROOM FOR ONE OF HIS CRAZY TRANSPORT MAT THINGIES THAT HE'S BEEN ABLE TO SNEAK IN WITH HIM.
WHAT? NO WAY.
I AM NOT GETTING ON ONE OF THOSE THINGS AGAIN.
YOU WON'T HAVE TO.
WHILE I'M GETTING TRANSPORTED INTO THE BUILDING...
YOU'RE ON THE OUTSIDE OF IT USING MY NOW STEALTH-ENHANCED BIKE--THANKS, BRIAN--TO LAND ON THE ROOF OF THE TOWER.
BUT I CAN ONLY GAIN ACCESS TO SO MANY FLOORS. HOW ARE YOU GOING TO GET TO THE TOP LEVEL? NOT TO MENTION AVOID ANY SECURITY?
SIMPLE...

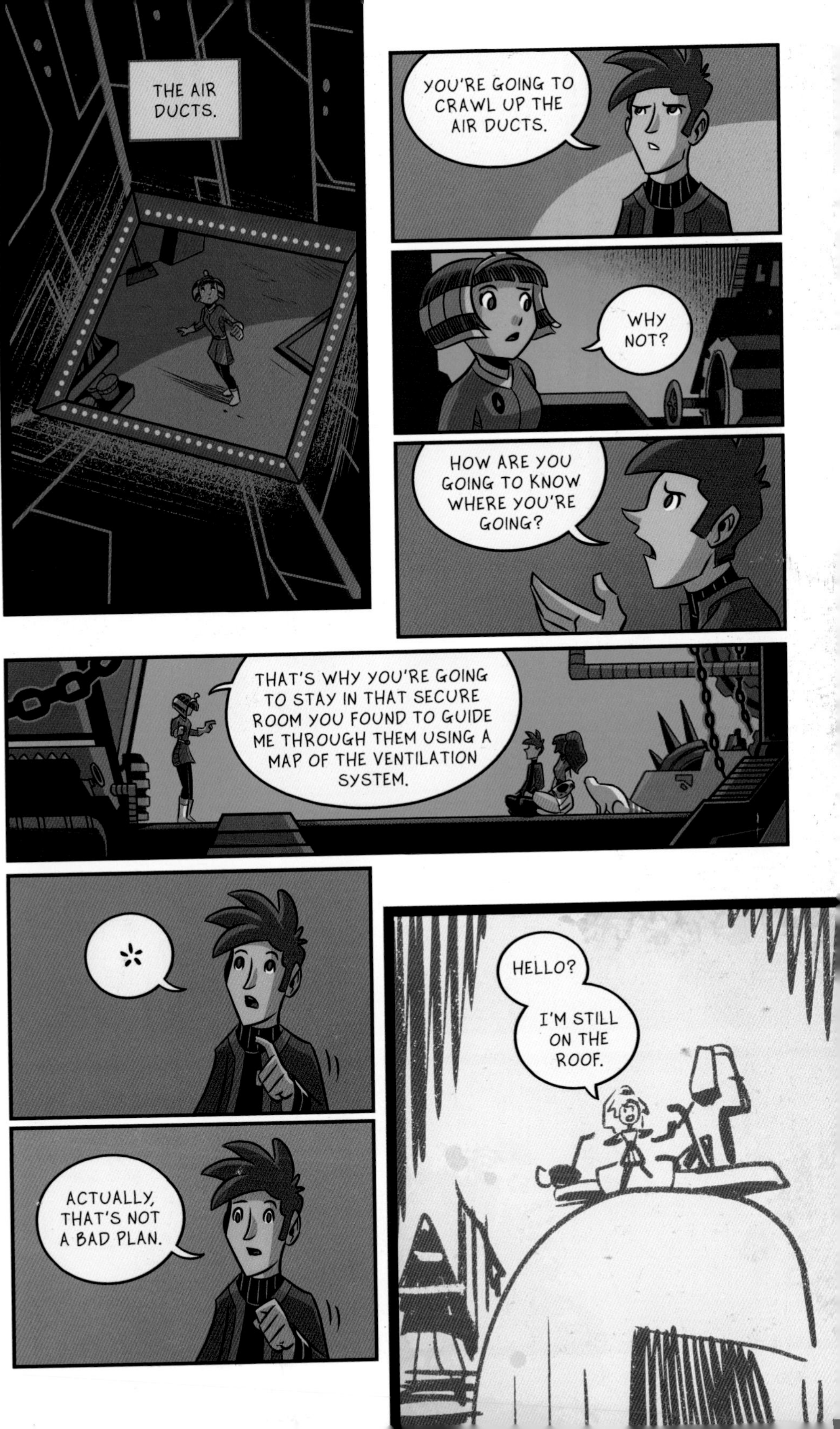
THE AIR DUCTS.
YOU'RE GOING TO CRAWL UP THE AIR DUCTS.
WHY NOT?
HOW ARE YOU GOING TO KNOW WHERE YOU'RE GOING?
THAT'S WHY YOU'RE GOING TO STAY IN THAT SECURE ROOM YOU FOUND TO GUIDE ME THROUGH THEM USING A MAP OF THE VENTILATION SYSTEM.
ACTUALLY, THAT'S NOT A BAD PLAN.
HELLO?
I'M STILL ON THE ROOF.

OH YEAH. YOU'RE GOING TO NEED A CABLE AND A HARNESS.

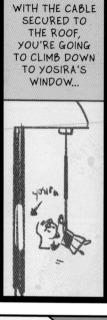

WITH THE CABLE SECURED TO THE ROOF, YOU'RE GOING TO CLIMB DOWN TO YOSIRA'S WINDOW...

YOSIRA

USE SUCTION CUPS TO ATTACH TO THE WALL...

AND INFORM ME WHEN IT'S SAFE TO ENTER HER ROOM.

ALL CLEAR!

WHY CAN'T I JUST HOVER IN FRONT OF HER WINDOW IN STEALTH MODE?

WELL, SURE. IF YOU WANT TO DO IT THE EASY WAY.

YES, CLEO! I WANT TO DO THIS THE EASY WAY!

FINE. SO WHILE AKILA IS HOVERING IN FRONT OF YOSIRA'S WINDOW...

WHICH DOES NOT SOUND CREEPY AT ALL.

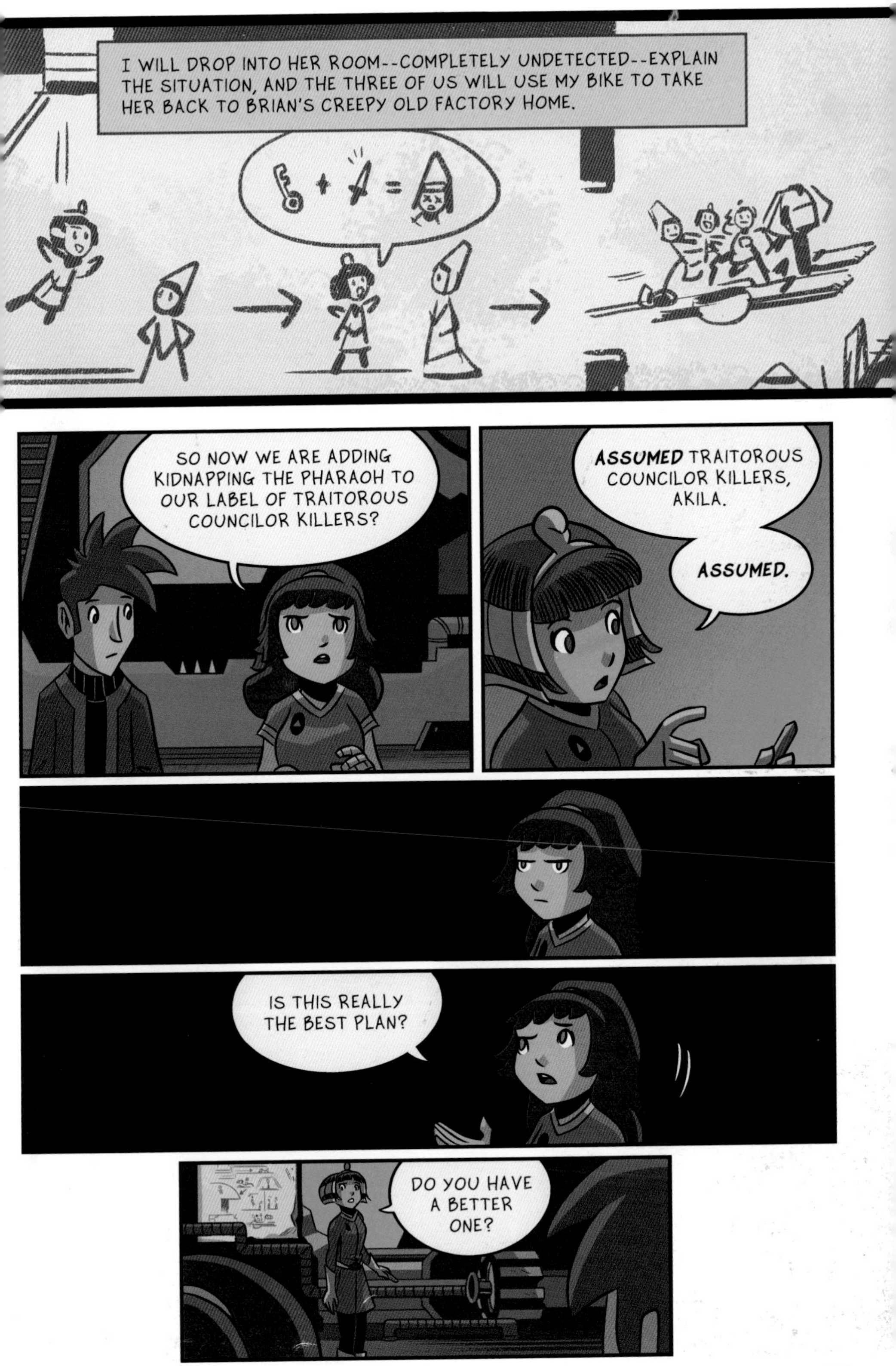
I WILL DROP INTO HER ROOM--COMPLETELY UNDETECTED--EXPLAIN THE SITUATION, AND THE THREE OF US WILL USE MY BIKE TO TAKE HER BACK TO BRIAN'S CREEPY OLD FACTORY HOME.
SO NOW WE ARE ADDING KIDNAPPING THE PHARAOH TO OUR LABEL OF TRAITOROUS COUNCILOR KILLERS?
ASSUMED TRAITOROUS COUNCILOR KILLERS, AKILA.
ASSUMED.
IS THIS REALLY THE BEST PLAN?
DO YOU HAVE A BETTER ONE?

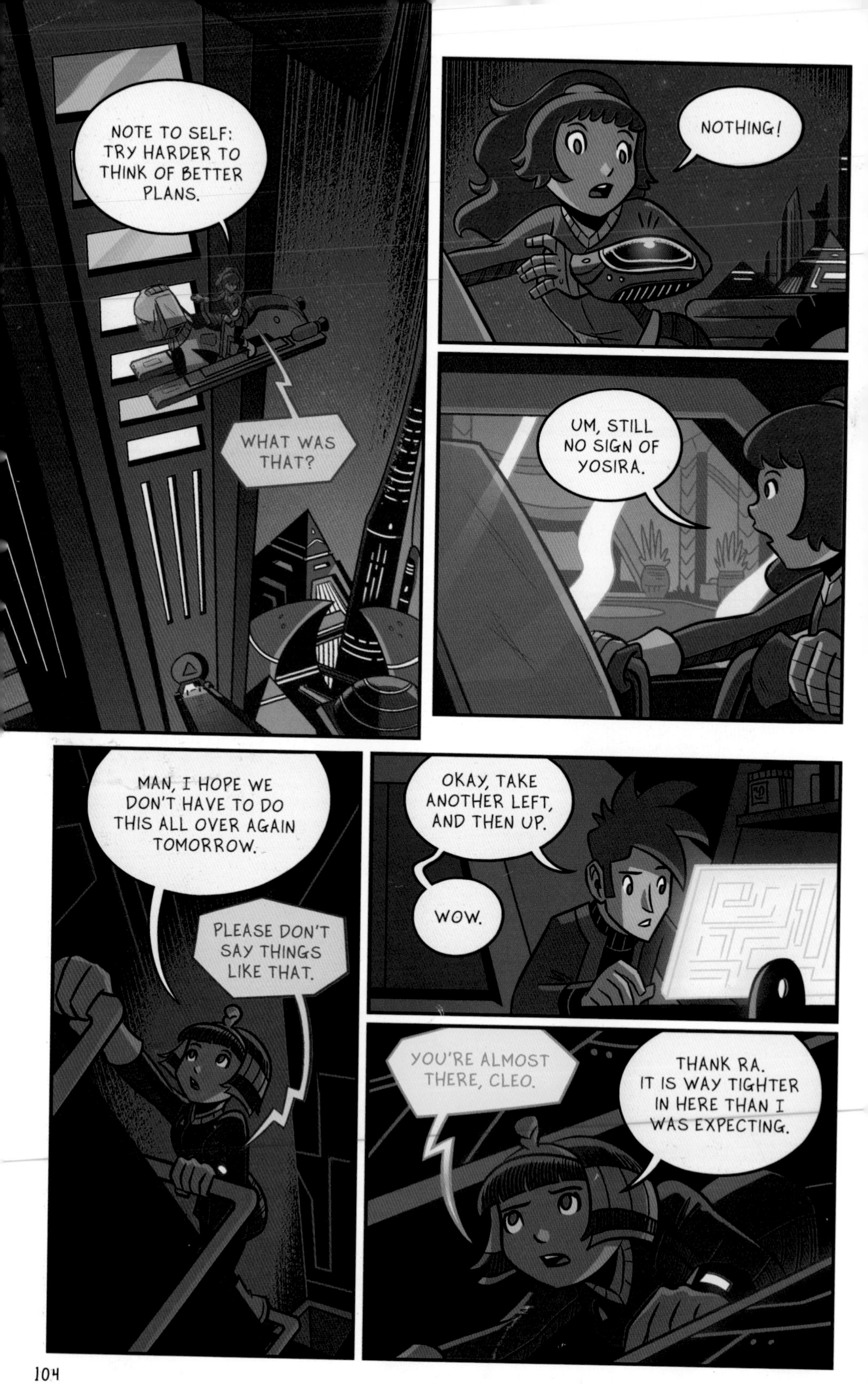
NOTE TO SELF: TRY HARDER TO THINK OF BETTER PLANS.
WHAT WAS THAT?
NOTHING!
UM, STILL NO SIGN OF YOSIRA.
MAN, I HOPE WE DON'T HAVE TO DO THIS ALL OVER AGAIN TOMORROW.
PLEASE DON'T SAY THINGS LIKE THAT.
OKAY, TAKE ANOTHER LEFT, AND THEN UP.
WOW.
YOU'RE ALMOST THERE, CLEO.
THANK RA. IT IS WAY TIGHTER IN HERE THAN I WAS EXPECTING.

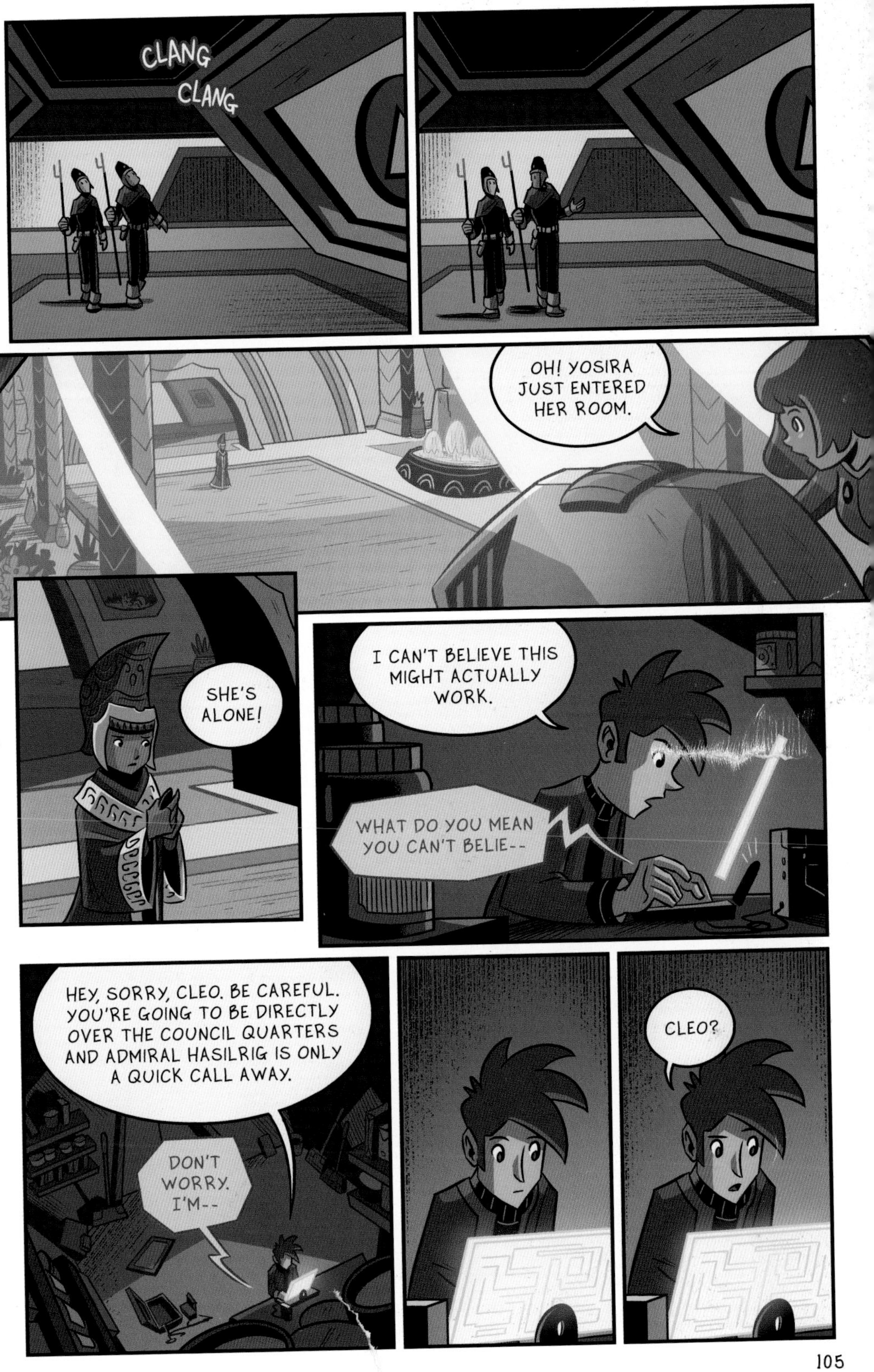
CLANG
CLANG
OH! YOSIRA JUST ENTERED HER ROOM.
SHE'S ALONE!
I CAN'T BELIEVE THIS MIGHT ACTUALLY WORK.
WHAT DO YOU MEAN YOU CAN'T BELIE--
HEY, SORRY, CLEO. BE CAREFUL. YOU'RE GOING TO BE DIRECTLY OVER THE COUNCIL QUARTERS AND ADMIRAL HASILRIG IS ONLY A QUICK CALL AWAY.
DON'T WORRY. I'M--
CLEO?

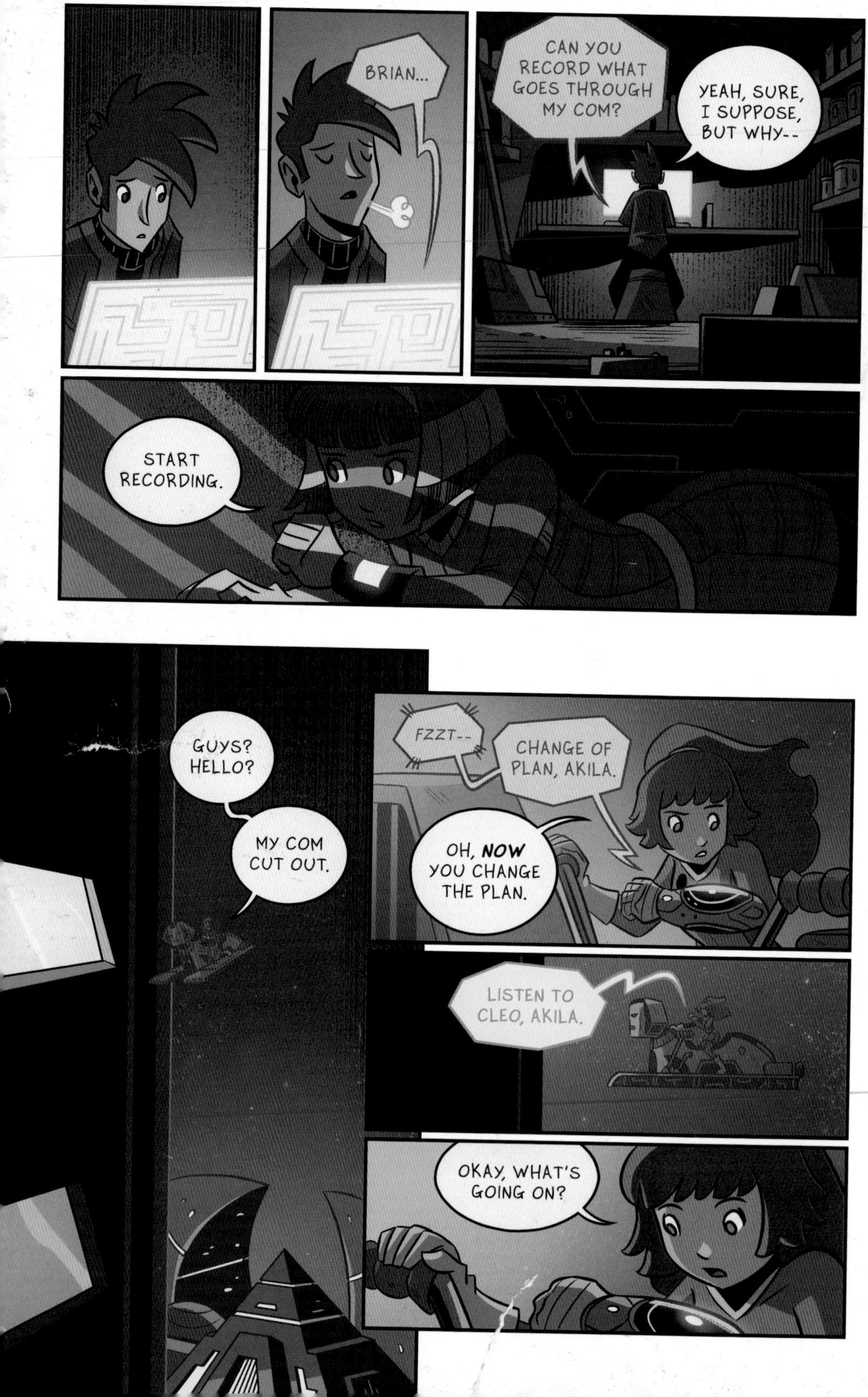
BRIAN...
CAN YOU RECORD WHAT GOES THROUGH MY COM?
YEAH, SURE, I SUPPOSE, BUT WHY--
START RECORDING.
GUYS? HELLO?
MY COM CUT OUT.
FZZT--
CHANGE OF PLAN, AKILA.
OH, **NOW** YOU CHANGE THE PLAN.
LISTEN TO CLEO, AKILA.
OKAY, WHAT'S GOING ON?

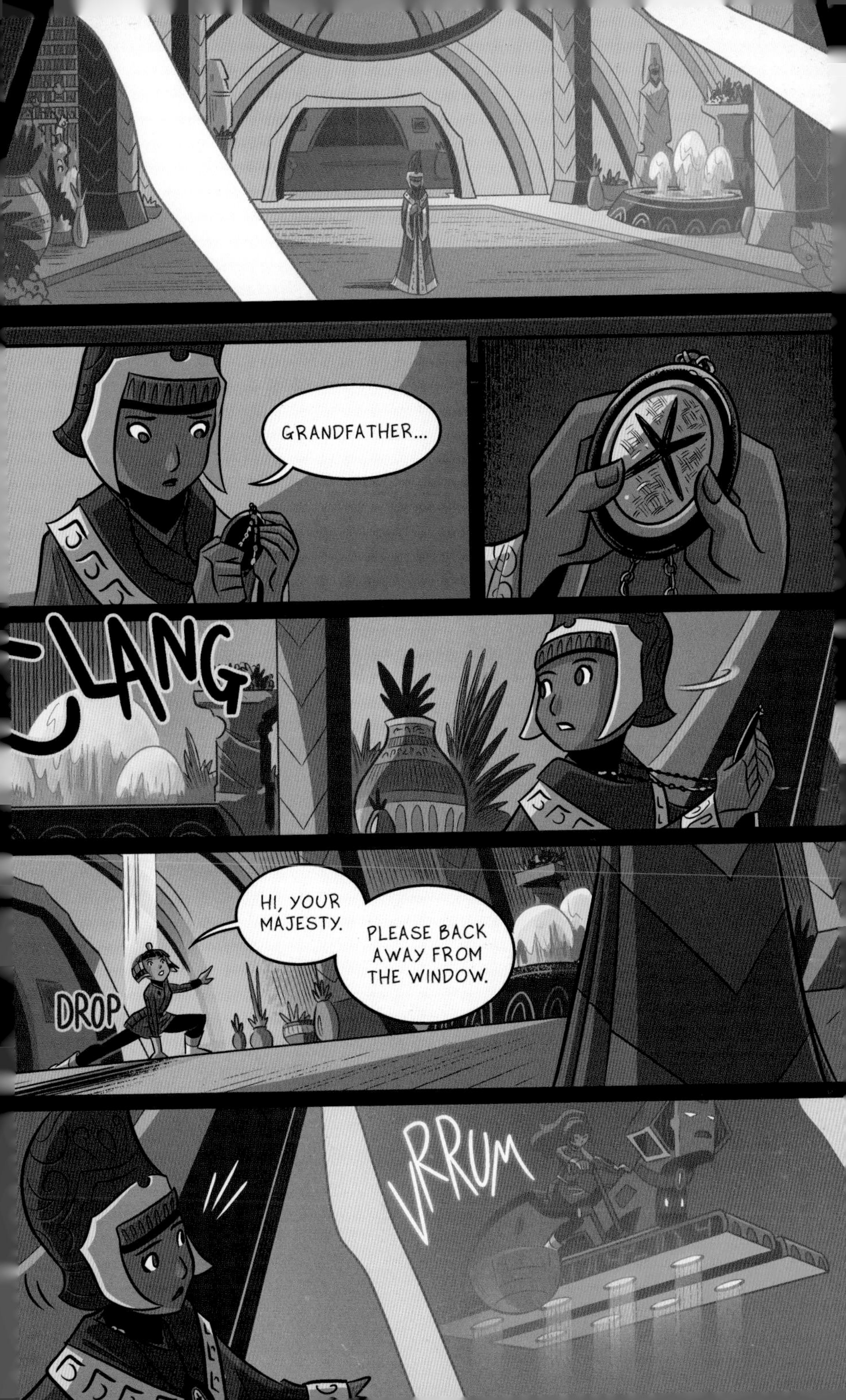
GRANDFATHER...
CLANG
HI, YOUR MAJESTY.
PLEASE BACK AWAY FROM THE WINDOW.
DROP
VRRUM

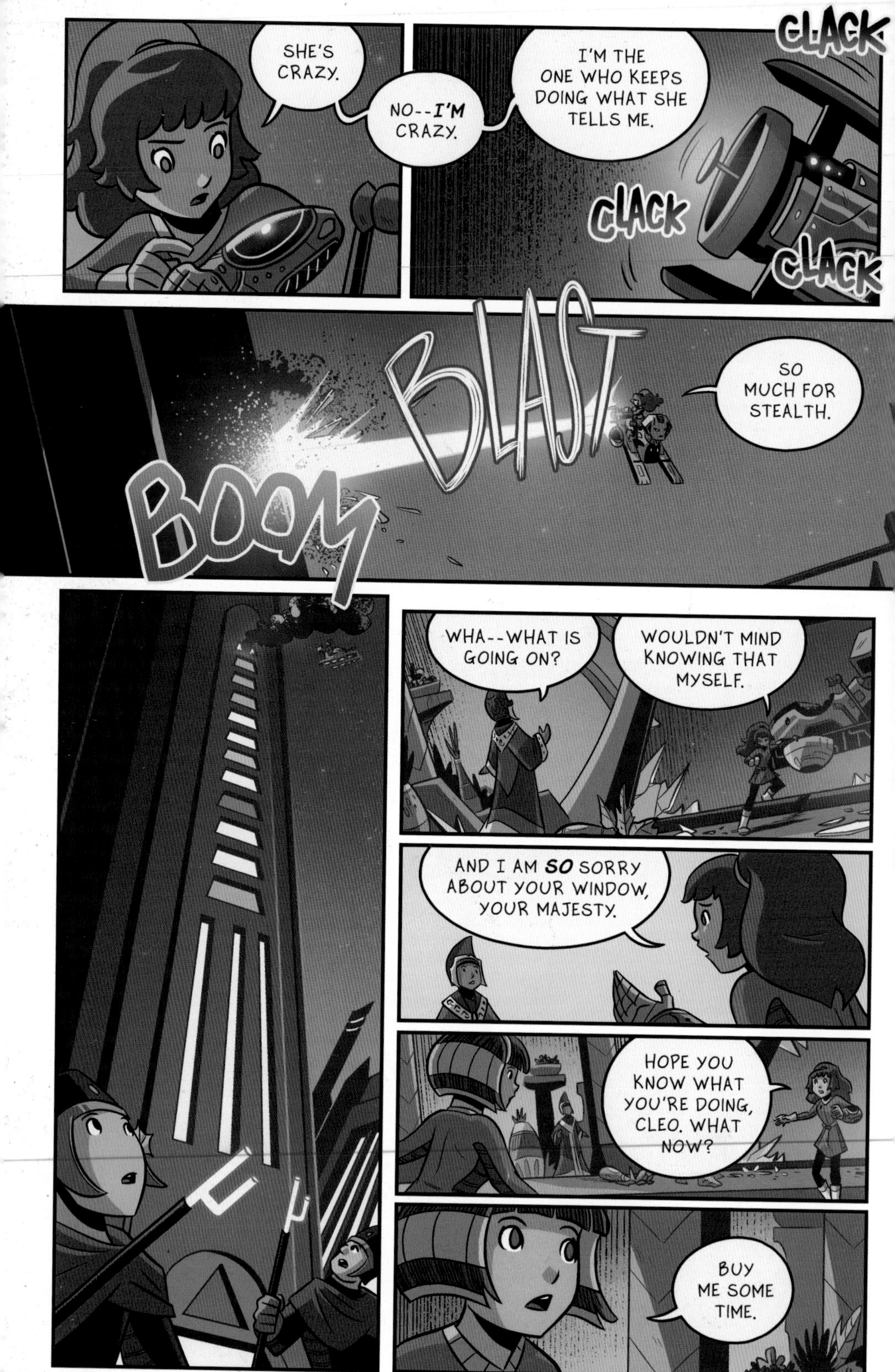
SHE'S CRAZY.
NO--*I'M* CRAZY.
I'M THE ONE WHO KEEPS DOING WHAT SHE TELLS ME.
CLACK
CLACK
CLACK
BLAST
BOOM
SO MUCH FOR STEALTH.
WHA--WHAT IS GOING ON?
WOULDN'T MIND KNOWING THAT MYSELF.
AND I AM ***SO*** SORRY ABOUT YOUR WINDOW, YOUR MAJESTY.
HOPE YOU KNOW WHAT YOU'RE DOING, CLEO. WHAT NOW?
BUY ME SOME TIME.

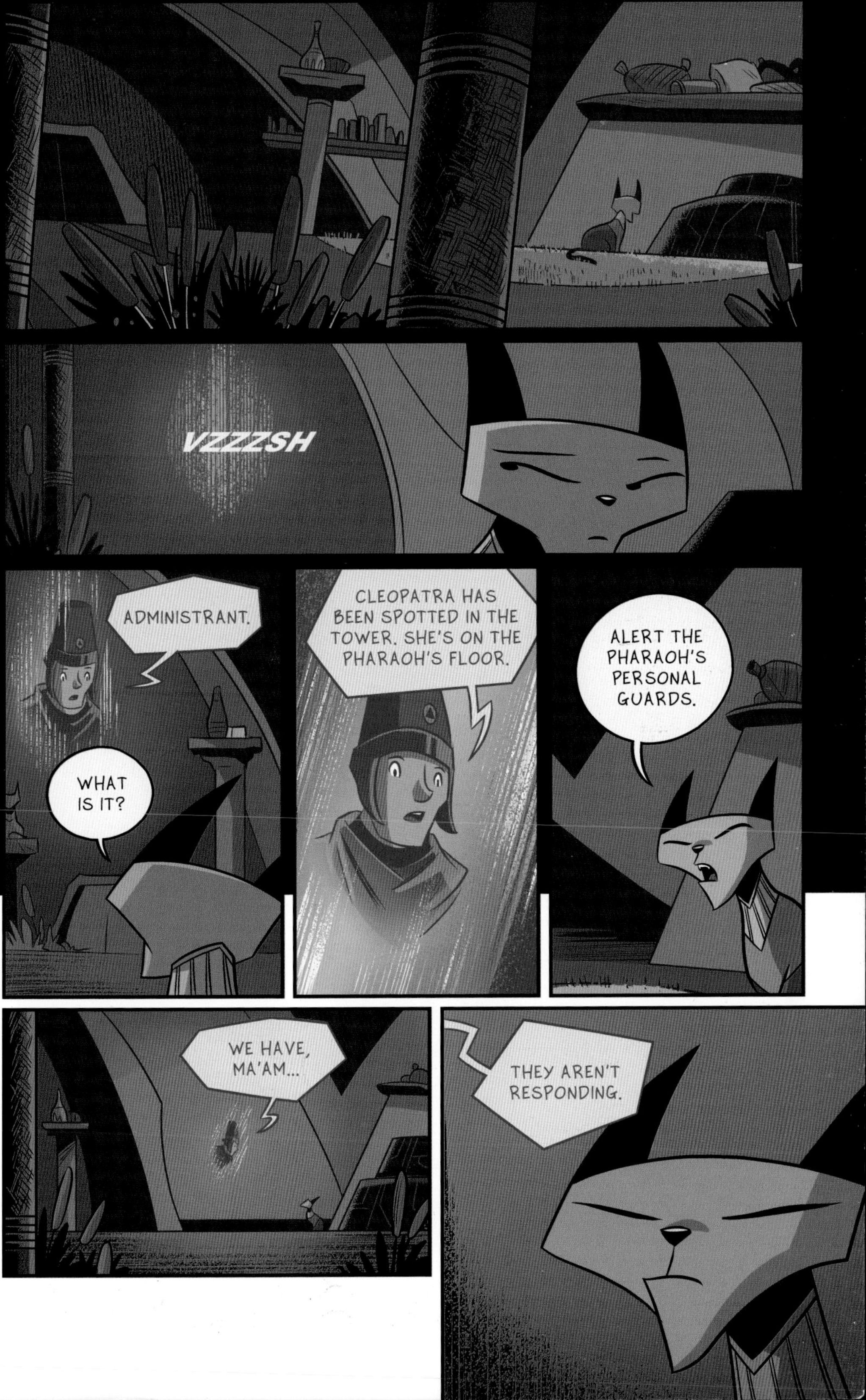
VZZZSH
ADMINISTRANT.
WHAT IS IT?
CLEOPATRA HAS BEEN SPOTTED IN THE TOWER. SHE'S ON THE PHARAOH'S FLOOR.
ALERT THE PHARAOH'S PERSONAL GUARDS.
WE HAVE, MA'AM...
THEY AREN'T RESPONDING.

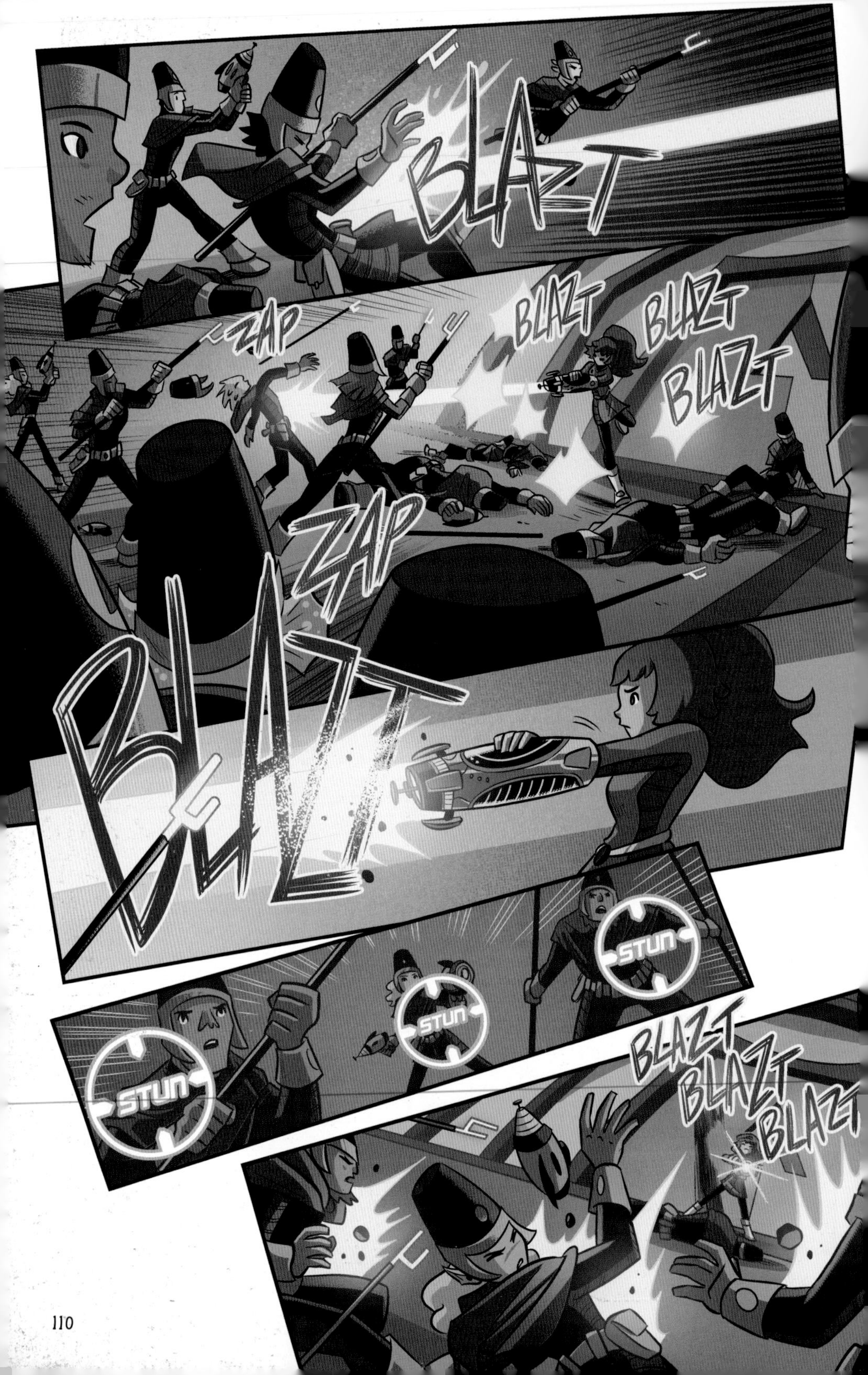
BLAZT
ZAP
BLAZT
BLAZT
BLAZT
ZAP
BLAZT
STUN
STUN
STUN
BLAZT
BLAZT
BLAZT

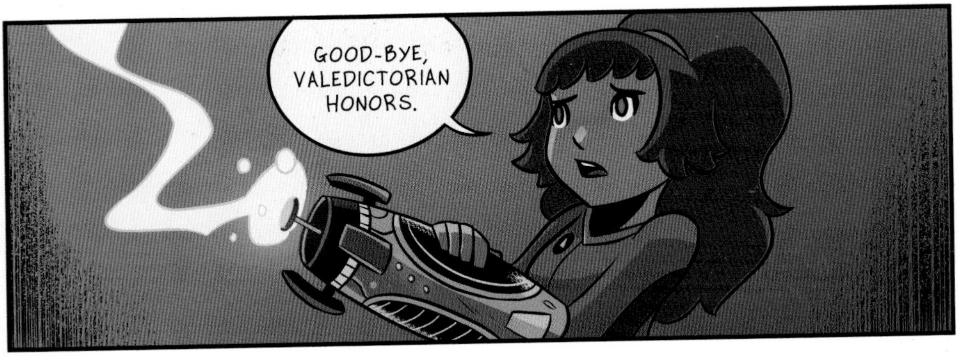
GOOD-BYE, VALEDICTORIAN HONORS.

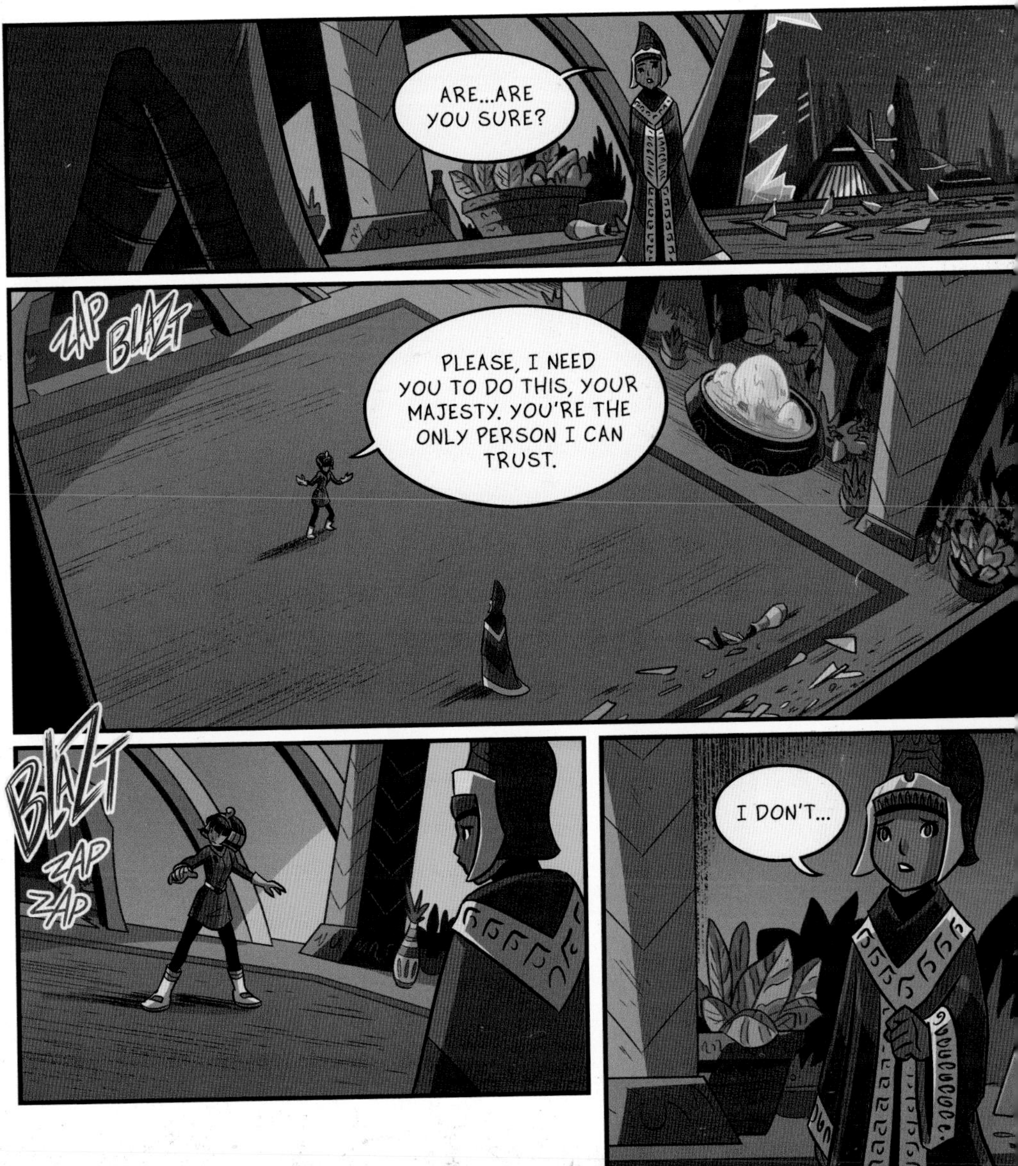
ARE...ARE YOU SURE?
ZAP
BLAZT
PLEASE, I NEED YOU TO DO THIS, YOUR MAJESTY. YOU'RE THE ONLY PERSON I CAN TRUST.
BLAZT
ZAP
ZAP
I DON'T...

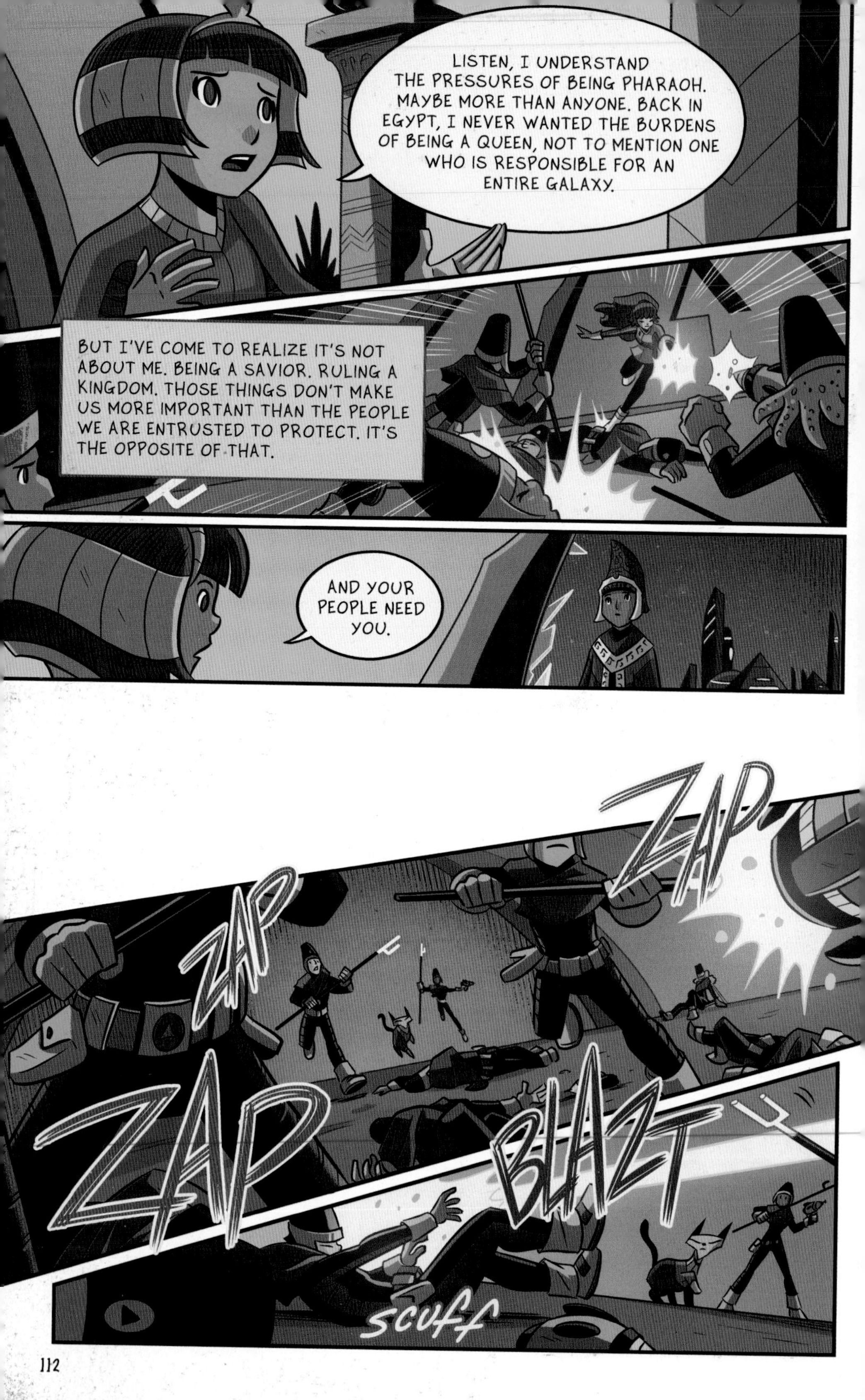
LISTEN, I UNDERSTAND THE PRESSURES OF BEING PHARAOH. MAYBE MORE THAN ANYONE. BACK IN EGYPT, I NEVER WANTED THE BURDENS OF BEING A QUEEN, NOT TO MENTION ONE WHO IS RESPONSIBLE FOR AN ENTIRE GALAXY.
BUT I'VE COME TO REALIZE IT'S NOT ABOUT ME. BEING A SAVIOR. RULING A KINGDOM. THOSE THINGS DON'T MAKE US MORE IMPORTANT THAN THE PEOPLE WE ARE ENTRUSTED TO PROTECT. IT'S THE OPPOSITE OF THAT.
AND YOUR PEOPLE NEED YOU.
ZAP
ZAP
ZAP
BLAZT
scuff

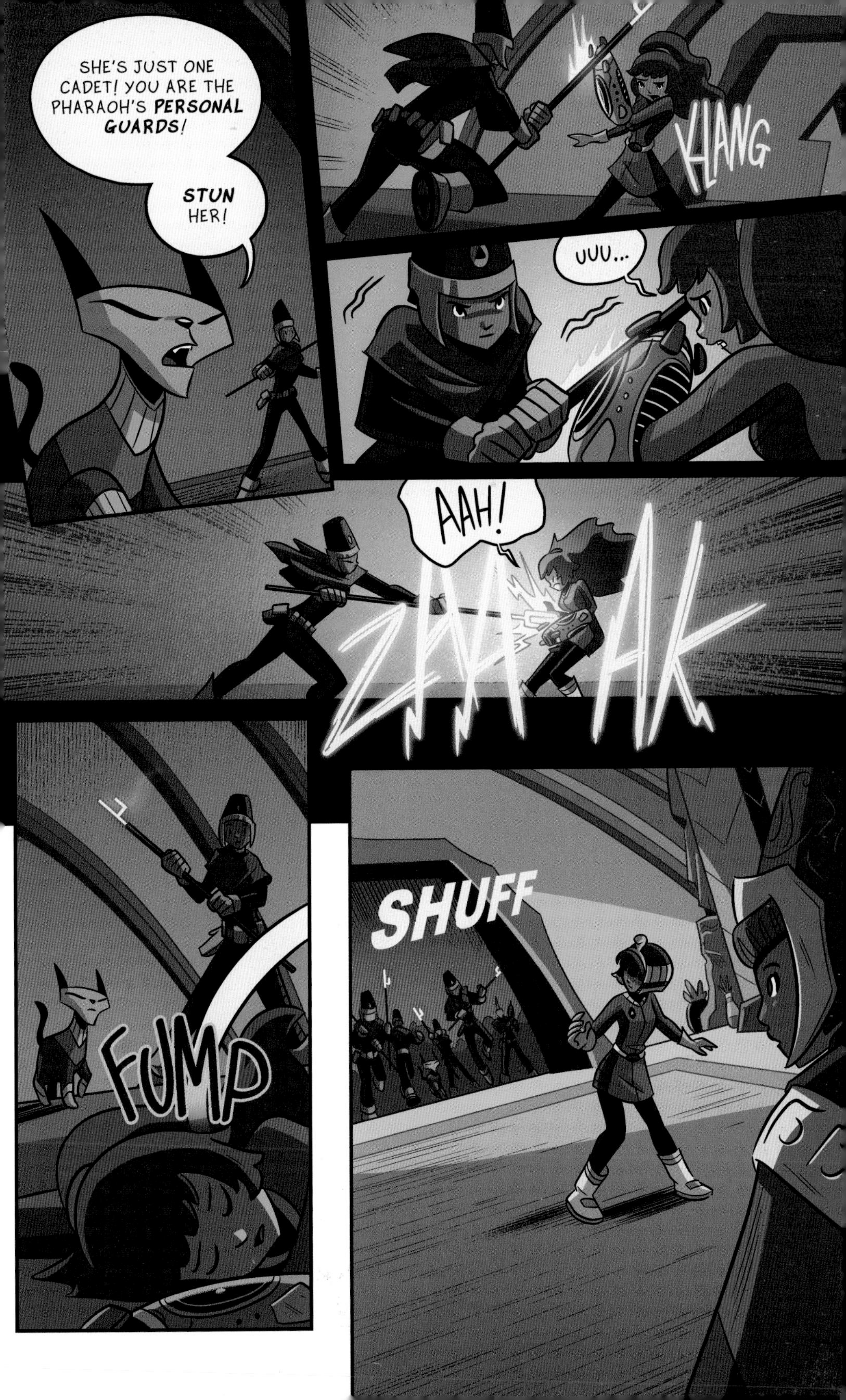
SHE'S JUST ONE CADET! YOU ARE THE PHARAOH'S **PERSONAL GUARDS**!
STUN HER!
KLANG
UUU...
AAH!
ZAAAK
FUMP
SHUFF

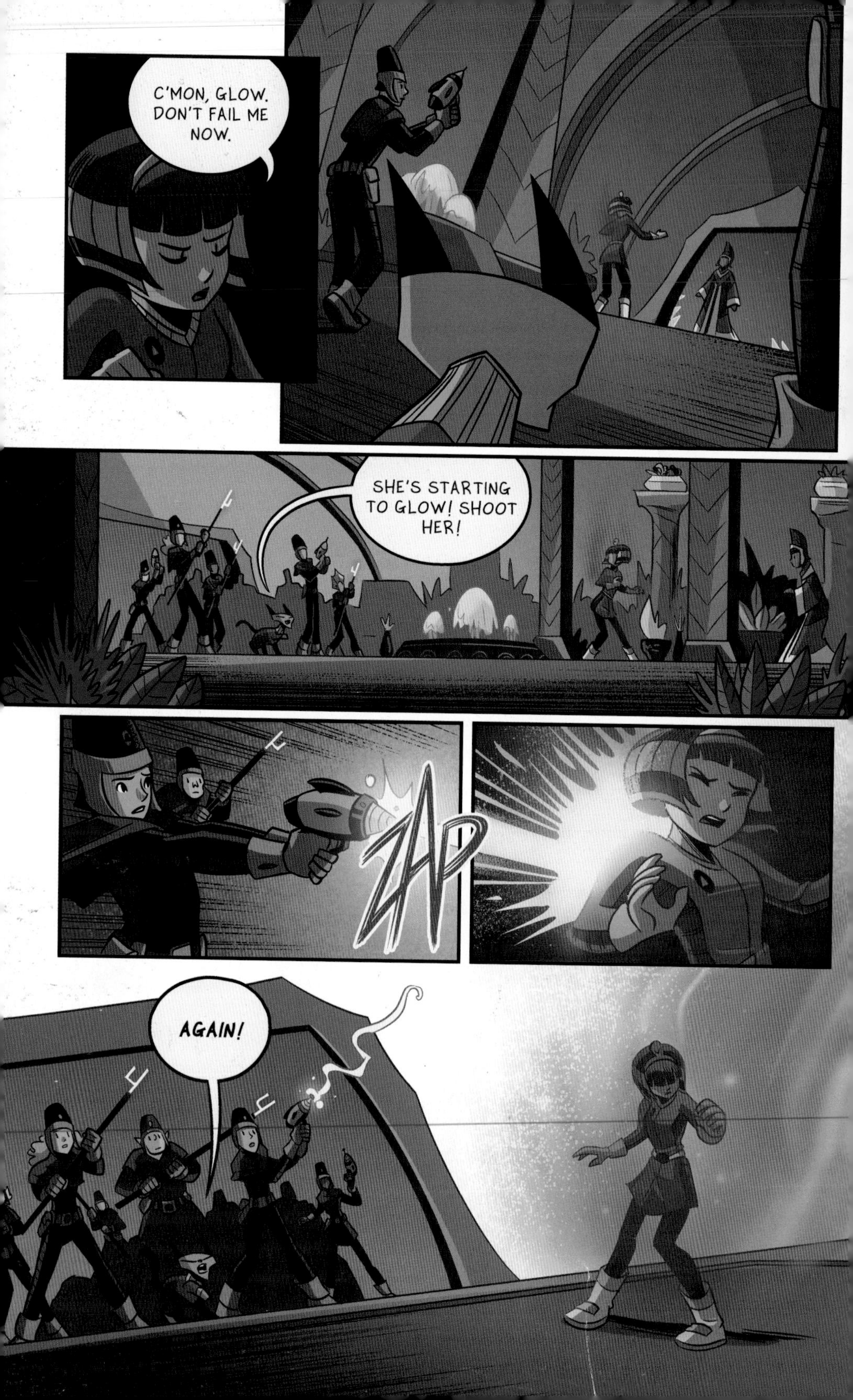
C'MON, GLOW. DON'T FAIL ME NOW.
SHE'S STARTING TO GLOW! SHOOT HER!
ZAP
AGAIN!

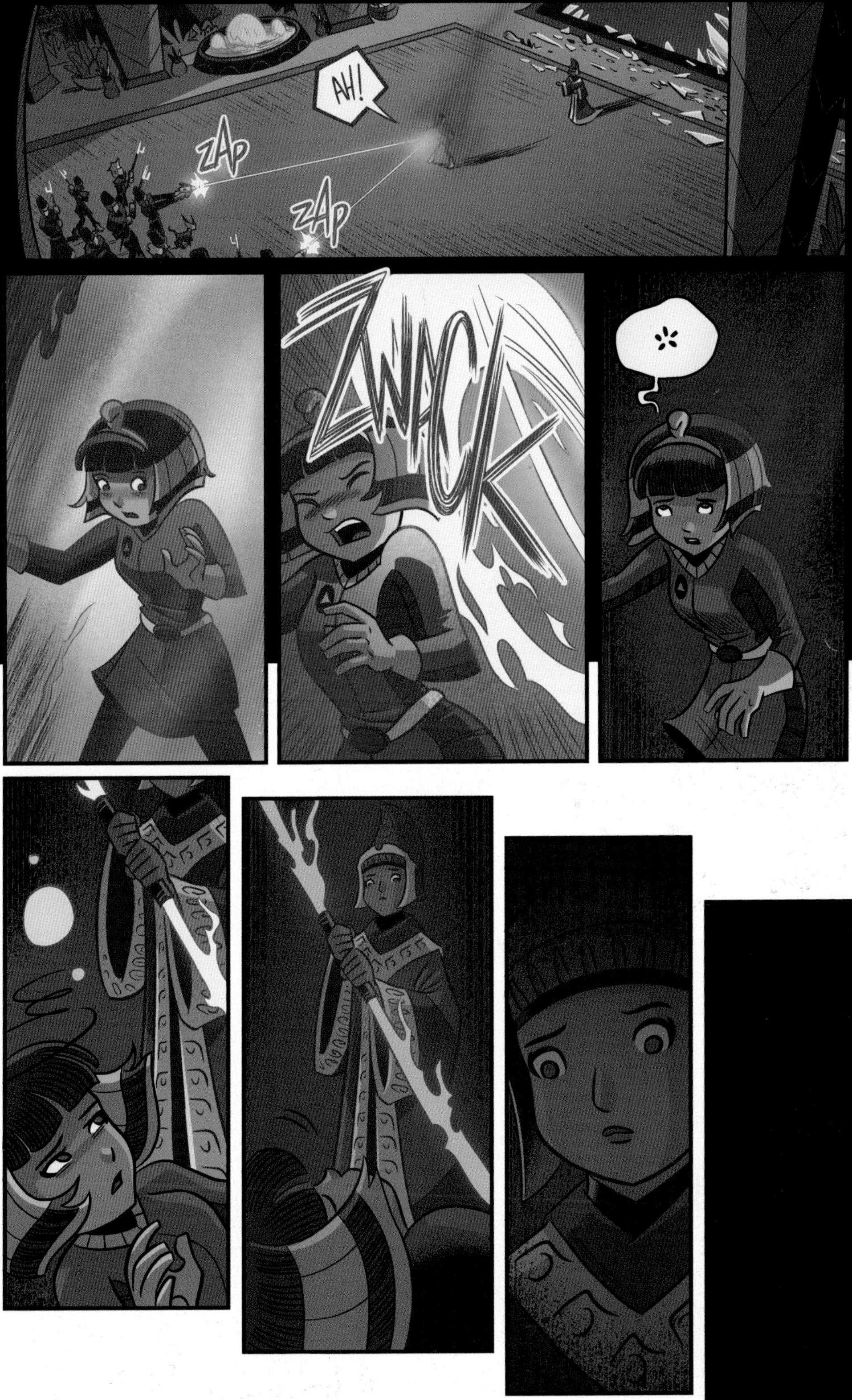
AH!
ZAP
ZAP
ZWACK

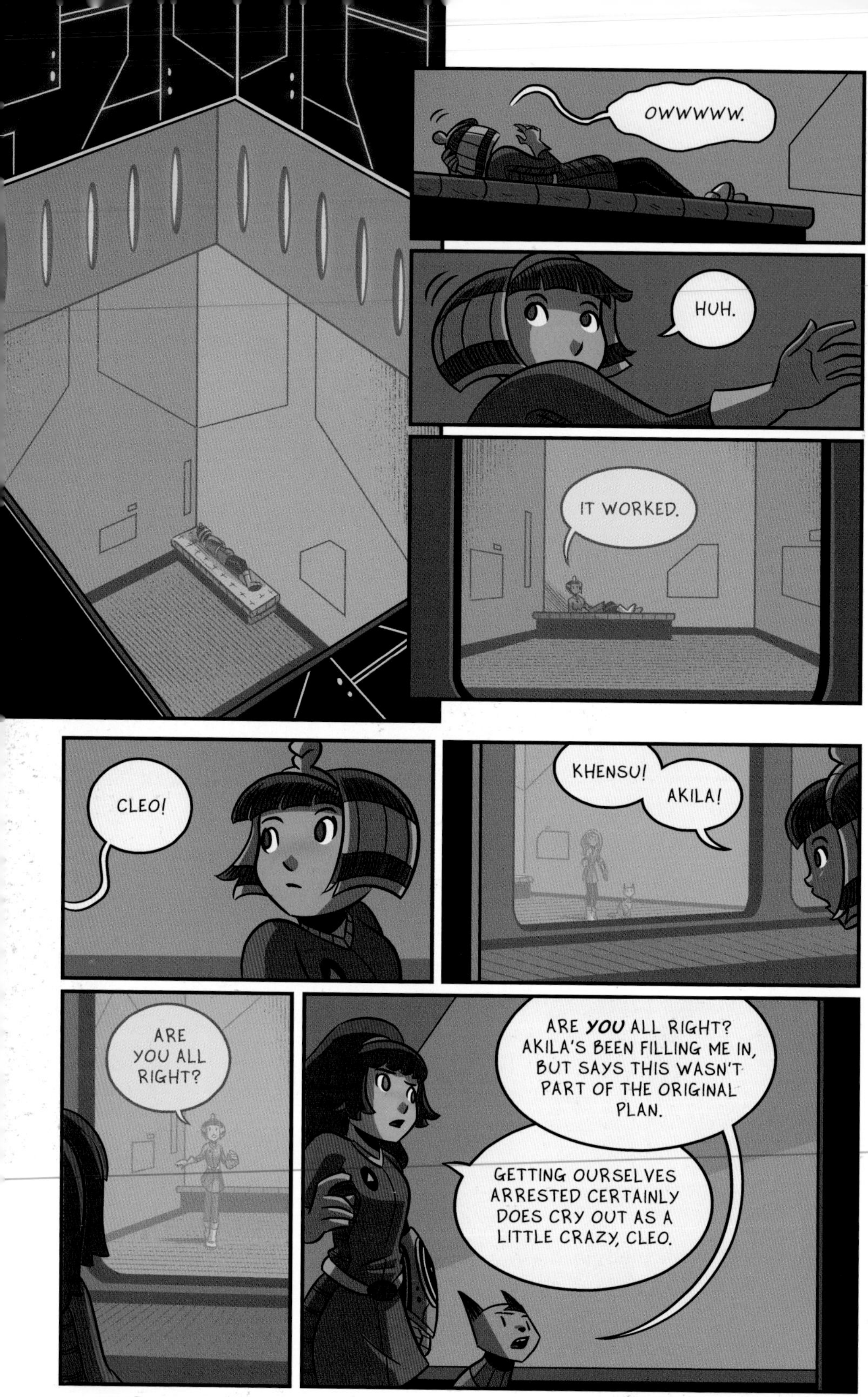

OWWWWW.
HUH.
IT WORKED.
CLEO!
KHENSU!
AKILA!
ARE YOU ALL RIGHT?
ARE *YOU* ALL RIGHT? AKILA'S BEEN FILLING ME IN, BUT SAYS THIS WASN'T PART OF THE ORIGINAL PLAN.
GETTING OURSELVES ARRESTED CERTAINLY DOES CRY OUT AS A LITTLE CRAZY, CLEO.

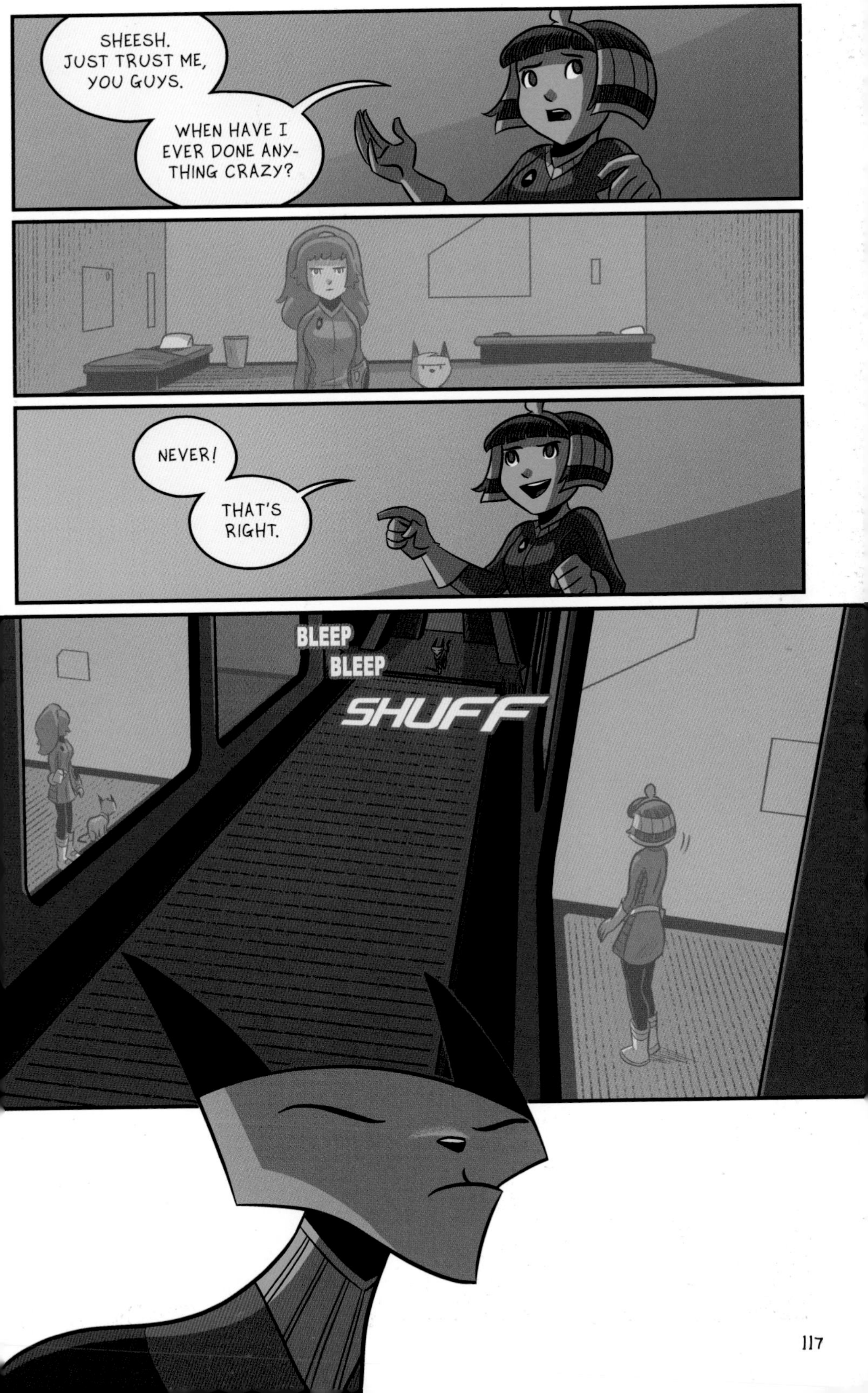
SHEESH. JUST TRUST ME, YOU GUYS.
WHEN HAVE I EVER DONE ANY-THING CRAZY?
NEVER!
THAT'S RIGHT.
BLEEP
BLEEP
SHUFF

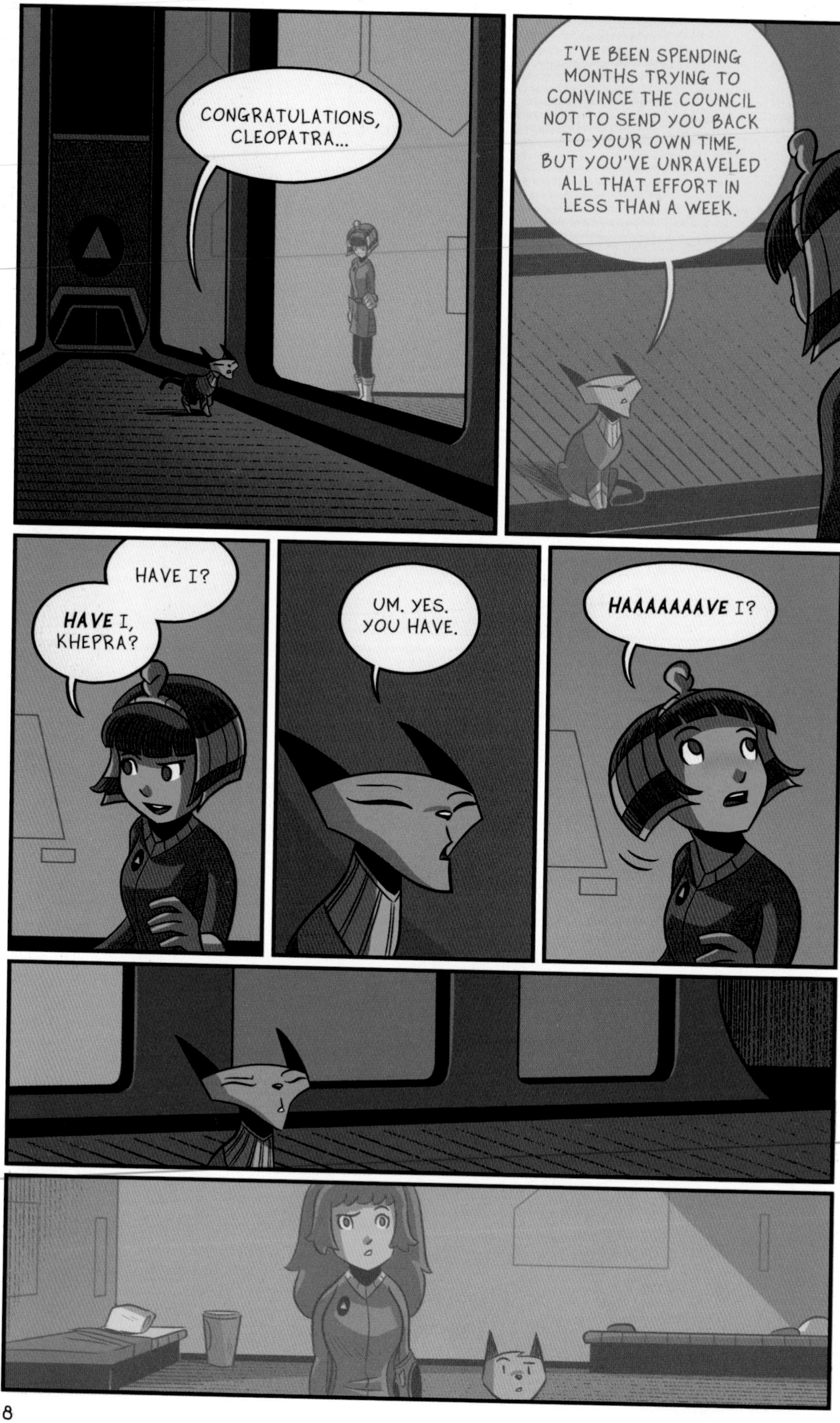

CONGRATULATIONS, CLEOPATRA...
I'VE BEEN SPENDING MONTHS TRYING TO CONVINCE THE COUNCIL NOT TO SEND YOU BACK TO YOUR OWN TIME, BUT YOU'VE UNRAVELED ALL THAT EFFORT IN LESS THAN A WEEK.
HAVE I?
HAVE I, KHEPRA?
UM. YES. YOU HAVE.
HAAAAAAAVE I?

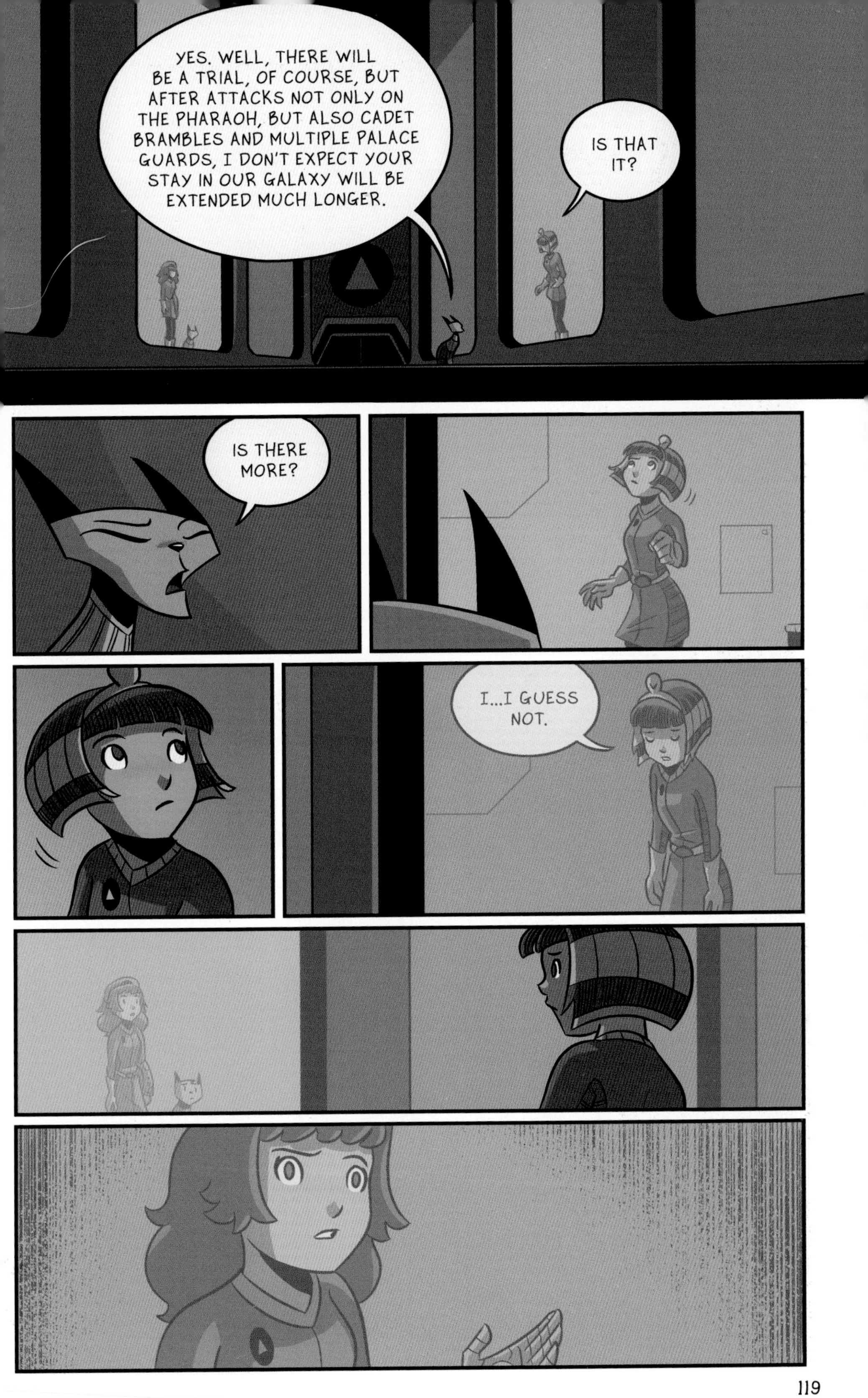
YES. WELL, THERE WILL BE A TRIAL, OF COURSE, BUT AFTER ATTACKS NOT ONLY ON THE PHARAOH, BUT ALSO CADET BRAMBLES AND MULTIPLE PALACE GUARDS, I DON'T EXPECT YOUR STAY IN OUR GALAXY WILL BE EXTENDED MUCH LONGER.
IS THAT IT?
IS THERE MORE?
I...I GUESS NOT.

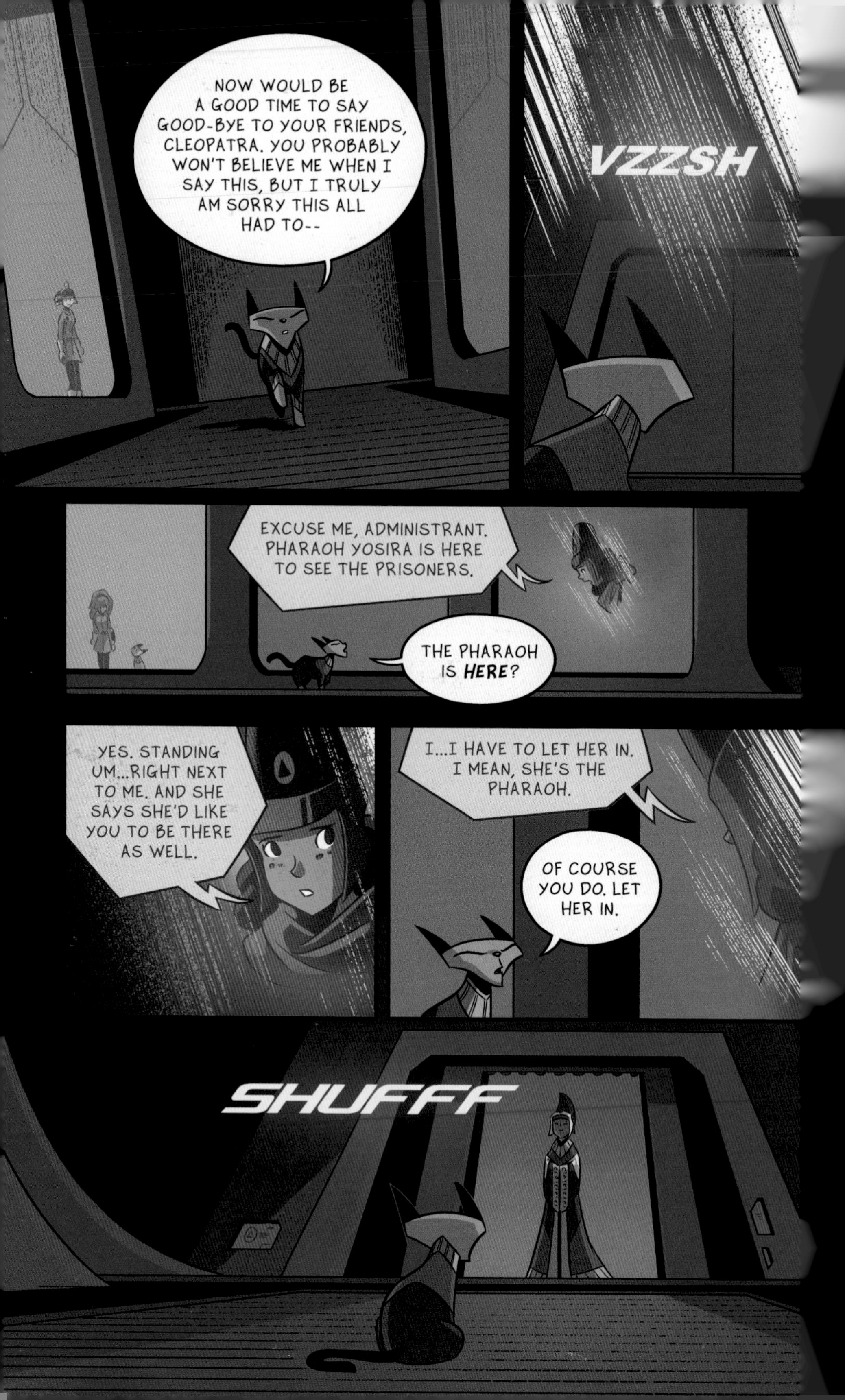
NOW WOULD BE A GOOD TIME TO SAY GOOD-BYE TO YOUR FRIENDS, CLEOPATRA. YOU PROBABLY WON'T BELIEVE ME WHEN I SAY THIS, BUT I TRULY AM SORRY THIS ALL HAD TO--
VZZSH
EXCUSE ME, ADMINISTRANT. PHARAOH YOSIRA IS HERE TO SEE THE PRISONERS.
THE PHARAOH IS **HERE**?
YES. STANDING UM...RIGHT NEXT TO ME. AND SHE SAYS SHE'D LIKE YOU TO BE THERE AS WELL.
I...I HAVE TO LET HER IN. I MEAN, SHE'S THE PHARAOH.
OF COURSE YOU DO. LET HER IN.
SHUFFF

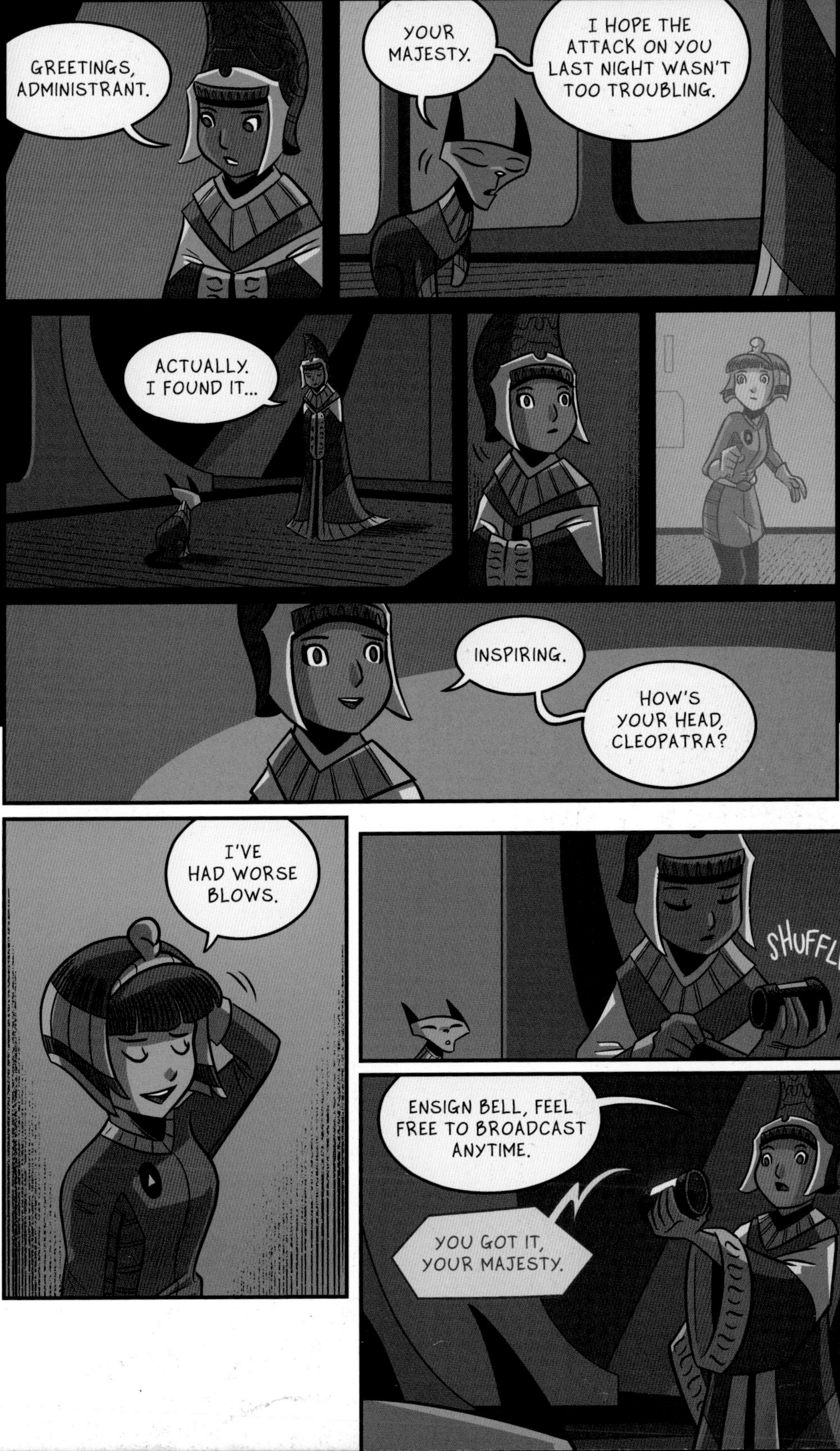
GREETINGS, ADMINISTRANT.
YOUR MAJESTY.
I HOPE THE ATTACK ON YOU LAST NIGHT WASN'T TOO TROUBLING.
ACTUALLY. I FOUND IT...
INSPIRING.
HOW'S YOUR HEAD, CLEOPATRA?
I'VE HAD WORSE BLOWS.
SHUFFLE
ENSIGN BELL, FEEL FREE TO BROADCAST ANYTIME.
YOU GOT IT, YOUR MAJESTY.

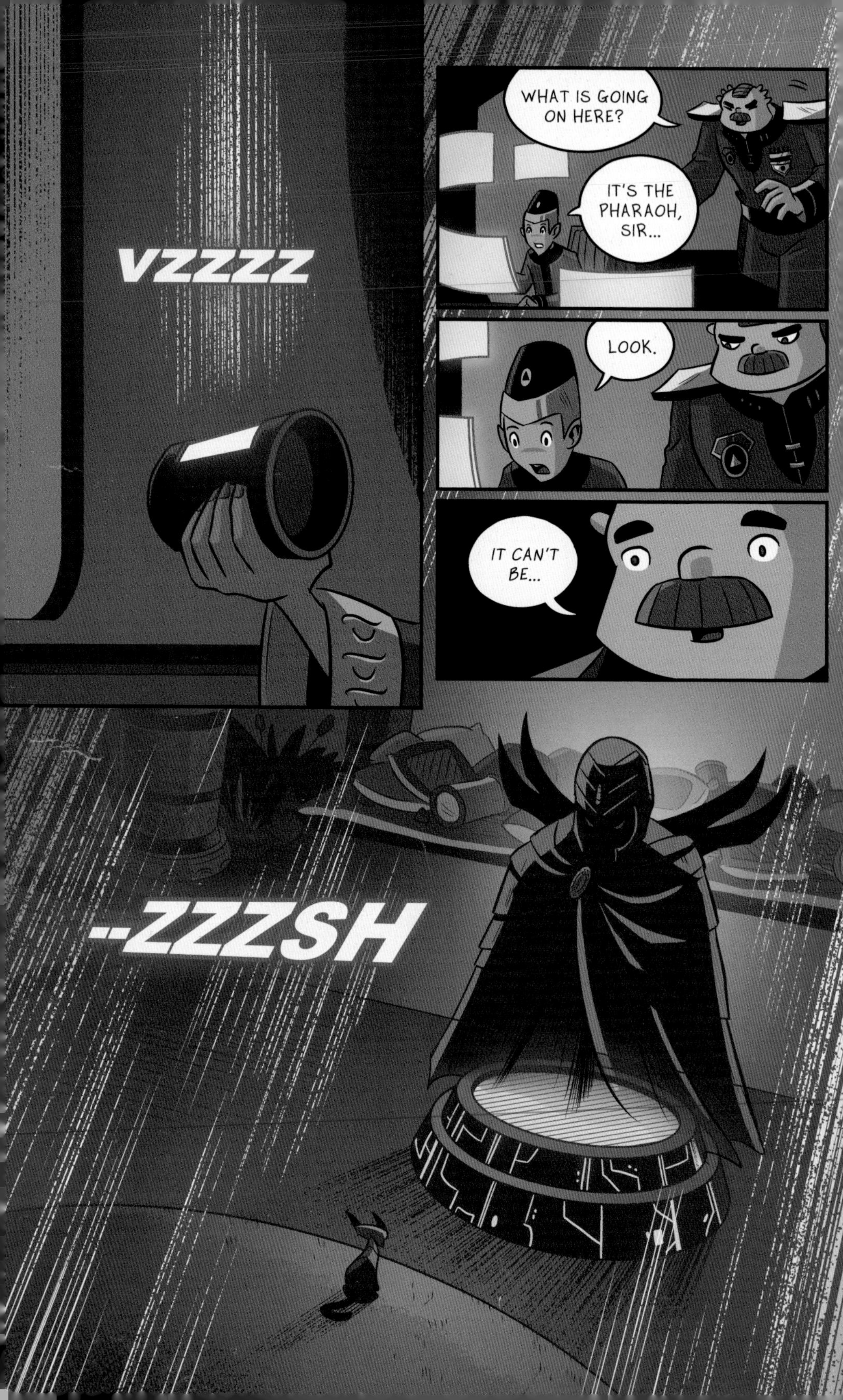
VZZZZ
WHAT IS GOING ON HERE?
IT'S THE PHARAOH, SIR...
LOOK.
IT CAN'T BE...
--ZZZSH

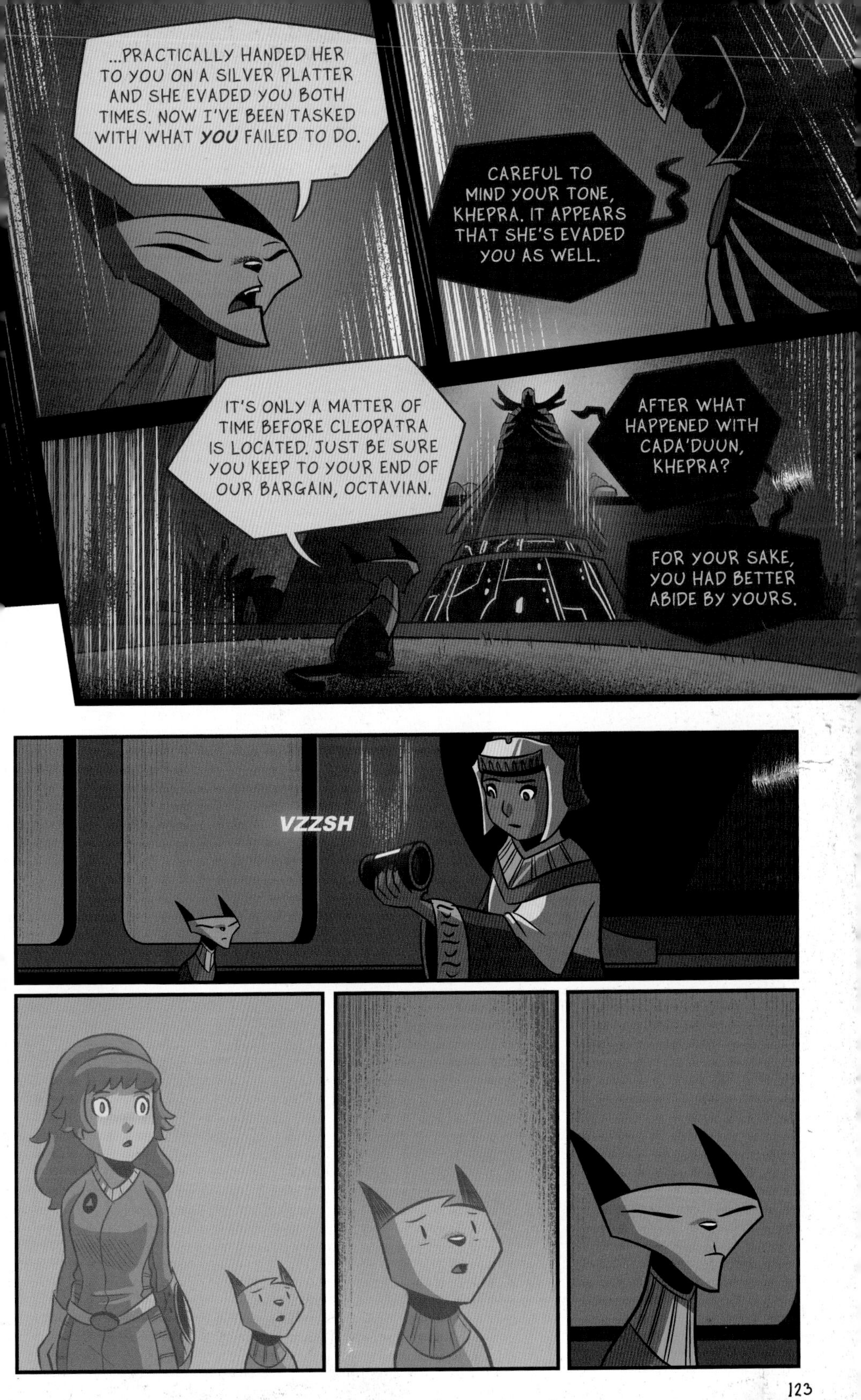
...PRACTICALLY HANDED HER TO YOU ON A SILVER PLATTER AND SHE EVADED YOU BOTH TIMES. NOW I'VE BEEN TASKED WITH WHAT *YOU* FAILED TO DO.
CAREFUL TO MIND YOUR TONE, KHEPRA. IT APPEARS THAT SHE'S EVADED YOU AS WELL.
IT'S ONLY A MATTER OF TIME BEFORE CLEOPATRA IS LOCATED. JUST BE SURE YOU KEEP TO YOUR END OF OUR BARGAIN, OCTAVIAN.
AFTER WHAT HAPPENED WITH CADA'DUUN, KHEPRA?
FOR YOUR SAKE, YOU HAD BETTER ABIDE BY YOURS.
VZZSH

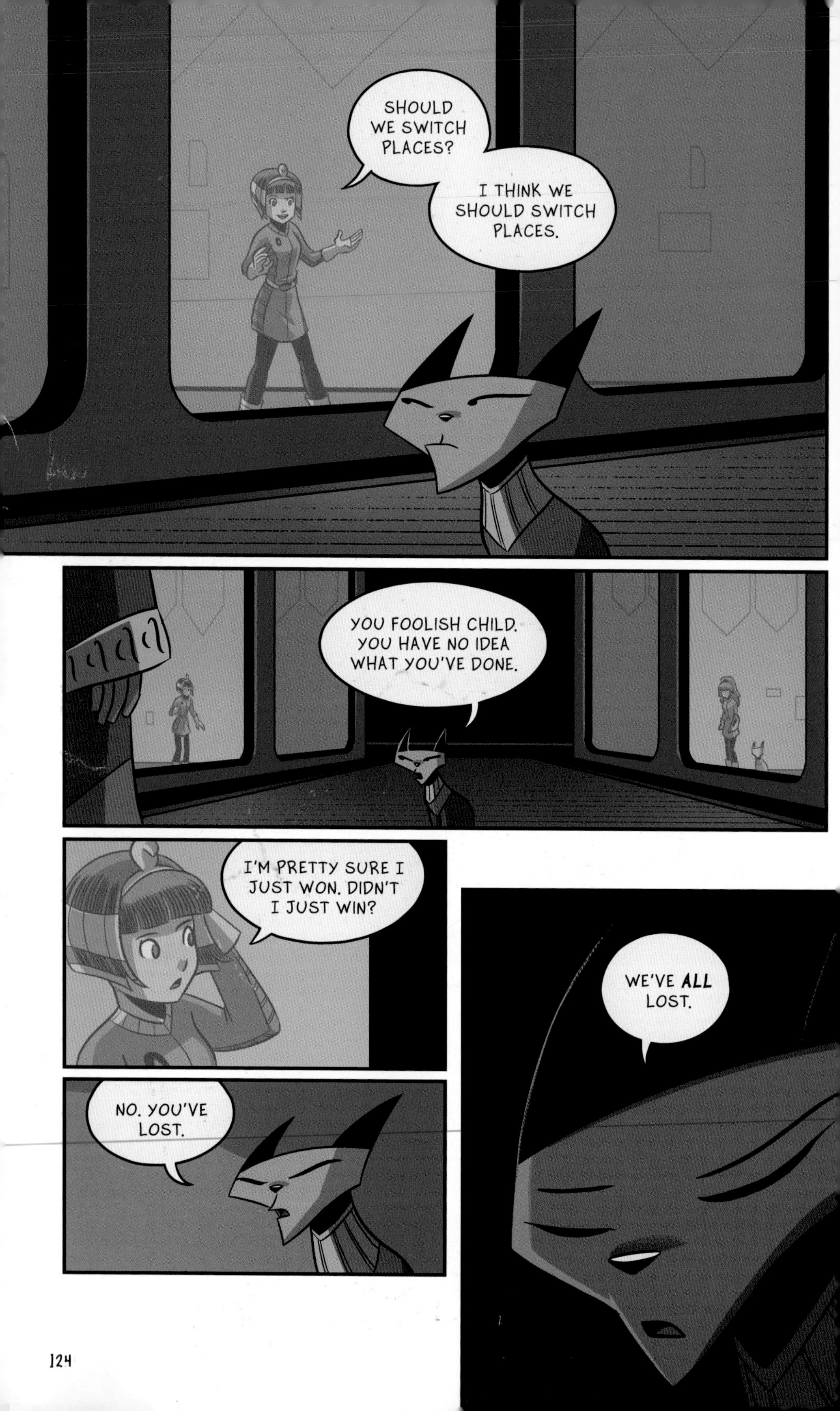
SHOULD WE SWITCH PLACES?
I THINK WE SHOULD SWITCH PLACES.
YOU FOOLISH CHILD. YOU HAVE NO IDEA WHAT YOU'VE DONE.
I'M PRETTY SURE I JUST WON. DIDN'T I JUST WIN?
NO. YOU'VE LOST.
WE'VE **ALL** LOST.

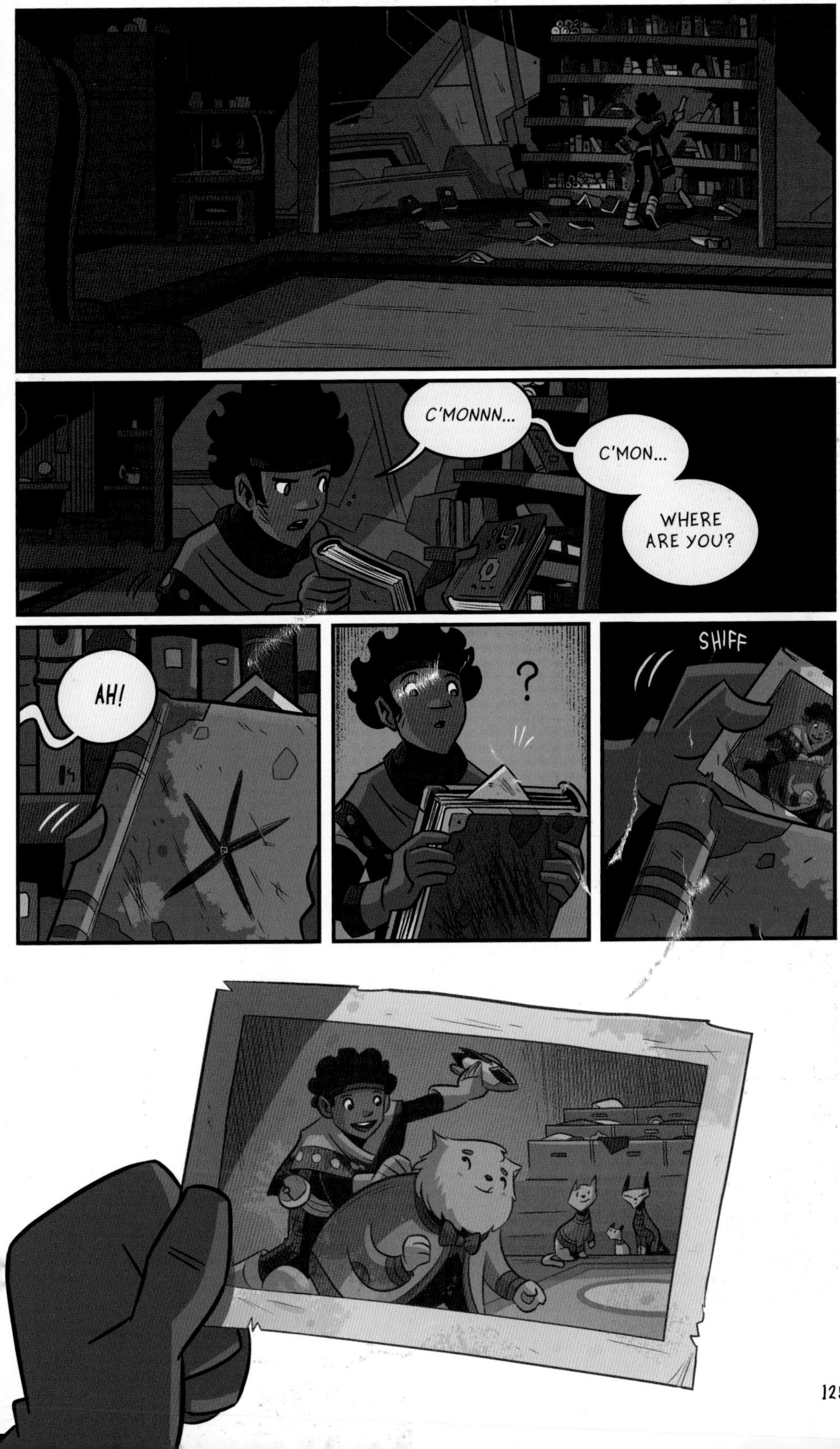
C'MONNN...
C'MON...
WHERE ARE YOU?
AH!
?
SHIFF

ALL THE KIDS ARE ON BOARD.

ANTONY!

SLAM

Shoff

LET'S GO.

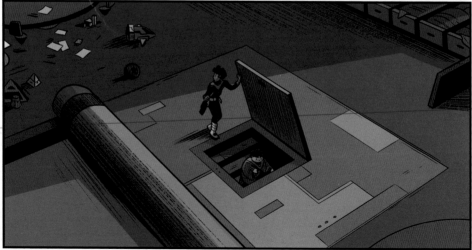

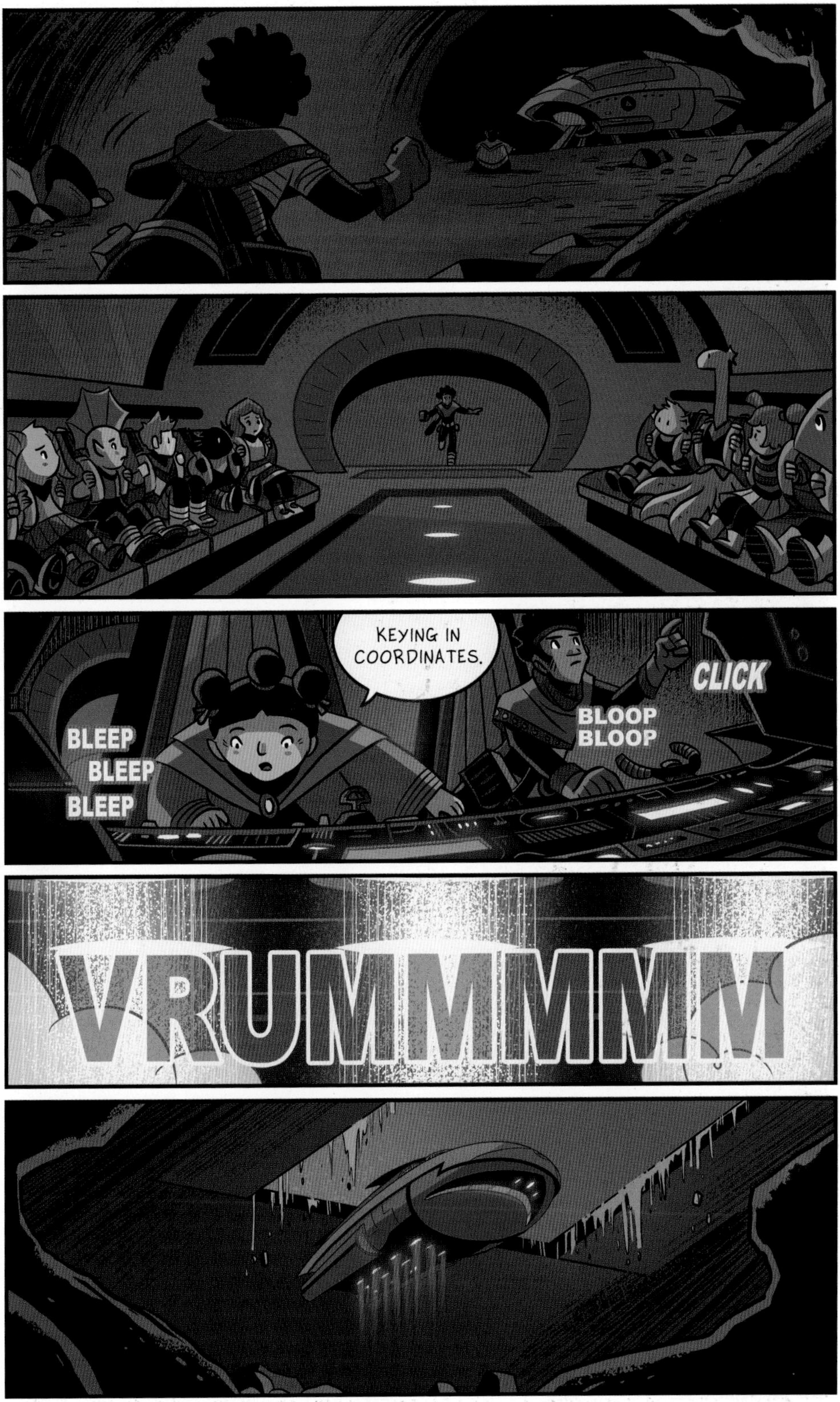

KEYING IN COORDINATES.
BLEEP
BLEEP
BLEEP
BLOOP
BLOOP
CLICK
VRUMMMMM

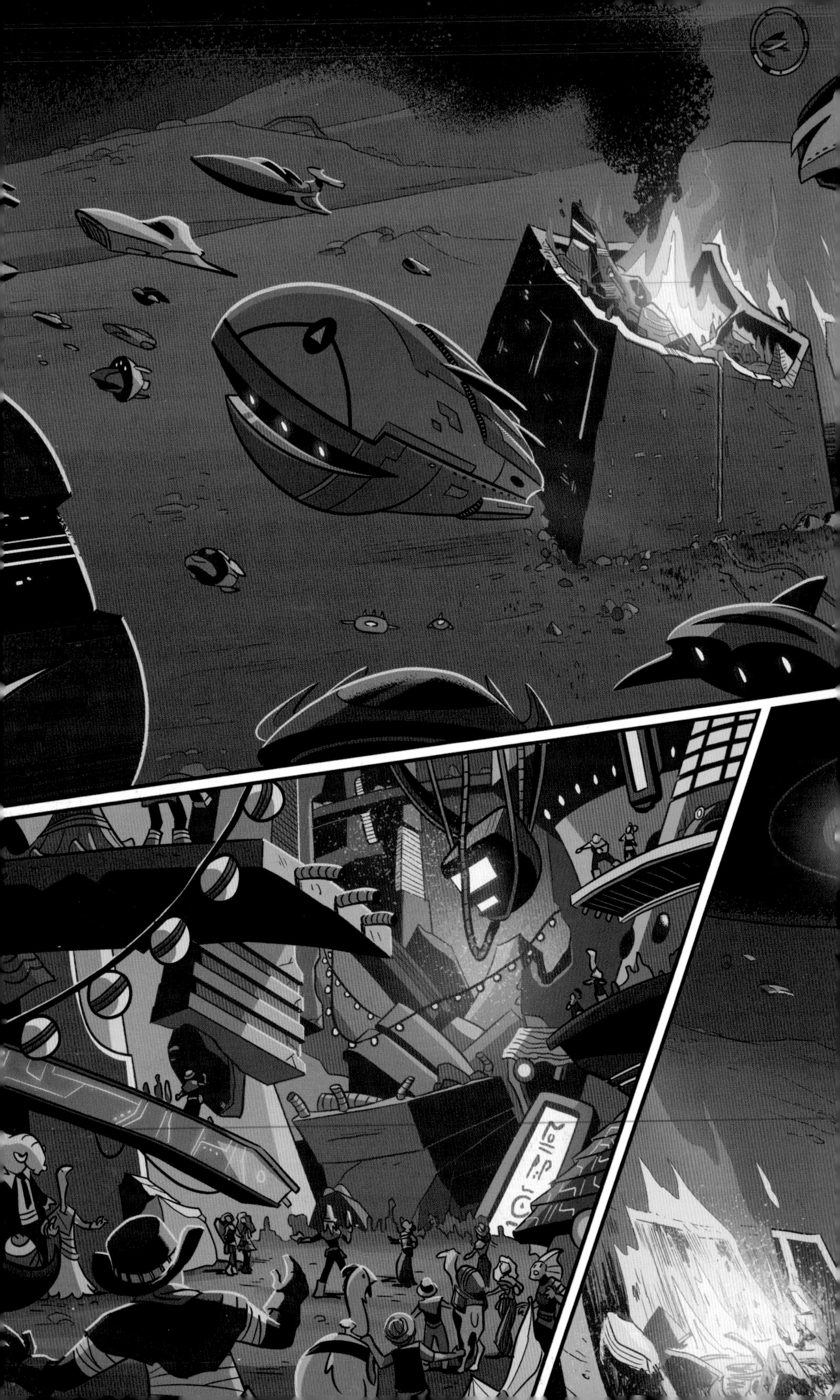

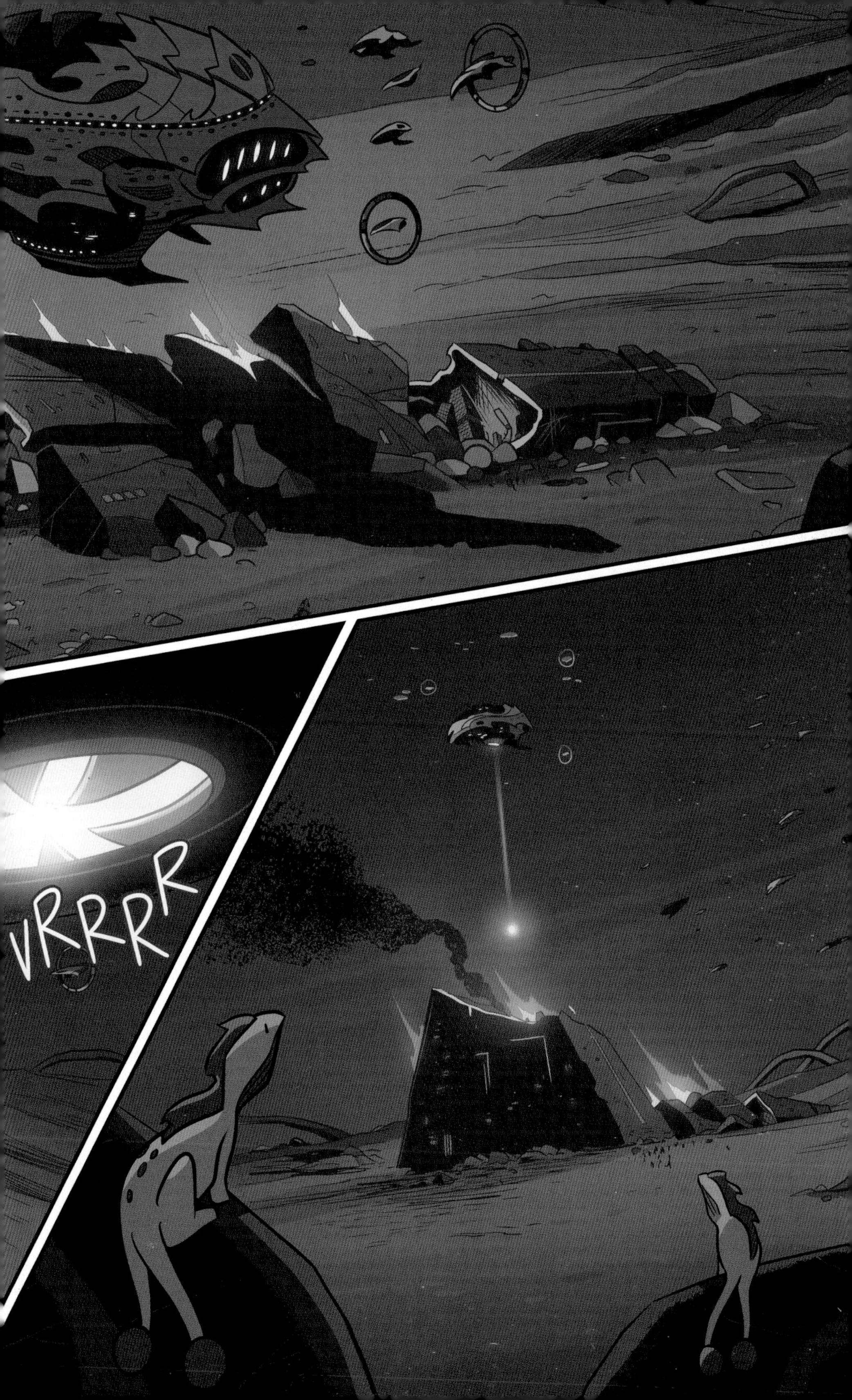
VRRRR

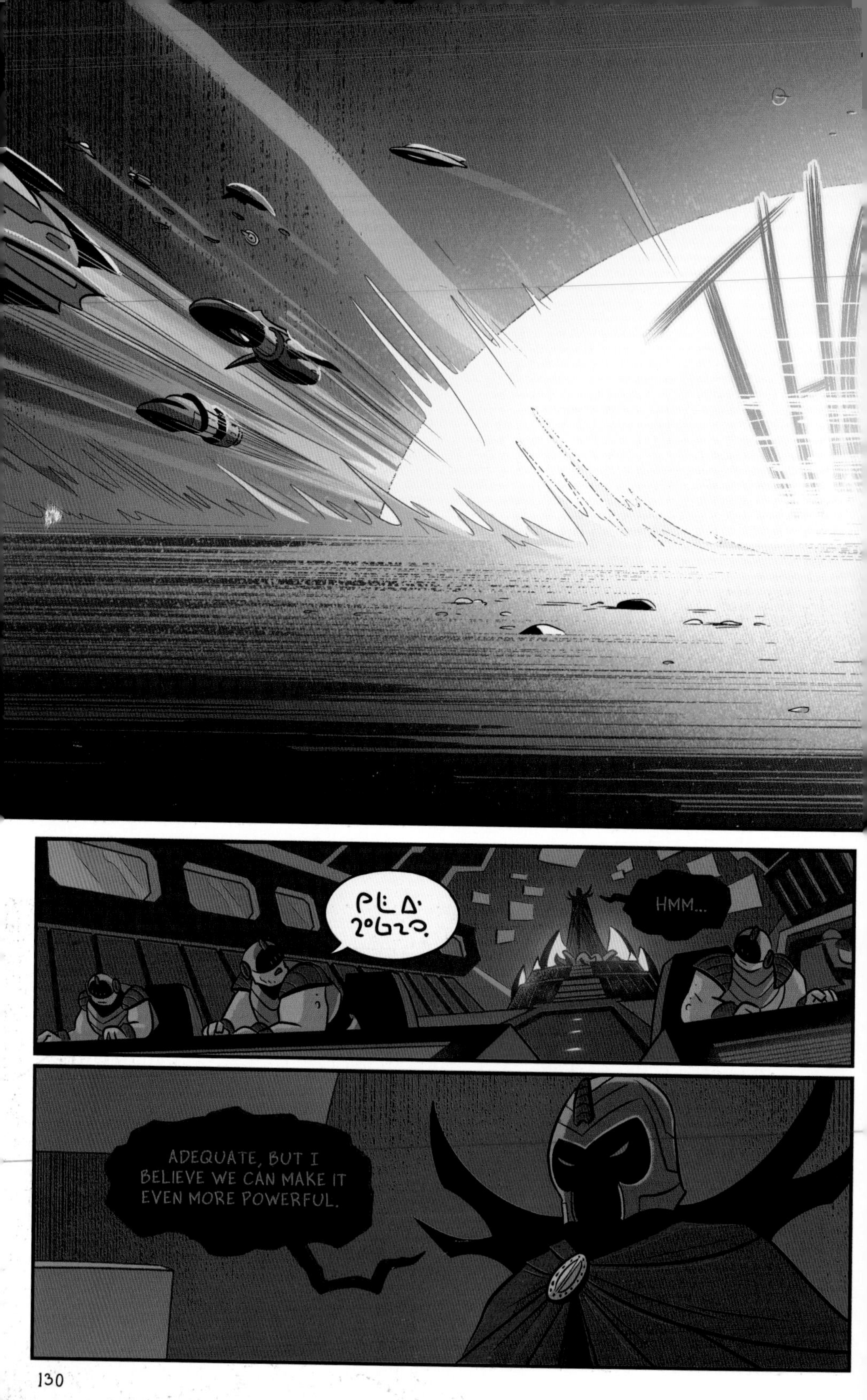
HMM...
ADEQUATE, BUT I BELIEVE WE CAN MAKE IT EVEN MORE POWERFUL.

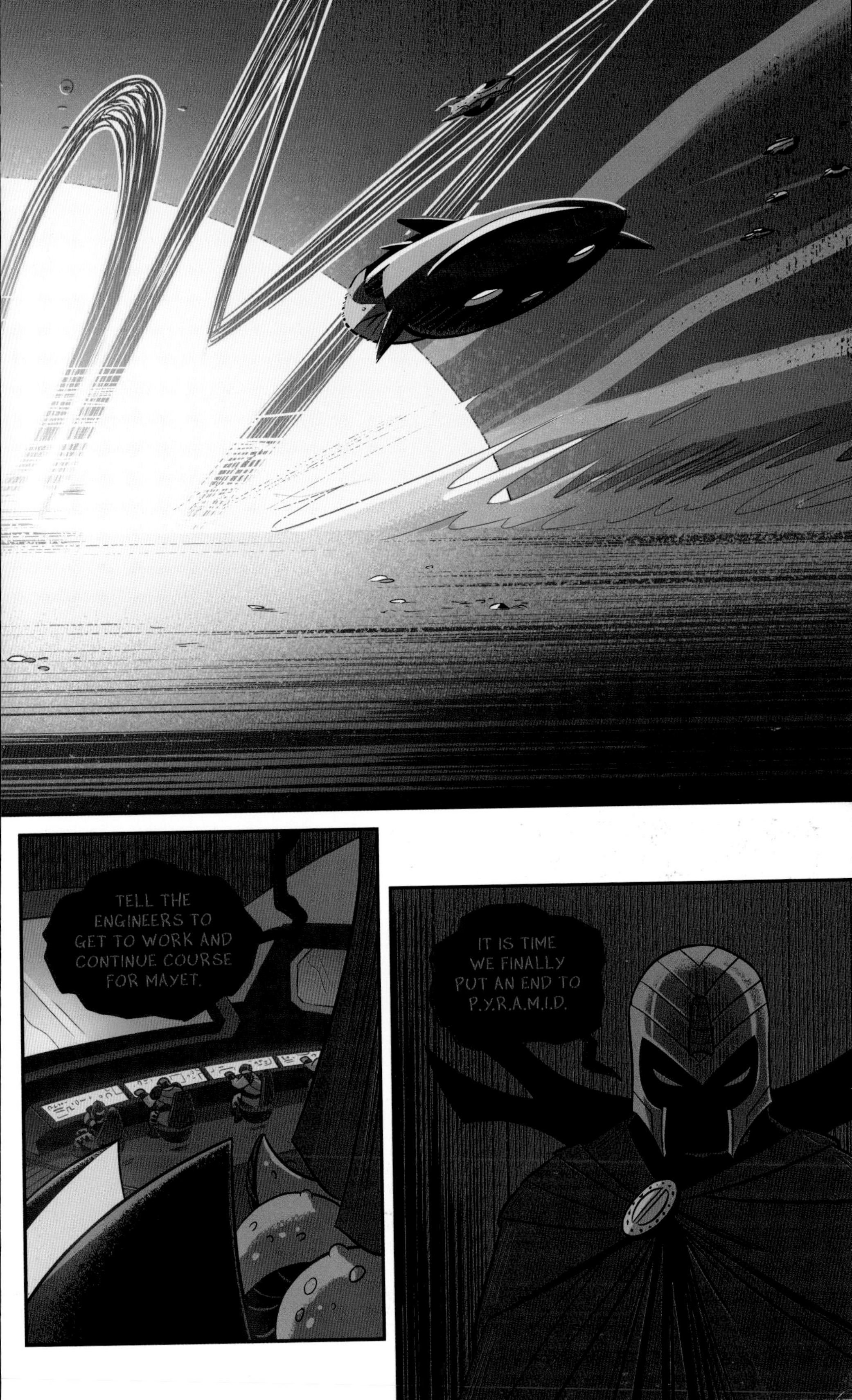
TELL THE ENGINEERS TO GET TO WORK AND CONTINUE COURSE FOR MAYET.
IT IS TIME WE FINALLY PUT AN END TO P.Y.R.A.M.I.D.

CHAPTER THREE

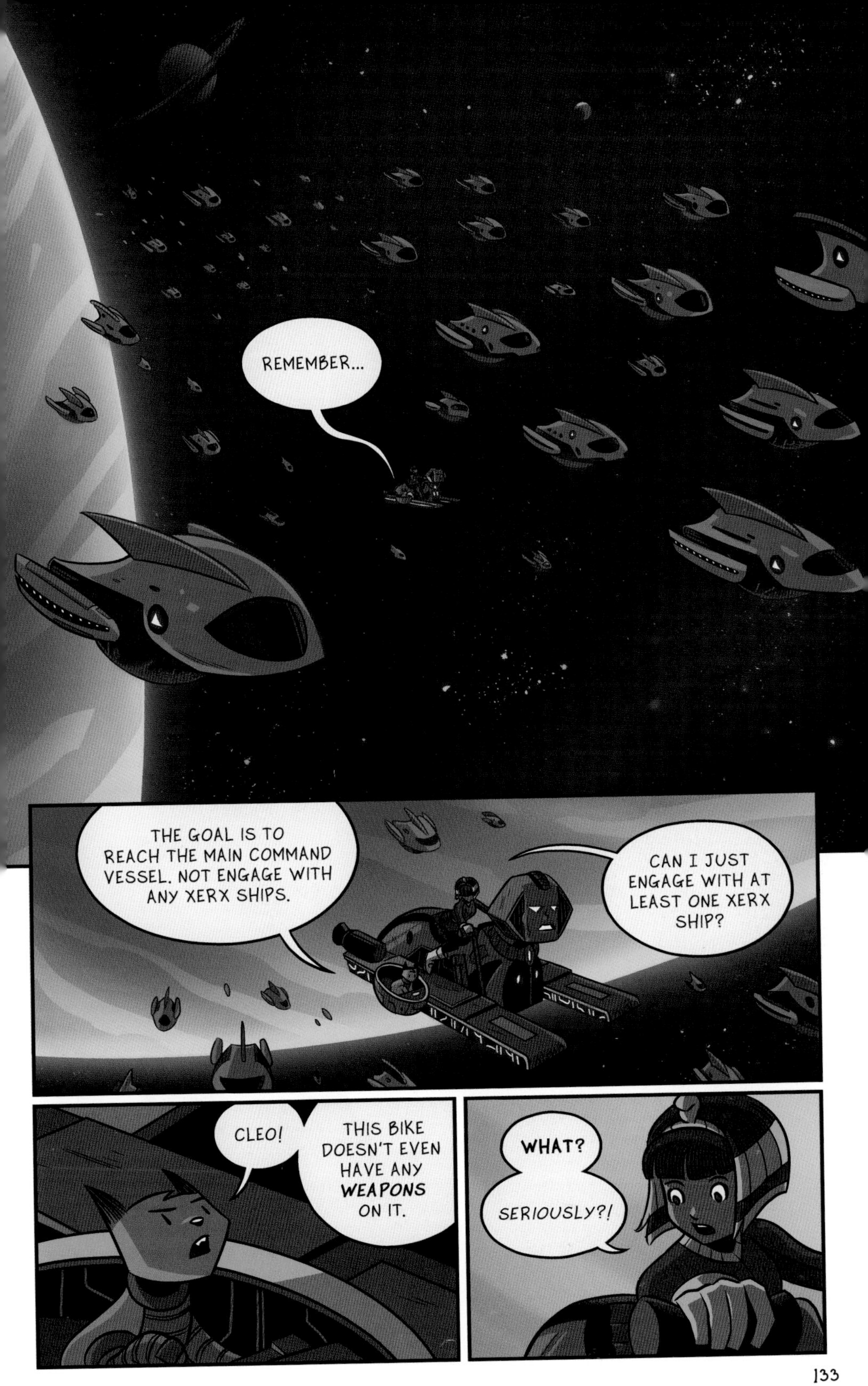
REMEMBER...
THE GOAL IS TO REACH THE MAIN COMMAND VESSEL. NOT ENGAGE WITH ANY XERX SHIPS.
CAN I JUST ENGAGE WITH AT LEAST ONE XERX SHIP?
CLEO!
THIS BIKE DOESN'T EVEN HAVE ANY **WEAPONS** ON IT.
WHAT?
SERIOUSLY?!

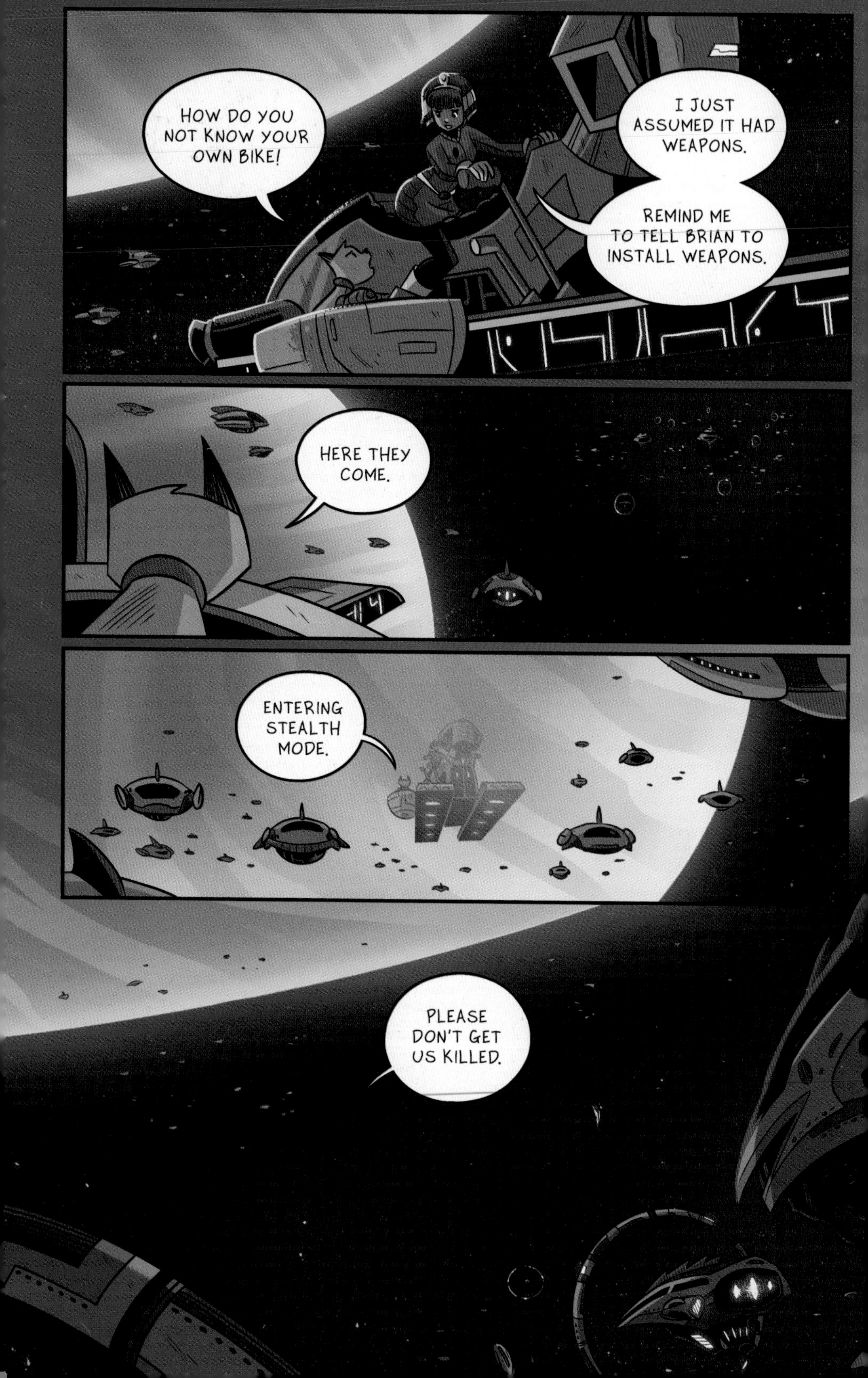
HOW DO YOU NOT KNOW YOUR OWN BIKE!
I JUST ASSUMED IT HAD WEAPONS.
REMIND ME TO TELL BRIAN TO INSTALL WEAPONS.
HERE THEY COME.
ENTERING STEALTH MODE.
PLEASE DON'T GET US KILLED.

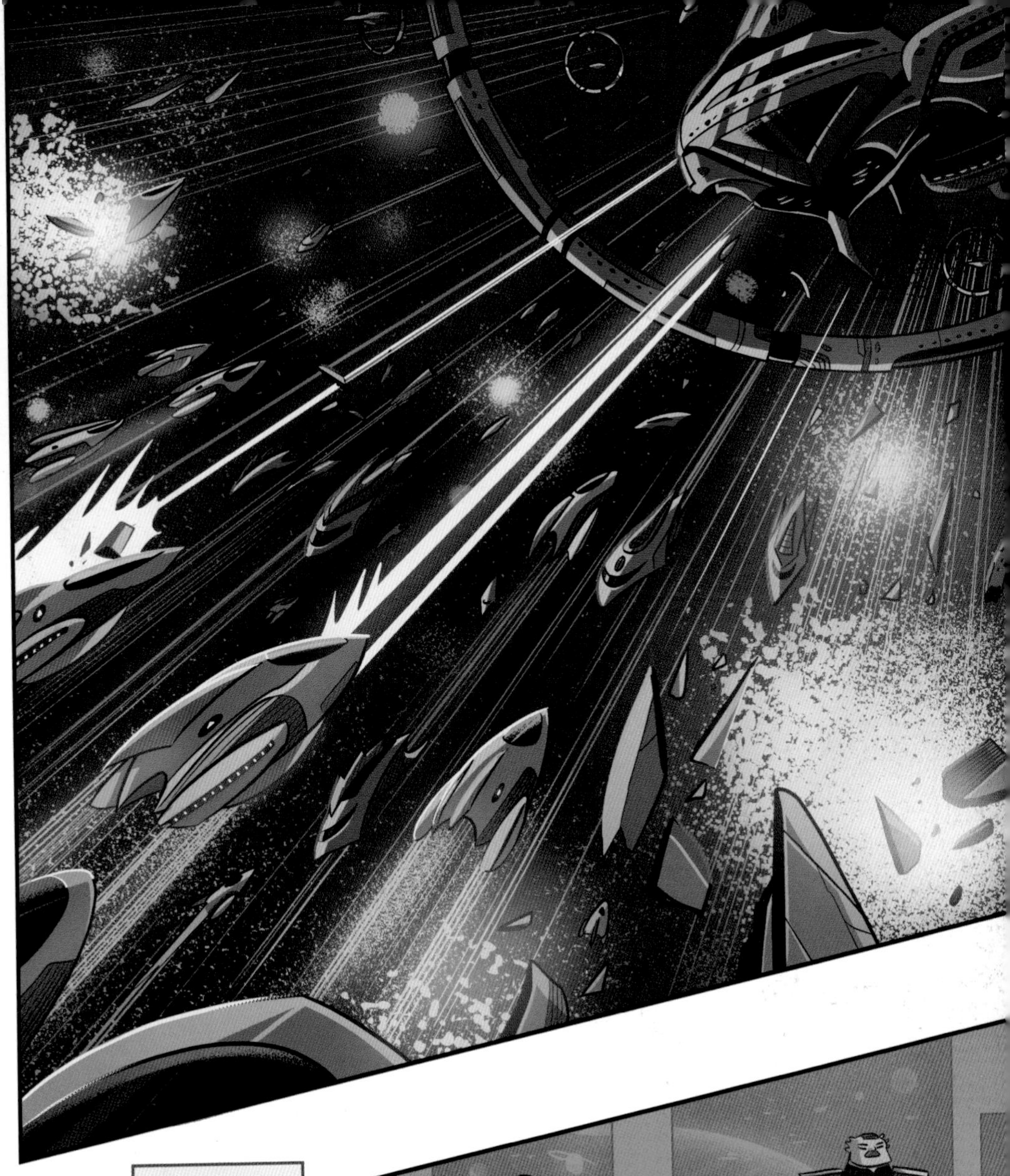

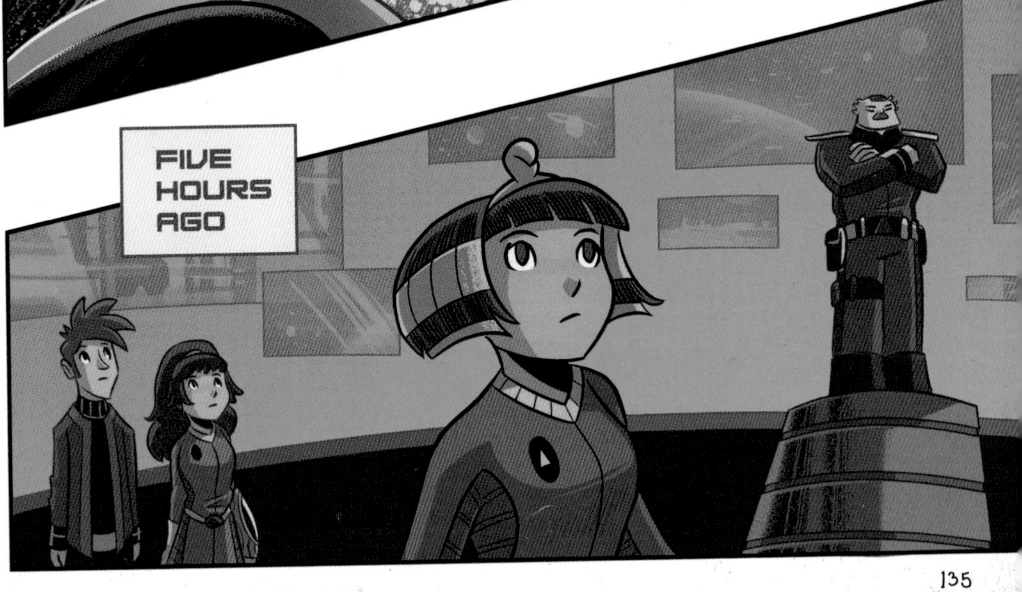
FIVE HOURS AGO

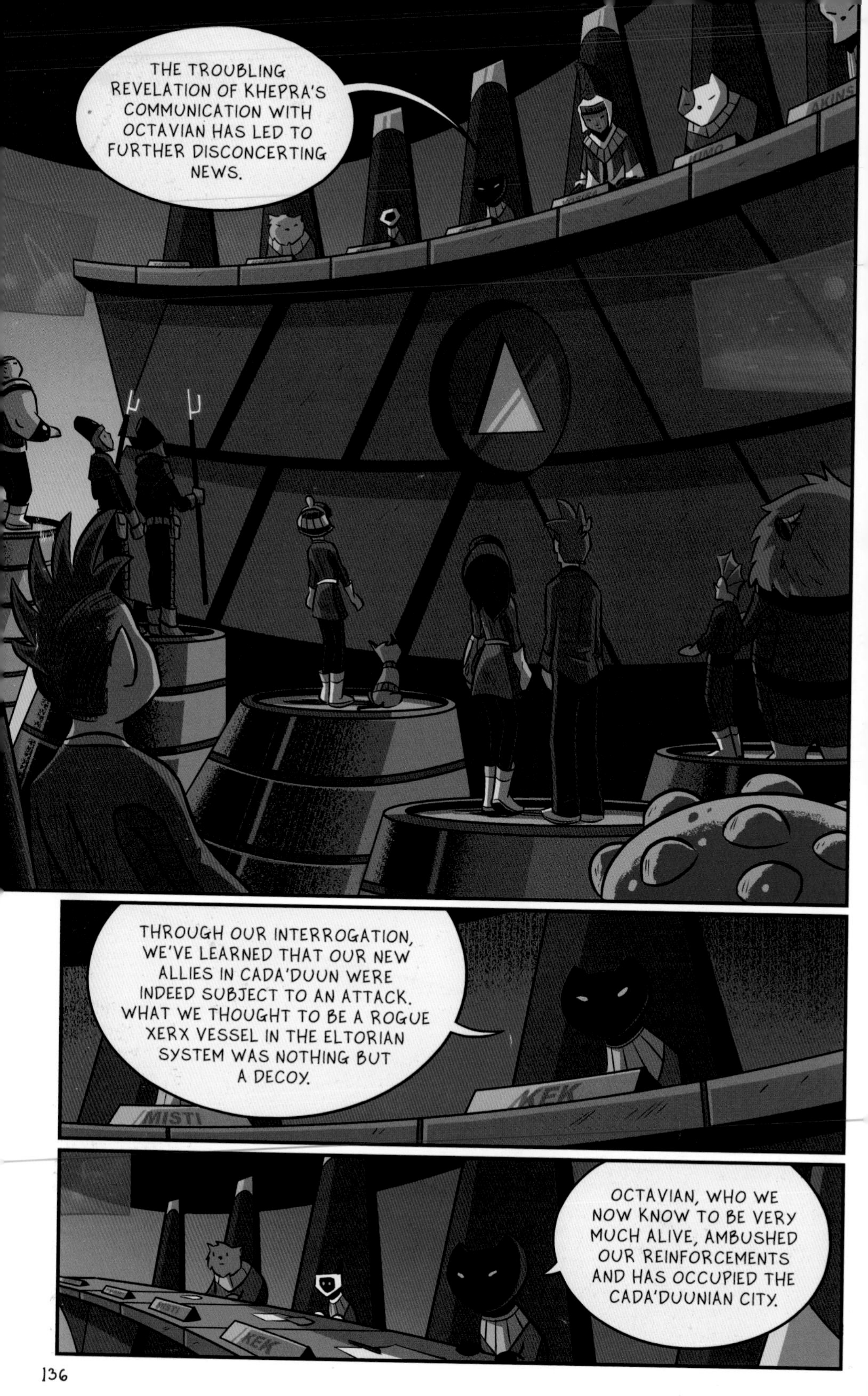
THE TROUBLING REVELATION OF KHEPRA'S COMMUNICATION WITH OCTAVIAN HAS LED TO FURTHER DISCONCERTING NEWS.
AKINS
THROUGH OUR INTERROGATION, WE'VE LEARNED THAT OUR NEW ALLIES IN CADA'DUUN WERE INDEED SUBJECT TO AN ATTACK. WHAT WE THOUGHT TO BE A ROGUE XERX VESSEL IN THE ELTORIAN SYSTEM WAS NOTHING BUT A DECOY.
MISTI
KEK
OCTAVIAN, WHO WE NOW KNOW TO BE VERY MUCH ALIVE, AMBUSHED OUR REINFORCEMENTS AND HAS OCCUPIED THE CADA'DUUNIAN CITY.
KEK

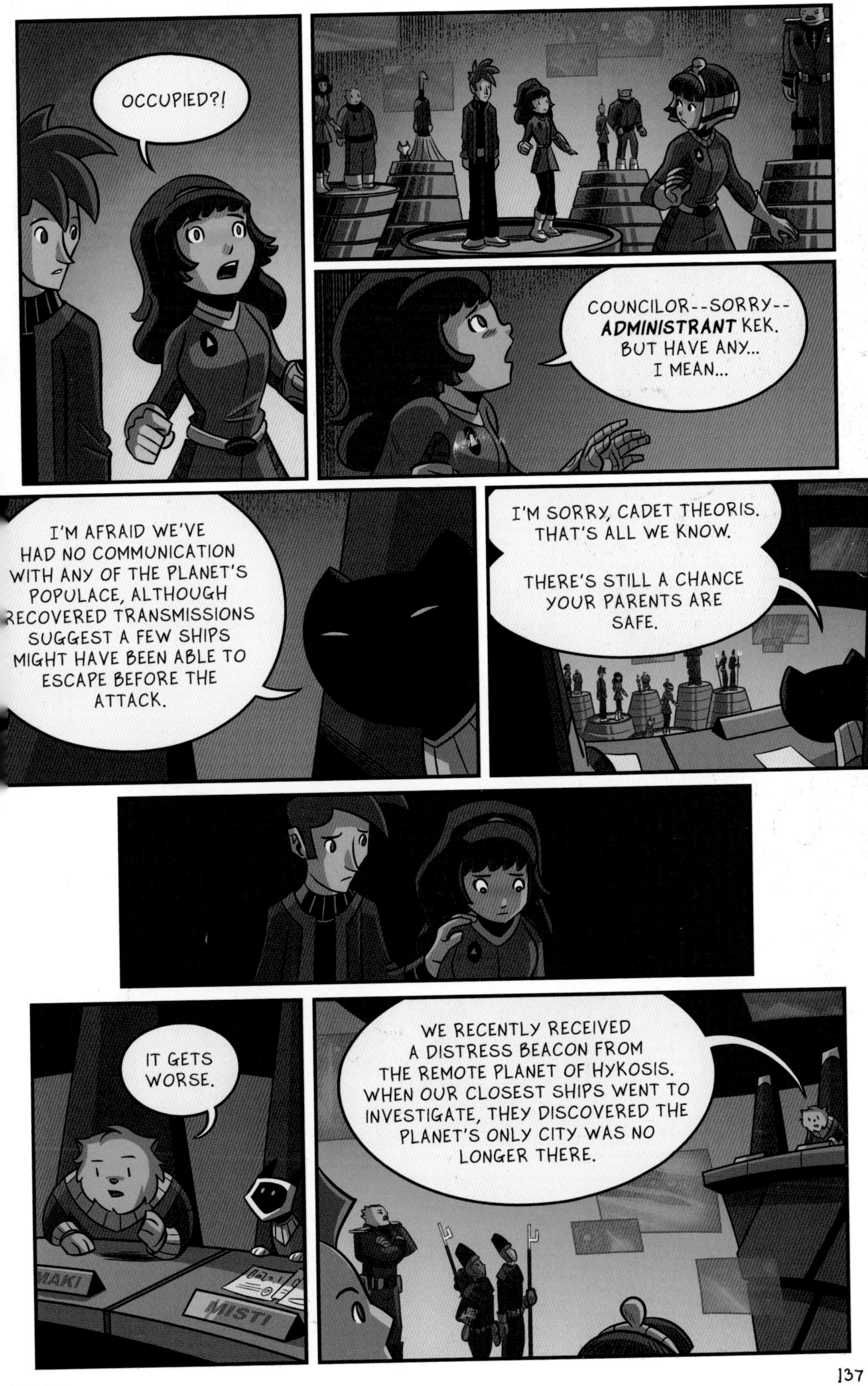
OCCUPIED?!
COUNCILOR--SORRY--**ADMINISTRANT** KEK. BUT HAVE ANY... I MEAN...
I'M AFRAID WE'VE HAD NO COMMUNICATION WITH ANY OF THE PLANET'S POPULACE, ALTHOUGH RECOVERED TRANSMISSIONS SUGGEST A FEW SHIPS MIGHT HAVE BEEN ABLE TO ESCAPE BEFORE THE ATTACK.
I'M SORRY, CADET THEORIS. THAT'S ALL WE KNOW.
THERE'S STILL A CHANCE YOUR PARENTS ARE SAFE.
IT GETS WORSE.
MAKI
MISTI
WE RECENTLY RECEIVED A DISTRESS BEACON FROM THE REMOTE PLANET OF HYKOSIS. WHEN OUR CLOSEST SHIPS WENT TO INVESTIGATE, THEY DISCOVERED THE PLANET'S ONLY CITY WAS NO LONGER THERE.

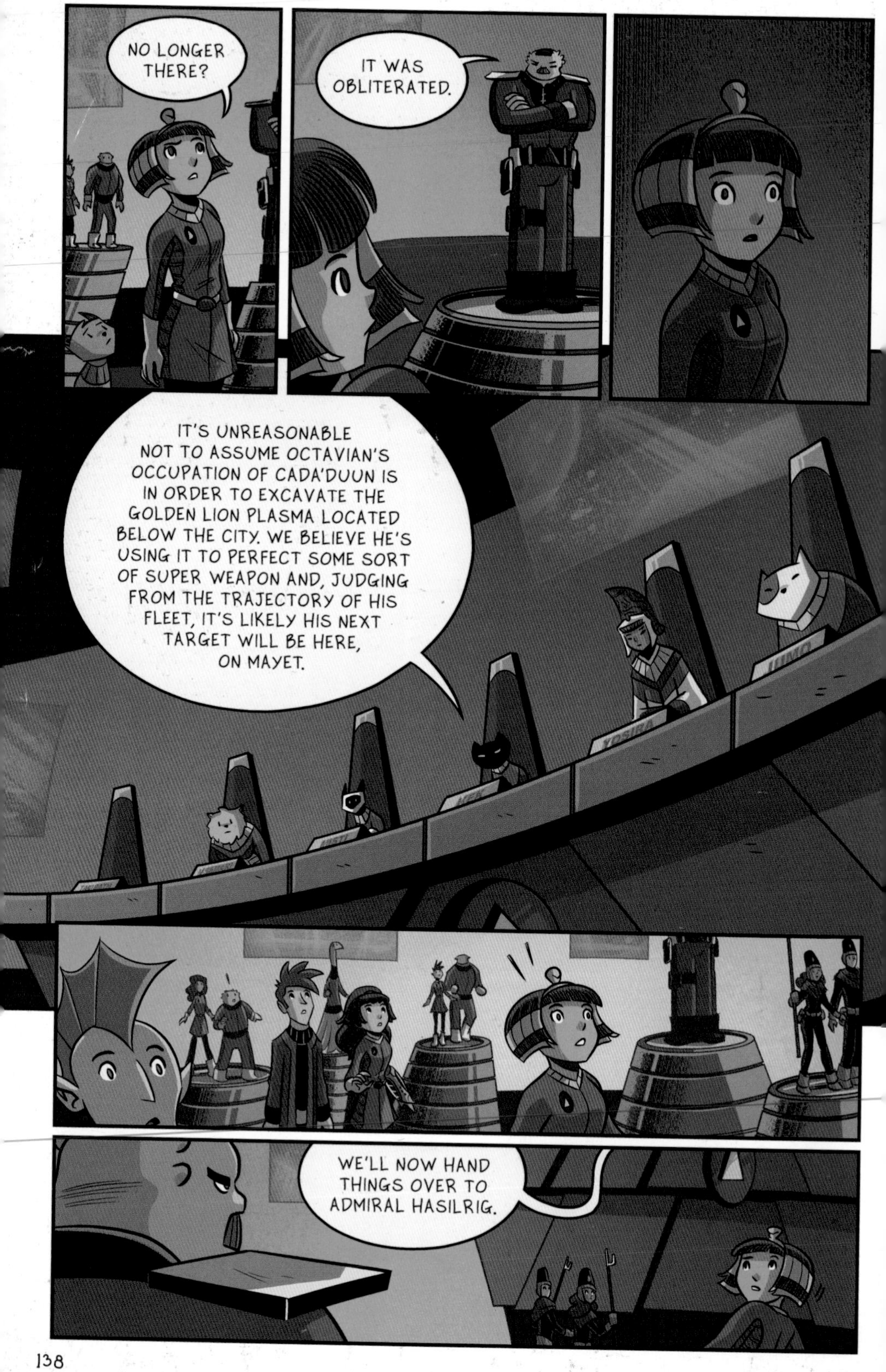
NO LONGER THERE?
IT WAS OBLITERATED.
IT'S UNREASONABLE NOT TO ASSUME OCTAVIAN'S OCCUPATION OF CADA'DUUN IS IN ORDER TO EXCAVATE THE GOLDEN LION PLASMA LOCATED BELOW THE CITY. WE BELIEVE HE'S USING IT TO PERFECT SOME SORT OF SUPER WEAPON AND, JUDGING FROM THE TRAJECTORY OF HIS FLEET, IT'S LIKELY HIS NEXT TARGET WILL BE HERE, ON MAYET.
WE'LL NOW HAND THINGS OVER TO ADMIRAL HASILRIG.

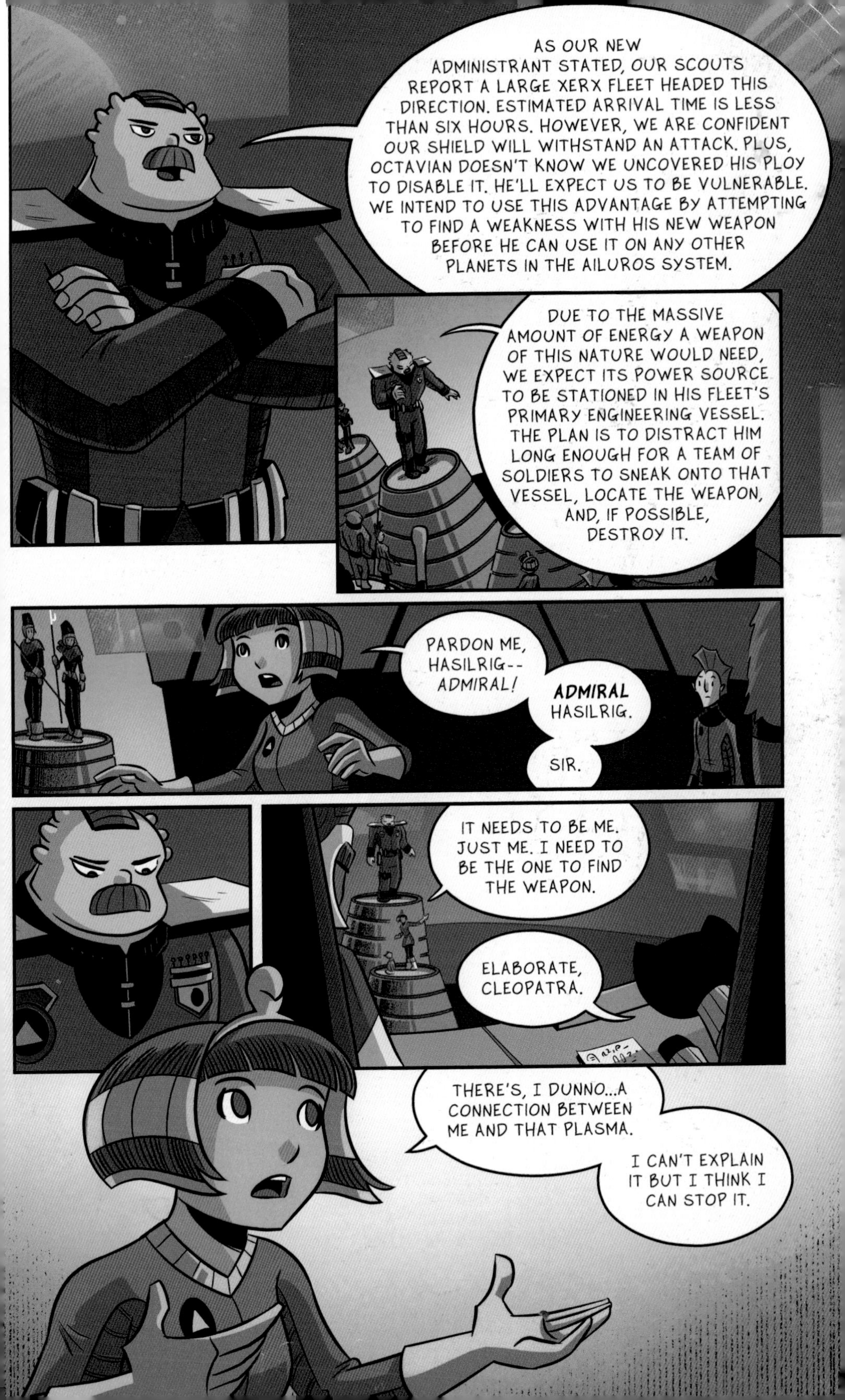
AS OUR NEW ADMINISTRANT STATED, OUR SCOUTS REPORT A LARGE XERX FLEET HEADED THIS DIRECTION. ESTIMATED ARRIVAL TIME IS LESS THAN SIX HOURS. HOWEVER, WE ARE CONFIDENT OUR SHIELD WILL WITHSTAND AN ATTACK. PLUS, OCTAVIAN DOESN'T KNOW WE UNCOVERED HIS PLOY TO DISABLE IT. HE'LL EXPECT US TO BE VULNERABLE. WE INTEND TO USE THIS ADVANTAGE BY ATTEMPTING TO FIND A WEAKNESS WITH HIS NEW WEAPON BEFORE HE CAN USE IT ON ANY OTHER PLANETS IN THE AILUROS SYSTEM.
DUE TO THE MASSIVE AMOUNT OF ENERGY A WEAPON OF THIS NATURE WOULD NEED, WE EXPECT ITS POWER SOURCE TO BE STATIONED IN HIS FLEET'S PRIMARY ENGINEERING VESSEL. THE PLAN IS TO DISTRACT HIM LONG ENOUGH FOR A TEAM OF SOLDIERS TO SNEAK ONTO THAT VESSEL, LOCATE THE WEAPON, AND, IF POSSIBLE, DESTROY IT.
PARDON ME, HASILRIG-- ADMIRAL!
ADMIRAL HASILRIG.
SIR.
IT NEEDS TO BE ME. JUST ME. I NEED TO BE THE ONE TO FIND THE WEAPON.
ELABORATE, CLEOPATRA.
THERE'S, I DUNNO...A CONNECTION BETWEEN ME AND THAT PLASMA.
I CAN'T EXPLAIN IT BUT I THINK I CAN STOP IT.

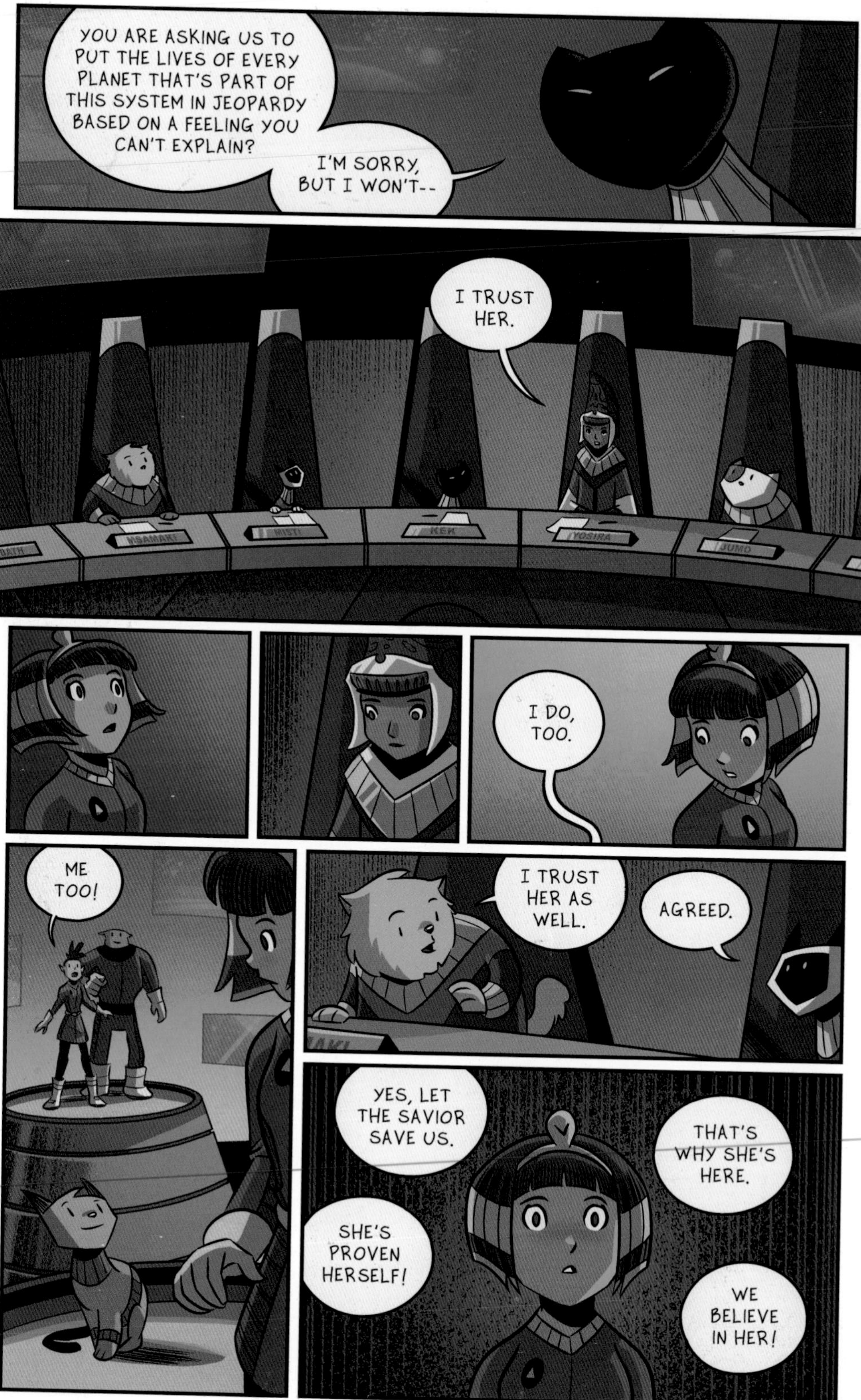
YOU ARE ASKING US TO PUT THE LIVES OF EVERY PLANET THAT'S PART OF THIS SYSTEM IN JEOPARDY BASED ON A FEELING YOU CAN'T EXPLAIN?
I'M SORRY, BUT I WON'T--
I TRUST HER.
I DO, TOO.
ME TOO!
I TRUST HER AS WELL.
AGREED.
YES, LET THE SAVIOR SAVE US.
THAT'S WHY SHE'S HERE.
SHE'S PROVEN HERSELF!
WE BELIEVE IN HER!

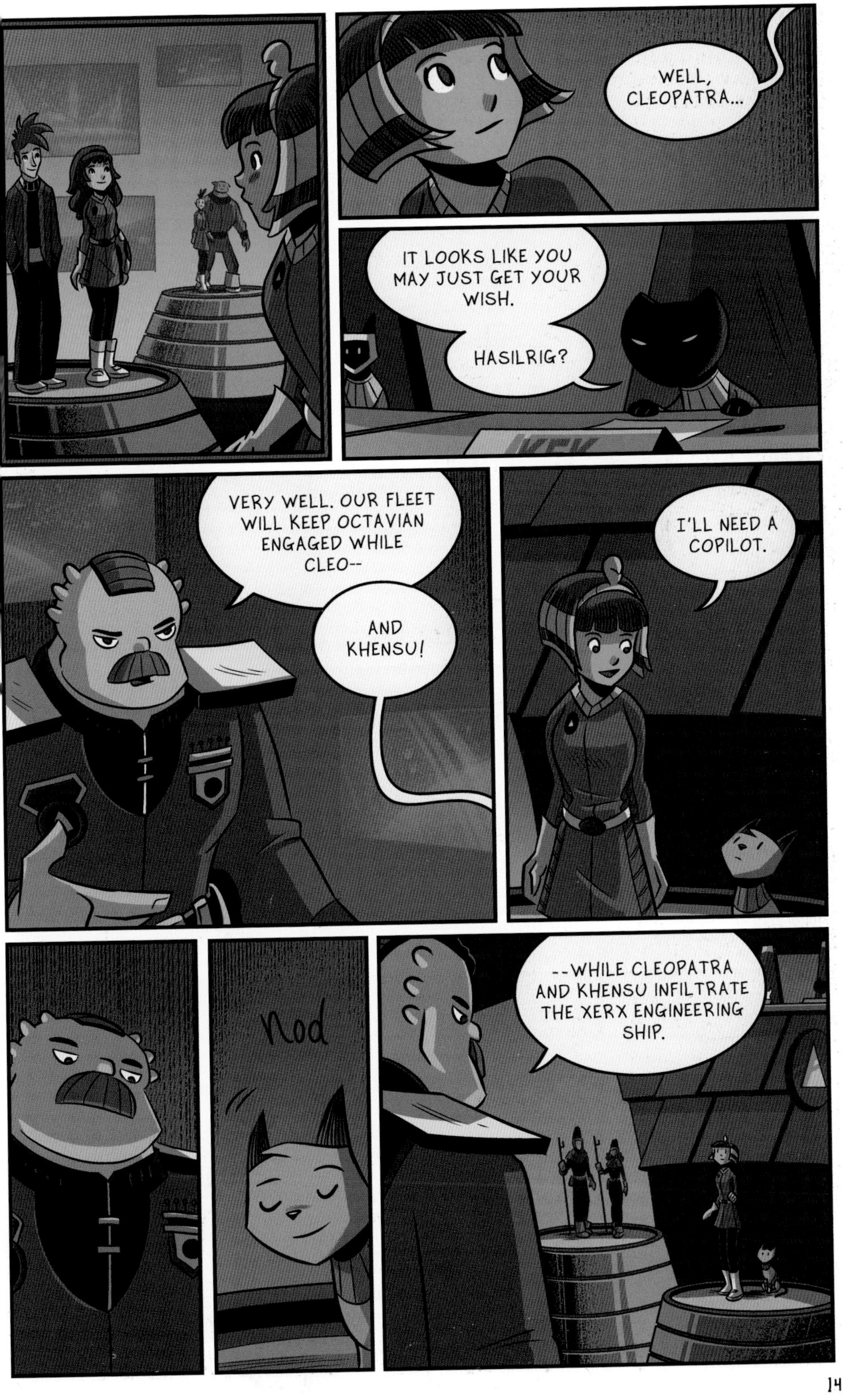
WELL,
CLEOPATRA...
IT LOOKS LIKE YOU MAY JUST GET YOUR WISH.
HASILRIG?
VERY WELL. OUR FLEET WILL KEEP OCTAVIAN ENGAGED WHILE CLEO--
AND KHENSU!
I'LL NEED A COPILOT.
nod
--WHILE CLEOPATRA AND KHENSU INFILTRATE THE XERX ENGINEERING SHIP.

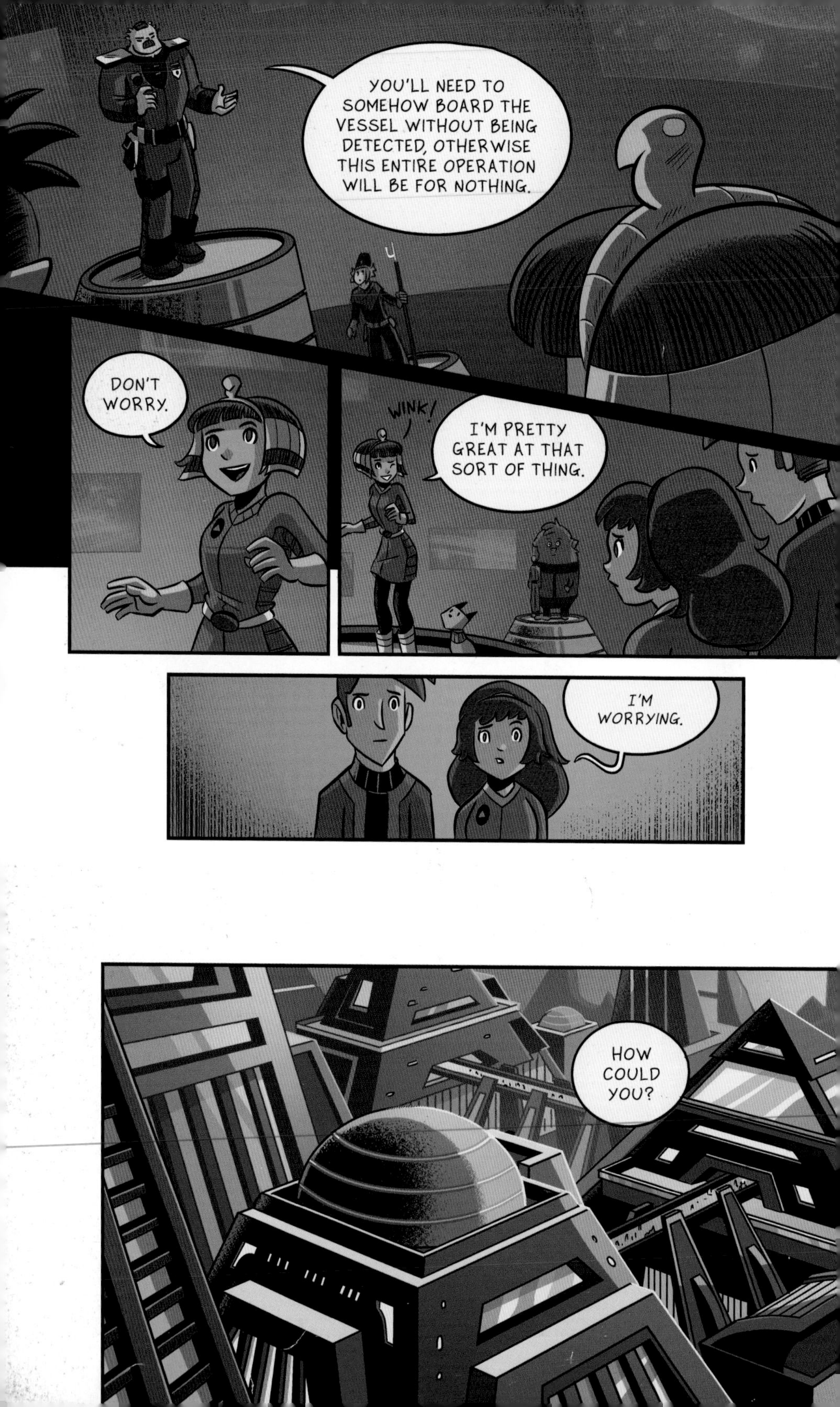
YOU'LL NEED TO SOMEHOW BOARD THE VESSEL WITHOUT BEING DETECTED, OTHERWISE THIS ENTIRE OPERATION WILL BE FOR NOTHING.
DON'T WORRY.
WINK!
I'M PRETTY GREAT AT THAT SORT OF THING.
I'M WORRYING.
HOW COULD YOU?

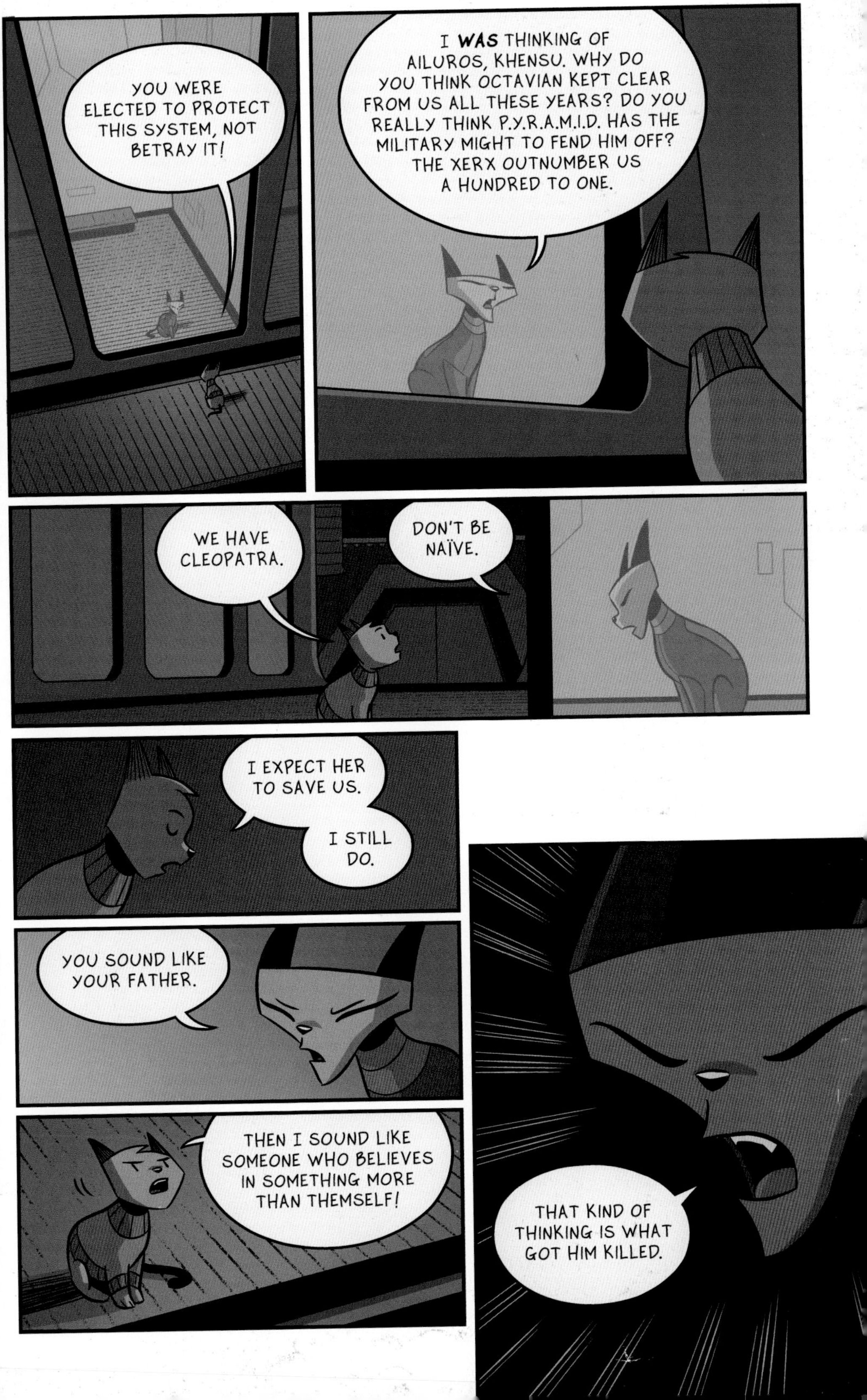
YOU WERE ELECTED TO PROTECT THIS SYSTEM, NOT BETRAY IT!
I **WAS** THINKING OF AILUROS, KHENSU. WHY DO YOU THINK OCTAVIAN KEPT CLEAR FROM US ALL THESE YEARS? DO YOU REALLY THINK P.Y.R.A.M.I.D. HAS THE MILITARY MIGHT TO FEND HIM OFF? THE XERX OUTNUMBER US A HUNDRED TO ONE.
WE HAVE CLEOPATRA.
DON'T BE NAÏVE.
I EXPECT HER TO SAVE US.
I STILL DO.
YOU SOUND LIKE YOUR FATHER.
THEN I SOUND LIKE SOMEONE WHO BELIEVES IN SOMETHING MORE THAN THEMSELF!
THAT KIND OF THINKING IS WHAT GOT HIM KILLED.

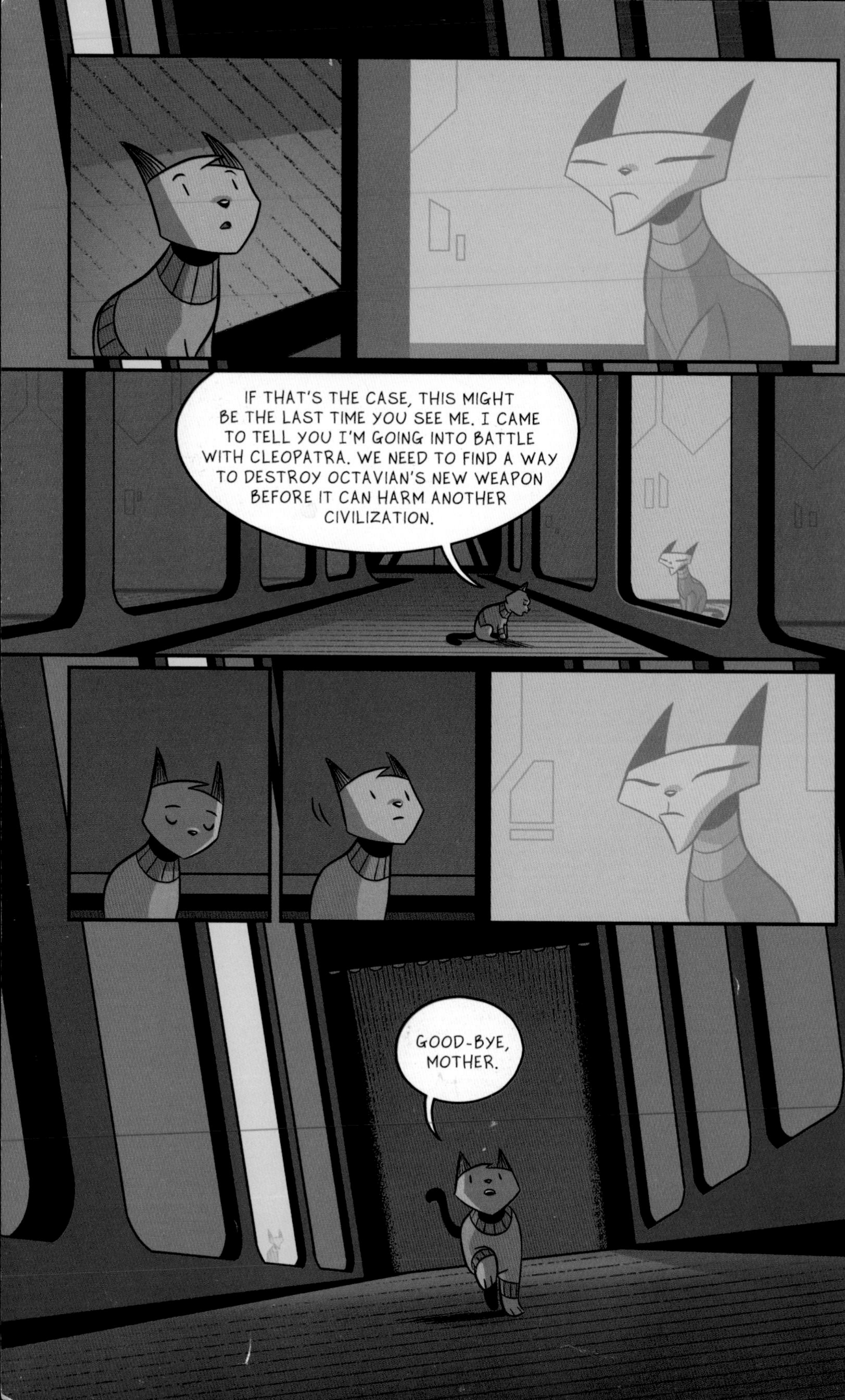
IF THAT'S THE CASE, THIS MIGHT BE THE LAST TIME YOU SEE ME. I CAME TO TELL YOU I'M GOING INTO BATTLE WITH CLEOPATRA. WE NEED TO FIND A WAY TO DESTROY OCTAVIAN'S NEW WEAPON BEFORE IT CAN HARM ANOTHER CIVILIZATION.
GOOD-BYE, MOTHER.

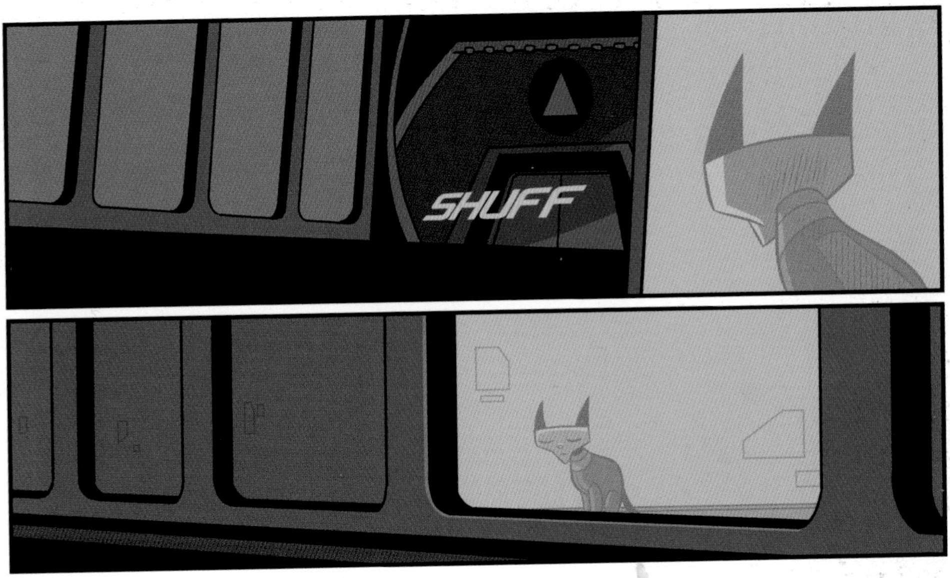
SHUFF

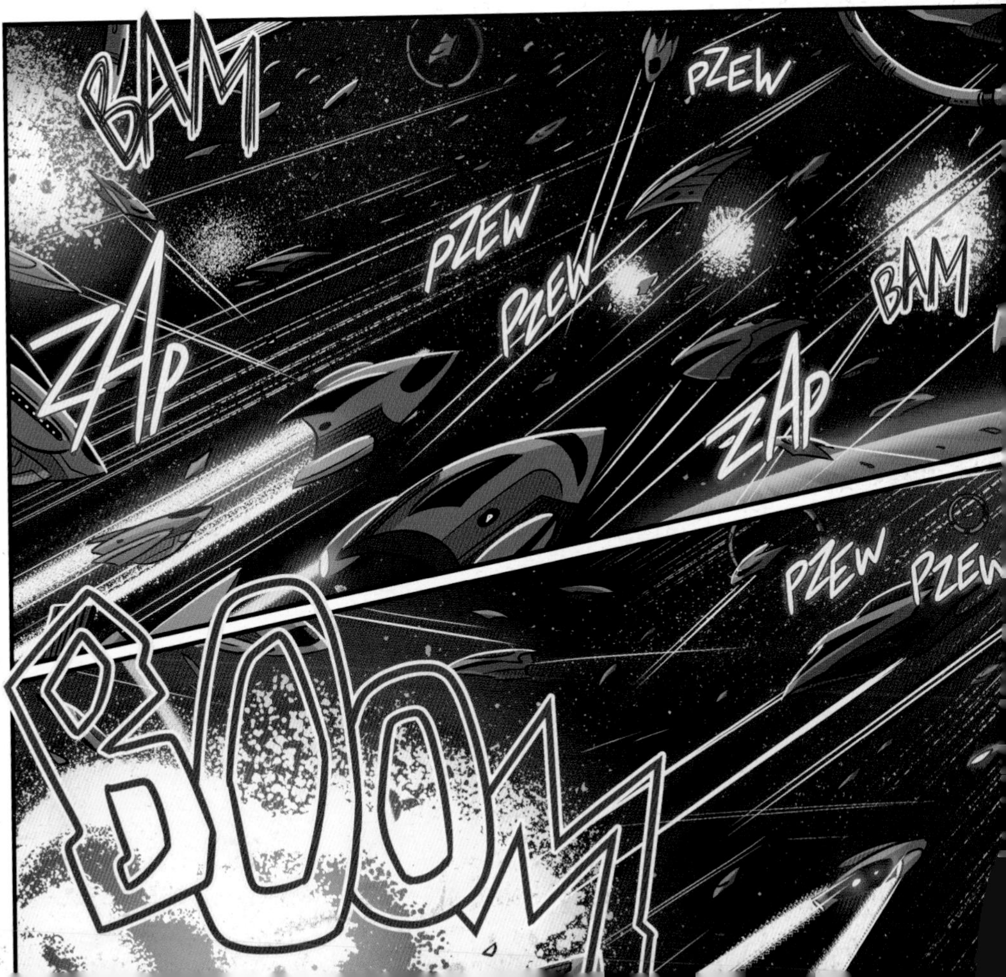
BAM
PZEW
PZEW
PZEW
ZAP
BAM
ZAP
PZEW
PZEW
BOOM

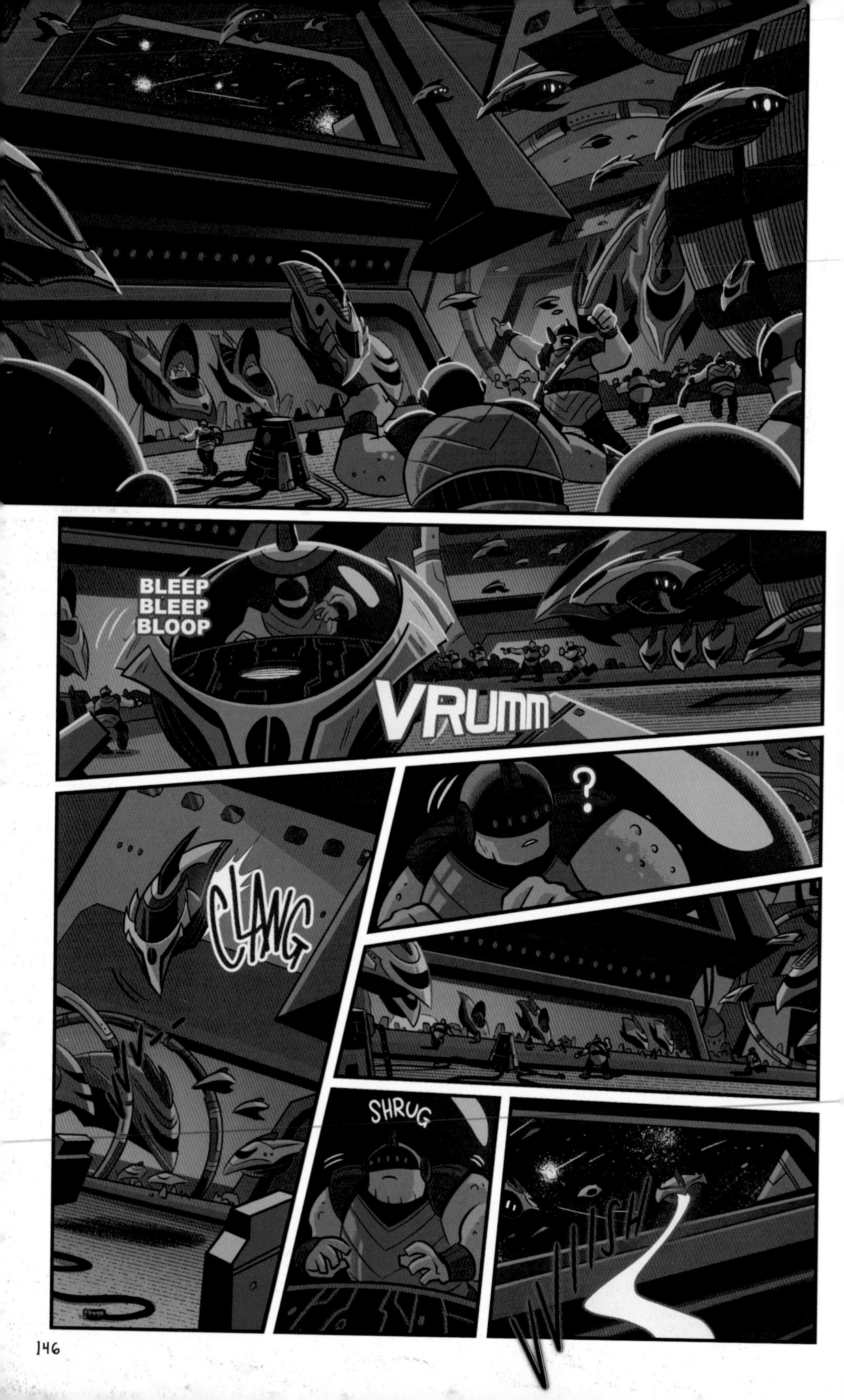
BLEEP
BLEEP
BLOOP
VRUMM
?
CLANG
SHRUG
WHISH

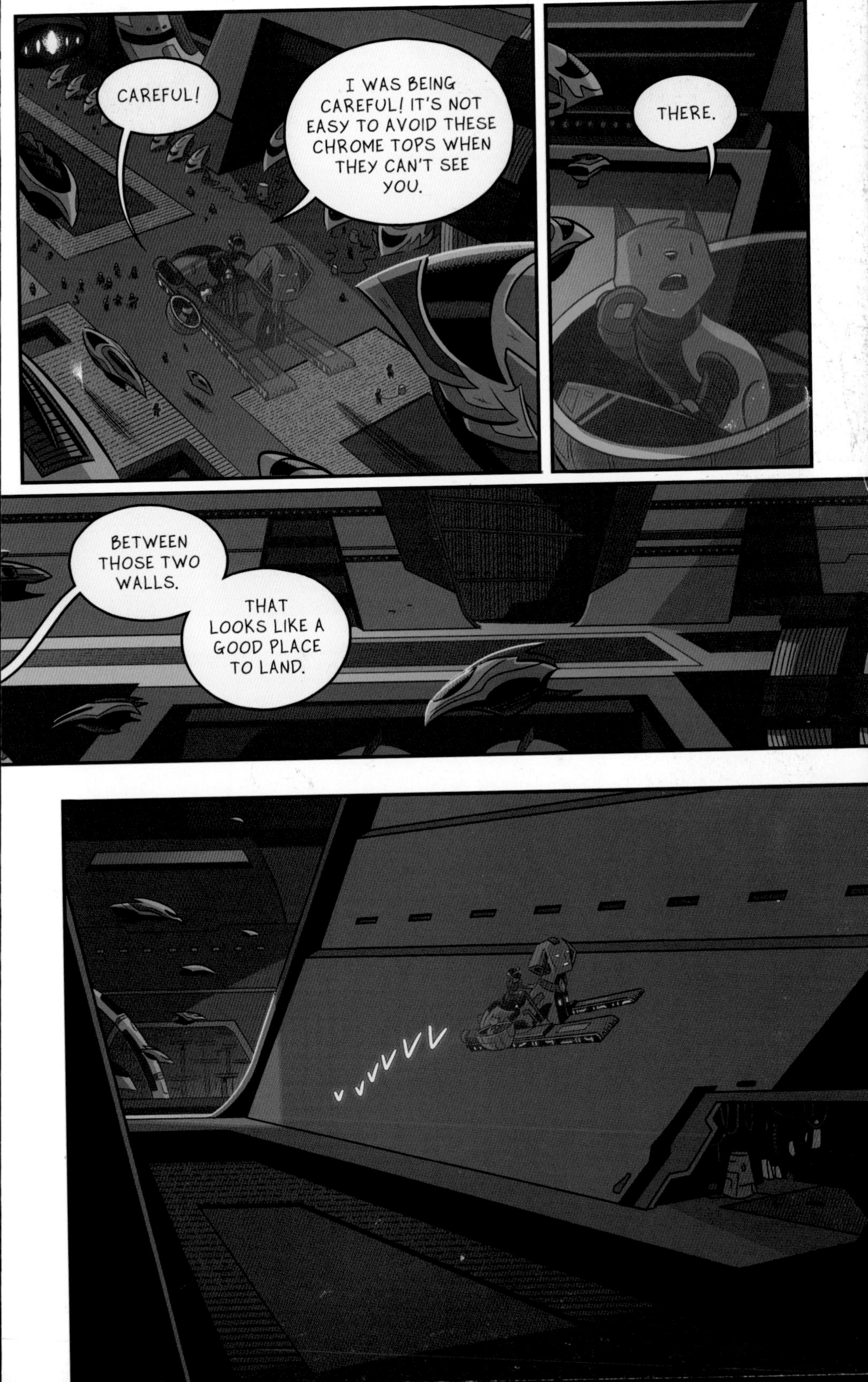
CAREFUL!
I WAS BEING CAREFUL! IT'S NOT EASY TO AVOID THESE CHROME TOPS WHEN THEY CAN'T SEE YOU.
THERE.
BETWEEN THOSE TWO WALLS.
THAT LOOKS LIKE A GOOD PLACE TO LAND.

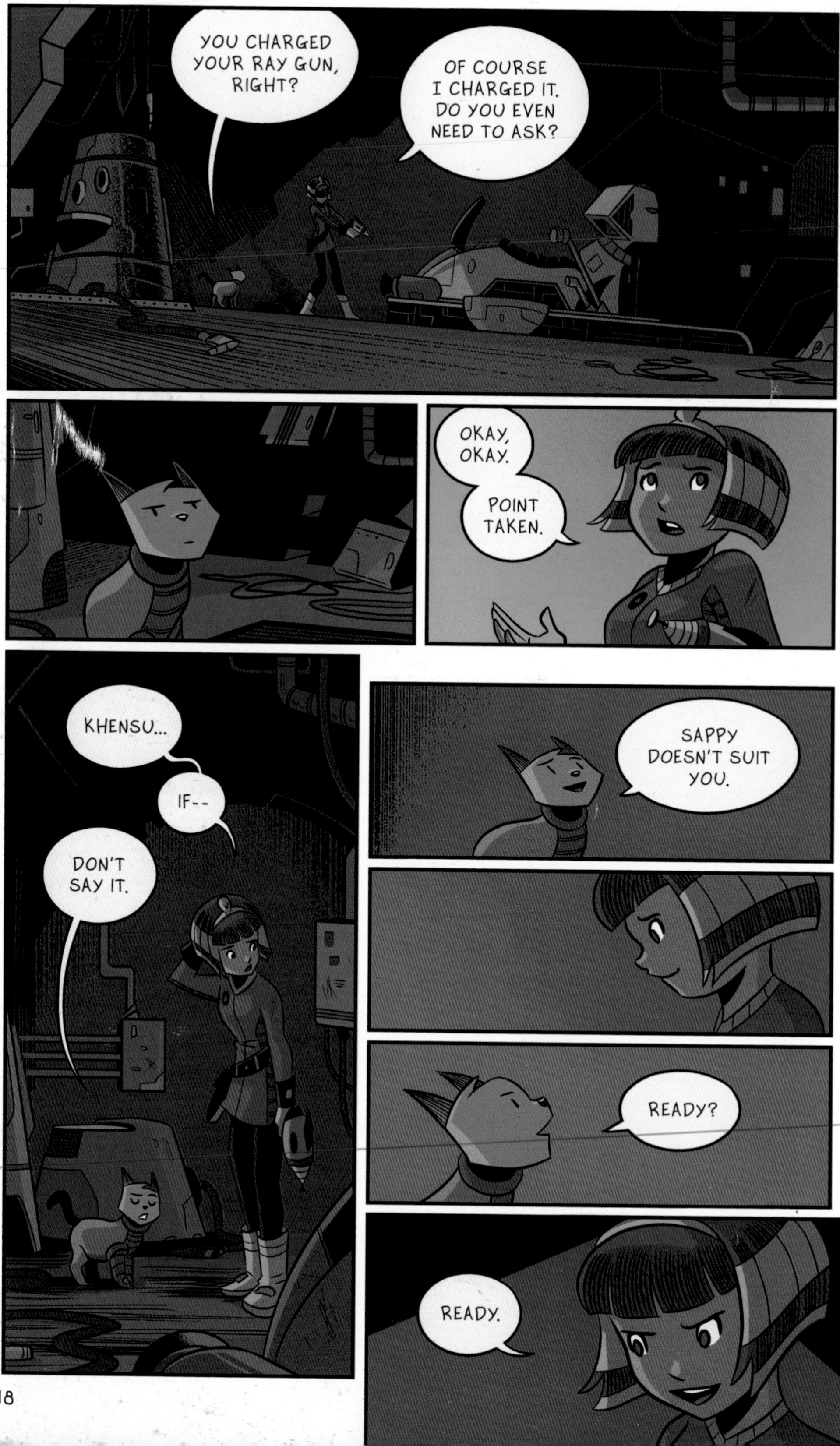
YOU CHARGED YOUR RAY GUN, RIGHT?
OF COURSE I CHARGED IT. DO YOU EVEN NEED TO ASK?
OKAY, OKAY.
POINT TAKEN.
KHENSU...
IF--
DON'T SAY IT.
SAPPY DOESN'T SUIT YOU.
READY?
READY.

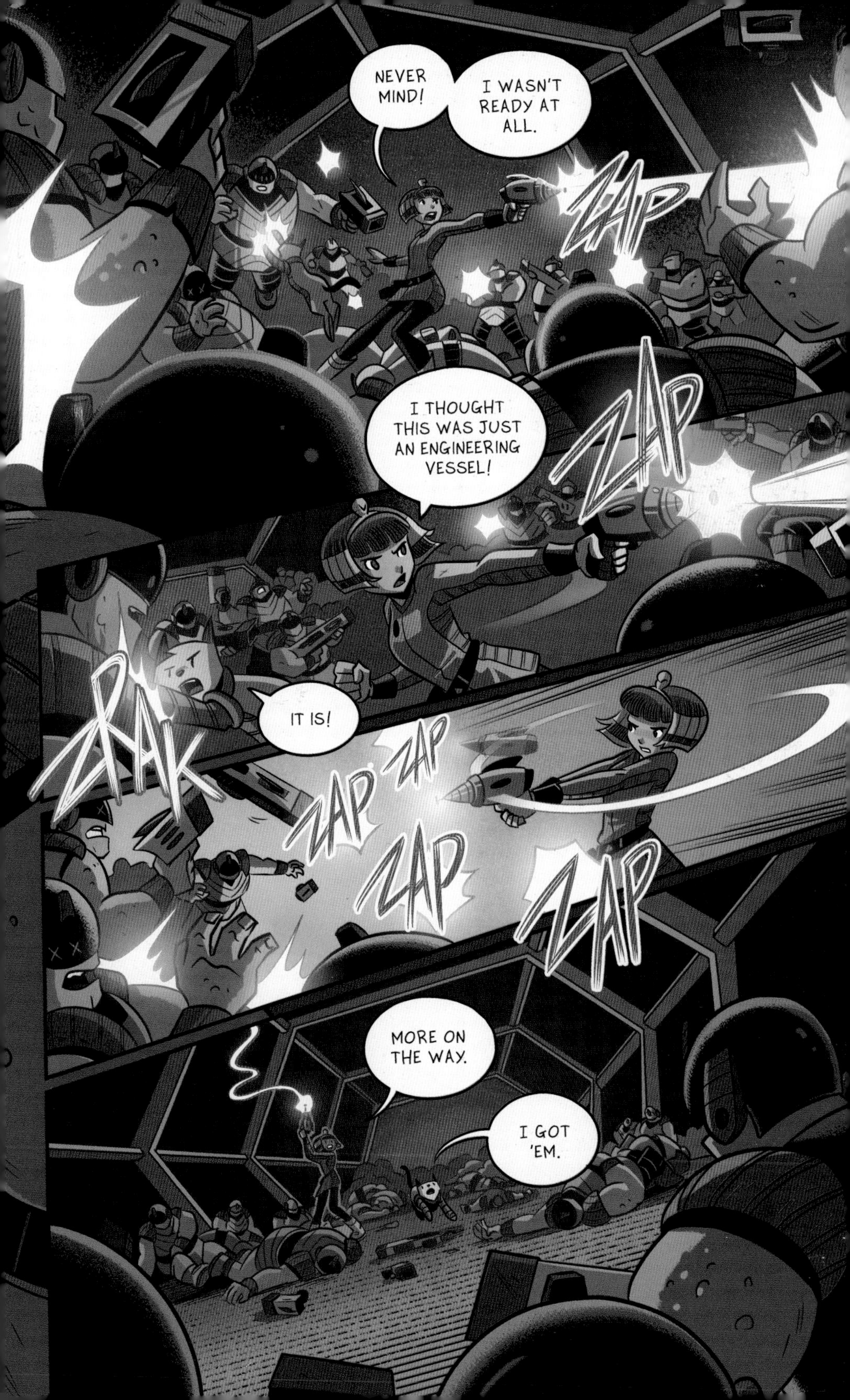
NEVER MIND!
I WASN'T READY AT ALL.
ZAP
I THOUGHT THIS WAS JUST AN ENGINEERING VESSEL!
ZAP
IT IS!
ZAP
ZAP
ZAP
ZAP
MORE ON THE WAY.
I GOT 'EM.

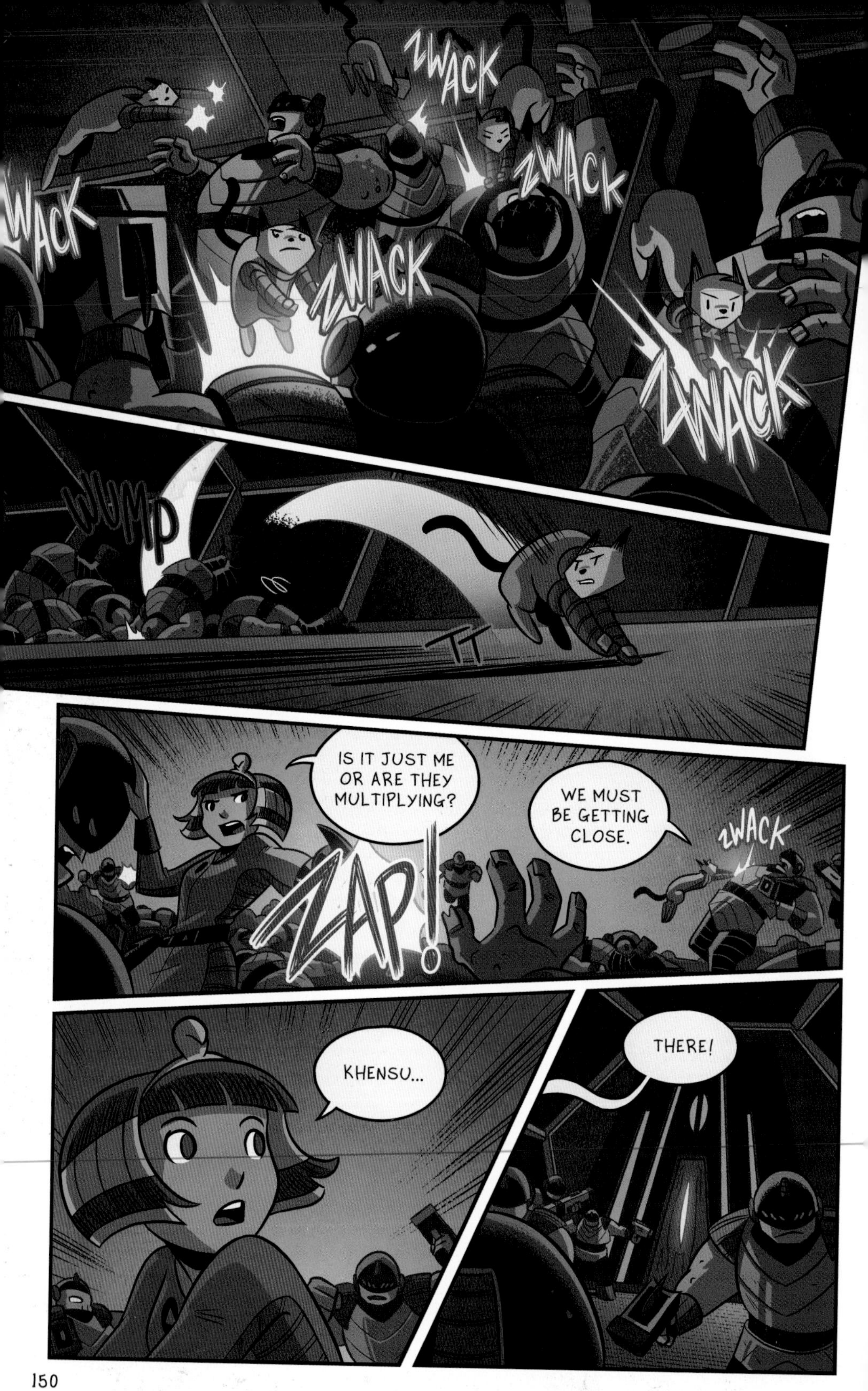
ZWACK
ZWACK
ZWACK
ZWACK
ZWACK
WUMP
TT
IS IT JUST ME OR ARE THEY MULTIPLYING?
WE MUST BE GETTING CLOSE.
ZWACK
ZAP!
KHENSU...
THERE!

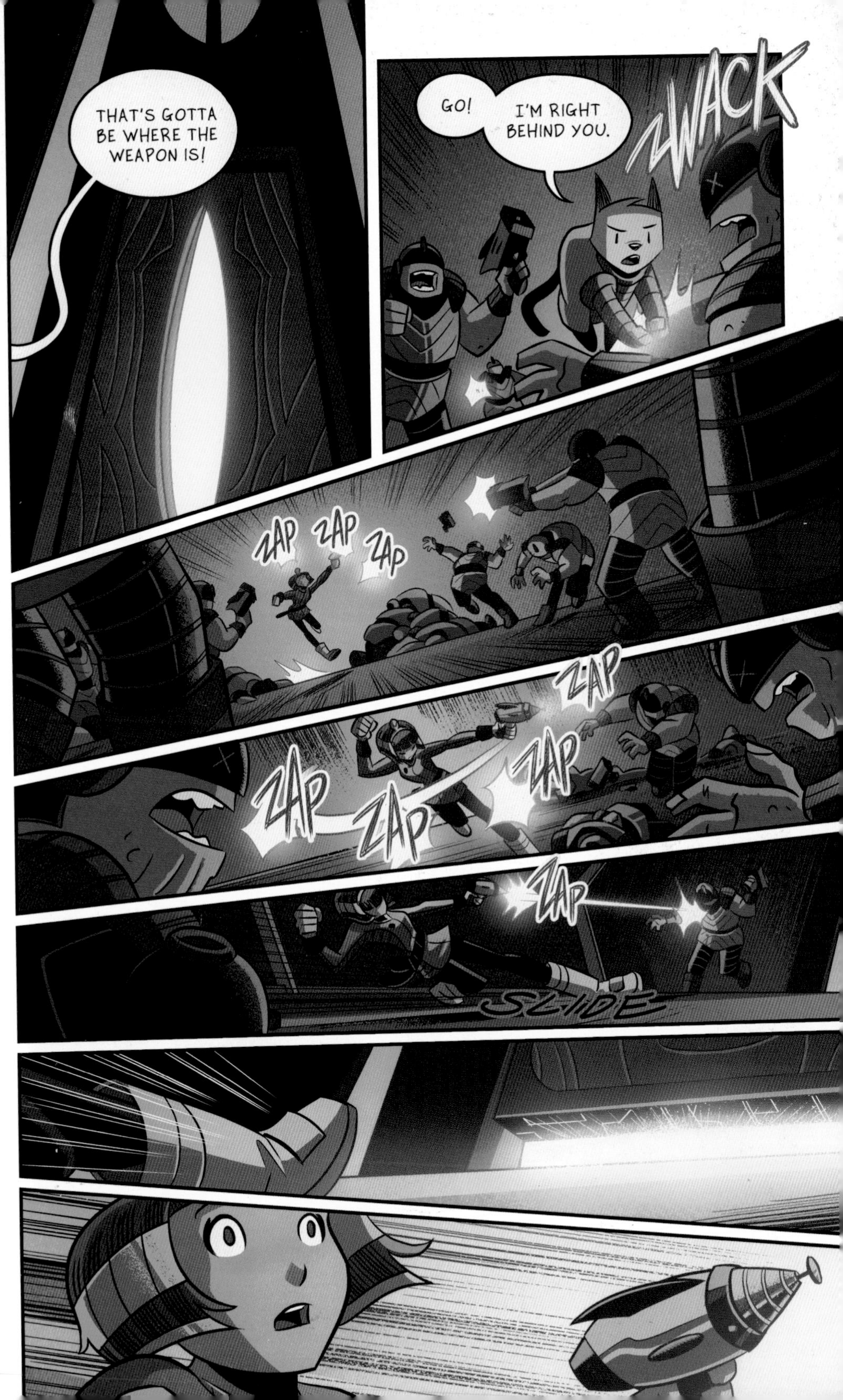
THAT'S GOTTA BE WHERE THE WEAPON IS!
GO!
I'M RIGHT BEHIND YOU.
WACK
ZAP ZAP ZAP
ZAP
ZAP ZAP ZAP
ZAP
SLIDE

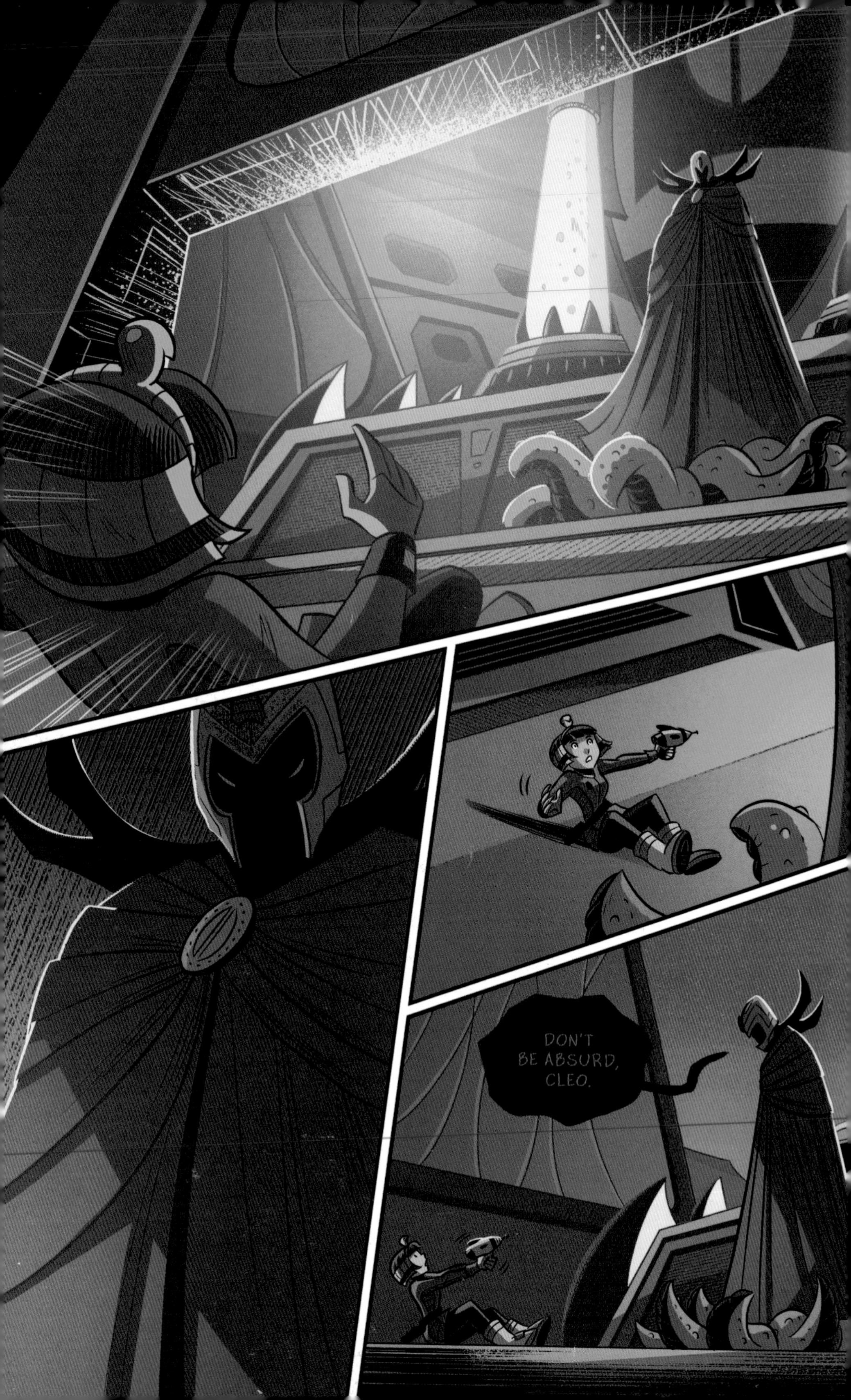
DON'T
BE ABSURD,
CLEO.

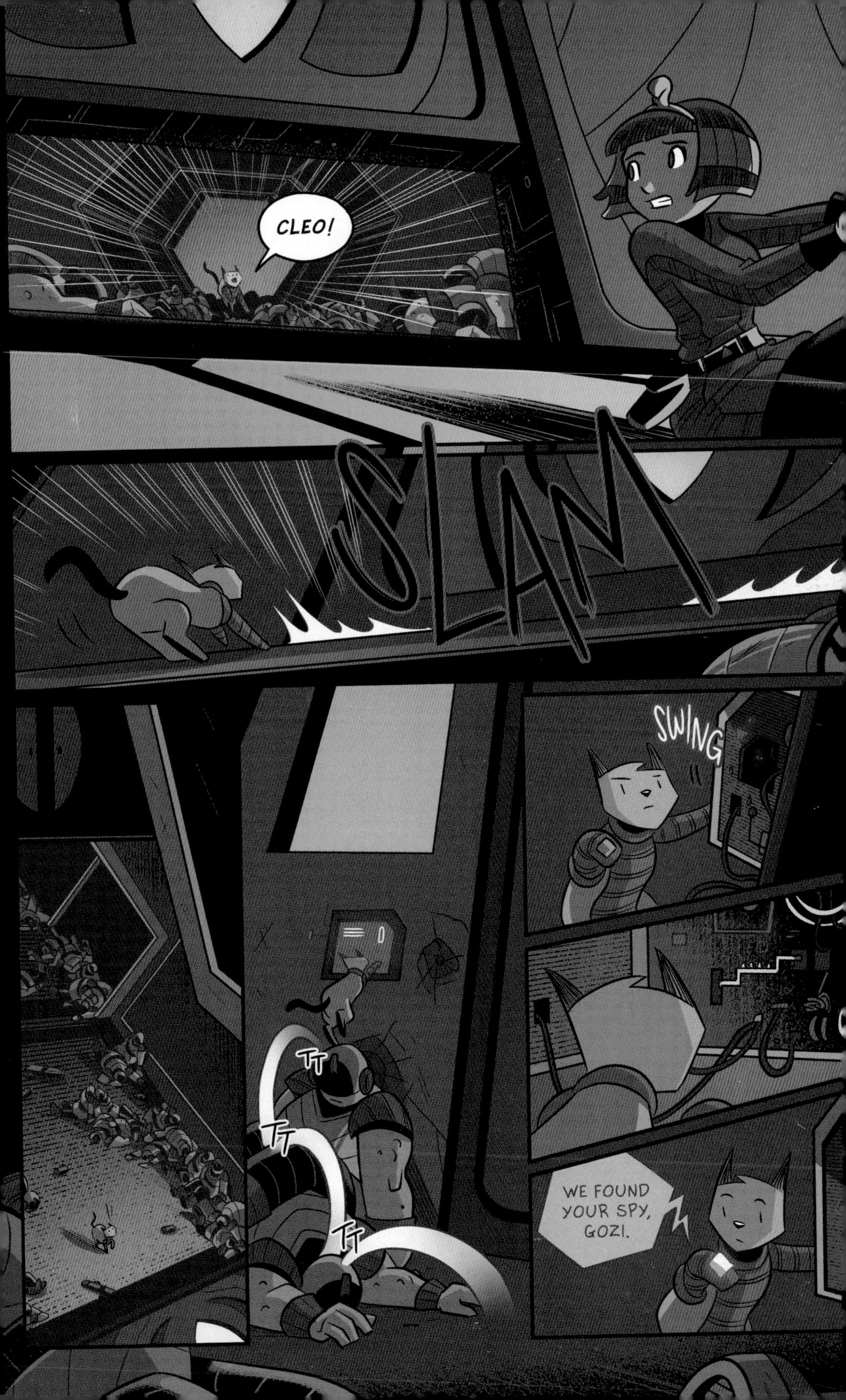
CLEO!
SLAM
SWING
TT
TT
TT
WE FOUND YOUR SPY, GOZI.

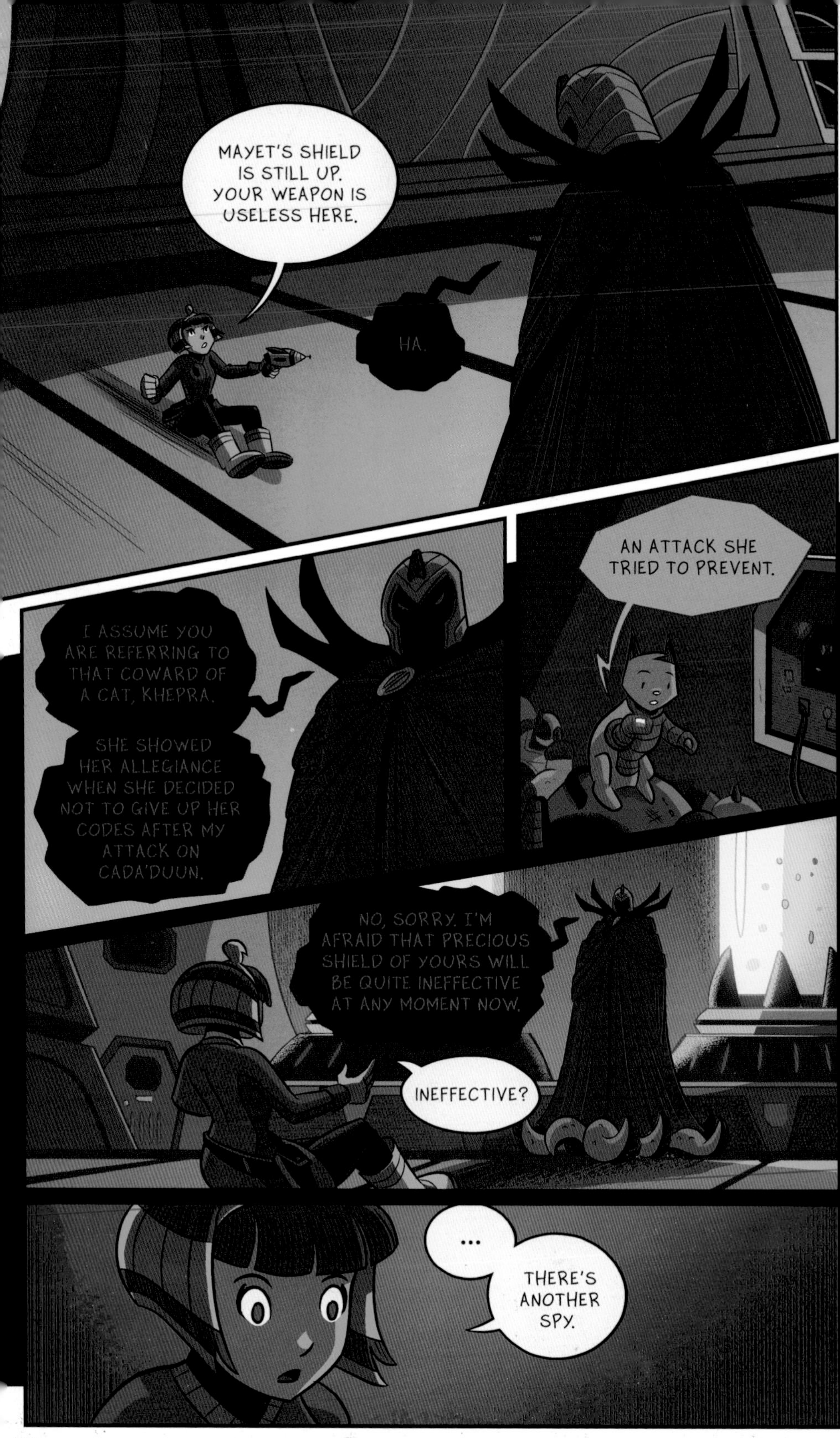
MAYET'S SHIELD IS STILL UP. YOUR WEAPON IS USELESS HERE.
HA.
I ASSUME YOU ARE REFERRING TO THAT COWARD OF A CAT, KHEPRA.
SHE SHOWED HER ALLEGIANCE WHEN SHE DECIDED NOT TO GIVE UP HER CODES AFTER MY ATTACK ON CADA'DUUN.
AN ATTACK SHE TRIED TO PREVENT.
NO, SORRY. I'M AFRAID THAT PRECIOUS SHIELD OF YOURS WILL BE QUITE INEFFECTIVE AT ANY MOMENT NOW.
INEFFECTIVE?
...
THERE'S ANOTHER SPY.

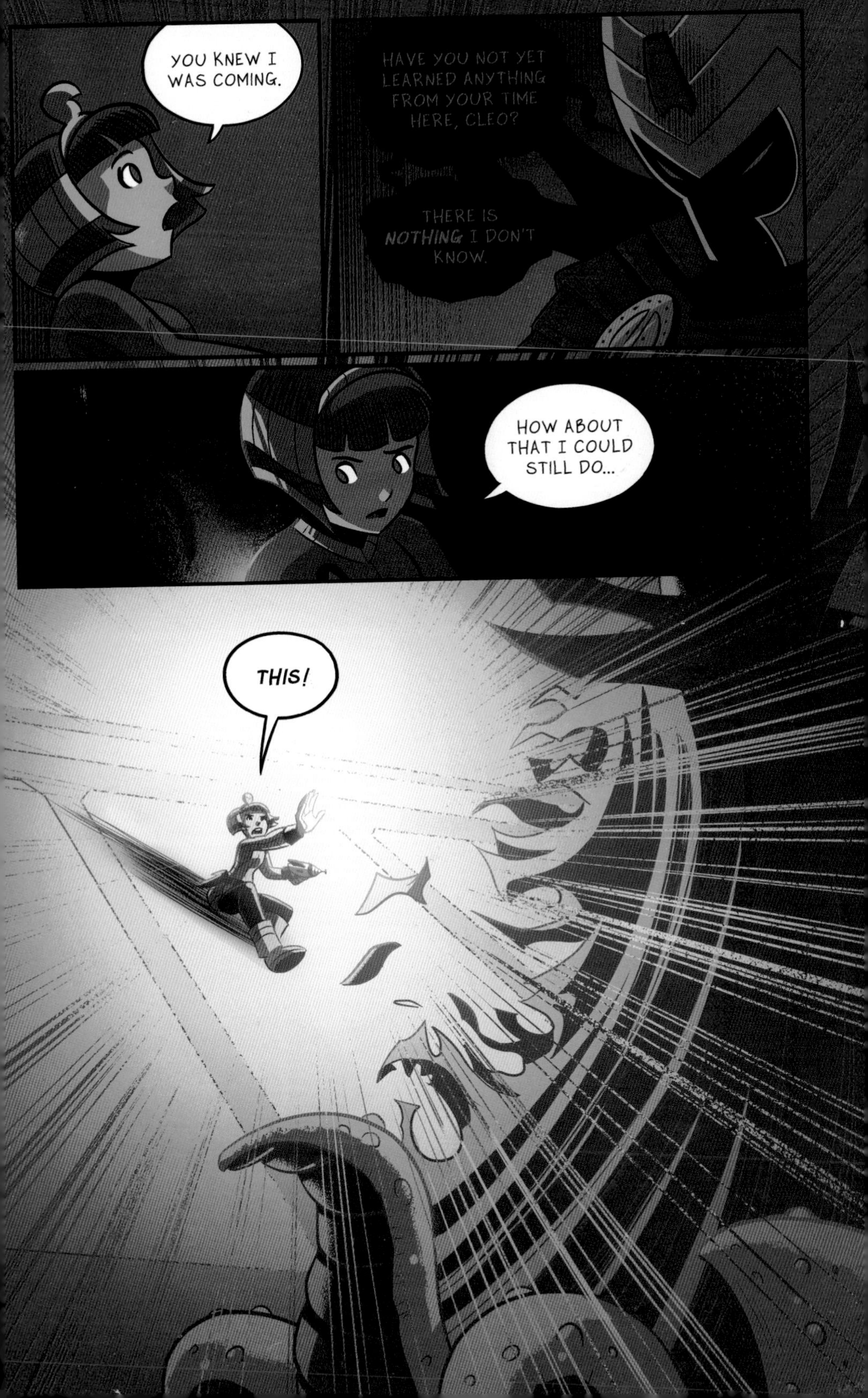

YOU KNEW I WAS COMING.
HAVE YOU NOT YET LEARNED ANYTHING FROM YOUR TIME HERE, CLEO?
THERE IS NOTHING I DON'T KNOW.
HOW ABOUT THAT I COULD STILL DO...
THIS!

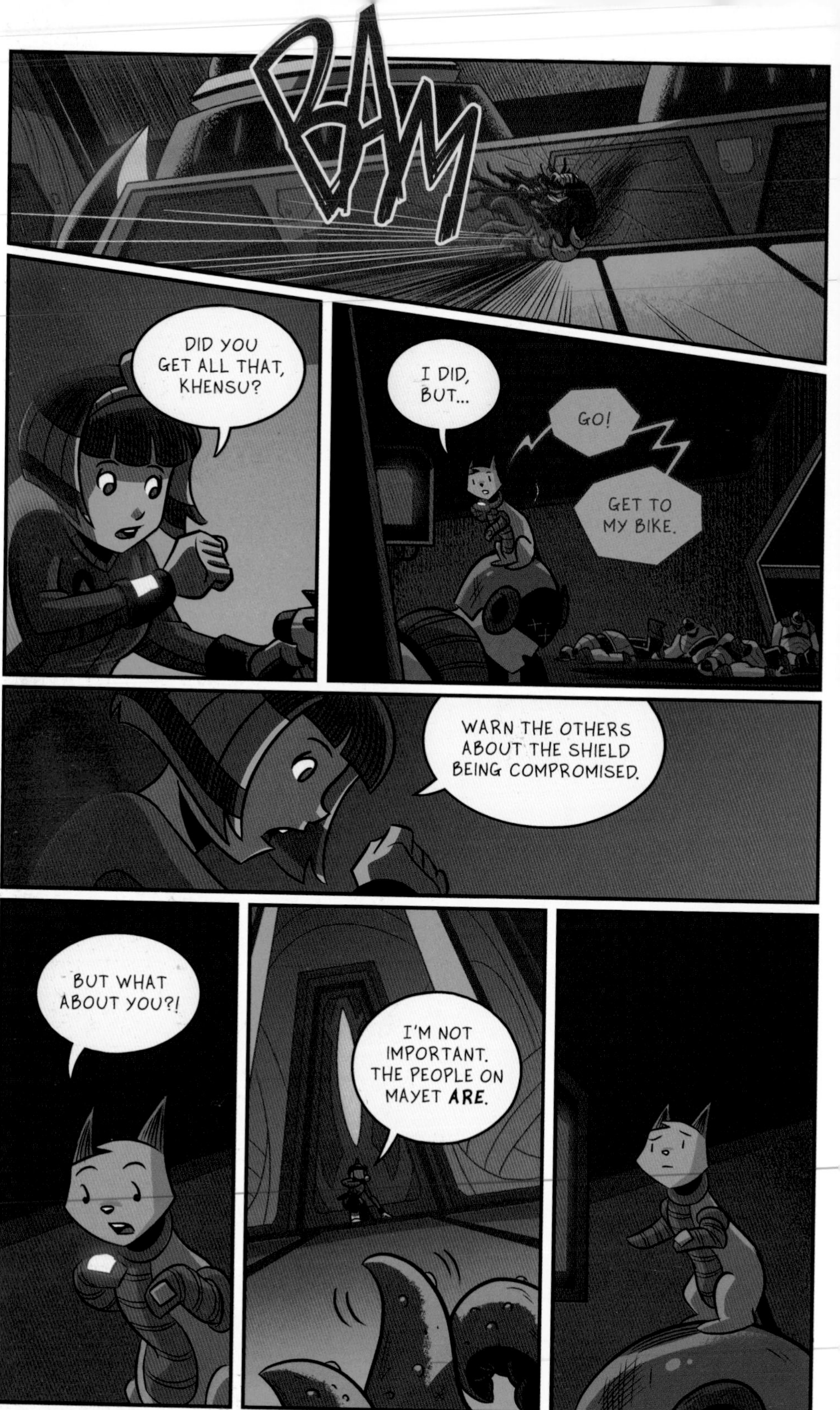
BAM
DID YOU GET ALL THAT, KHENSU?
I DID, BUT...
GO!
GET TO MY BIKE.
WARN THE OTHERS ABOUT THE SHIELD BEING COMPROMISED.
BUT WHAT ABOUT YOU?!
I'M NOT IMPORTANT. THE PEOPLE ON MAYET **ARE**.

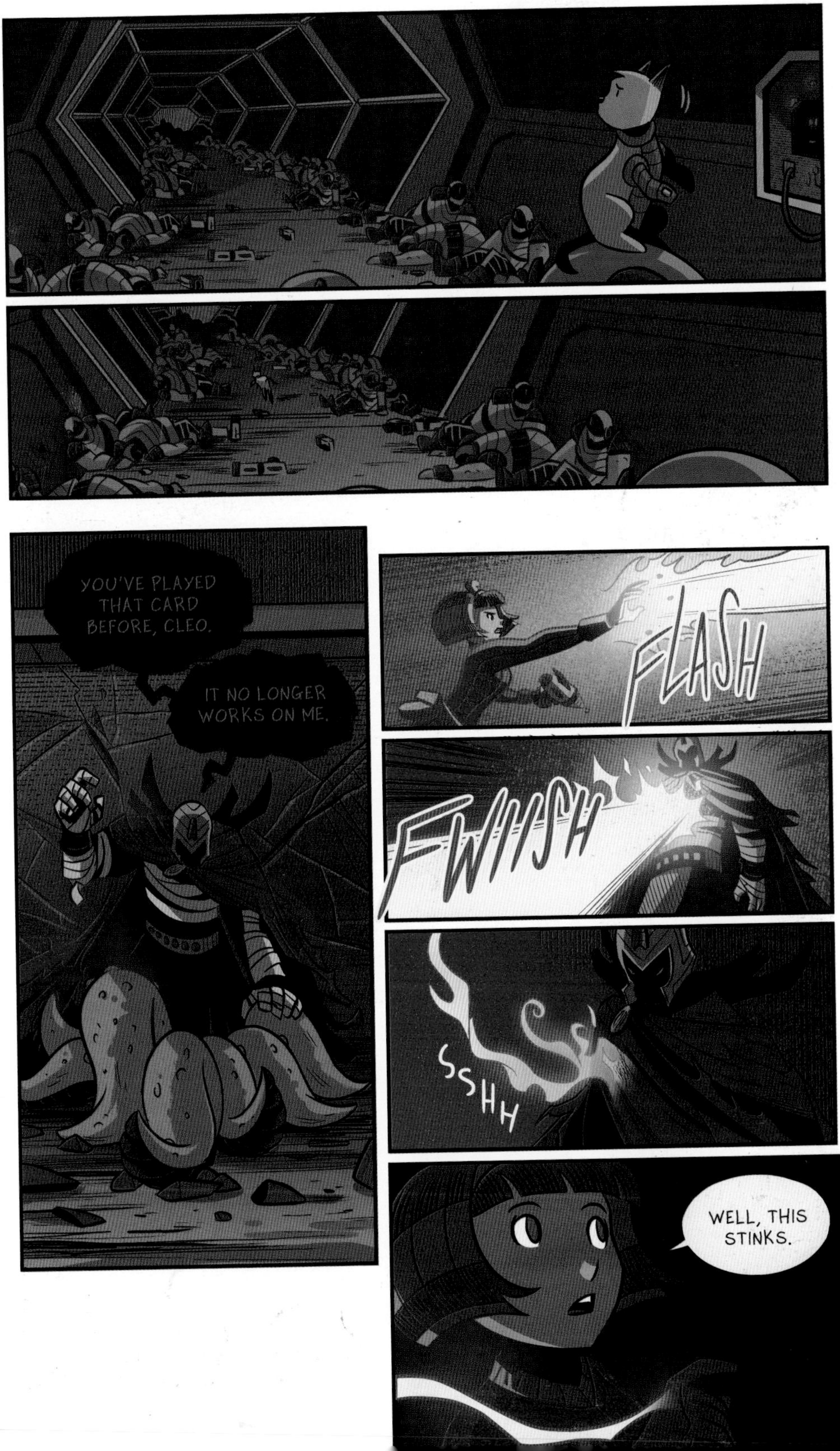
YOU'VE PLAYED THAT CARD BEFORE, CLEO.
IT NO LONGER WORKS ON ME.
FLASH
FWISH
SSHH
WELL, THIS STINKS.

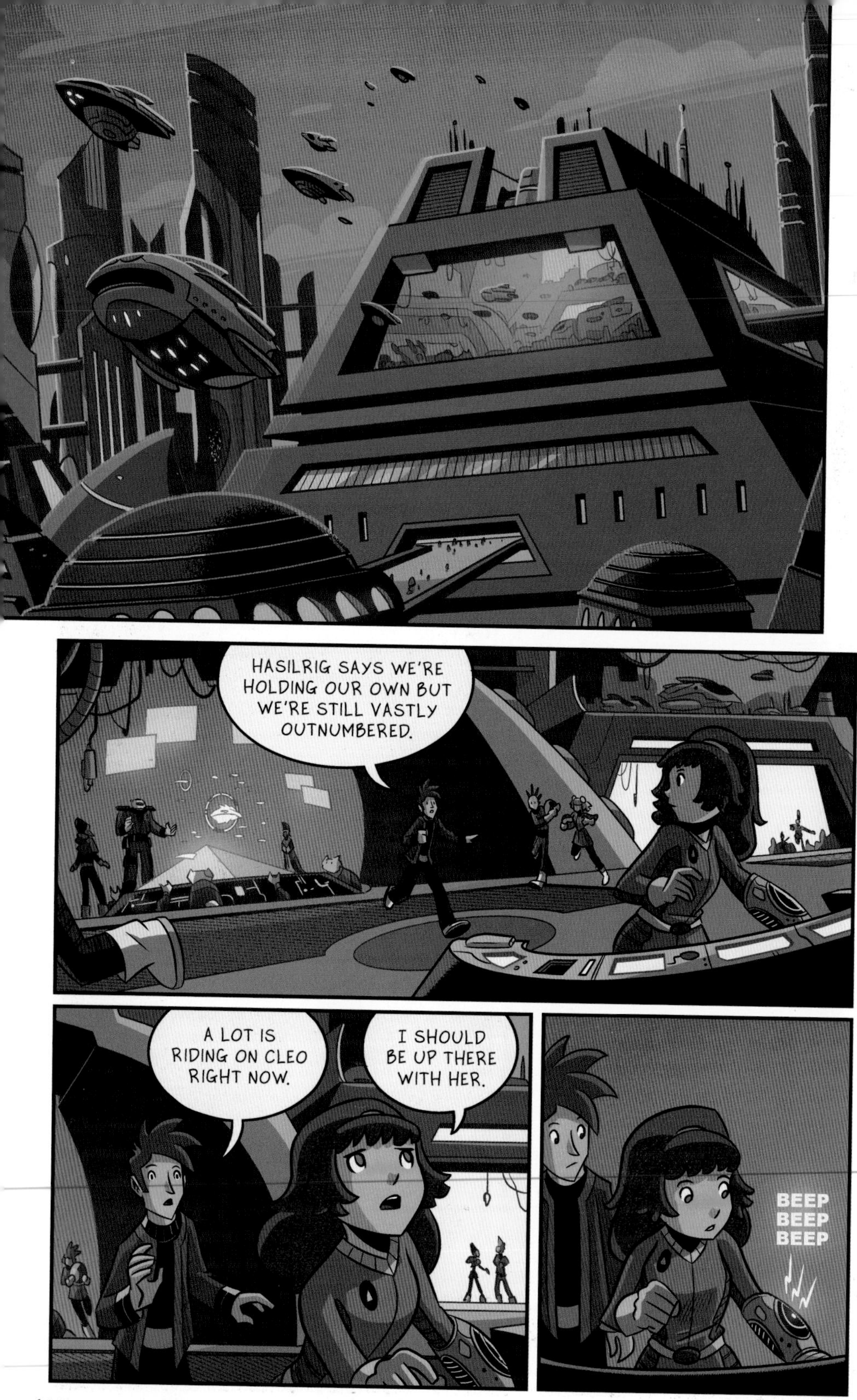
HASILRIG SAYS WE'RE HOLDING OUR OWN BUT WE'RE STILL VASTLY OUTNUMBERED.
A LOT IS RIDING ON CLEO RIGHT NOW.
I SHOULD BE UP THERE WITH HER.
BEEP BEEP BEEP

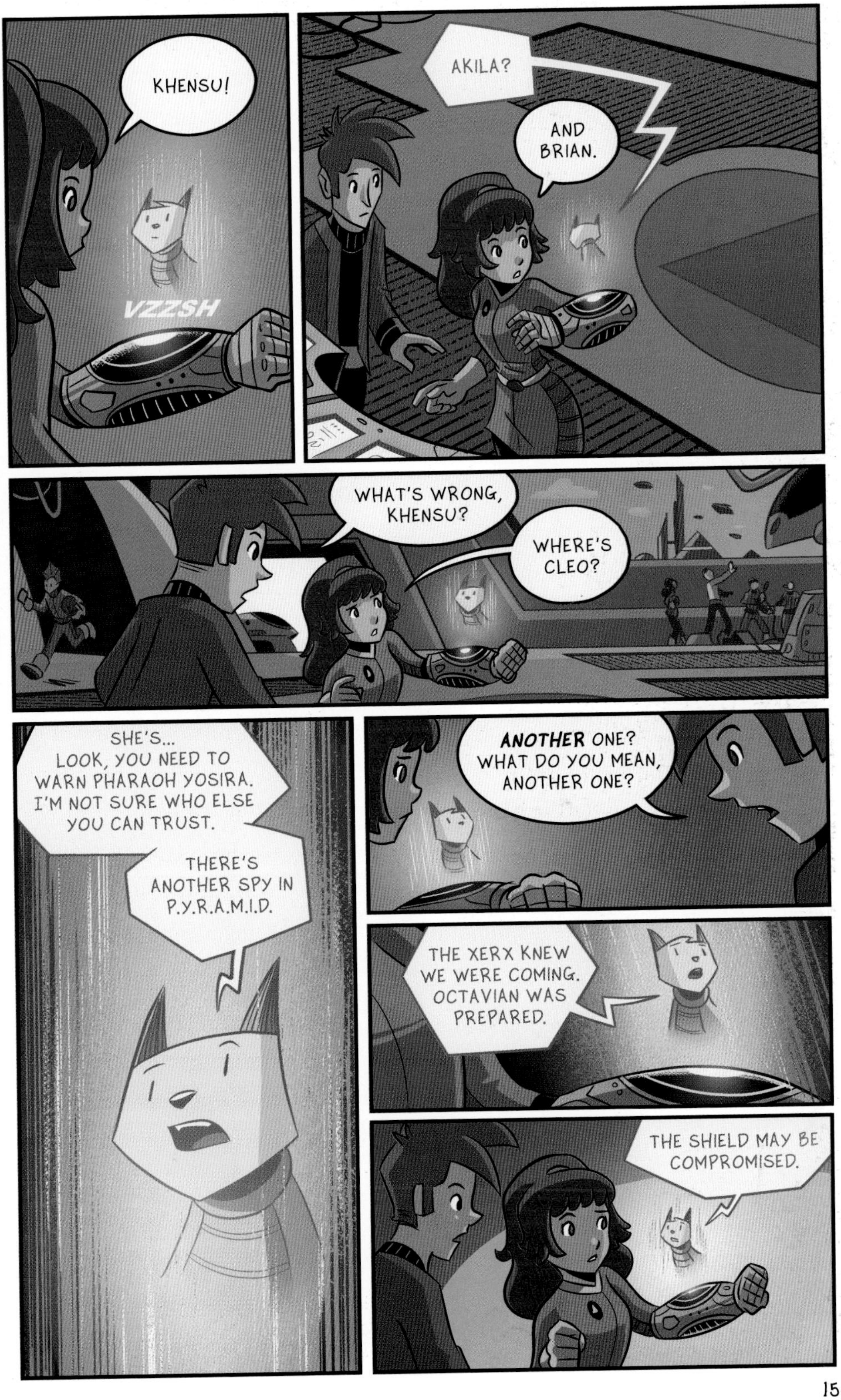
KHENSU!
VZZSH
AKILA?
AND BRIAN.
WHAT'S WRONG, KHENSU?
WHERE'S CLEO?
SHE'S... LOOK, YOU NEED TO WARN PHARAOH YOSIRA. I'M NOT SURE WHO ELSE YOU CAN TRUST.
THERE'S ANOTHER SPY IN P.Y.R.A.M.I.D.
ANOTHER ONE? WHAT DO YOU MEAN, ANOTHER ONE?
THE XERX KNEW WE WERE COMING. OCTAVIAN WAS PREPARED.
THE SHIELD MAY BE COMPROMISED.

IT'S OKAY. EVEN IF THERE IS ANOTHER SPY, ADMINISTRANT KHEPRA WAS THE ONLY ONE WITH THE KEY CODES AND SHE'S...

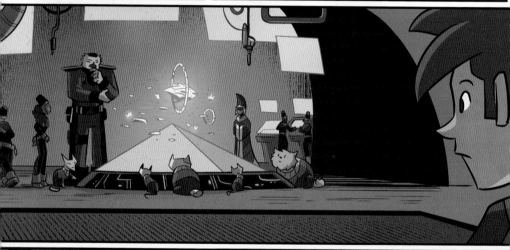

WHERE'S...

WHAT IS IT?

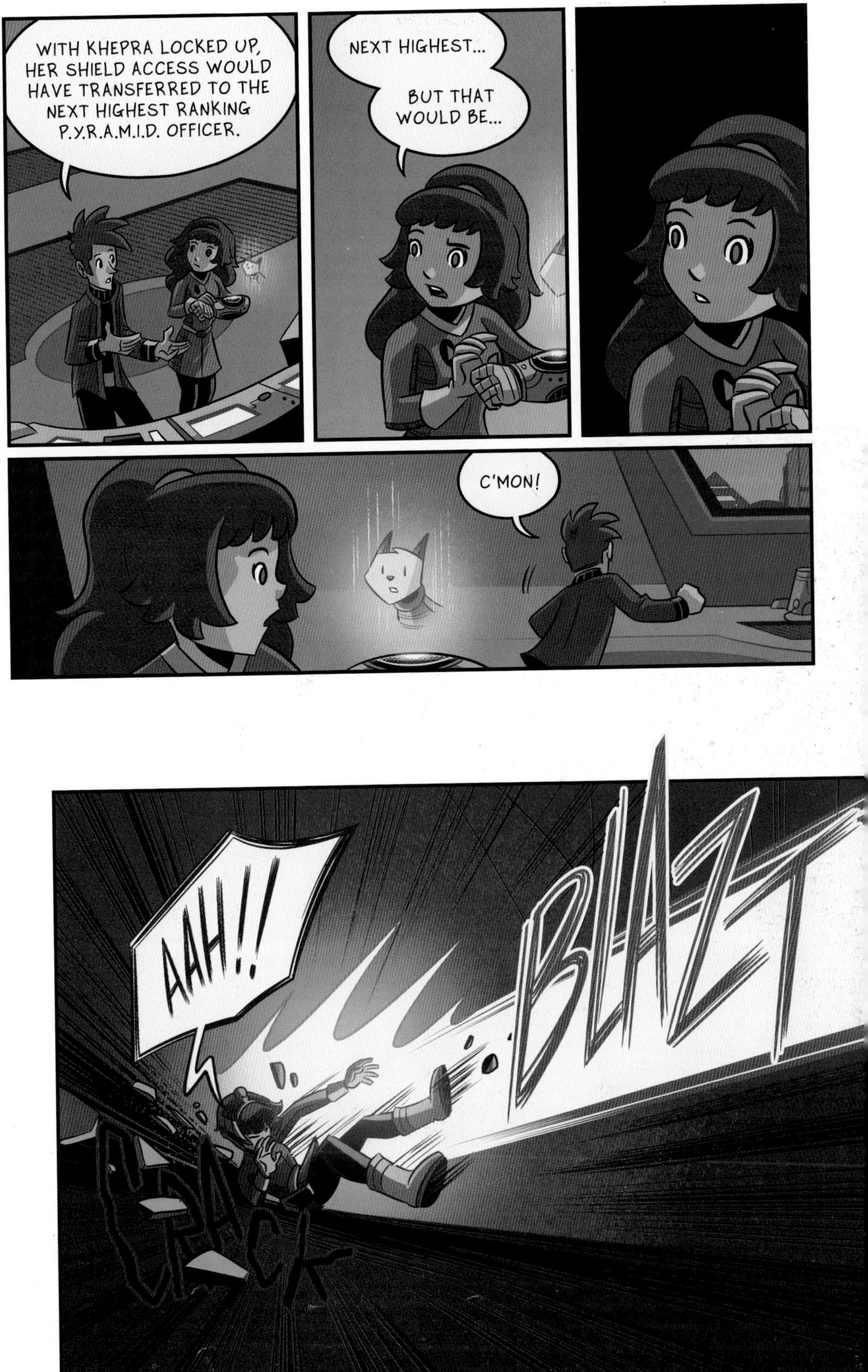
WITH KHEPRA LOCKED UP, HER SHIELD ACCESS WOULD HAVE TRANSFERRED TO THE NEXT HIGHEST RANKING P.Y.R.A.M.I.D. OFFICER.
NEXT HIGHEST...
BUT THAT WOULD BE...
C'MON!
AAH!!
BLAZT
CRACK

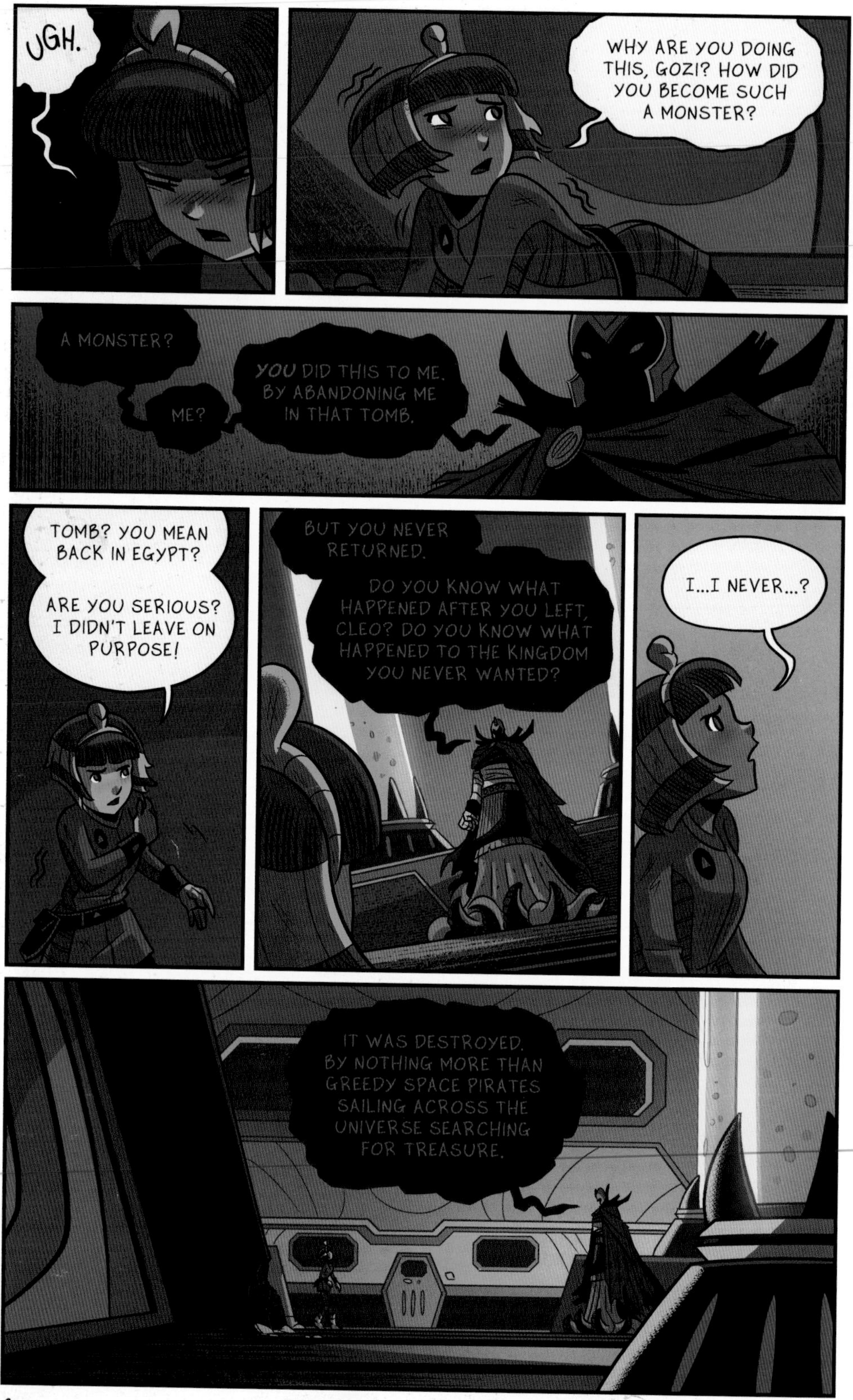
UGH.
WHY ARE YOU DOING THIS, GOZI? HOW DID YOU BECOME SUCH A MONSTER?
A MONSTER?
ME?
YOU DID THIS TO ME. BY ABANDONING ME IN THAT TOMB.
TOMB? YOU MEAN BACK IN EGYPT?
ARE YOU SERIOUS? I DIDN'T LEAVE ON PURPOSE!
BUT YOU NEVER RETURNED.
DO YOU KNOW WHAT HAPPENED AFTER YOU LEFT, CLEO? DO YOU KNOW WHAT HAPPENED TO THE KINGDOM YOU NEVER WANTED?
I...I NEVER...?
IT WAS DESTROYED. BY NOTHING MORE THAN GREEDY SPACE PIRATES SAILING ACROSS THE UNIVERSE SEARCHING FOR TREASURE.

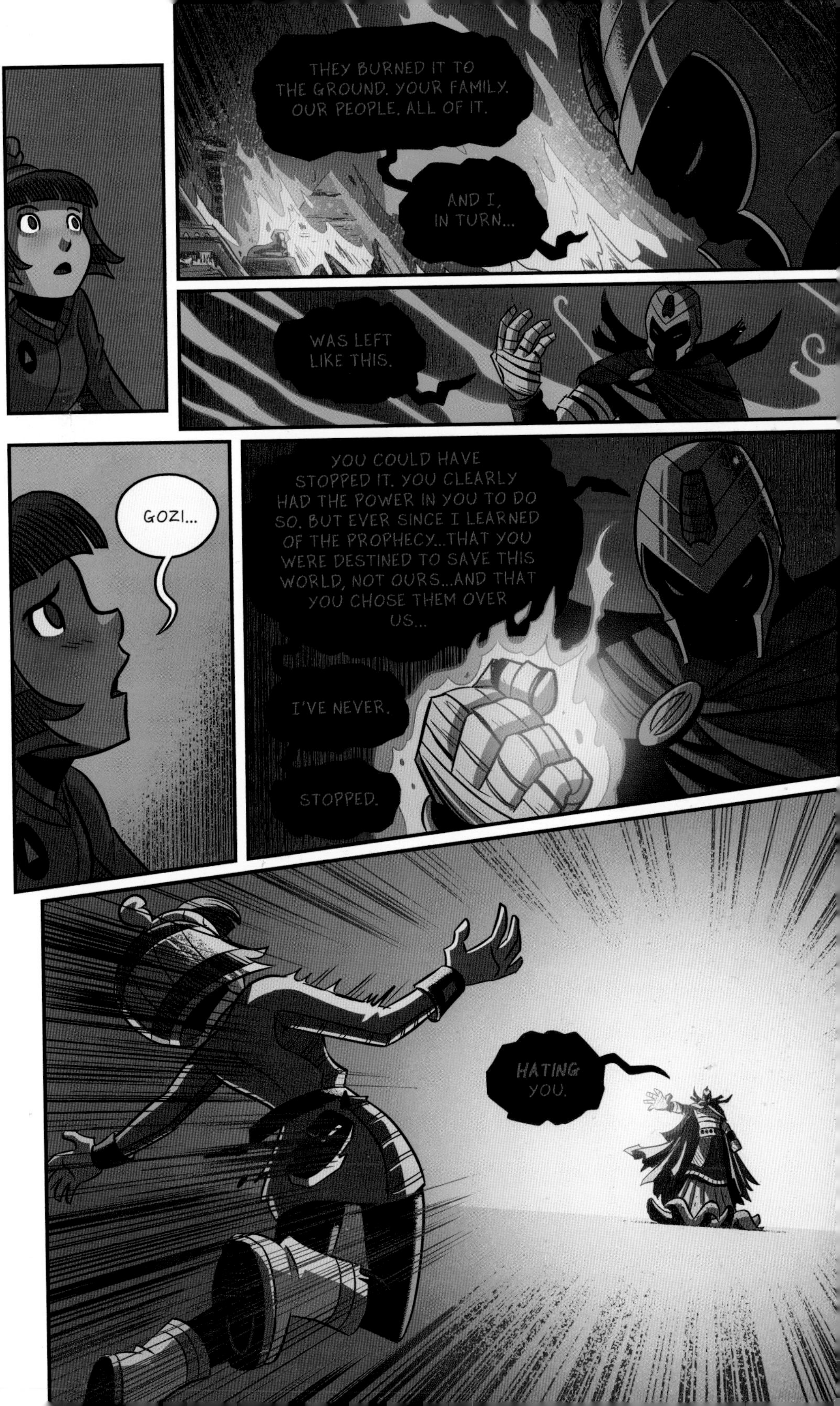
THEY BURNED IT TO THE GROUND. YOUR FAMILY. OUR PEOPLE. ALL OF IT.
AND I, IN TURN...
WAS LEFT LIKE THIS.
GOZI...
YOU COULD HAVE STOPPED IT. YOU CLEARLY HAD THE POWER IN YOU TO DO SO. BUT EVER SINCE I LEARNED OF THE PROPHECY...THAT YOU WERE DESTINED TO SAVE THIS WORLD, NOT OURS...AND THAT YOU CHOSE THEM OVER US...
I'VE NEVER.
STOPPED.
HATING YOU.

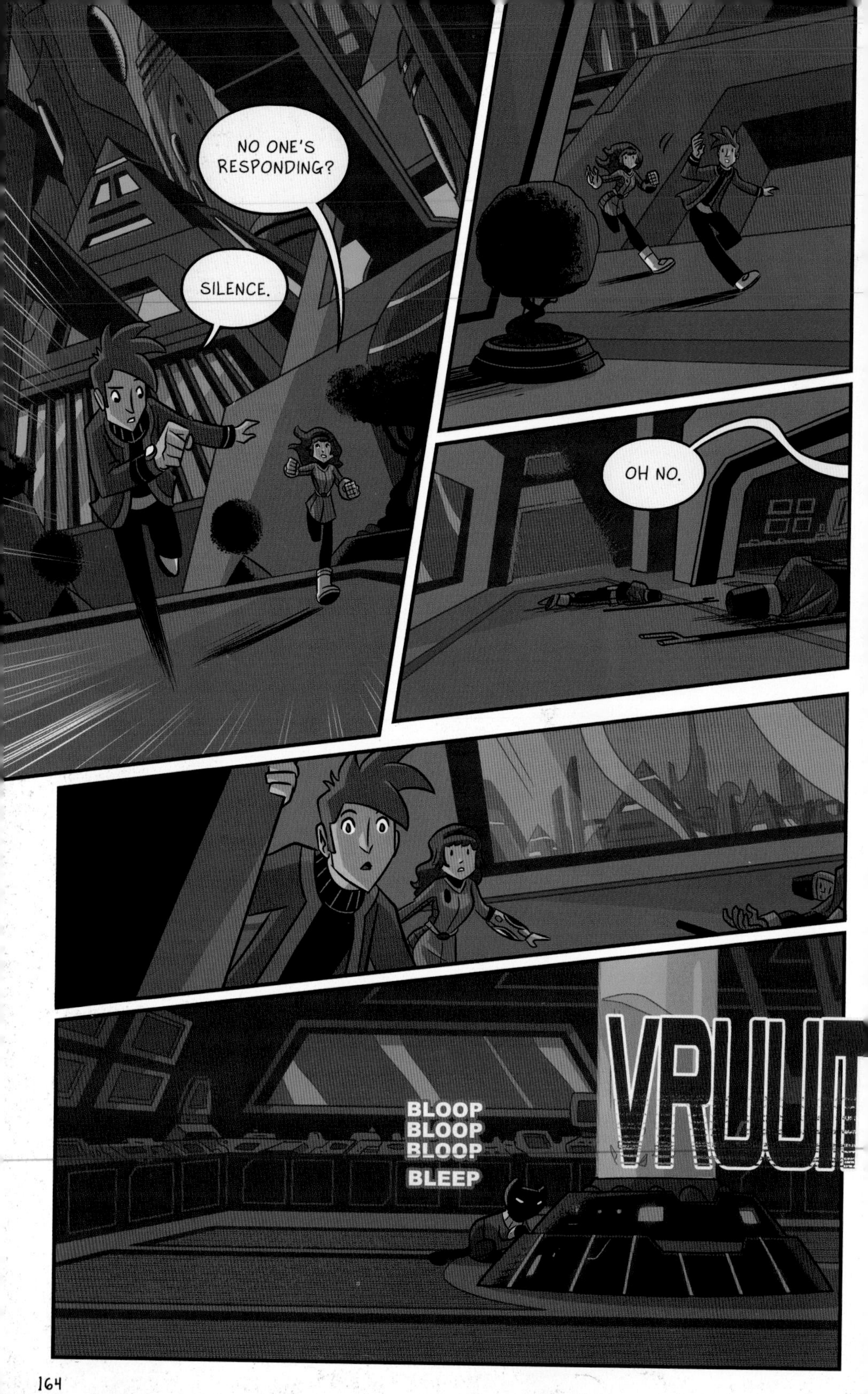
NO ONE'S RESPONDING?
SILENCE.
OH NO.
BLOOP
BLOOP
BLOOP
BLEEP
VRUUM

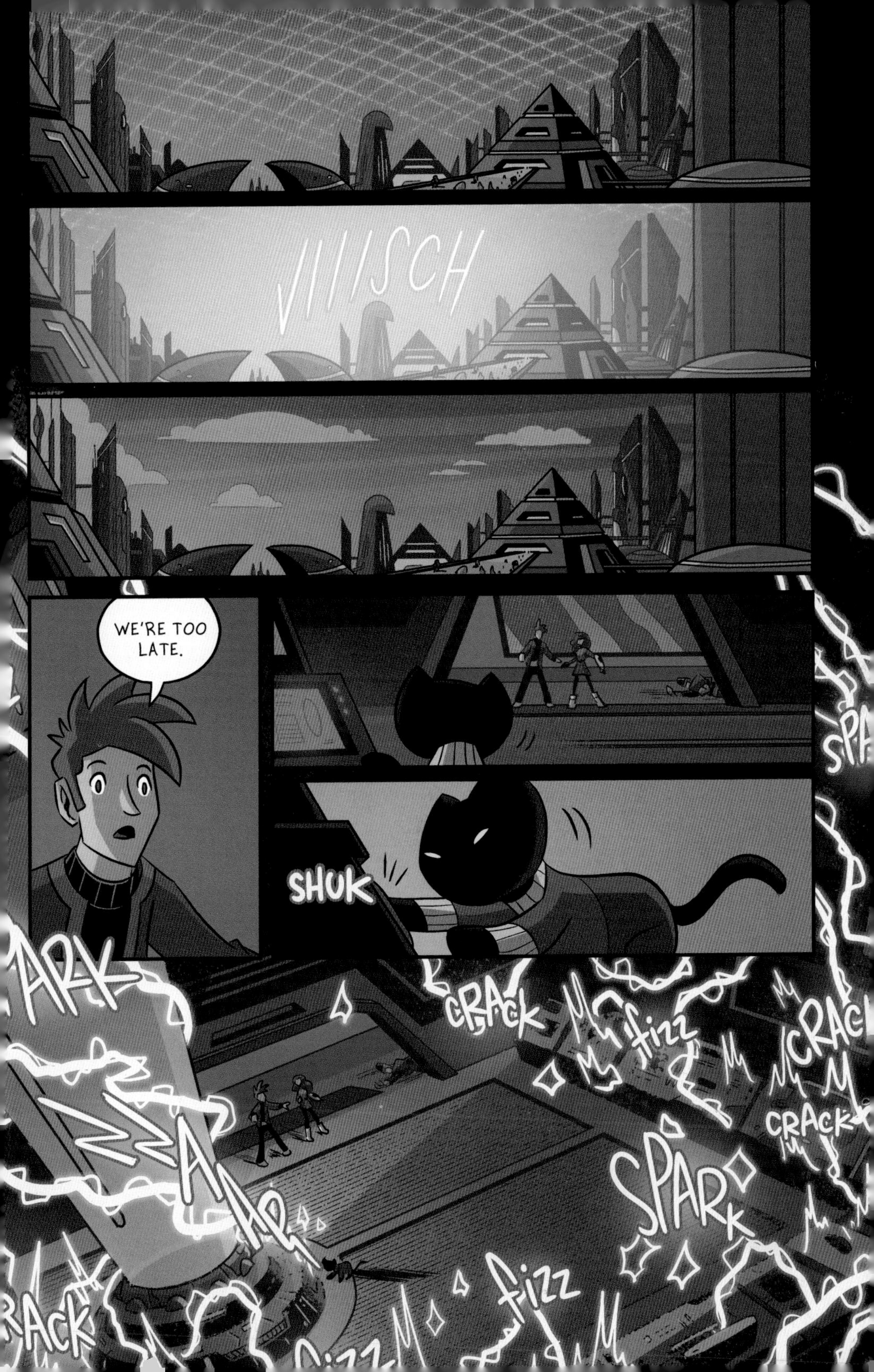
VIIISCH
WE'RE TOO LATE.
SHUK
SPARK
CRACK
fizz
CRACK
CRACK
SPARK
ZZZAAP
fizz

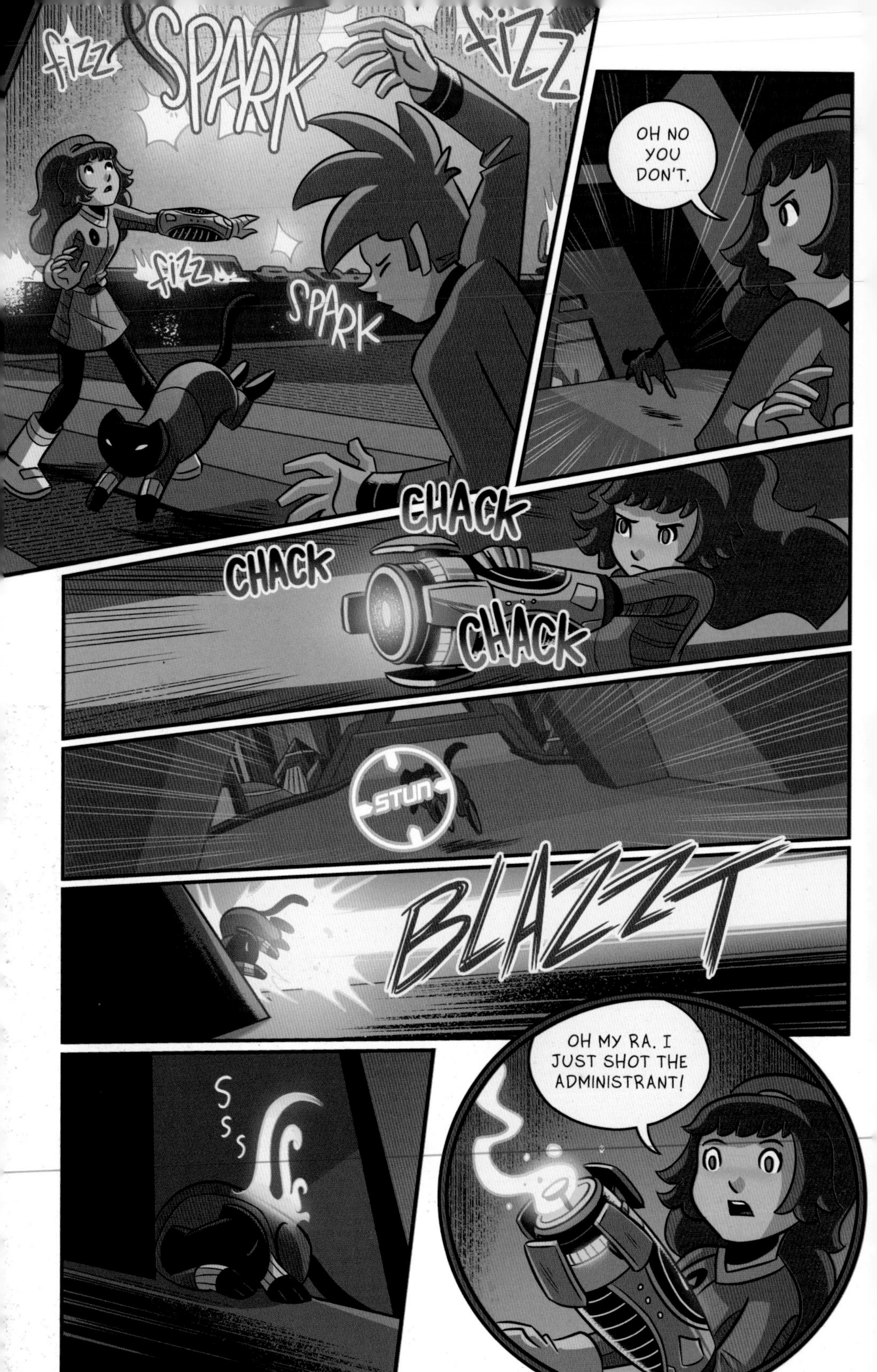
fizz
SPARK
fizz
fizz
SPARK
OH NO YOU DON'T.
CHACK
CHACK
CHACK
STUN
BLAZZT
SSS
OH MY RA. I JUST SHOT THE ADMINISTRANT!

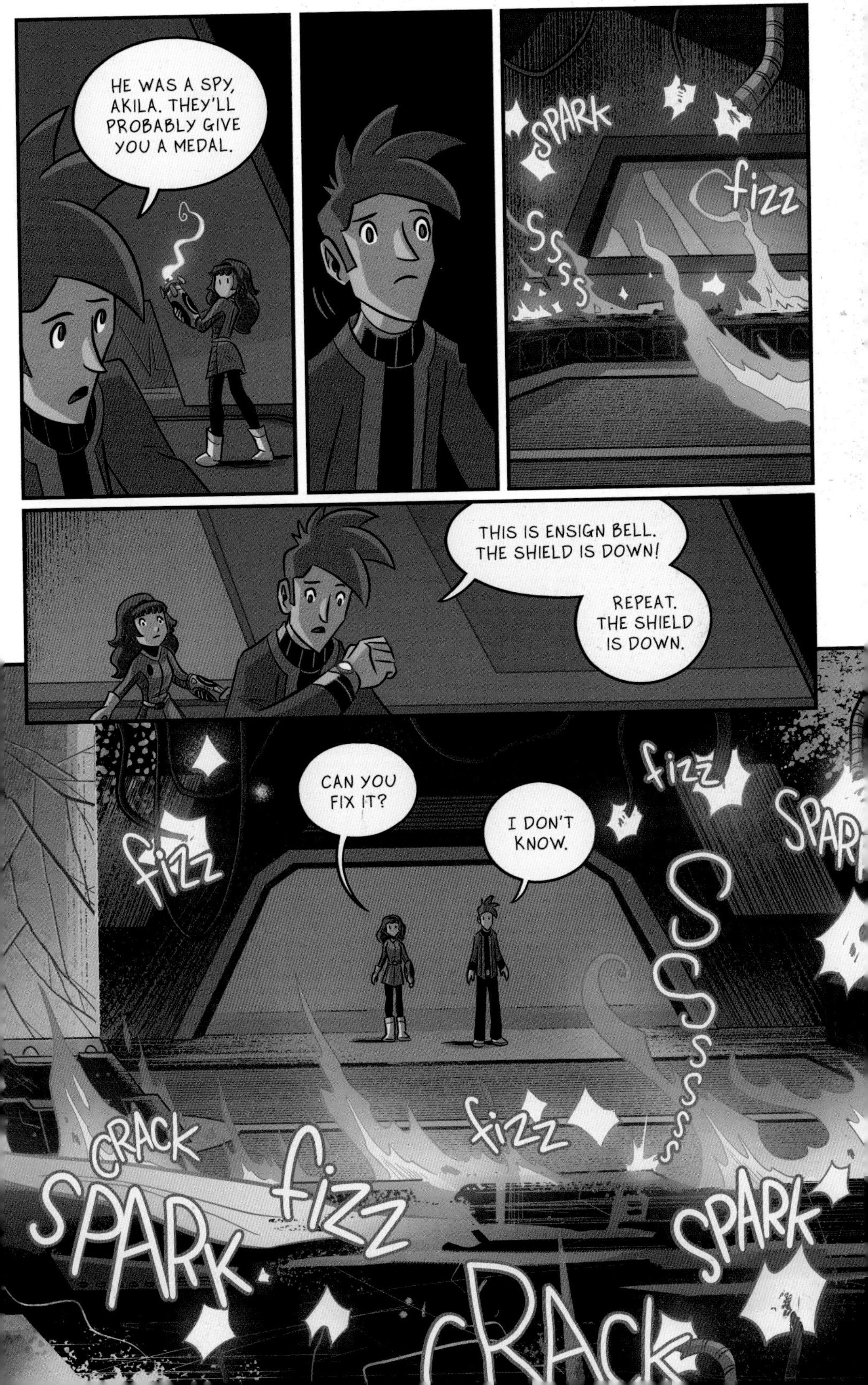
HE WAS A SPY, AKILA. THEY'LL PROBABLY GIVE YOU A MEDAL.
SPARK
fizz
SSSS
THIS IS ENSIGN BELL. THE SHIELD IS DOWN!
REPEAT. THE SHIELD IS DOWN.
CAN YOU FIX IT?
I DON'T KNOW.
fizz
fizz
SPAR
SSSSSSSS
fizz
CRACK
SPARK
fizz
SPARK
CRACK

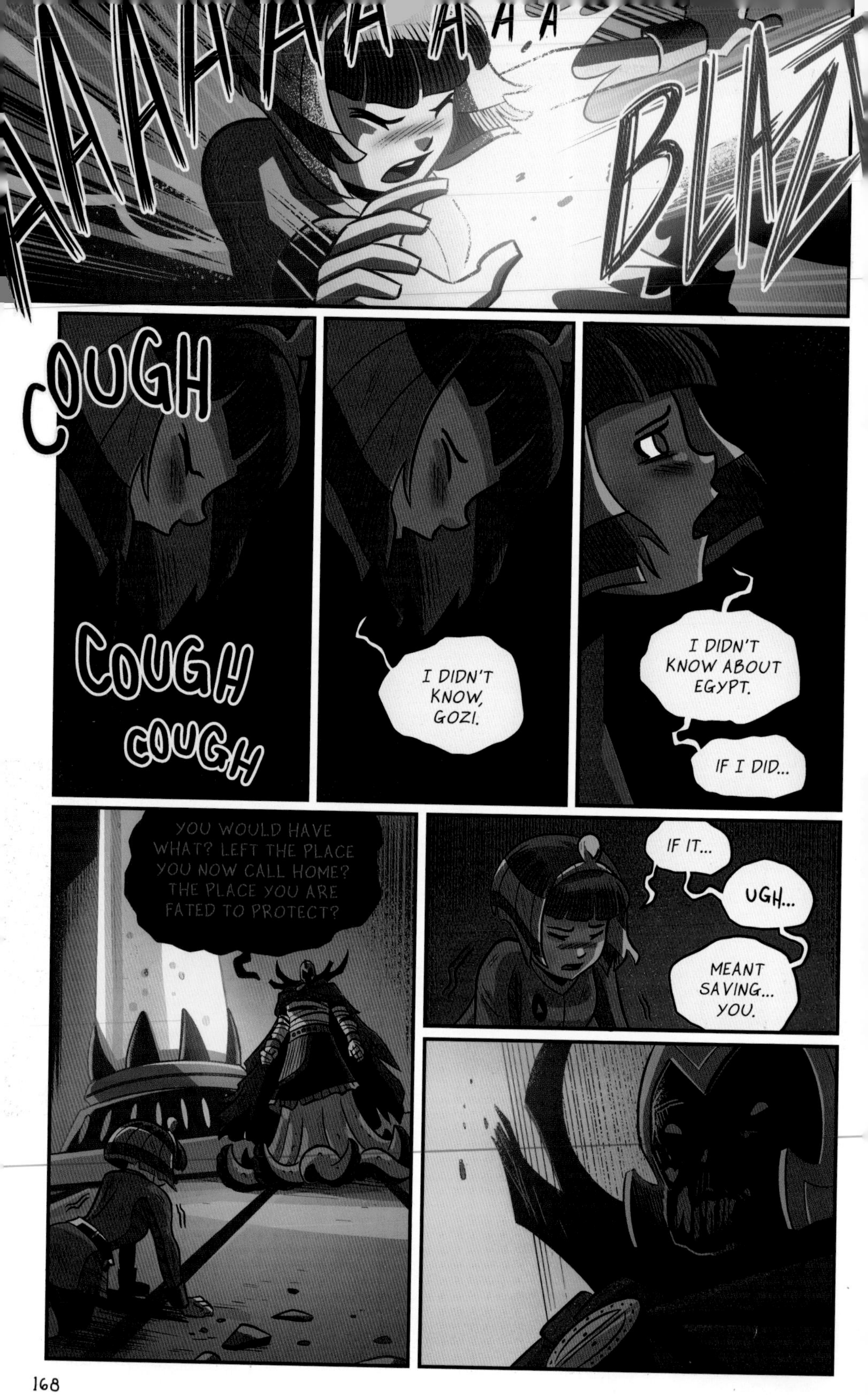
AAAAAAAAA
BLAZT
COUGH
COUGH
COUGH
I DIDN'T KNOW, GOZI.
I DIDN'T KNOW ABOUT EGYPT.
IF I DID...
YOU WOULD HAVE WHAT? LEFT THE PLACE YOU NOW CALL HOME? THE PLACE YOU ARE FATED TO PROTECT?
IF IT...
UGH...
MEANT SAVING... YOU.

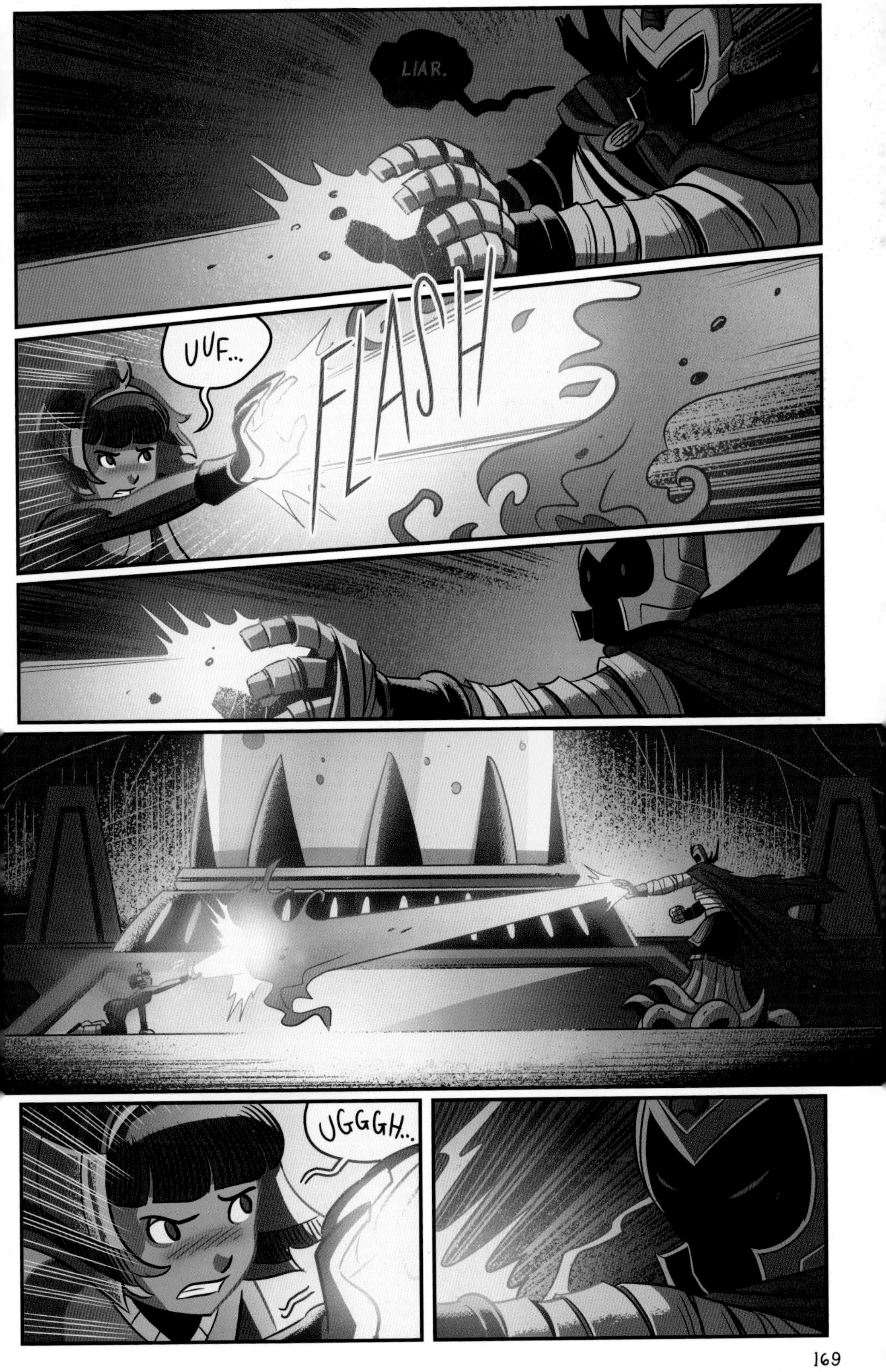
LIAR.
UUF...
FLASH
UGGGH...

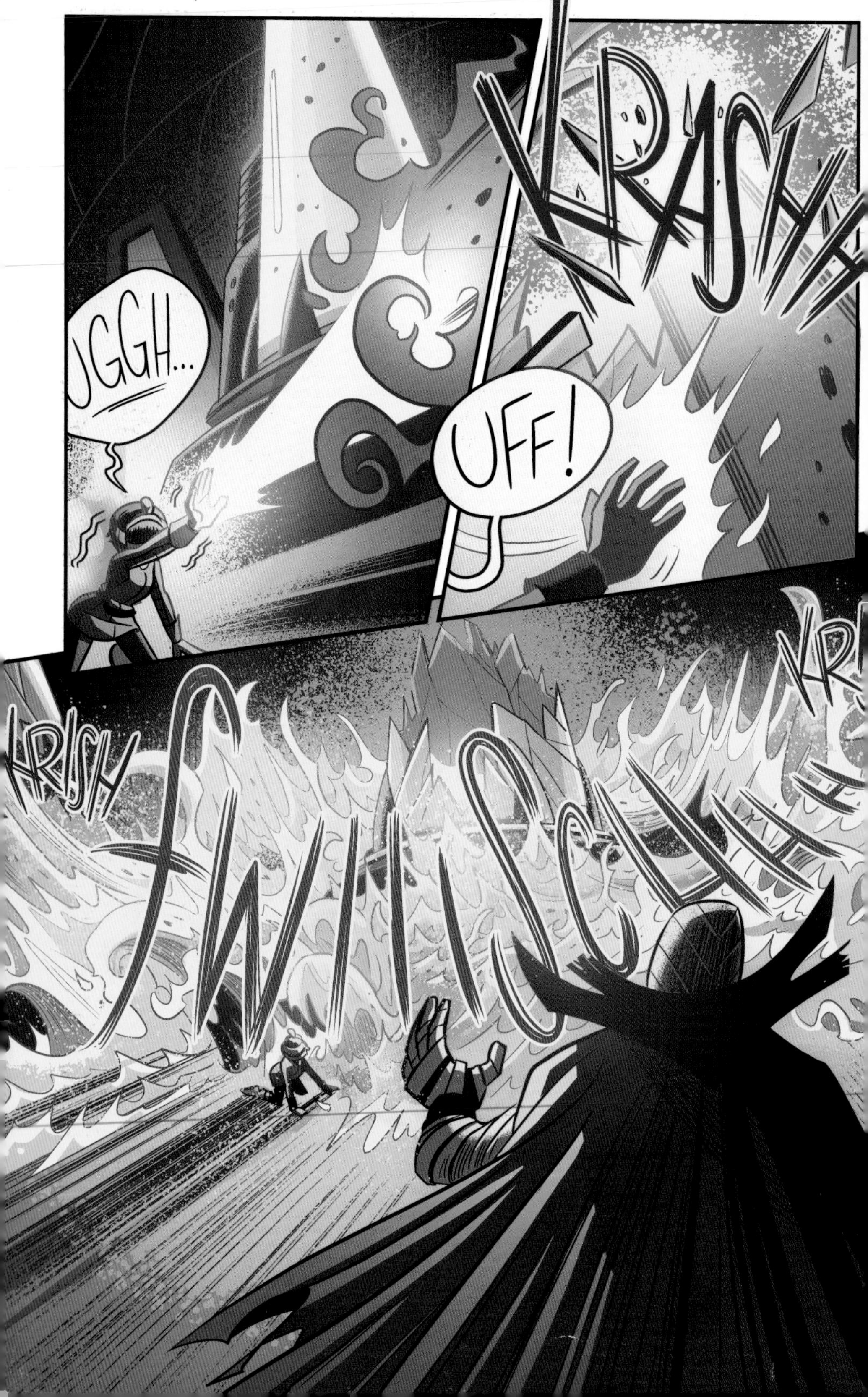
UGGH...
KRASH
UFF!
KRISH

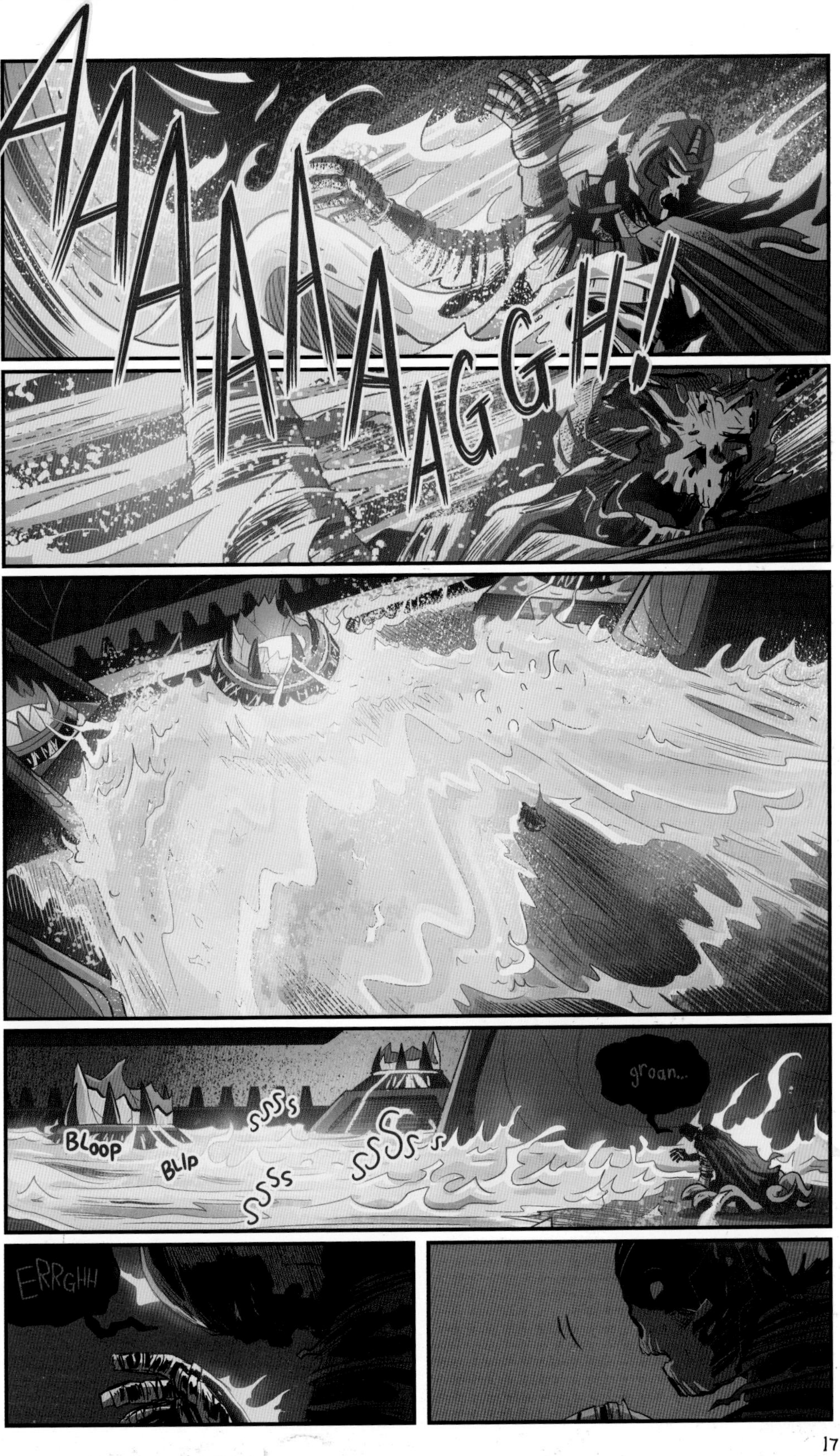
AAAAAAAGGH!
SSSS
BLOOP
BLIP
SSSSS
SSSS
groan...
ERRGHH

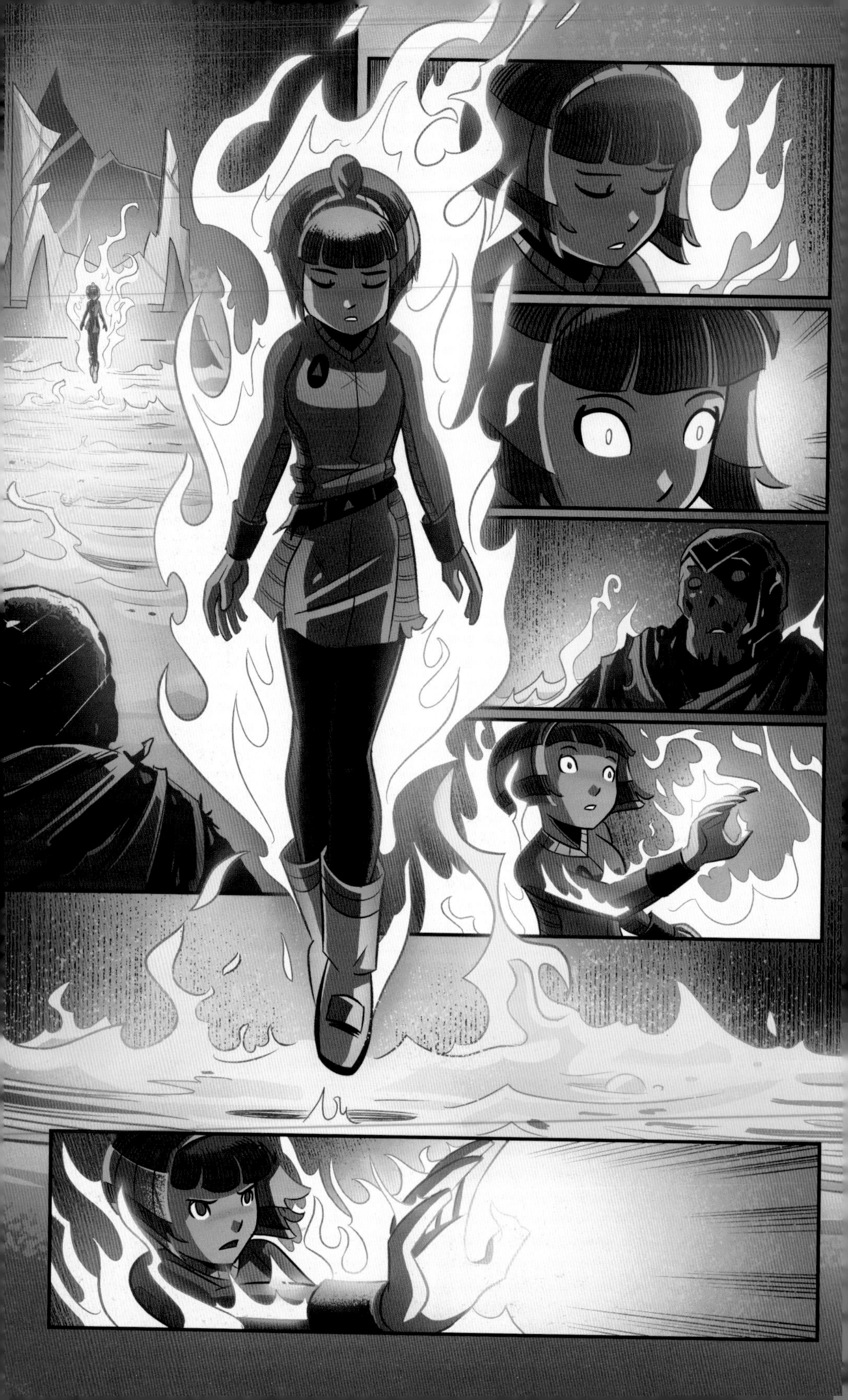

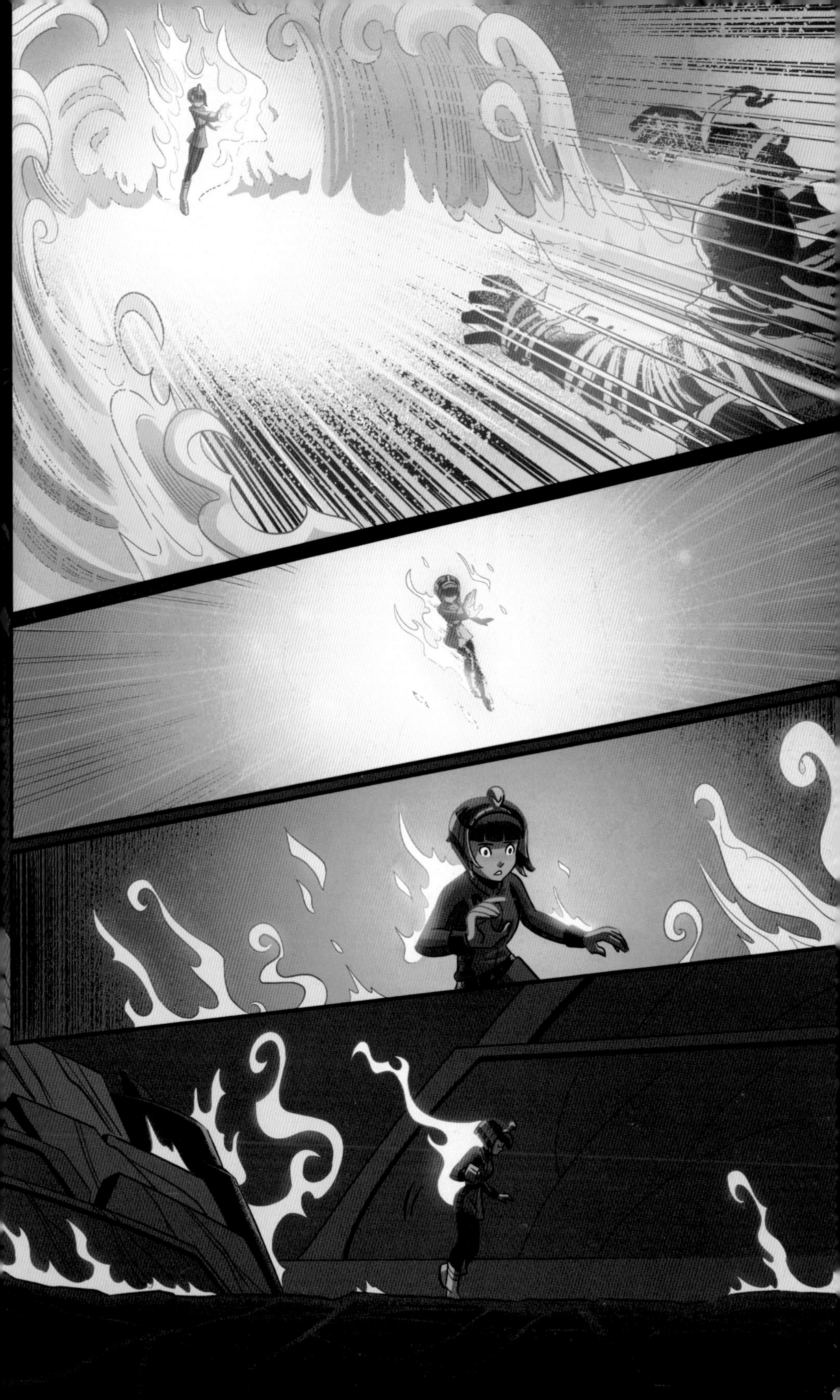

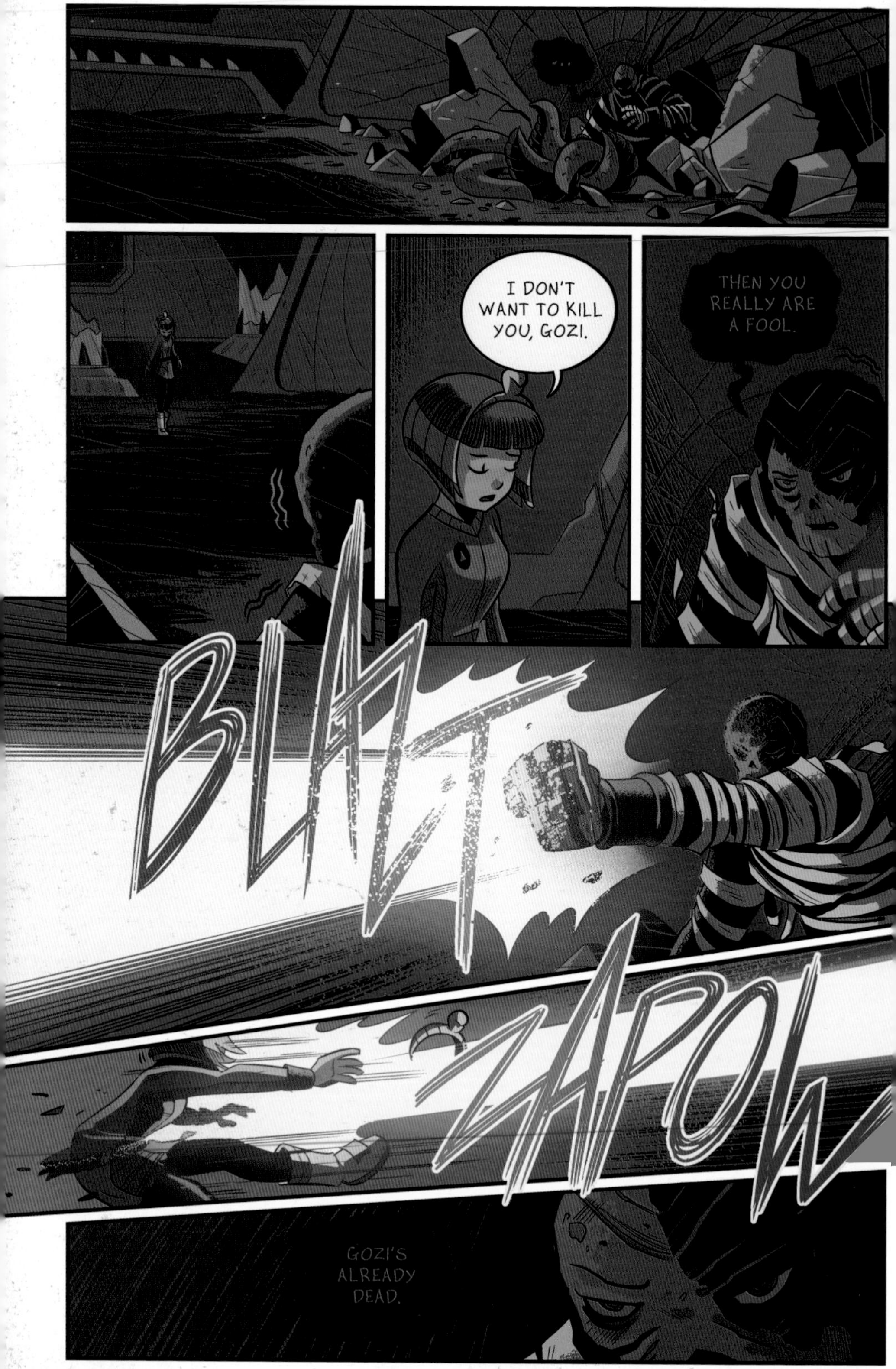
I DON'T WANT TO KILL YOU, GOZI.
THEN YOU REALLY ARE A FOOL.
BLAST
ZAPOW
GOZI'S ALREADY DEAD.

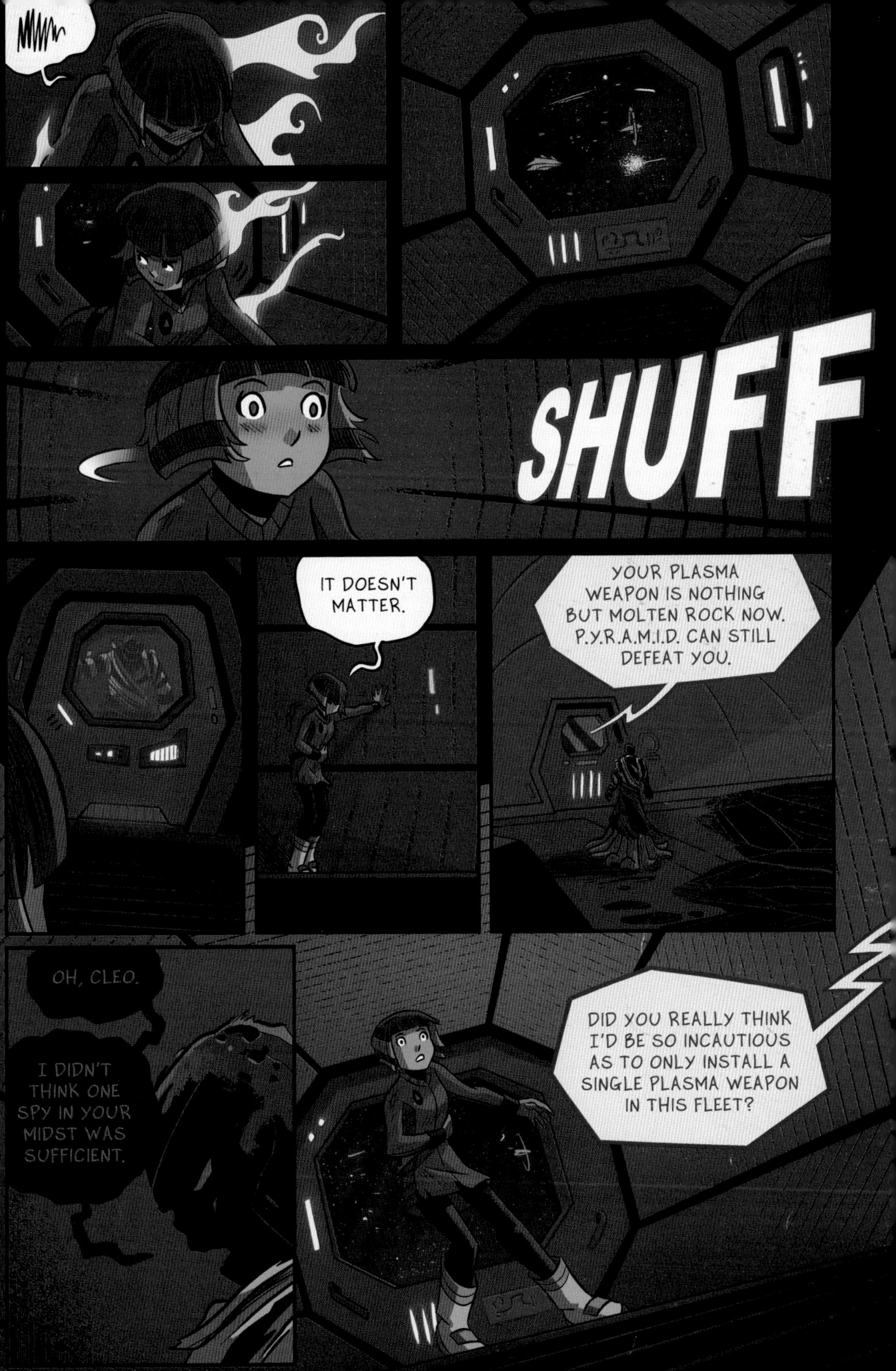
MMMM
SHUFF
IT DOESN'T MATTER.
YOUR PLASMA WEAPON IS NOTHING BUT MOLTEN ROCK NOW. P.Y.R.A.M.I.D. CAN STILL DEFEAT YOU.
OH, CLEO.
I DIDN'T THINK ONE SPY IN YOUR MIDST WAS SUFFICIENT.
DID YOU REALLY THINK I'D BE SO INCAUTIOUS AS TO ONLY INSTALL A SINGLE PLASMA WEAPON IN THIS FLEET?

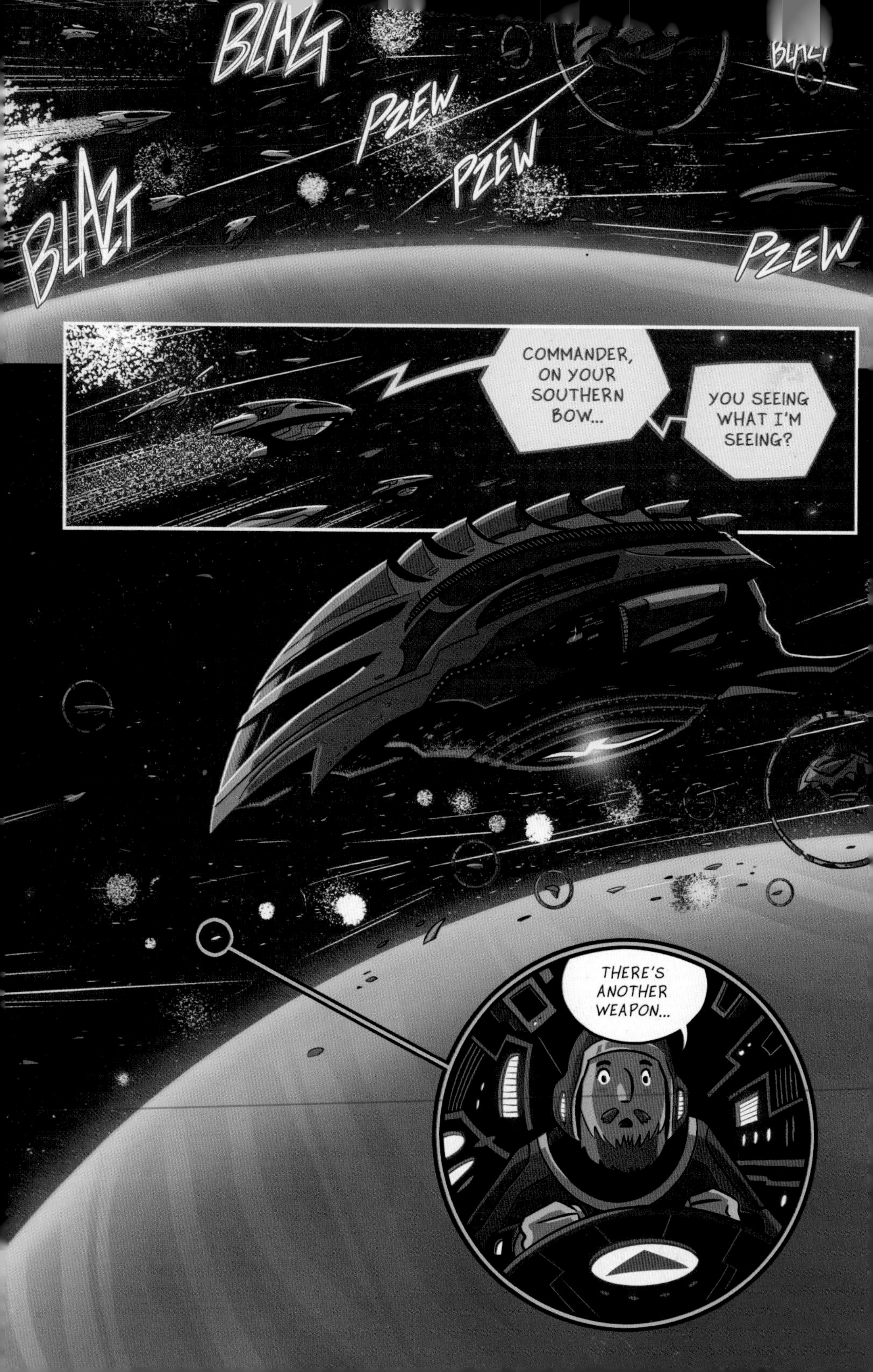

BLAZT
PZEW
PZEW
BLAZT
BLAZT
PZEW
COMMANDER, ON YOUR SOUTHERN BOW...
YOU SEEING WHAT I'M SEEING?
THERE'S ANOTHER WEAPON...

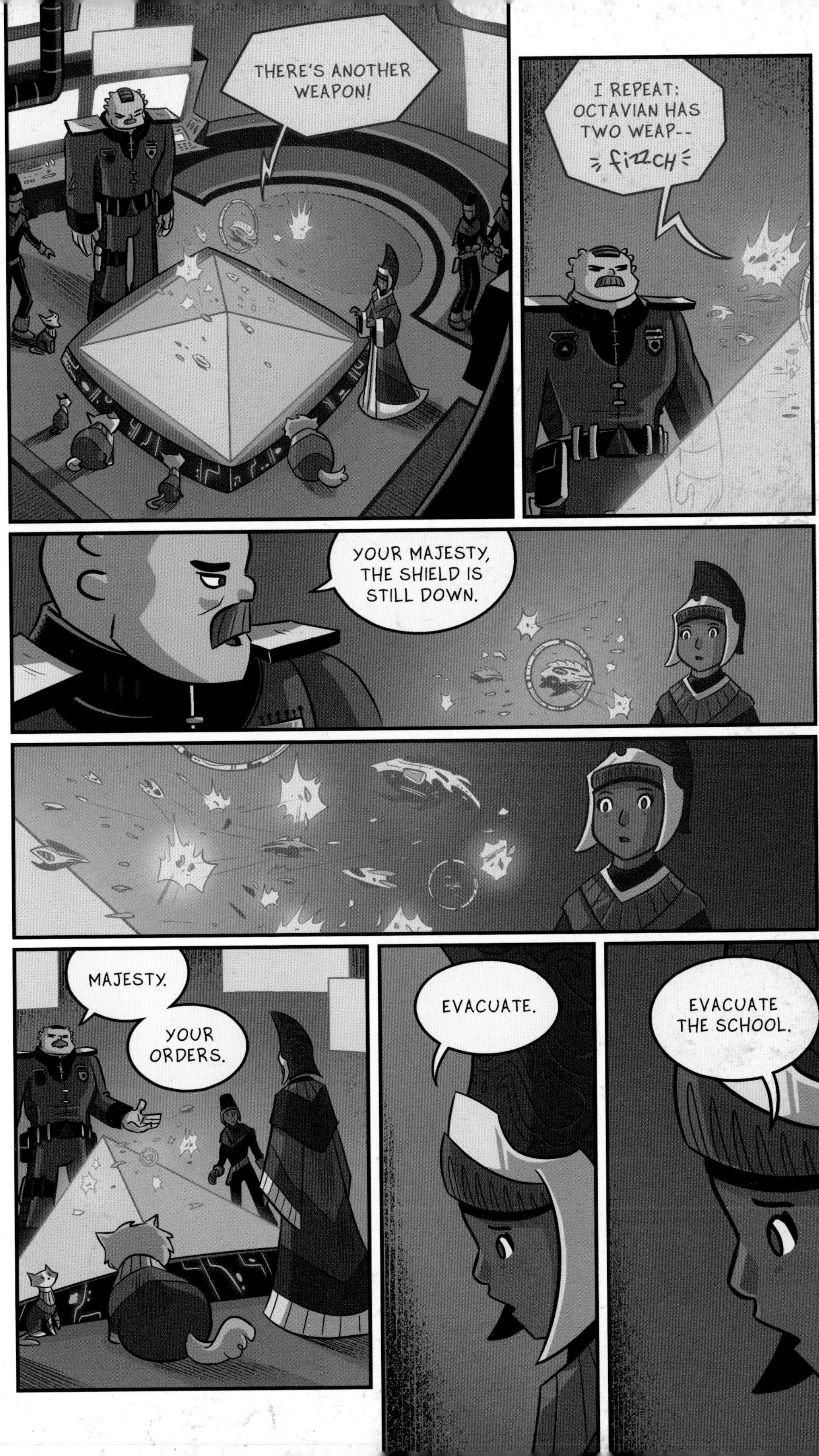
THERE'S ANOTHER WEAPON!
I REPEAT: OCTAVIAN HAS TWO WEAP--
fizzch
YOUR MAJESTY, THE SHIELD IS STILL DOWN.
MAJESTY.
YOUR ORDERS.
EVACUATE.
EVACUATE THE SCHOOL.

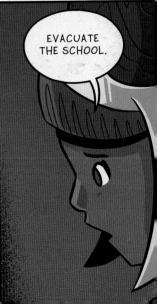

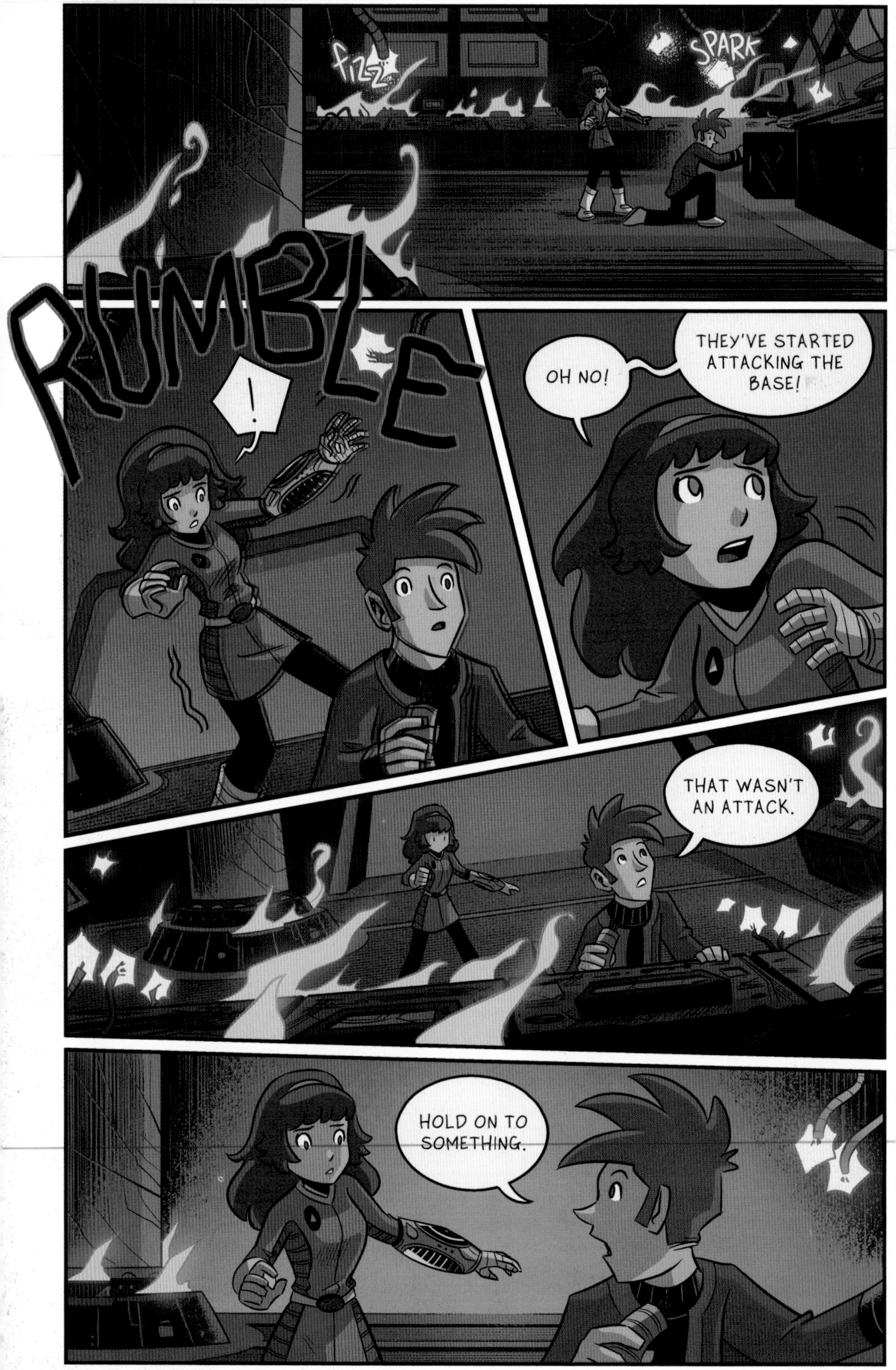
fizzz
SPARK
RUMBLE
!
OH NO!
THEY'VE STARTED ATTACKING THE BASE!
THAT WASN'T AN ATTACK.
HOLD ON TO SOMETHING.

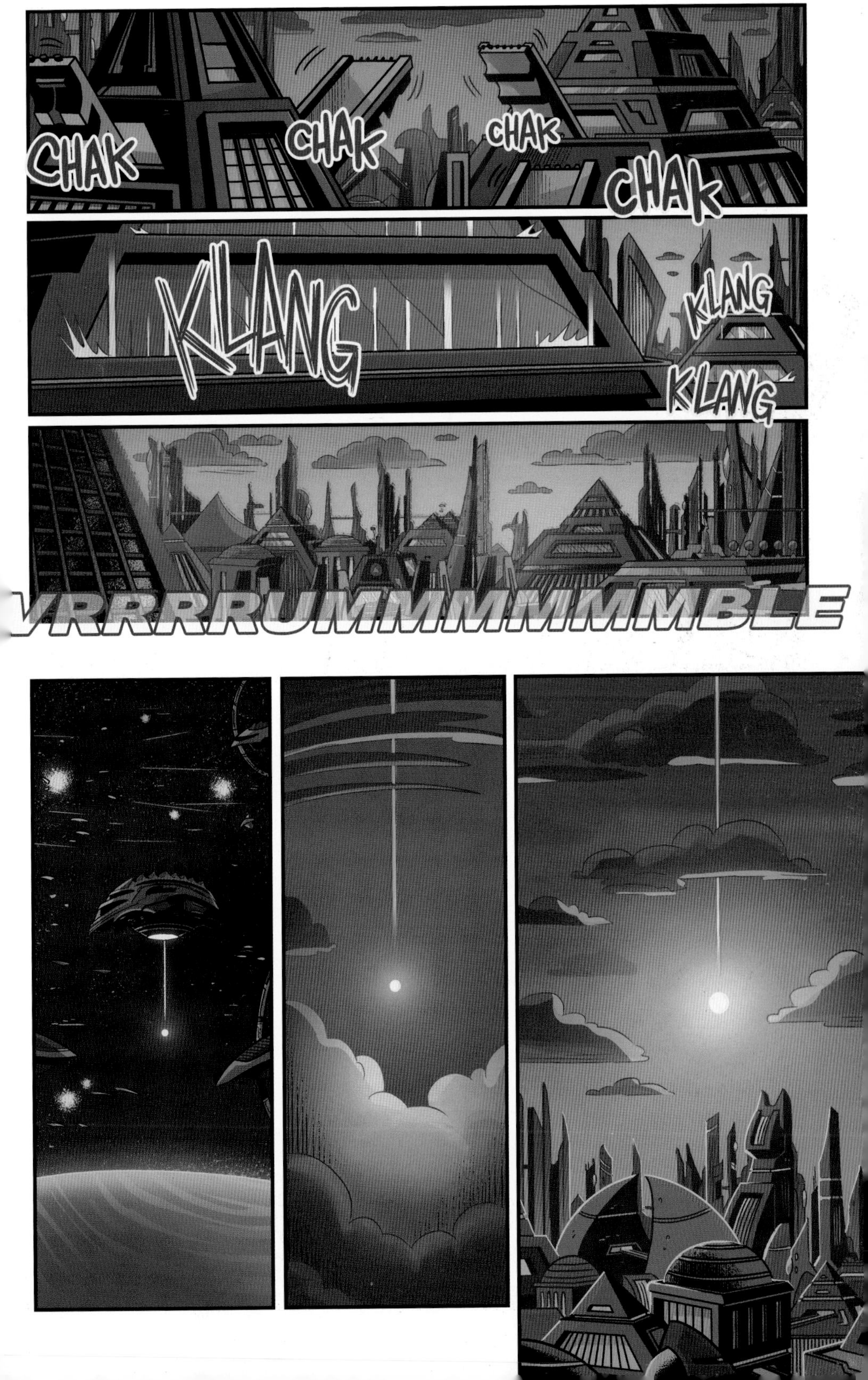
CHAK
CHAK
CHAK
CHAK
KLANG
KLANG
KLANG
VRRRRUMMMMMMMBLE

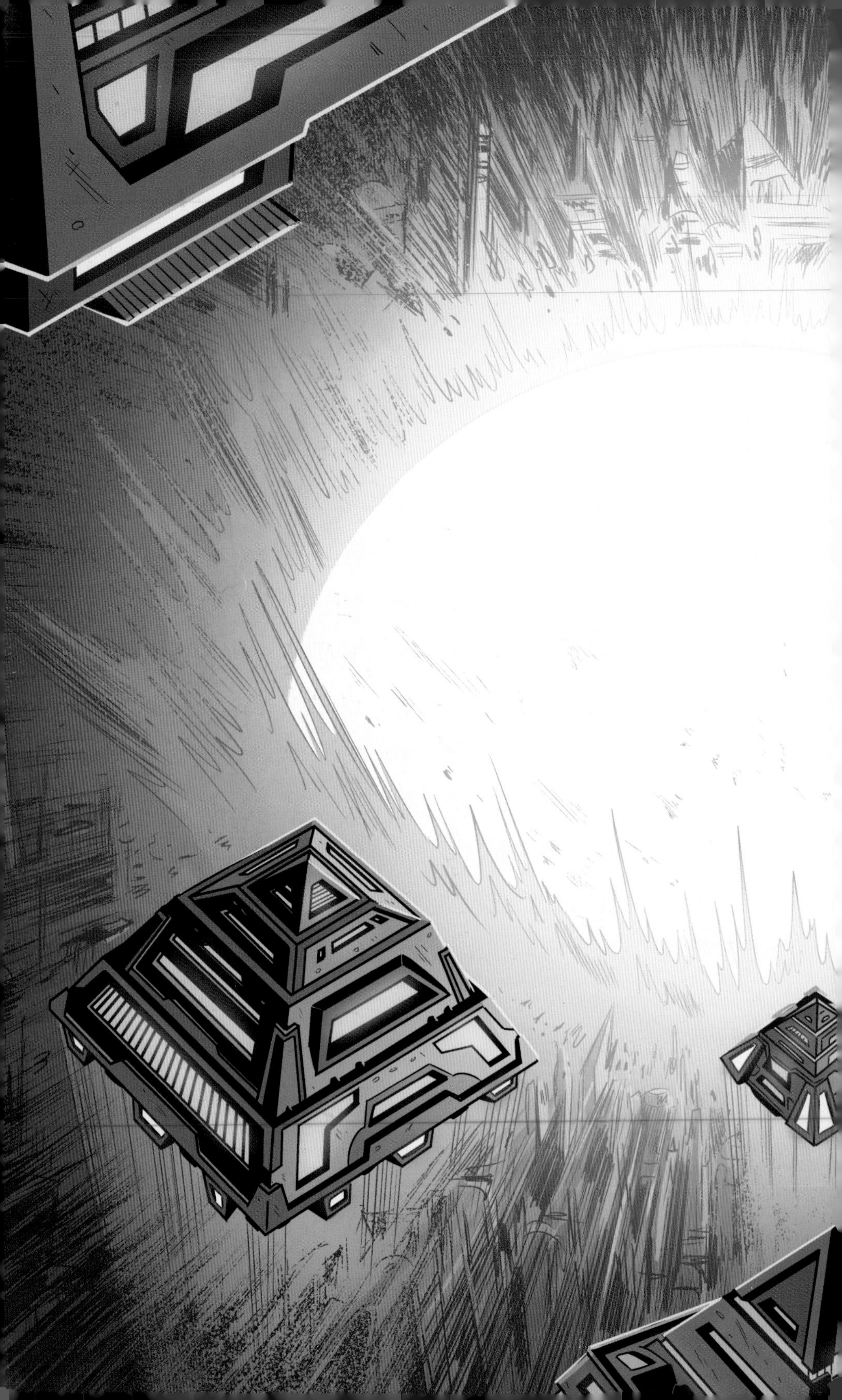

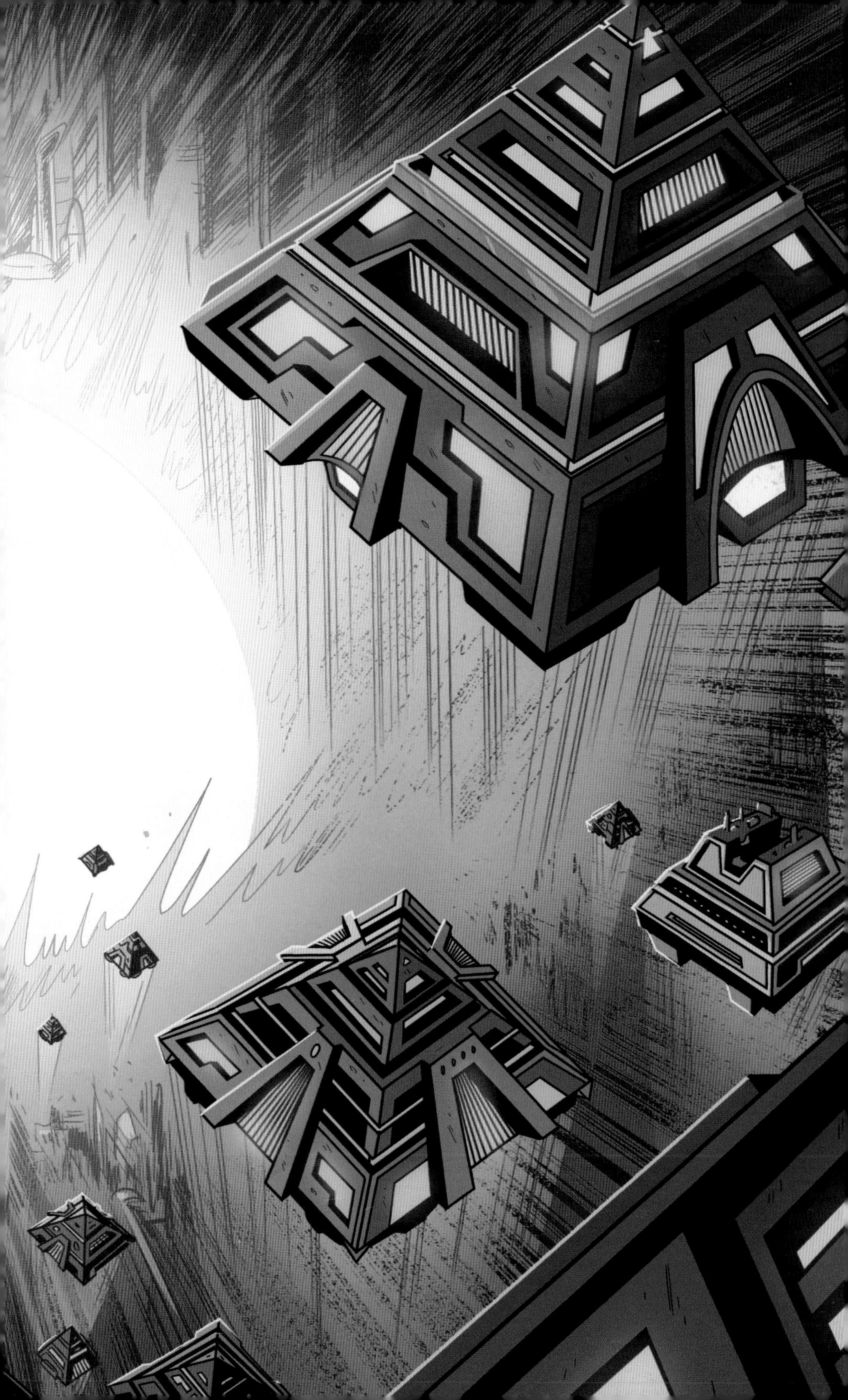

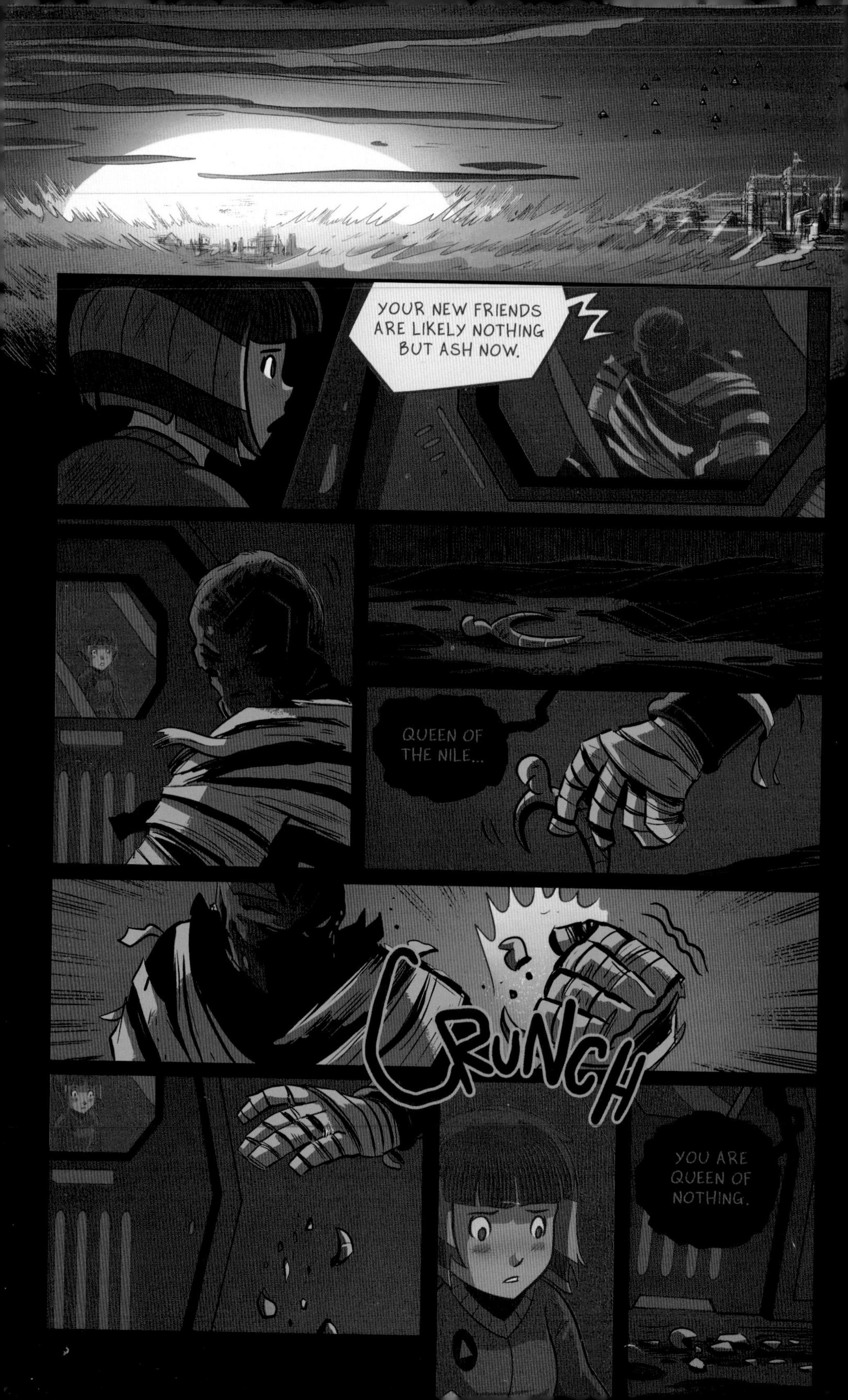
YOUR NEW FRIENDS ARE LIKELY NOTHING BUT ASH NOW.
QUEEN OF THE NILE...
CRUNCH
YOU ARE QUEEN OF NOTHING.

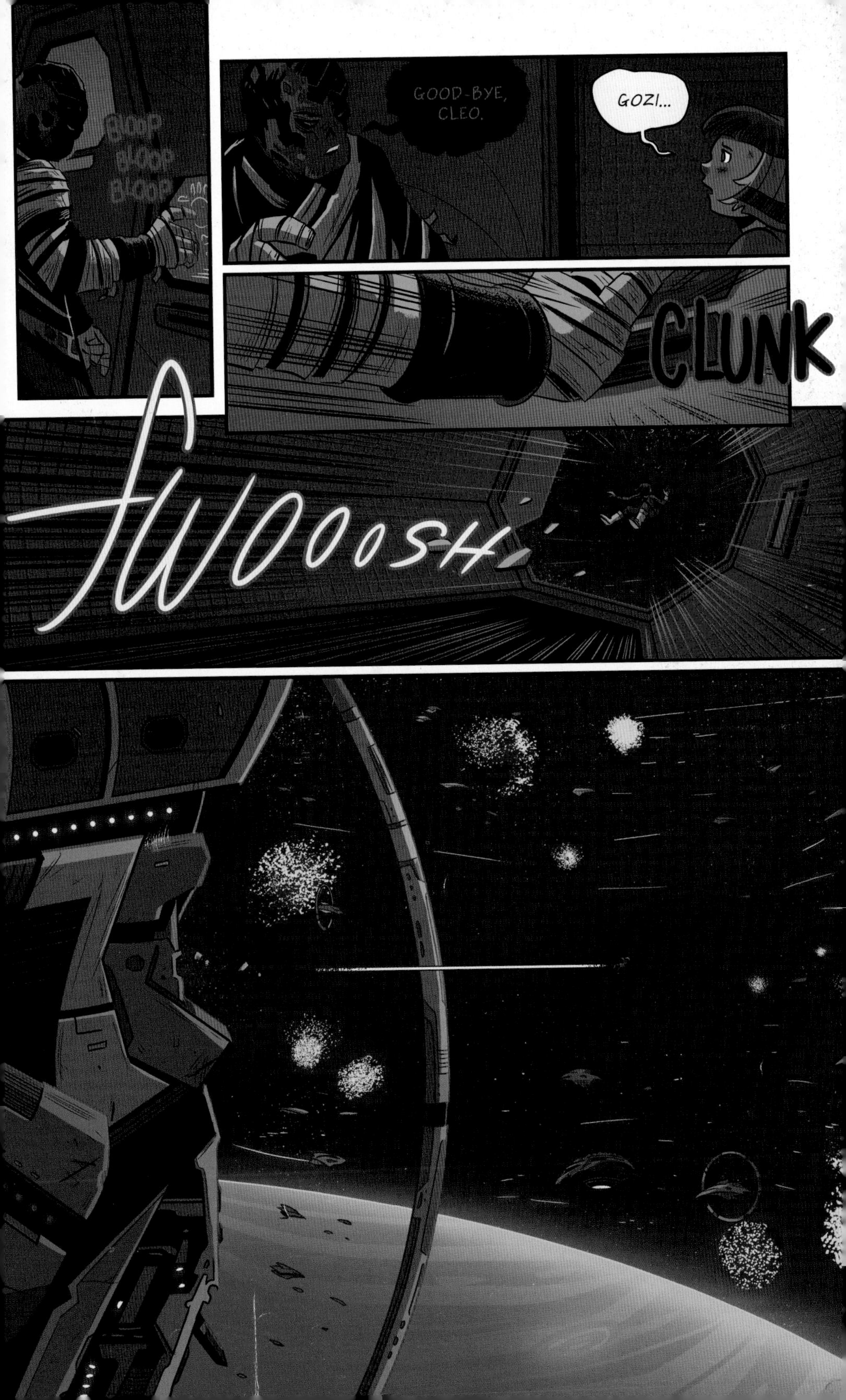
BLOOP
BLOOP
BLOOP
GOOD-BYE, CLEO.
GOZI...
CLUNK
FWOOOOSH

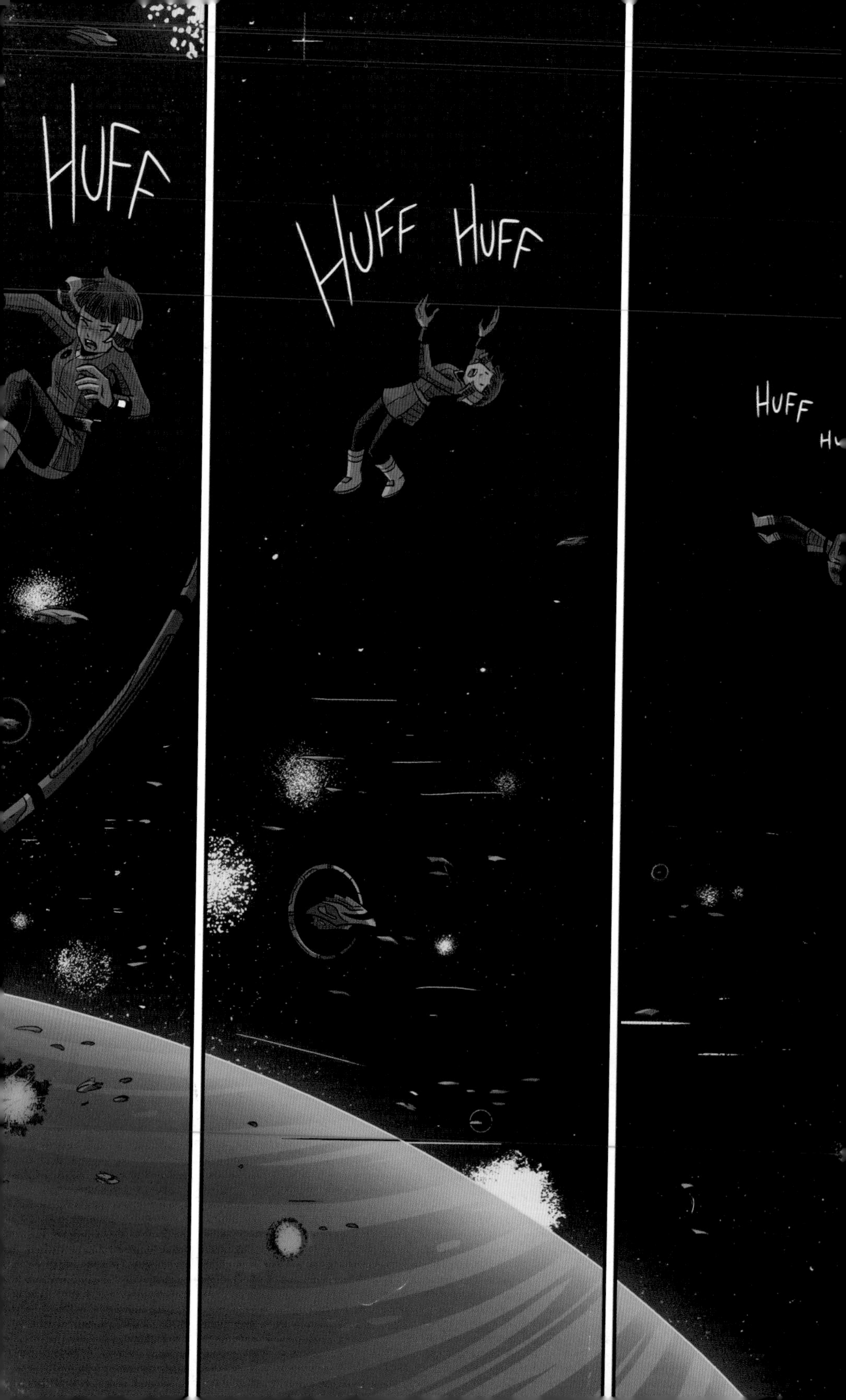
HUFF
HUFF HUFF
HUFF

AUTHOR

ABOUT THE AUTHOR

A graduate of the Columbus College of Art & Design, Mike Maihack spends his time drawing comics, writing comics, talking about comics, and whatever one does to ensure his house doesn't collapse from two boys bouncing around inside it (which sometimes involves comics). He's contributed to several books, including Sensation Comics Featuring Wonder Woman; *Parable*; Jim Henson's *The Storyteller*; *Cow Boy*; *Geeks, Girls, and Secret Identities*; and *Comic Book Tattoo*. The first book in the Cleopatra in Space series, *Target Practice*, was a Florida Book Award winner, a YALSA Great Graphic Novel for Teens, and a YALSA Quick Pick. Mike lives in Lutz, Florida, with his family.

The creation of *Fallen Empires* took seventeen months, sixteen of which were spent growing that beard in the above drawing. To learn more (about Mike, not growing a beard), visit him online at www.mikemaihack.com.

ALSO BY MIKE MAIHACK

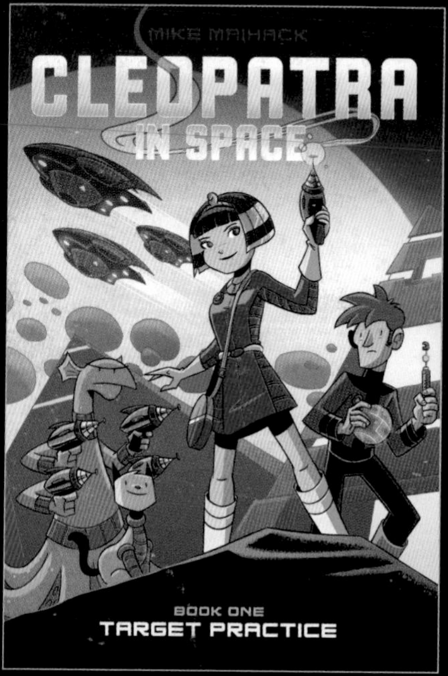
MIKE MAIHACK
CLEOPATRA
IN SPACE
BOOK ONE
TARGET PRACTICE

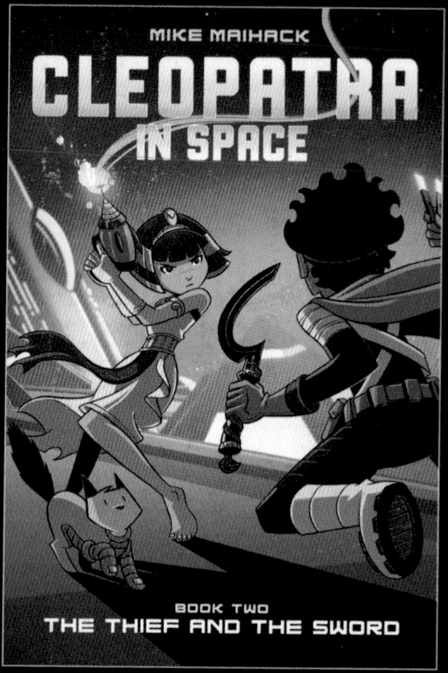
MIKE MAIHACK
CLEOPATRA
IN SPACE
BOOK TWO
THE THIEF AND THE SWORD

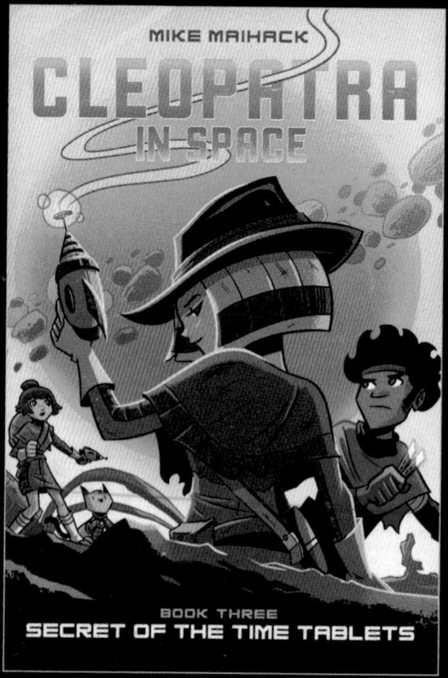
MIKE MAIHACK
CLEOPATRA
IN SPACE
BOOK THREE
SECRET OF THE TIME TABLETS

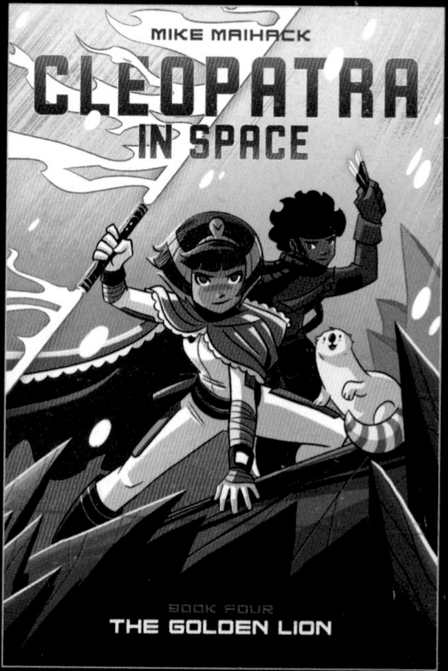
MIKE MAIHACK
CLEOPATRA
IN SPACE
BOOK FOUR
THE GOLDEN LION